CRITICAL ACCLAIM FOR
NEW YORK TIMES BESTSELLING AUTHOR ELLEN TANNER MARSH, WINNER OF THE *ROMANTIC TIMES* LIFETIME ACHIEVEMENT AWARD

"A superb novel by one of the romance genre's finest."
—*Affaire de Coeur,* on *The Enchanted Prince*

"Ellen Tanner Marsh has penned an enchanting tale brimming with true-to-life characters and emotions that will have you eagerly turning the pages."
—*Romantic Times,* on *The Enchanted Prince*

"Tumultuous and exciting!"
—*Publishers Weekly,* on *In My Wildest Dreams*

"You don't read a book by Ellen Tanner Marsh, you live it!"
—*Romantic Times,* on *In My Wildest Dreams*

"Good, solid storytelling from the first page to the last. The only disappointment is that the book has to end."
—*Publishers Weekly,* on *Tame the Wild Heart*

D0958861

SWEET POISON

"What's wrong?" he taunted softly. "Afraid?"

"No! I mean, of what?"

"That I might kiss you?"

He saw her pupils widen until those damnably purple eyes were nearly black.

"Y-you wouldn't!"

"Oh no?" His big hands curved boldly over her hips. Still smiling, he drew her slowly toward him until they were standing center to center. Maura's heart seemed to stop beating as the crinkly taffeta of her ball dress was crushed between them. One of Ross's hands settled in the small of her back while the other cupped her chin, tipping it up so that he could look into her eyes. She tried to turn away but couldn't. So she twisted her fingers in the lapels of his coat, as though hanging on for dear life. Maybe she was.

"Still afraid?" he whispered.

"No."

"Don't you want me to kiss you?"

"I'd rather drink poison!"

But Ross only laughed and, bending his head, slanted his mouth across her own.

Maura went rigid in his arms. She knew that she should struggle, should cry out for help—but all she could think of was that she would die if anything were to stop this kiss.

PROMISE ME PARADISE

ELLEN TANNER MARSH

LEISURE BOOKS   NEW YORK CITY

For Nicholas, who'd rather play soccer.

A LEISURE BOOK®

September 1998

Published by

Dorchester Publishing Co., Inc.
276 Fifth Avenue
New York, NY 10001

ISBN 0-8439-4426-9

Chapter One

Bombay, India
Early April, 1866

The morning was windy and very hot. Across the ocean, a finger of land showed against the humid sky. The railing of the steamer *Viceroy of India* was crowded with passengers eager for their first glimpse of Indian soil.

Beneath the shade of an awning on the upper deck, Maura Adams brushed the windblown hair from her eyes. Unlike the others, she had not come topside merely to enjoy the view. After all, she had known Bombay as a child and could well remember the dazzling beauty of its curving harbor. What she truly wanted to savor after all these years was the way India *smelled:* the mingled scents of cooking oil, sandalwood, dust and burning cow dung that were

9

unfamiliar to most European noses, but not to hers. Oh no, not to hers.

The steamer was now close enough to make out the native houses, painted in gaudy pinks and yellows, that crowded the waterfront. Behind them, grand European buildings and Islamic mosques filled the sky. By now the sounds of India were apparent as well: the liquid dialects of Hindi, the jingling of cart bells, the lowing of sacred market cows. Pariah dogs growled, parrots shrieked, and the ropes were made fast amid the excited shouts of those gathered on the dock waiting to welcome the travelers ashore.

"Oh, Maura, isn't it wonderful?"

Maura turned as her cousin appeared beside her. Poor Lydia was perspiring heavily in her green muslin frock and chip-straw bonnet. Dark brown hair clung in damp ringlets to her temples, but her young face glowed with excitement.

"Do you think Terence is somewhere down there waiting to meet us? Mama says it would be much too forward considering that we aren't formally engaged, but I was rather hoping—" Lydia's voice trailed away and she blushed pinkly.

"It's much too far from Delhi," Maura reminded her gently. "He couldn't have earned enough leave to make the journey."

"I suppose you're right." Lydia Carlyon smiled brightly to show it didn't matter, but Maura knew better. Lydia was more than a little anxious to meet the fiancé with whom she had been corresponding faithfully for the past two years but had yet to meet.

Lydia and Maura were first cousins. Although both were seventeen, they could not have looked less alike. Lydia had inherited the slight build and dark coloring of the Carlyons from her father's side, while Maura had been born with the bright red locks that immediately proclaimed her an Adams. As well, she had inherited her father's height and her mother's slimness. Only her features were her own; neither the Carlyons nor the Adamses could lay claim to the dark violet of her thickly fringed eyes . . . or to the slim, upturned nose and disturbingly full mouth that was set rather mockingly beneath it.

Unlike her cousin, Maura was delighted to be back in India once again. She had spent the long voyage patiently copying long passages of Hindustani from the books she had brought with her so as to polish her command of the difficult language. Now, as discordant snatches of conversation floated to her from the Hindu lascars clambering topside to make fast the ropes, she smiled to herself. Those endless hours had been well worth their pain. She had not forgotten.

"We'd better look for Mama," Lydia was saying. "She'll be wondering what's keeping us. I think—" She broke off as the gangway below them was finally cleared and a huge crowd surged on board. "Goodness! What do all those people want?"

"Friends and loved ones," Maura guessed. "No doubt it's been years since any of them have seen—" Her words were drowned out by the shrill scream of a stout British matron, whose fashionable hat had just been attacked by a monkey carried on board by a Hindu merchant. Terrified, the little creature abandoned the artificial fruits pinned to its brim and launched itself over the railing where Maura and her cousin stood.

Lydia screamed as the monkey skittered past her to land on Maura's shoulder. There it clung, chattering and afraid, while a crowd gathered round.

"Don't move, miss!"

"Keep still!"

"It may bite!"

"Oh, please!" Lydia wailed. "Somebody do something!"

"Certainly," came a deep, amused voice from somewhere in the crowd. "What?"

Maura looked up to see a tall Englishman push his way to the front of the onlookers. He seemed to be the only one among them who hadn't succumbed to panic. Standing there with his hands on his hips and his full lips twitching, he looked ready to laugh.

"Oh, please!" Lydia cried. "Take that—that creature away!"

Both Maura and the Englishman looked at the monkey. It was still clinging to Maura's shoulder, tiny hands fisted in the material of her gray traveling gown.

A dimple appeared in Maura's cheek. Looking up, her eyes met the bright blue ones of the Englishman.

"Do you want me to take him?" he inquired politely, "or would you rather hand him over yourself?"

Laughing, Maura gave him the animal and watched as he waded back through the crowd to deliver a stinging lecture in fluent Hindustani to its embarrassed owner. He might have been Italian or Spanish given the darkness of his skin and the raven's-wing black of his hair, but Maura knew better. Not only the bright blue of his eyes and that clipped, Oxford accent proclaimed him an Englishman, but his rough-hewn features reflected the harshness of many years in Eastern climes. Maura had instantly recognized from his manner the air of an old India hand.

"Lydia, Maura!"

The crowd parted to allow a pale and breathless Daphne Carlyon through. "Oh, my dears! What happened? Are you hurt? Someone said you'd been attacked by an animal!"

"A monkey, Aunt Daphne," Maura soothed. "It's been caught."

"Oh, thank heaven!" Mrs. Carlyon collapsed on a bench and fanned herself vigorously with the sheaf of papers she carried. "Vicious creatures! I can't understand why anyone would want to keep them as pets!"

Sensing that the excitement was over, the crowd drifted away. Maura looked around for the tall Englishman, but he, too, had vanished. What a shame. She would have liked to thank him for his calm handling of so silly a situation.

"Can we go now, Mama?" Lydia asked eagerly. "Is Papa waiting? Have you seen him yet?"

"Oh, my dears," Aunt Daphne answered with a dramatic catch in her voice, "my dears, I'm afraid I have the most dreadful news!"

Lydia suddenly became aware of the letters her mother carried. "Terence!" she shrieked. "Something's happened to Terence!"

"No, no, dear, Terence is fine. But I'm afraid the pressure of work has detained your father in Delhi. He won't be able to meet us here." Mrs. Carlyon rose to pat her daughter's cheek. "I know how very disappointed you must be after waiting all these years to see him again. He writes that he regrets the delay. Unbearably."

"So how are we to get to Delhi?" Maura asked.

"Captain Hamilton has already made the necessary arrangements. We'll be traveling by rail. I understand the Delhi train has Ladies Only compartments that should prove quite comfortable.

And just think! In a few days we'll be home in Bhunapore."

"Who," asked Maura, "is Captain Hamilton?"

Aunt Daphne looked bewildered. "Why, he was here just a moment ago. A charming man. Your Uncle Lawrence sent him to escort us, and I quite think—Why, there he is! Yoo hoo!" Aunt Daphne lifted her parasol and waved. "Captain Hamilton!"

Maura turned to see the black-haired Englishman who had rescued her from the monkey crossing the deck toward them. Her brows drew together. Surely this tall man with the wide shoulders and commanding air couldn't possibly be the mere assistant of Lawrence Carlyon, the mildest, most deferential man Maura knew?

Apparently he could. When he reached them, introductions were made by the beaming Aunt Daphne. Although Maura was tall, she found that she had to tilt her chin in order to look into the man's eyes.

"How do you do, Captain Hamilton?"

"Miss Adams." He bowed briefly before releasing her hand. There was nothing in his tone to suggest that they had just met under slightly more dramatic circumstances.

Aunt Daphne was eyeing him with open approval. "So glad to have you with us, Captain. Tell me, how long will we be staying in Bombay before our train leaves? I have friends I wish to see, and of course the girls will want to do some sightseeing."

"I'm afraid there's no time at all, ma'am. The Delhi train leaves in two hours. I've just sent my bearer ahead with your luggage."

Aunt Daphne paled. "Two hours! Oh, but that's not at all acceptable! Can't we take a later one?"

The rough-hewn features didn't soften. "Certainly. If you care to wait a week or more."

"A week—!" Aunt Daphne put a hand to her ample bosom. "No, of course not. Maura, Lydia, we'd better hurry along. Though I must say I'm dreadfully disappointed. I hope you're coming too, Captain Hamilton?"

He looked down at her from his great height with a smile that reminded Maura more of a grimace. "I wouldn't miss it for the world, ma'am."

The Bombay train station was unbelievably crowded. With Captain Hamilton in the lead, the Carlyon ladies pushed their way through herds of goats and stray cattle and throngs of Indian families camping out on the platforms. The noise was deafening. Babies wailed and women argued while men shouted and gesticulated. Cooking stoves, bedrolls and baskets of squawking chickens took up every available inch of space. Skinny pariah dogs wove in and out looking for something to steal. Beggars and religious fanatics harassed the passersby for handouts.

Aunt Daphne marched with her bosom thrust firmly ahead, ignoring them all, while Lydia clung fearfully to Captain Hamilton's arm. She had never seen so many dirty, dark-skinned people in all her life. And the beggars—horrible! Nearly every last one of them was grossly disfigured or maimed in some way, and she felt quite sick at the smell of them.

Maura, unlike her cousin, found endless fascination in the tumultuous scene. Lagging behind, she paused to admire the wares offered for sale in countless stalls along the tracks. There were piles of sweets, date palms and figs, brass hookahs, palm baskets, toys, prayer rugs and books and, unbelievably, current copies of *Strand* magazine from home.

"Miss-sahib?"

She turned and found herself confronted by a vendor wearing nothing more than the traditional Hindu loincloth known as the dhoti. He was holding aloft a bottle of soda water. "For the train. You will be thirsty, yes?"

Maura nodded and held up two fingers to show that she wished to purchase another. Aunt Daphne hadn't thought to bring refreshments for the journey.

"The miss-sahib has not given me enough money," he protested when Maura tucked the bottles beneath her arm.

She frowned. "I gave you a rupee."

He shook his head. "*Nahin*, miss-sahib. It was but an anna."

Maura's chin tipped. "Show me."

The vendor held out his hand. Sure enough, a single copper coin lay innocently in his leathery palm.

Maura's eyes narrowed. This was a part of Indian life she had forgotten: the sleight-of-hand skills practiced by dishonest marketplace vendors.

Behind her a train whistle blew. For a moment Maura thought she could hear someone calling her name. It sounded like Aunt Daphne. "I don't have time for this," she told the vendor in annoyance.

"Then perhaps a constable should be called," he suggested blandly. "To settle our dispute."

"You must be joking!"

The train whistle blew again, insistently.

"Well?" he prodded.

Maura promptly lost her temper. "Thou misbegotten son of a dog!" she exploded in the Hindi vernacular. "Call him then, so that I may explain how thou hast wrongly cheated a memsahib!"

The vendor's eyes widened into saucers. *Hai mai*, the miss-sahib understood his language! Oh, but this was inauspicious! Perhaps he had made an error, he told her hastily. He would look again. Yes, yes, it was just as he had feared. The rupee was here. He had placed it in the left pocket, not the right. A thousand pardons for inconveniencing the gracious miss-sahib. He hoped she was not angry. He was a poor man, and simple minded. If she would prefer—

"If you don't come away this moment, Miss Adams," a deep British voice interrupted his tirade, "you'll miss the Delhi train. And your aunt, I might add, is frantic at the thought. She sent me to fetch you."

Maura turned to find Ross Hamilton scowling down at her from his great height. He really was intimidating considering his size and those craggy features of his. She much preferred him when he was smiling.

Not that she preferred him at all, mind!

"Are you quite ready?" he continued crisply, "or do you have anything else of equal charm to say to this poor fellow?"

"Thank you, no." She did her best to sound haughty even though her eyes were dancing. "I think I've said enough."

Apparently she had. The vendor practically brushed the platform with his nose as he bowed them out of his stall.

Captain Hamilton's lips twitched as he escorted Maura back through the crowds and into the railway car. He wasn't nearly as annoyed with her as he had made himself out to be. No, he'd quite enjoyed the lively scene he'd witnessed out on the platform. Very few Englishwomen fresh off the Malta steamer could possibly dress a Hindu vendor down so neatly.

A frantic Aunt Daphne met them at the top of the steps. "Oh, my dear, what a scare you gave us! Why, if Captain Hamilton hadn't gone looking for you, you could well have been left behind!"

"I'm sorry, Aunt," Maura said contritely.

"What were you doing down there?" Lydia demanded.

"Buying something to drink."

"From one of those—those people?" Lydia was aghast. "Weren't you scared?"

"No. Thirsty."

"Well, at least we're together now," Aunt Daphne stated happily.

"Here's your compartment, ladies." Captain Hamilton slid open a brass-plated door halfway down the length of the car.

Aunt Daphne made a close inspection of the padded benches, the overhead luggage shelf and tiny fold-out tables and pronounced herself satisfied. "But, my goodness!" she exclaimed. "Why on earth is the window barred?"

"To deter the *budmarshes*," Maura answered, stowing her bottled water beneath the seat.

"The what?"

Maura chuckled, realizing that she had used the Hindustani word without thinking. "Sorry, Aunt. I meant bad men, thieves."

Mrs. Carlyon jerked upright in alarm. "Thieves! Oh, Captain Hamilton, surely—"

"You'll be quite safe here," Ross interrupted from the doorway. His cold blue eyes shot a warning glance at Maura.

"Yes, of course we will," Maura answered quickly, although the answering look she sent Captain Hamilton was equally frosty. Why on earth was he bothering to protect her aunt from the truth? Even after spending the last ten years in England she couldn't have forgotten what India was like!

Annoying meddler, she thought.

Stubborn Irish beauty, Ross thought. She was going to have a lot of trouble fitting into Bhunapore society, that was for sure!

The train whistle wailed. Ross straightened with relief. "That's it, then. I'll bid you a pleasant journey and be off."

"Aren't you traveling with us?" Lydia asked, dismayed.

His eyes twinkled. Maura realized that they had yet to twinkle when he looked at *her*. "This is a Ladies Only carriage, Miss Carlyon."

The whistle blew another long, piercing blast, and the train shuddered. Captain Hamilton quickly made his farewells and disappeared.

The moment he was gone a dense cloud of black ash came swirling through the window. Lydia gave a choked cry and pressed a handkerchief to her mouth and nose.

Maura rose quickly to pull down the blind. "Better get used to it."

With a screeching of wheels the train rolled out of the station. Gathering speed, it chuffed across an ancient riverbed with the emerald hills of Bombay falling behind.

They were underway at last.

Maura found that she couldn't sit still. She ached to drink in each and every passing mile, for she had been all of seven years old when she had looked her last upon this golden land.

"Where are you going?" Aunt Daphne demanded as she slid open the compartment door.

"Out," Maura responded cheerfully. "I won't be long."

19

Holding aside her wide tarlatan skirts, she pushed past the travelers who had gathered in the aisle to gossip, and made her way down the swaying corridor. After inspecting the washroom and glancing into the adjoining car, she stood for a long time at the rear window simply watching the landscape roll past. How well she remembered these scenes: the cane brakes and tangled jungle, the countless villages with their stone wells, ancient temples and mud-baked houses, and the oxen dozing in the shade beneath the yellow blossoms of the thorny *kikar* trees along the tracks.

I can't believe it, she thought with a long, blissful sigh. I'm home, home at last!

Behind her the connecting door opened and a man stepped inside. Maura was annoyed to find herself blushing as she recognized Ross Hamilton. She was well aware that he disapproved of her.

Indeed, his voice held absolutely no warmth as he halted in front of her and said, "It isn't at all wise to leave your compartment, Miss Adams."

"Oh? Why not?"

He frowned into her wide violet eyes. They were as dark as the night sky, he realized, a soft, pansy purple, and he wondered briefly if she used kohl pencils to make them tilt so artfully at the corners. His tone was suddenly brusque. "A young lady's virtue could well be compromised out here in a public area."

"In a Ladies Only carriage?" Maura shot back. "With no men in sight?"

"I'm here, aren't I?" he growled.

"Don't tell me *you* intend to compromise my virtue?"

She didn't so much as blink an eye as she uttered those outrageous words, and Ross couldn't help

20

feeling a flash of admiration for her—once he got over the shock. Immediately afterward came the urge to laugh aloud. And the desire to shake her until she exhibited some sense. He decided on a few choice words of warning instead.

"Miss Adams—"

A shrill scream from one of the compartments interrupted him. Both of them whirled.

Maura gasped as the screams continued, growing louder. "Why, it's my aunt!" She took off at a run with Ross right behind her, cursing her inwardly because her skirts were so wide that he couldn't push past them and be the first through the door. Didn't the damned girl have *any* sense?

Bursting into the compartment, Maura found her cousin and aunt clinging to each other on the bench beneath the window. Above them, on the outside of the train, a grinning native in a filthy turban was reaching inside with a long, curved stick and doing his best to hook the largest of their bags.

Without hesitation, Maura snatched up her aunt's umbrella. Before she could take a single step toward him, however, she was caught fast from behind.

"Allow me," growled a voice in her ear.

Setting her aside—none too gently—Captain Hamilton reached through the bars and grabbed the would-be thief by the collar. The Hindu gave a yelp of pain as a lean, whipcord arm shot out to deliver a devastating blow. Moments later his dark face disappeared from view and the scenery reverted to foothills once again.

"I'll wager he'll think twice before trying that again," Ross said, calmly dusting off his hands.

"Oh, my word!" Mrs. Carlyon squeaked from her seat. "Captain, please! Call the conductor! Tell him to stop the train!"

Ross looked startled. "Whatever for?"

"Why, to catch that man! Have him arrested!"

"I'm afraid he's long gone by now."

Mrs. Carlyon took a shuddering breath. "Yes, yes, I suppose you're right."

"How on earth did he get up there?" Lydia wanted to know.

Ross shrugged. "No doubt he climbed onto the roof while we were still in the station. Ladies Only compartments make admirable targets for railway thieves."

"Why don't the authorities do more to protect us?" Lydia inquired indignantly.

Ross's eyes sparked with amusement. "Because this is India, Miss Carlyon."

"And what exactly does that mean?"

Ross didn't bother to answer. "I'll check in on you more often," he promised.

"You've been ever so kind," Aunt Daphne murmured emotionally.

"Glad to be of service." Ross bowed to her and then to Lydia. In the doorway he halted in front of Maura, who was still brandishing her aunt's umbrella. "In India," he said in a voice meant for her ears alone, "it's wiser to leave the heroics to the men."

Maura's eyes flashed. Who the devil did he think he was, lecturing her like that? "Is that so?"

"I assure you, Miss Adams—" He broke off abruptly, a glint of amusement entering his eyes. "Perhaps you'd like to put away the parasol? Or am I mistaken in imagining you'd like to use it on me?"

Since Maura had been thinking precisely along those lines, she blushed hotly and thrust the umbrella behind her back. Before she could think of a stinging retort, however, he had brushed past her and disappeared down the corridor, his soft laughter echoing in her ears.

Chapter Two

Fortunately another attack on the Carlyon railway car never occurred, and the journey progressed uneventfully. So uneventfully, in fact, that after a few days boredom set in. Aunt Daphne and Lydia were soon complaining of headaches that were brought on, so Maura suspected, by the boredom as much as the heat. They took to relieving their discomfort by napping for hours on end, and it was only at night, when the heat relented a little, that they met with the other ladies in the aisle to gossip and nag and trade endless complaints. No one, it seemed, had anything kind to say about India.

Except Maura. She alone found nothing to criticize about the country of her birth; she alone found endless fascination in watching the sun rise every morning in a wash of saffron over the sacred rivers, where elephants bathed and egrets posed along the curving sandbanks.

24

Every evening she watched as that same sun set over folding plains dotted with jackal packs and herds of magnificent blackbuck. At night she watched the jungle steam beneath the bleached light of the moon, and wondered how anyone could ever grow tired of this ever-changing vista. The spell of India had caught her in its enchanted web once again and she was blissfully happy.

Because the Delhi train had no dining car, Captain Hamilton had taken over the responsibility of disembarking at every station to barter for the ladies' meals. Even Maura had to admit—grudgingly—that he knew how to handle the natives, and that they were never lacking the freshest fruits and coldest bottled drinks. At one stop he even managed to procure a small cooking stove on which Maura and Lydia brewed welcome cups of tea and Bovril every morning.

In larger towns the train stopped for an hour or more to allow leisurely meals inside the station where the ladies could enjoy the relative comforts of the ladies' waiting rooms, which were equipped with baths attended by Indian maidservants.

Nevertheless, and despite Maura's undiminished enthusiasm, the journey proved a long one. Often their progress was slowed by flooding or by elephants on the tracks, but eventually the great plains of Rajasthan were crossed and the journey was seen to draw to a close. The mood of the passengers brightened, and Lydia talked excitedly of meeting her Terence at last.

That night, their last on board, Mrs. Carlyon hosted a farewell celebration. Captain Hamilton was invited to attend, and a bottle of champagne was donated by a generous neighbor. The festivities were slated to begin at seven o'clock, and it was just at that hour, as the guests were filing in and the first of the glasses were being poured, that the train rounded a curve in the tracks and hit a mudslide.

The sun had already set by then, and the faint glow in the western sky was fading into blackness. Maura had just opened the compartment door to invite the conductor in for a toast when the world exploded around her. There was a deafening crash and a screeching of metal and in an instant she was thrown off her feet. Striking her head against the window frame across the aisle, she sagged to the floor.

The car was instantly plunged into darkness. The ladies screamed and trampled one another in a mad rush to get outside. Lydia and her mother were among those swept along in the panic. A tall figure caught up with them at the door. Gasping her relief, Aunt Daphne caught at his arm.

"Captain Hamilton, thank goodness you're here! What on earth has happened?"

"I believe the train's been derailed. Careful, now." He shouldered his way down the aisle, making a path for them. At the steps he paused, scowling. "Where is Miss Adams?"

Aunt Daphne looked around, bewildered. "Why, I've no idea! She was just here with us. . . ."

Cursing beneath his breath, Ross waded back down the corridor. There was still no sign of Maura. He swore again as he suddenly caught sight of her lying beneath the window, barely out of reach of the shoving, trampling crowd. Bending swiftly, he lifted her to safety.

"Miss Adams, are you all right?"

Maura moaned but made no answer.

Kneeling with his arm beneath her shoulders,

Ross shook her insistently. "Miss Adams, you must get up. The train's been derailed."

She stirred and lifted huge, unfocused eyes to his face. "What?"

"I said the train's been derailed. We'll be safer outside. Can you walk?"

"I-I think so." But she didn't move. She merely sighed and turned her aching head against his shoulder.

Ross's expression softened abruptly. Something stirred deep inside him, a strange emotion that was replaced, before he could even name it, by unreasoning anger. "Miss Adams!" His voice was hard now, like a slap in the face.

Peevishly Maura lifted her throbbing head to find his scowling face only inches from hers. "Oh, what is it?"

"I asked if you were able to walk. We've got to get out. Do you need my help?"

"What if I do? Do you intend to carry me?"

"If I have to," he snapped.

"You're a very unlikable man, do you know that, Captain Hamilton?"

"And you are a very difficult woman, Miss Adams."

"I know." Amazingly, she was smiling a little. "So I've been told for most of my life."

"Now why am I not at all surprised to hear that?"

Maura bristled. "I don't believe, Captain Hamilton, that you have any right to say—"

"Oh, no, you don't. I've more important things to do at the moment than endure another of your lectures." Scooping her effortlessly into his arms, he carried her to the steps and swung her down to the ground.

"Maura! Oh, my dear, thank goodness you're here!"

Aunt Daphne and Lydia crowded around her, fussing and weeping. A compress was applied to the bump on her head while one of the passengers insisted on making a rough pallet for her to lie on. Maura refused. Her dizziness was fading and she found that she could finally open her eyes without feeling ill.

Looking around the circle of worried faces she saw that Captain Hamilton's was no longer among them. Absurdly, and despite the fact that she was furious with him, she felt a pang of disappointment. Really, he could at least have *pretended* some concern!

But instead he stayed away for what seemed a very long time. When he finally did return, he brought dismaying news. The train's locomotive and first four cars had derailed. It would take days to clear the wreckage.

"Days?" Lydia squeaked.

"Whatever shall we do?" Aunt Daphne quavered.

Captain Hamilton led them a short distance away from the others. "I've made arrangements to put you up in the nearest *dâk*-bungalow tonight."

"A what?" Lydia breathed.

"A *dâk*," her mother explained, remembering. "It's an inn maintained by our government, for British travelers only. I'm afraid they're somewhat primitive. Oh, dear, and terribly cramped as I recall. Are you certain, Captain, that they'll have enough room for us?"

"I've sent my bearer ahead to make certain. Now, if you'll excuse me? I'd better see to your luggage. There'll be time in the morning to arrange some other transportation to Delhi."

"You've been ever so kind," Aunt Daphne said emotionally. "Lawrence probably had no idea what he was putting you through."

Ross smiled wryly. "All grist in the mill of the service, ma'am. Now, if you don't mind, I'll see to that luggage. Please stay here until the *dâk-gharry* arrives."

"Captain Hamilton," Maura said as Ross brushed past her.

He paused to look at her, saying nothing, his expression impossible to read. Maura was glad for the darkness that surrounded them because she found it difficult all of a sudden to meet his gaze without blushing. Common decency demanded that she thank him for his earlier assistance, but she suddenly found herself extremely unwilling to give voice to her feelings—a decidedly new and unpleasant situation for her.

"Miss Adams?" he prodded when she said nothing, only stood there looking up at him with dark, solemn eyes.

She took a deep breath. "I—I wanted to thank you for your assistance in the carriage earlier, when I hit my head."

"No need to. I was merely doing my duty. Now, if you'll excuse me? I've much to do."

She stared after him as he disappeared into the darkness. Well! He certainly was an arrogant besom, wasn't he? Maybe he'd do her the kindness of stepping on a scorpion out there in the jungle!

The three of them, Maura, Lydia, and Daphne Carlyon, were covered with dust and utterly exhausted by the time they descended from the jolting, horse-drawn conveyance that brought them from the train tracks to the *dâk*-bungalow door. Adding insult to injury was the discovery that, while Captain Hamilton had indeed procured lodgings for them, they were expected to share them with nearly a dozen other refugees.

At least the intervention of Captain Hamilton's bearer had guaranteed them a trio of rickety string beds known as charpoys, although the fact that the Carlyon women would not be sleeping on the floor like everyone else earned them the thinly disguised hostility of their roommates. In frosty silence the entire party of fifteen irritable females settled themselves on the verandah steps to eat supper from wooden trays. The meal was skimpy and overcooked; a stew of inedible chicken and sticky rice washed down with tepid tea.

Afterward, Maura retired at once to bed. She had no desire to listen to the others moan and complain about their predicament. Unlacing her corset and stripping down to her petticoat and camisole, she stretched out on the hard canvas mat. Her head throbbed and the greasy chicken she'd eaten for supper lay like a lump in her belly. Closing her eyes, she willed herself to sleep.

Impossible. The lamps had been extinguished earlier to discourage the invasion of insects, and with nothing else to do, the rest of the room's occupants now retired as well. Their whispered conversations were nearly as noisy as those of the menfolk who remained on the verandah outside.

The night was very hot. Somewhere in the jungle a jackal howled. One by one the other ladies withdrew to their pallets and the room grew still at last. But only for a while. Soon someone in the far corner began to snore while somebody else tossed and muttered in uneasy sleep.

Gritting her teeth, Maura turned onto her side

and tried to ignore them. After a moment she gave an exclamation of disgust and sat up. Sliding quietly from the bed she threw a shawl over her shoulders and tiptoed to the door. On the threshold she paused to make certain that none of the servants who were stretched out on the verandah remained awake. Quietly she descended the uneven steps and walked barefoot across the grass.

A fragrant breeze had sprung up now that the darkened earth had cooled. Overhead whirred the ubiquitous fruitbats of India, and in the jungle countless fireflies winked like stars. Off in the distance came the throbbing of drums, a long forgotten sound. Listening to them, Maura could feel her weariness and pain beginning to fade. A measure of peace crept into her sore heart.

How wonderful to be outside at last, freed from the sooty confines of the railway carriage! This spicy, moonlit jungle was the India she had craved, not the squalid bazaars of Bombay or the crowded train.

Standing there with the breeze tugging her unbound hair, she drew in a deep, deep breath of happiness. She couldn't remember the last time she had felt so alive. Certainly never during the long years of her confinement in England! Oh, not that England had been unlivable or the Carlyons unkind! In fact, Maura was well aware that she owed them a huge debt of gratitude for having welcomed her so willingly into their lives.

Eighteen long years ago, when Aunt Daphne had first discovered that she was expecting a child, she had promptly been dispatched back to England by her husband, even though Uncle Lawrence's work for the Indian Civil Service in Delhi had prevented him from accompanying her. Like all dutiful wives

31

whose husbands served the British Raj, Aunt Daphne had accepted the long years of separation that followed without complaint. In fact, she had been delighted to raise Lydia in England inasmuch as everyone knew that India was literally littered with the graves of English children.

Unlike Lydia, Maura had been born in India, and raised until the age of seven in her parents' home in Lucknow. Then, considered old enough to obtain a proper English education, she had been dispatched to the Carlyons' home in Norfolk by her father, Colonel Archibald Adams. Maura's mother, ignoring her sister Daphne's pleas, had chosen to remain behind, an unconventional decision that had cost her her life when she had been murdered along with her husband in the bloody mutiny staged by native infantry soldiers during the following year.

Upon being told that she had been orphaned, a grief-stricken Maura had despaired of ever seeing India again. But now those endless years of waiting were over at last, and as she strolled through the fragrant darkness beyond the bungalow steps she could have shouted aloud with happiness.

How she wished she had someone to talk to! Someone who could understand her joy and share it! Not Aunt Daphne, who considered India a sentence to be endured for the sake of family, or Lydia, who proclaimed it ugly and overwhelming and was frightened of the natives and the wild animals lurking in the jungle.

I wish . . . thought Maura, only to stumble without warning over an unseen tree root and fall heavily to her knees.

Instantly something—or someone—scrambled upright in the darkness behind her. Maura cried out as a hand clamped itself around her upper arm and jerked her to her feet.

"*Wah!*" exclaimed a startled voice in Hindustani. "I believe I have captured a woman, Brother!"

"Art thou certain it is not a thief?" came another voice, also speaking in the venacular.

"No. She is dressed like an *Angrezi* memsahib."

Maura, whose eyes had by now adjusted to the darkness, saw that she had tripped over a tent rope, not a root. Dismayed, she realized that she had wandered unknowingly into a men's camp—wearing nothing but a petticoat and camisole! She began to struggle in earnest, but the Hindu merely tightened his grip.

"An *Angrezi* memsahib?" By now the second man had emerged from the tent. "Thou art mistaken, Brother. No proper British lady would leave the safety of a *dâk*–bungalow at night. Assuredly thou hast caught a thief."

"Nay, I have not! Look closely."

"Let me go!" Maura demanded in the same breath, struggling harder to break free.

"By God!" The second man strode hastily toward them. "Is that you, Miss Adams?"

Maura's eyes widened as Ross Hamilton's astonished face appeared through the darkness. "Oh, no. . . ."

Taking one look at her he burst into deep, resounding laughter.

"What's so funny?" she demanded, quivering with outrage.

"I might have known that a young lady who thinks nothing of attacking train robbers with an umbrella would be equally unconcerned about roaming the jungle at this hour!"

"I was not roaming," Maura retorted, still trying

33

to free herself from the Hindu's bruising grip. "Now will you *please* tell your bearer to let me go?"

"Then what were you doing?" Ross inquired, ignoring her request.

"I couldn't sleep. I was taking a walk."

"In considerable dishabille," he observed, still sounding wretchedly amused. But at least he signed to the Hindu to let her go. "You really are a little savage, aren't you?" he continued conversationally. "Don't you even own a shawl?"

"I dropped it when I fell," Maura answered frostily. "And you, sir, are no gentleman."

"My dear girl, at this moment you honestly have no right to be calling the kettle black."

"Oh!" Maura gasped. "You—you—"

"Go on," he invited when she broke off and stamped her foot out of sheer frustration. "I'm extremely interested to hear your opinion of me. Will it be vented in English or Hindustani, I wonder, and as charming as the choice things you said to that poor vendor in the Bombay station?"

He grinned as he spoke, a disarming grin that made him look young and devilishly handsome, and all at once, and quite without warning, Maura's anger vanished. Oh, she was aware that Captain Hamilton was making fun of her, that he was deriving unfair amusement at her expense, but though she knew that she should be furious with him, she felt like. . . . like laughing instead!

Lips twitching, she tipped her chin and tried hard to glare at him. The wind whipped her unbound hair behind her as their gazes clashed and held, and all at once the smile on Ross's lips faded and a look entered his eyes that Maura had never seen before. She shivered as something strange thrilled through her blood, making her heart beat faster. Her lips parted unwittingly and the color rose high in her cheeks.

"You damnable little wretch," Ross growled.

In the stillness they looked at each other, steadily and with something very like hostility. Neither was aware of how long the moment lasted, or of the Hindu bearer, Ghoda Lal, looking on with considerable interest.

I wonder what she'd do if I kissed her, Ross was thinking darkly. Surely that would serve to wipe the arrogance from her pretty face!

It was a very tempting thought.

He ought to be slapped, Maura was thinking haughtily. Staring at me like that, making no move to avert his eyes, while I have to stand here in front of him half undressed—!

Both of them flinched violently as a loud crash came from the *dâk*-bungalow behind them; a sound that was instantly followed by shrill screams. In a flash Ross seized Maura by the wrist and thrust her behind him.

"What are you doing?" she demanded furiously.

"Quiet!" Without releasing her he spoke sharply to his bearer, who melted away in the darkness.

"Captain Hamilton!" Maura's eyes widened as he drew a pistol from his waistband.

He glared at her. "Not going to get hysterical on me, are you?"

"Certainly not! But if you intend to shoot that thing I'd like to remind you that gunfire attracts attention."

"Obviously."

"But I'm not wearing—"

"I'm aware of that, too. Stay behind me if you wish to keep what's left of your dignity."

Her eyes sparked with fury. "You are absolutely insufferable, do you know that?"

"So you've told me before."

By now lights had sprung on throughout the bungalow. Footsteps pounded across the verandah, accompanied by the confused babble of the servants. The screams continued, louder than ever.

"Why, that's Aunt Daphne!" Maura exclaimed suddenly.

"No, you don't! Not again!" Ross made a grab for her, but she dodged past him and took off at a run. Cursing savagely, he followed, though he didn't catch up with her until she'd reached the verandah steps.

"Let me go!" she cried as he pinned her roughly beneath his arm.

"Just what do you intend to do?" he shot back. "You don't even have an umbrella this time!"

"I don't care!"

"Or much in the way of clothes, either!"

At that she went slack in his grasp. Grimly satisfied, he let her go. His eyes were like shards of flint as he looked her up and down. "Stay behind me and you may yet walk out of this with your reputation intact."

"But—"

"Do you understand me?"

Fuming but obedient, Maura followed him up the steps and into the bungalow. By now Aunt Daphne had stopped screaming, but she was standing at the foot of her bed with her hands pressed to her mouth and her ample bosom heaving. The rest of the room's occupants, including a very hysterical Lydia, were still running about in considerable confusion.

Pushing past the jibbering servants, Ross quickly dispersed the other women and took Aunt Daphne by the arm. Shaking her a little, he demanded to know what had happened.

"A man," gasped Aunt Daphne, "in our room! I woke to find him tugging on my ring!" She lifted a shaking hand to show him the wedding band on her finger. "He didn't manage to get it, but, oh, it was dreadful!"

"Where is he now?" inquired one of the gentlemen piling through the door.

"When I screamed he ran away. Can't someone catch him?"

"I've already sent my bearer in pursuit," Ross told her, "though I doubt he'll have any luck."

"So do I," agreed a man in the doorway. "I've heard that the bloody devils grease themselves with butter. Makes 'em too slippery to catch."

Sure enough, when Ghoda Lal returned a few minutes later, it was to report that the well-greased thief had managed to elude him. By this time Aunt Daphne had regained her composure sufficiently to realize with horror that neither she nor her young charges or any of the other ladies were decently attired. The impropriety of this was enough to bring about a complete return of her senses and, with the polite help of Captain Hamilton, she swiftly cleared the room. Ross remained behind long enough to arrange for a pair of servants to stand watch the remainder of the night.

"I suggest you push something heavy against the door as well," he added before he left.

In the doorway his eyes fell for a brief moment on Maura. When she saw that his lips were twitching, she lifted her chin and gave him a baleful stare.

"I hope we'll have no more disturbances tonight," he added meaningfully, then turned on his heel and disappeared.

No sooner had the sound of his footsteps died away on the verandah than Maura scooted into bed. No one had to tell her that she'd been extremely lucky not to have been missed in all the confusion. Aunt Daphne would have been horrified had she known that her niece had been carrying on a clandestine conversation in the darkness with a gentleman while wearing nothing more than her undergarments!

Thinking back on it, Maura couldn't help feeling annoyed. Ross Hamilton was certainly no gentleman. He'd had no right to laugh at her just because she'd been wandering around in the dark in her petticoats!

On the other hand, she had to admit that she'd been fortunate he hadn't marched her straight back into the bungalow in order to confront Aunt Daphne with her scandalous behavior. Still, Maura wasn't about to feel charitable toward him. Not when she was still so angry with him for laughing at her. Oh, and the way he had laughed, making her shiver as he looked at her with those intensely glowing blue eyes!

He was an unsettling man, if not a particularly likable one.

And why on earth are you still thinking about him? Maura asked herself scornfully. If anything, she should be thinking about Aunt Daphne, who'd endured more than enough since arriving in Bombay!

Poor Aunt Daphne, she thought belatedly. I shall have to make it up to her. Be kinder, watch out for her more than I have been.

Heaven knows, it couldn't hurt. Maybe that way Captain Hamilton wouldn't have to involve himself in their lives so much anymore. Maybe that way he'd leave them alone and stop preying on her thoughts this way. In fact, the sooner she stopped thinking about him, the better.

To prove that she could, Maura rolled onto her back and closed her eyes. And a scant minute later she had dropped off into a deep and thoroughly untroubled sleep.

Chapter Three

"It would seem your nighttime visitor did manage to steal something after all, though fortunately he ended up dropping it."

Maura froze, her tea cup suspended in the air, as Ross Hamilton crossed the verandah to the breakfast table where the three of them were seated.

"Why, it's your shawl, Maura!" Lydia exclaimed in surprise.

Mrs. Carlyon stared. "So it is! How very kind of you to return it, Captain."

"My pleasure," he answered, offering the garment to Maura.

"Thank you," she murmured, eyes downcast.

He inclined his dark head and clicked his booted heels together. "You're most welcome, Miss Adams."

Ooh, how his gallantry set her teeth on edge! She knew perfectly well that he enjoyed tormenting her.

"I only wonder," he went on glibly, "why he bothered stealing just a simple shawl? My bearer suggested that perhaps, seeing as it happens to be cashmere—"

"A thief wouldn't care what it's made of," Maura snapped, glaring at him.

"Precisely my own thoughts. Which is why I can't understand why he took the shawl and nothing else?"

Looking up into his laughing eyes, Maura wondered what he would do if she decided to poke a breakfast fork up his nose. "I couldn't imagine."

Lydia said thoughtfully, "Maybe that was all he could get his hands on after you screamed, Mama."

Mrs. Carlyon shuddered. "Can we talk about something else, please?"

Instantly Ross straightened and stepped away from Maura's side. "Of course. No reason to discuss anything so unpleasant for you."

Aunt Daphne smiled at him. Maura could tell that she was deeply touched by his thoughtfulness. She herself itched to turn the tea pot over on his head.

"Why don't you take breakfast with us?" Aunt Daphne invited.

To Maura's relief Ross declined, saying that he had breakfasted earlier. Furthermore, he had quite a bit of work to do if they were to leave on schedule that morning.

"Today?" Mrs. Carlyon exclaimed, startled. "But the others aren't going until tomorrow! Aren't we taking the same *dâk-gharry?*"

Ross shook his head. "I'm afraid there isn't room. I had to bribe the driver handsomely just to make certain your trunks went along."

"Then what is it we're going to do?" Mrs. Carlyon demanded.

"My bearer is in the nearby village at the moment procuring horses for us."

"You mean we'll have to ride?" Aunt Daphne's voice had grown faint.

Ross's lips twitched as he studied her plump, unathletic form. "Never fear, madam. He has instructions to bring a carriage as well."

"I should like to ride," Maura said eagerly.

"Oh, my dear—" Mrs. Carlyon began doubtfully, but Ross interrupted.

"I was rather hoping one of you would. It's doubtful there'll be room for all three in the carriage."

"But, Captain, surely you can't expect—"

"I do," Ross said more forcibly. "This isn't Bombay. We don't have limitless choices."

"I see. Well, if we must. . . . Although I've no idea what Mr. Carlyon will say about this. Are you certain you don't mind, Maura?"

Smiling, Maura shook her head and saluted Ross with her teacup, letting him know that all was forgiven.

When Ghoda Lal returned a scant hour later he was driving a high-wheeled *ekka* whose narrow seat was indeed only wide enough for Lydia and Aunt Daphne. Behind the *ekka* plodded a pair of down country mares, both half-starved and considerably mean looking.

"Oh, but they will never do!" Aunt Daphne protested at the sight of them. It was one thing to allow her niece to ride a well-schooled hack, but one of these ill-bred creatures?

"There was nothing else to be had," Ross told her. "Our fellow travelers have put a considerable strain on the local resources."

"Please don't worry, Aunt Daphne," Maura added

42

quickly. "Ghoda Lal can drive the two of you, and Captain Hamilton and I shall ride."

"Ghoda Lal? Who is Ghoda Lal?"

"Why, Captain Hamilton's bearer."

Aunt Daphne looked at her. "However did you know his name?"

"I—" Maura broke off and looked helplessly at Ross.

"The miss-sahib sought me out this morning," Ghoda Lal answered quickly, bowing to Aunt Daphne. "She wished to thank me for attempting to catch the thief last night."

"You've trained him well," Maura said in an undertone to Ross. "He tells lies as well as you do."

"On the contrary, I've learned most of what I know from him. He's usually the one plucking *me* out of hot water." To Aunt Daphne Ross added politely, "Well, ma'am?"

"Oh, dear, I don't know! Maura, are you certain you wish to ride?"

"Quite sure," Maura answered cheerfully.

"Very well, then. But, Captain, you'll keep a close eye on her, won't you?"

Ross's bland expression never changed. "Rest assured that I will, ma'am."

Clenching her teeth in what she hoped would pass for an agreeable smile, Maura took up the reins and waited for him to help her into the saddle. When he tossed her up like a sack of oats she whirled to give him a healthy blow with her whip, but by then the mare was already proving herself every bit as ill-spirited as she appeared. By the time Maura had gotten the bucking creature under control, Ross had moved away to help Aunt Daphne and Lydia into the *ekka*.

At any rate, Maura's mood quickly lifted the mo-

43

ment she found herself astride, free at long last from confinement following the endless weeks at sea and those wearying hours on the Bombay train. Her eyes glowed, her anger was forgotten, and she trotted quite companionably beside Ross past acres of mustard fields with the morning sun warm on her back. Monkeys chattered in the trees above them while peacocks strutted in the gold-barred shadows, their haunting calls the sound of home.

The villages through which they passed that day were filled with friendly natives who offered them milk and *chupattis*, the flour cakes of India, to sustain them on their journey. Maura and Ross ate them while they rode, and shared a bottle of raspberry-ade left over from the train. They didn't speak at all, for the *ekka*'s wheels rumbled deafeningly over the rocky road directly behind them, but the silence between them was for once free of hostility.

I suppose we've made a truce of sorts, Maura thought contentedly. She had forgiven him everything, in fact, and he in turn seemed to have relaxed when it became apparent that she intended to mind her manners while astride.

For the time being, at any rate.

Maura was wearing a wide-brimmed straw hat to protect her from the strong sun, but by evening her cheeks and the bridge of her nose were burned a charming pink. She was tired and covered with dust, but completely, mindlessly happy by the time they stopped at last in a grassy clearing near the banks of a river. Twilight was falling and the first stars were winking in the black canopy of the sky.

Dismounting, Ross came around the side of her horse to help her down.

"I'm fine, thank you," she assured him, looping up

the reins and sliding from the saddle. But her legs buckled the moment they touched the ground, and Ross had to move quickly to catch her before she fell.

She laughed ruefully. "I guess I'm not as fit as I thought."

"You've managed six hours in the saddle," he pointed out gruffly.

Her laughter died at his tone. Up swept her eyes to meet his. In the breathless stillness that settled over them she became aware that he hadn't released her yet; that his strong hands were still clasped about her waist. His nearness and the intimacy of his touch made her heart catch oddly.

"Captain Hamilton! Why on earth are we stopping here?"

The *ekka* had drawn alongside and a puzzled Aunt Daphne was descending on Ghoda Lal's arm. In the distance, the lights of a village winked through the trees, and the murmurous water from the nearby river carried with it the bleating of goats and the voices of children. The smell of cooking fires hung heavy in the warm air.

"This is where we're going to make camp," Ross explained, releasing Maura and stepping away. He was frowning, the way he usually did whenever something annoyed him.

"Camp?" Lydia glanced fearfully around her. On the far side of the river the jungle pressed close, the yawning darkness alive—so she imagined—with hungry tigers and legions of snakes.

"Camp!" her mother echoed faintly. "But Captain Hamilton, surely you can't mean—"

"You'll find every last *dâk* around here over-flowing with Europeans," Ross interrupted with the first hint of impatience Maura had ever heard him

45

exhibit toward her aunt. "Not only are our fellow passengers heading in the same direction, but one of the largest trunk roads in the district passes right through here. It's a heavily traveled route."

"Oh, my," breathed Mrs. Carlyon. "I had no idea. I didn't realize—" Her voice trailed away and she looked as though she wanted to cry.

"Where will we sleep?" Maura asked with interest. "Your bearer didn't happen to bring along the tent you were using last night?"

"What tent is that?" Lydia asked, sounding close to tears.

Ross wisely ignored her. "You'll be quite comfortable under the carriage. My bearer brought blankets." In an undertone to Maura he added, "Unfortunately, the tent wasn't ours."

"So we'll be sleeping outside?" She was intrigued by the idea. "Under the wagon? I wonder what Aunt Daphne has to say about that?"

Both of them looked inquiringly at Mrs. Carlyon, but apparently Maura's plump little aunt had decided to face this latest ordeal with proper British fortitude. Taking a handkerchief from her fichu she dried Lydia's tears and murmured something about all of them accepting the fact that the lives of frontier memsahibs were endlessly difficult and that they must now show a bit of backbone for the benefit of poor Mr. Carlyon, who would no doubt be frantic once the Bombay train failed to arrive.

Over her daughter's head her surprisingly calm gaze sought Ross's. "If your bearer would be so kind as to build us a fire, Captain Hamilton? That way we can cook a meal from our provisions. And if you would check the safety of the riverbank before it gets too dark? The girls and I will need to wash before going to bed."

Ross inclined his head, and Maura, seeing his lips twitch, knew that he was trying to suppress a smile. Her heart warmed, aware that he was feeling something very like fondness for her aunt.

"I'd be more than happy to, madam."

By the time the cooking fire had burned low and the simple meal of fried *chupattis* and honey-glazed fruit had been consumed, Lydia seemed to have accepted their situation. Aunt Daphne had helped to distract her by regaling everyone with fascinating tales of her newlywed life in India.

Captain Hamilton, too, had spoken a little about his early days on the Northwest Frontier, which had surprised Maura because she had already come to realize that he was by nature a quiet man. Listening to his recollections of patrolling the notorious Khyber Pass and bringing Afghani thieves to justice, she found herself wondering again why he had been reduced to serving in the role of military attaché to the British Resident of a tiny backwater like Bhunapore. Surely he was qualified to undertake far more important assignments?

Eventually the fire died to glowing embers and the night wind began crooning through the trees.

"I think," said Aunt Daphne, "it's time we all went to bed."

While the women went down to the river to wash, Ross hobbled the horses and Ghoda Lal spread rough blankets on the grass beneath the *ekka*. Maura was the first to return from the river, and she paused briefly beneath the tree where Ghoda Lal was making himself comfortable with his saddle and rifle to thank him for his efforts. She had unpinned her hair while down at the water, and Ross, coming into the clearing from the far side of the

47

road, saw the glint of crimson as it swung in a curtain to her hips. She had just said something to Ghoda Lal that had made him laugh, and as she tossed back her head to join him, Ross could see the smooth, womanly column of her slim white throat.

A flash of unreasoning anger hit him. Since when did Ghoda Lal make it a habit to trade jests with a memsahib? Like any devout Hindu, he had always steered well clear of them, disapproving, as most of his race did, of the open way British ladies consorted with their men, danced with them in public while wearing shockingly low-cut dresses, and refused to veil their faces in the presence of strangers.

But Ghoda Lal was a young man, and obviously not immune to a lovely face, whether it was sloe-eyed and brown or smooth as a lily petal and framed with the most riotous gold-red hair Ross himself had ever seen.

Perhaps, he reflected grimly, it was a good thing that Delhi lay barely another day's journey across the plain. With luck they should reach its great red walls before nightfall tomorrow. Lawrence Carlyon had friends in the city, friends who would willingly take his wife, daughter, and niece under their wing until arrangements could be made to transport them comfortably—and properly—across the twenty-odd miles remaining between Delhi and Bhunapore.

And I will have discharged my duty and can consider myself finished with them, Ross thought with grim relief.

"Captain Hamilton."

He looked around, frowning, to see that Maura had crossed the clearing to join him where he stood brooding amid the shadows. The night was moonless but not so dark as to conceal the white stains that were Maura's dress and bare arms. Her magnificent hair spilled down her shoulders and breasts, and Ross found that he had to look deliberately away.

"Miss Adams?" he said brusquely when she ventured to say nothing more, only stood there looking at him with a faint frown pulling at the corners of her lovely mouth.

"I wanted to ask you something before my aunt and cousin return."

"Oh?" His arms, which had been crossed before him, fell away as he straightened. He was beginning to know Miss Maura Adams very well indeed, and thought it wise to prepare himself for whatever preposterous query was about to tumble from her innocent-seeming lips.

"How can you be certain they'll be safe sleeping under the wagon?"

"Who?"

"My aunt and cousin."

Ross frowned. "Why shouldn't they?"

She hesitated. "I remembering being told as a child that it . . . um . . . that it's dangerous for English ladies to sleep out in the open on Indian roads. Aunt Daphne seems to have forgotten, but my father always said—"

"What did he say?" Ross prodded when she fell silent.

She bit her lip, and despite the dim starlight Ross could see the color surging to her cheeks. Sudden understanding hit him, but instead of wanting to laugh, he found himself consumed with the same odd anger that had washed over him when he had watched Maura and Ghoda Lal laughing together in the shadows.

"My dear Miss Adams," he said icily, "do you hon-

49

estly believe I'd permit the three of you to camp here if there was the least danger that you'd end up losing your virtue to roving *budmarshes?*"

Maura was by nature an outspoken girl, but no one had ever spoken so baldly to her about rape before, especially not a man like Ross Hamilton, who disconcerted her as no man ever had. She felt the heat of her embarrassment wash up and over her, and without another word she turned from him and fled.

With unsteady fingers Ross reached into his coat pocket and drew out a cigarette. Lighting it, he inhaled deeply, then grimaced and crushed it impatiently beneath his heel.

"Hell!" he said savagely although he had no idea at whom he was directing his anger. Surely the chit must know that he'd be damned before he let that happen!

Some time during the night, while Ross and Ghoda Lal kept watch over the sleeping women, clouds blew in from the foothills and it began to rain. Neither man had expected it, and Ghoda Lal swore savagely as he crawled more deeply into the thickets with his rifle and bedroll. Ross had no choice but to take cover beneath the *ekka,* although there was little room. Mrs. Carlyon and her daughter had made themselves comfortable beneath the rear axle while Maura slept on a blanket toward the front.

Ross seated himself quietly with his back to one of the front wheels, his head bent to prevent it from striking the floorboards above. Beside him Maura lay without moving, her cheek cradled on an outstretched arm. Ross sat for a while watching her, marveling at how innocent she appeared while asleep—and how her breasts rose and fell to the quiet rhythm of her breathing.

Quite without warning he found himself having to avert his eyes. Propping his rifle across his knees, he shifted angrily to relieve the uncomfortable pressure in his loins. Scowling, he cursed the rain as energetically as Ghoda Lal had done earlier.

What in hell was the matter with him? This annoying Irish redhead had a way of getting under his skin that was nothing short of infuriating! The last thing he wanted was to start lusting after her, by God! Not only was Maura Adams not at all to his taste, but she was Lawrence Carlyon's niece, of all people! Why couldn't the damnable chit be more like Carlyon's shy, unassuming daughter?

Leaning his head against the carriage wheel, Ross stubbornly closed his eyes. Unfortunately it took quite some time before the heat faded and sleep finally claimed him.

A few hours later the rain ended and the air became fresh and cool. Stars winked in the clearing skies. Across the murmurous river an owl hooted. A jackal barked shrilly in the jungle, and the sound awoke Maura from sound slumber.

Opening her eyes she saw above her the floorboards of the *ekka*. The ground beneath her was rocky and hard, but she was aware of a strange sense of well being, as though she had slept for endless hours on the softest of beds. How on earth was that possible?

Turning her head a little, she felt her cheek brush against something solid and warm. After a moment, and with a curious lack of surprise, she realized that it was a man; Ross Hamilton, to be exact, who lay stretched out beside her beneath the front wheels of

51

the *ekka*. She became aware that she was lying curled against his hip, as though she had sought out his warmth as the night air grew cool.

From the sound of his deep, even breathing, Maura realized that he was asleep. She realized, too—again with a complete lack of surprise—that she didn't feel the least bit embarrassed to find herself lying with the hard curves of his chest beneath her cheek. Instead she knew again that odd sense of comfort that had overwhelmed her in his arms on board the Bombay train after it had derailed; a sense of safety and belonging the likes of which she hadn't known since her parents had sent her away from home.

Holding her breath, Maura raised herself slowly up on one elbow. Ross did not stir. He must be very tired, she thought, to sleep so deeply.

Shamelessly she studied his face in the starlight. His expression was unguarded for once, his face almost unrecognizable relaxed in sleep. Strange, but she had never noticed before how young he looked with his black hair tumbling over his brow, or how his mouth had a tendency to curve almost sensuously now that he wasn't berating her or smiling wryly at yet another of Aunt Daphne's hysterical posturings.

For the first time Maura wondered how a man as proud as this one must have felt upon being pressed into the role of chaperone for three such tiresome women. It had been obvious to her from the very first that Ross preferred far more vigorous duties out in the rugged wilds of the Indian frontier with only Ghoda Lal for company. Nevertheless, he had been unfailingly polite to all of them so far, even, admittedly, to her. Not once had he let them see how irritating he found their presence or how much he chafed to be done with them.

"You're a lot nicer than you want other people to think," Maura told him softly. "Aren't you, Ross Hamilton?"

No answer. Nor had she expected one. Even if Ross had overheard her impertinent question he would never have chosen to answer it. Maura was beginning to know him very well, and suspected that he was not the sort to let anyone, especially a woman, become privy to the secrets of his soul.

Which was just as well. At the moment she was truly uninterested in the workings of Ross Hamilton's heart. What she wanted more than anything was the warmth that his nearness provided. Lying down, she curled her shivering body shamelessly against the protective curve of his hip and, closing her eyes, drifted off into a sleep that was as deep and dreamless as his own.

Chapter Four

Lawrence Carlyon's house stood just inside the tall front gates of Bhunapore's sprawling British settlement. Owing to his distinguished position as British Resident of Bhunapore—a tiny state lying no more than a day's journey north of Delhi—Mr. Carlyon had been given a rambling, whitewashed residency which was larger and more modern than the bungalows on the far side of the cantonment street . . . but only just. The walls were made of simple mud bricks and the roof was topped with thatch. Owing to the destructive nature of termites and white ants, the floor was not made of wood, but packed earth covered with primitive rush mats. There were few windows, and those were suffocatingly small and covered during the day by thick wooden shutters to keep out the sun.

At least the size of the Residency was such that Lydia and Maura both had rooms to themselves, although they were stark, with furniture constructed of rough wooden planks and walls hung with mil- dewed brocade. The mirrors were tarnished, and the beds, covered with mosquito netting, stood in pans of water to discourage crawling insects.

Surprisingly, Mrs. Carlyon declared herself un- daunted by the bleakness of their new home. She had brought many household items with her from England, including porcelain, candleholders and yards of bright chintz. Once these had been un- packed and the material converted into cushions, hangings and slipcovers, she assured them that the Residency would take on a considerably cosier air.

Besides, as she pointed out to her utterly dis- mayed daughter, they were actually quite fortunate. The Residency had its own drawing room, which opened onto the verandah by way of tall French win- dows covered by split-cane *chiks*. That and the lovely little parlor on the opposite end were marks of distinction that separated the home of the British Resident from all the others.

Tomorrow, said Mrs. Carlyon, they would visit the Bhunapore bazaar to see what sort of furniture they could purchase, and this would go a long way toward making the place seem more like the home they had left behind.

"I hope you're right, Mama," Lydia had said doubtfully.

Unlike her cousin, Maura did not find her new surroundings oppressive or strange. Before the first day was out she had managed to make friends with Meera, the middle-aged Hindu woman who would be serving both English girls as personal maid, or *ayah*. Within the space of an hour, she had also learned all the current gossip concerning everyone, European and native alike, who lived in the Bhu-

55

napore cantonment. Maura had forgotten that in British India secrets were simply not kept, and now, remembering, it seemed perfectly natural for her to discover that Meera and the other Residency servants spent their days doing what everyone else around them did: gossiping endlessly about themselves and each other.

Not surprisingly, she already felt quite at home in the rambling residency house, which reminded her in no small measure of the roomy bungalow in the city of Lucknow where she had been born. She did not mind the lizards, rats, or myriad insects that invaded every dark corner of the walls and cupboards. And she thought it wonderful to sit in the shade of the verandah every evening listening to the creaking of the well rope in the garden, the subdued conversation of the servants, and the crows cawing out on the plains while the sun set in a pageant of pearlescent color that was breathtaking to behold.

Lawrence Carlyon was delighted to have his family about him once again. Although his daughter and niece were no longer the little girls in frilled pantalettes and sashes he remembered from his last visit to England six long years before, he pronounced himself bewitched by the lovely young ladies into which they had grown. He hinted that Terence Shadwell, the young clerk to whom Lydia was unofficially affianced, would also be enchanted, and the remark brought a pretty blush to his daughter's cheeks.

"I've invited him to dine tomorrow evening. You'll meet him then. As for you, Maura—" Lawrence twinkled at his niece—"I've a surprise for you too."

Maura smiled across the breakfast table into his kind, chubby face. "I hope you haven't been so bold as to pick out a suitor for me, Uncle Lawrence."

"Have you no intention of marrying, dear?" Aunt Daphne asked with a sudden frown. The thought seemed inconceivable to her. Why else did young ladies come out to India if not to find themselves a husband among the countless bachelors, who outnumbered the women three to one?

"I think Maura already has someone in mind," Lydia said wickedly.

Maura laughed. "Do I? Pray enlighten me."

"Why, Captain Hamilton, of course. No, I mean it," Lydia insisted as Maura's brows shot up. "He's ever so handsome and kind, don't you think?"

"Better not let young Terence hear you talking that way," her father said with a hearty laugh. "And leave Ross out of it, will you? Never had a better man serving under me, and I've no desire to see him snapped up in matrimony any time soon."

"Where is he, by the way?" inquired Aunt Daphne, who suddenly realized that she had seen nothing of the captain since their arrival two days earlier.

"Gone shooting with his bearer. Figured he'd be needing leave after playing nursemaid to the three of you." Chuckling, Lawrence gave his wife a fond kiss on the cheek.

Maura was glad when the *khidmatgar*, the Residency's head waiter, entered with the tea and so brought an end to the conversation. She didn't want to talk about Ross Hamilton, or even think about him. Not when she was still chafing at the way he had treated her on that last day before reaching Delhi: all but ignoring her, or speaking to her only when he absolutely had to—and then in a stiffly formal tone that made her feel like some osseous octagenarian, not the young woman against whose side he had slept for the duration of a cold, damp night!

57

It might never have happened, Maura thought resentfully, recalling how she had felt upon crawling out from under the ekka that morning to find Ross in a thoroughly grumpy and uncommunicative mood—but only toward her! Why, he had all but gone out of his way to be kind to Aunt Daphne and Lydia while abandoning her to the care of his indifferent bearer!

Crabby man. She should have tweaked that hawkish nose of his, or given his ear a proper twist instead of behaving as though she didn't care.

Which she didn't!

Maura was doubly glad now that her uncle had granted Ross leave to go hunting. By the time he returned she would be totally immersed in this new life of hers, and he would once again be reduced to nothing more than a lowly member of her uncle's staff. Her chin tipped haughtily. As if he had ever been anything else!

The following evening, after hours of agonized waiting on the part of poor Lydia, Terence Shadwell made his appearance on the Residency doorstep. Maura was delighted to find him a pleasant young man with kindly brown eyes and a shy, appealing manner. Not only did he present his betrothed with a bouquet of flowers, but he had brought gifts for Maura and Aunt Daphne as well.

It was obvious that the British Resident thought highly of him, a sentiment that appeared to be shared by his daughter, who blushed pinkly whenever Terence so much as looked at her. He in turn seemed smitten by the picture Lydia presented in a sprigged frock of pale blue satin and with her dark hair artfully rolled in a chignon. Aunt Daphne dabbed emotionally at her eyes as she watched them exchange their first, tentative smiles.

After the introductions were behind them, Uncle Lawrence suggested that everyone retire to the parlor. Their progress was halted, however, by the turbanned *chupprassi*, who announced yet another arrival.

"That will be Charles," Terence said, brightening.

"Who is Charles?" Aunt Daphne wished to know. "Lawrence, you didn't say anything about another guest!"

Her husband's eyes twinkled. "Didn't I? What about that surprise I mentioned, the dinner partner for Maura?"

Oh, no! Maura thought in panic, but by then it was too late. The *chupprassi* had already shown him in: a tall, smartly dressed Englishman in his early thirties with bold black eyes and impressive sideburns who went by the name of Charles Burton-Pascal. Another round of introductions followed in which the womenfolk learned that he was distantly related to Terence on his mother's side, an aristocrat on a grand tour of India who was so enamored of the country that he had decided to prolong his stay indefinitely.

Before Maura could warm to him, however, Charles went on to elaborate on the rough shooting he had been doing since his arrival last winter and how he had bagged no fewer than three tigers and an elephant in the last month alone. Maura, who championed the very un-British view of condoning hunting only when there were hungry mouths to feed, immediately lost interest in him.

During dinner, Mr. Burton-Pascal nevertheless showed himself to be both charming and skilled at conversation. Mrs. Carlyon, watching both young couples with a matronly eye, was delighted by her niece's uncharacteristic stillness as she sat dutifully beside him. Could the girl actually be feeling shy in the presence of a gentleman? What a delightful notion! Not only did Lydia and her young man appear most taken with each other, but here dear Maura had wasted no time in finding Someone Special as well! How clever of Lawrence to have arranged it. One could only hope that Mr. Burton-Pascal chose to stay in the area long enough to press a stronger suit.

"Terence is so very handsome," Lydia confided breathlessly to Maura as the two girls readied themselves for bed that night. "He is every bit as wonderful as I imagined from his letters."

"Only his portrait did not do him justice, did it?" Maura teased.

Lydia sighed dreamily. "No. He is *sooo* much better looking in real life. Do you know, Maura, he intends to speak to Papa as early as next week! Do you think Papa will approve?"

Maura unpinned her hair and shook out the tangled red curls. "I don't see why not."

"As for Mr. Burton-Pascal . . ." Lydia added slyly.

Maura put a finger to her lips. "Now, where on earth has my nightgown gone? Be a dear, Lyddie, and ask Meera to fetch it for me, will you?"

Later, as a bone white moon rose over the garden and the bamboo brake beyond the house rustled and sighed to the crooning of the wind, Maura lay in bed thinking about Charles Burton-Pascal—but not in the favorable light her family would have hoped. It was clear to her that Lydia, happily in love and soon to be married, yearned to bestow similar blessings upon her cousin. Even Aunt Daphne seemed to feel the same.

Well, why shouldn't they? English girls came out to India all the time to be married—sometimes, like Lydia, after entering into courtships that had taken place entirely through letters, and sometimes without any prospects at all. The practice was so common, in fact, that the ships which brought these hopeful young brides out to India were dubbed, rather unkindly, the "fishing fleets."

The problem was that Maura did not wish to be married. Not now; not ever. All her life she had wanted nothing more than to come home to India, and now that she was here, she was not about to rush into an unwanted relationship simply because the tenets of the day and age demanded it.

"And if I ever do get married, which I doubt, it certainly won't be to a puffed up toady like Charles Burton-Pascal!" Maura told herself aloud. "Or—or anyone else!" Rolling over, she shut her eyes and gave the matter no more thought.

"Now I know why Mama insisted we bring so many clothes with us," groaned Lydia one humid afternoon several days later. She was standing in her dressing room waiting for Meera to lace up her corset. Guests were expected at the Residency within the hour for an impromptu birthday party honoring the Carlyons' prospective son-in-law. There would be light sandwiches, curry puffs, and even a birthday cake. Mrs. Delaney, the popular wife of a local subaltern, was going to sing, and a juggler from the bazaar had been hired to perform tricks with his trained parrots and monkeys.

The Residency had already become the fashionable place for Bhunapore's residents to gather, with Mrs. Carlyon appointed the station's Senior Memsahib. In keeping with such an exalted position, she had begun entertaining three or four times a week, transforming her abode with plants, wicker, brass, and chintz into a surprisingly elegant domicile. The other memsahibs of the station had hurried to pay calls, and invitations to Residency socials were already being vied for quite fiercely.

"We had lots of parties in Lucknow when my parents were alive," Maura remembered now. "I suppose it's the accepted way of life here in India."

She was sitting beneath the cooling breeze of the *punkah* fan in her petticoat and crinolines waiting for her turn to dress. An afternoon party demanded a complete change of wardrobe from the demure frocks that had served for morning calls, and now Maura did her best to stand patiently while Meera slipped a ruffled white party gown over her head.

The gown was made of tulle, the spreading skirts gathered up in flounces that were held in place by stitched bouquets of tea-rose yellow camellias. The white of the ballgown warmed Maura's fair skin, and in it her figure was revealed to possess a breathtaking slimness. Meera clucked approvingly as she combed and twisted and pinned her young mistress's red hair in a manner that lent fresh beauty to the girl's clean-cut features.

"Thou wilt be the loveliest miss-sahib at the party tonight," she murmured in the venacular.

Maura responded with an unladylike snort. The moment Meera was finished with her she escaped to the drawing room only to find there a scene of considerable foment as Aunt Daphne exhorted the servants to put this here, place that there, rearrange the flowers, bring in more napkins and lay out the huge array of sandwiches and side dishes. The servants obeyed, looking even more harassed than

Aunt Daphne, and Maura wisely fled to the verandah.

The afternoon was very warm and still. Only a slight breeze stirred the plumbago hedges fringing the entrance of the Residency. The head gardener, the *mali*, an elderly Mussulman by the name of Mohammed Akbar, was weeding the flowerbeds near the front gate. Maura wandered over to inquire after his granddaughter, who had fallen from the stable roof two days earlier and broken her arm.

They spoke politely for several minutes before Maura bid him farewell and strolled away. Her uncle's office, a small cottage separated from the Residency proper by a sand walkway and a cluster of pepper trees, lay before her. As she approached, the front door opened from within so unexpectedly that Maura had to step quickly out of the way. Looking up indignantly, she found herself gazing into the startled eyes of Ross Hamilton.

For a moment they stared at one another without speaking. Maura had not seen him since he had brought them to Delhi nearly a week before, and she had not known that he had returned from hunting. She noticed that he looked tired and harassed and immediately her indignation faded. In its stead rose a thoroughly unexpected impulse: the temptation to reach up and smooth away the weary lines that etched his brow.

Mortified, she thrust her hands behind her back, but Ross appeared not to notice. He, too, had been taken aback by her sudden appearance—not because he hadn't expected it, but because of the way she looked. For some reason, the Maura Adams of his memory did not square with this lovely creature in the flounced white balldress, who wore her bright red hair pinned in soft waves to her head and whose

63

slimly seductive waist and curving breasts were revealed by the elegant cut of her gown. On the long and admittedly tiresome journey from Bombay she had never looked quite like this: so young and freshly virginal, and at the same time so poised and unattainable, and stirringly desirable.

"I hadn't realized you were back, Captain Hamilton," she said when the silence between them became painfully obvious. She looked down at her hands, striving to sound casual. "When did you return?"

"Late last night."

"Was your hunting successful?"

Ross shrugged his broad shoulders. "I've had better days. The heat, I think, has driven the *nilghai* too far into the hills."

"Will you be joining us for Mr. Shadwell's birthday party?"

A birthday party. Ah. That explained the elegant balldress and the seed pearl combs that caught up the shining waves of her hair.

"Mr. Carlyon mentioned something about it," Ross admitted, "but I'm afraid I have—" He broke off because he saw that Maura was no longer listening. She was peering over his shoulder, her pansy eyes wide, and Ross turned quickly to see a high–wheeled carriage passing beneath the Residency gates with two men seated inside. He recognized one of them as Terence Shadwell, Lydia Carlyon's betrothed, while the other was a dangerous looking fellow with handsome features whom he had never seen before.

He turned back to Maura. "Who is that?"

"Charles Burton-Pascal. An—an acquaintance of Mr. Shadwell's."

There was something in her tone that Ross had

never heard before. Dismay? Dislike? Or, perhaps, admiration? Whatever it was, it had changed her. The breathless expectancy that had so transformed her a moment earlier was gone.

Ross frowned, and Maura, turning and catching sight of it, forced herself to laugh lightly. "You haven't answered my question, Captain Hamilton. Are you coming to the party?"

"Yes," Ross heard himself say although a moment ago nothing had been further from his mind. He was not by nature a sociable man, but now, abruptly, he smiled at Maura, although the humor of the smile didn't quite reach his eyes. "I'd better change into something more suitable, don't you think?" Without waiting for her answer, he bowed and walked away.

When he stepped into the Residency's drawing room some twenty minutes later, the party was in full swing. Girls in bright party dresses laughed and flirted with the officers who had gathered, most of them wearing the gorgeous dress uniforms of regiments that had never been heard of outside India. The civilian men were all high-ranking representatives of the British Raj, and many of them sported medals and orders to prove as much. Bhunapore, although tiny as far as Indian territories went, had an admirable representation of Britain's Indian political and civil service.

Ross recognized most of the people there. Because this was his first public appearance in quite some time, he was instantly monopolized; greeted with obvious pleasure by the men already gathered— and by quite a number of the ladies. Maura, who had been speaking with the commanding officer of Bhunapore's modest infantry when Ross came in, did not fail to notice the way the other ladies' fans began fluttering the moment he appeared. Judging from the way most of the mamas in attendance were nudging their daughters in his direction, she guessed that Captain Hamilton was considered a highly eligible catch.

For some reason the thought annoyed her. Granted, there was no denying that Ross Hamilton was the most arresting man at the party. Tall and broad shouldered, he seemed to possess the magnificent lines of a jungle cat as he prowled among the guests, and he certainly looked handsome enough in his scarlet regimentals, which enhanced his dark masculinity so that he appeared both dashing and mysterious. But who on earth would wish to marry such a difficult, temperamental man?

I certainly wouldn't, Maura thought.

Watching him without acknowledging that she was, she saw him pause in front of a stout British matron whose name she couldn't remember. Greeting the woman politely, he then turned to her flaxen-haired daughter, bowed over her hand and said something that made her give vent to a tinkling little laugh. Scowling, Maura saw that Ross was laughing too, his handsome face far more relaxed than she had ever seen it.

"I'm sorry," she said, turning deliberately back to her companion. "What were you saying, Major Clapham?"

After the birthday cake had been presented to the blushing Terence and he had made a clumsy but touching speech, the dancing began. Bhunapore's tiny regimental band had graciously agreed to provide entertainment, and the moment it burst into a noisy rendition of "El Dorado," eager couples flocked to the floor.

In keeping with the impromptu spirit of the party, Mrs. Carlyon had done away with the formal etiquette of dance cards, and Maura found herself inundated by would-be partners every time the band struck up another tune. Captain Hamilton, she couldn't help noticing, danced surprisingly well. Nor was he lacking for eager partners, she thought resentfully, judging from the furious blushes that crept into comely cheeks whenever he asked for this hand or that. But he did not once, that entire afternoon, ask to dance with her.

Not that she cared. Bhunapore might be a small British station, but, as elsewhere in India, it was not lacking for eligible men. She made a point of smiling sweetly at each and every one who escorted her onto the floor, and listening with apparent interest to everything that was said.

But she could not prevent a small, unwilling frown from knitting her brow sometime later when Charles Burton-Pascal appeared before her and, bowing deeply, requested another dance. Maura had already granted him a mazurka and two reels, and she had no real desire to have him partner her in this, the far more intimate waltz. She was about to open her mouth and tell him as much when a shadow fell across her.

"Sorry," Ross said curtly to Charles. "I believe this dance has been promised to me." Without waiting for a reply, he took Maura's arm and led her away.

The hour, meanwhile, had grown late. Turbanned servants were pulling back the *chik* blinds over the French windows. Long shadows lay across the garden outside. The more elderly of the guests were already taking their leave even though the band continued its valiant puffing and scraping and plucking away on humidity-tarnished instruments. Even the dance floor was no longer as crowded as before.

Maura didn't notice. She was aware of nothing

67

but the heat rising to her cheeks as Ross took her hand in his and turned her until she was facing him. She searched desperately for something casual to say, something that would prove to him—and her—that she was not anywhere near as flustered as she appeared.

She settled at last on the truth. "Thank you. I had no wish to dance with Mr. Burton-Pascal again."

"No need to thank me," Ross said curtly. "Only thing for a gentleman to do." Seeing her blank look, he frowned. "Surely you're aware, Miss Adams, that to dance four times in a single afternoon with the same man is tantamount to becoming engaged to him?"

No, Maura hadn't realized. And the fact that Ross had led her out merely to foil Burton-Pascal's request—and not because he had actually desired to dance with her—made her feel angry and wounded and very foolish. But she wasn't about to let him know.

"I'd forgotten that the social rules here in India are more strict than those in England," she said coolly.

"I can assure you that no one else has forgotten. Not for a moment. You'd do well always to remember that everyone here is far more narrow-minded than you think."

Maura looked at him, surprised by his biting tone. "Then why do you stay here, if you dislike everyone so? Surely someone of your talent and experience would have no trouble finding work back home?"

"I stay because of India," Ross told her grimly. "India *is* my home."

Maura had never heard anyone admit aloud what she had always felt in her heart. She could only stare at Ross, amazed. "Mine, too," she confessed in an aching whisper.

Startled, Ross glanced down at her. Their eyes met and they exchanged a long, steady look. Flustered, Maura didn't even notice when the music ended and he led her back to the approving smiles of Aunt Daphne.

"I'm quite amazed at how well you dance, Captain Hamilton. You'll have to join us more often."

But that was the last thing Ross wanted. He had managed for most of his life to avoid the romantic entanglements that preoccupied the bored men and flighty women on British stations across the length and breadth of India. Socializing, flirting, seducing trembling virgins and jaded memsahibs were commonly accepted games that had never been to his taste. Whatever dark desires stirred him had always been appeased elsewhere, usually in the arms of a skilled Indian courtesan who knew how to be discreet.

No, Ross reflected, savagely dismissing the stirrings of desire he had felt while holding Maura Adams's slim body in his arms. He was not the sort to change his ways merely because he had felt the pull of a young girl's winsome smiles. Especially Maura Adams, who was in truth no more than a fishing-fleet bride—albeit lovely enough to reel in any husband she wished.

Pleading a heavy load of evening work, he excused himself from Mrs. Carlyon, and gave Maura a curt nod before vanishing through the door.

"He certainly is a temperamental man," remarked Aunt Daphne, sighing. "I think he can be downright difficult at times, don't you? Oh, look, dear. Mr. Burton–Pascal is coming this way. I'm not at all sure it's quite the thing for you to dance with him again.

On the other hand, one must allow that convention—"

But Maura had heard enough. She had no desire to face Charles Burton-Pascal, not after Ross Hamilton had just quitted the party as though he couldn't get away from her fast enough! Without a word to her aunt, she fled to the verandah.

Afternoon had waned and the brief Indian twilight was closing over the land. The sky was a luminous turquoise in which the first faint stars were pulsing to life. The sound of a conch braying from a distant temple mingled on the breeze with the harsh cries of the Residency peacocks. Fruitbats and night birds were stirring, and the air was alive with the whirring of wings. Maura stood quietly at the railing, forgetting her heartache and confusion as she breathed in the enchantment of the coming night.

A murmur of voices drew her attention to the front gate. Turning her head she saw the Residency's *chowkidar*, the night watchman, making a respectful obeisance to Captain Hamilton, who was sitting astride a restless horse waiting for the gate to be opened.

In response to the *chowkidar's* greeting, Ross sketched a brief salute of his own before turning his mount onto the road—albeit to the left, which would take him into the town of Bhunapore, rather than back to his own bungalow, which lay on the far side of the cantonment to the right.

How strange, Maura thought. He had told Aunt Daphne that he had work to do. Why, then, was he riding into town, where by now the streets would be deserted save for the beggars and the *pi* dogs?

Chapter Five

The week following Terence Shadwell's birthday party was a busy one for the Carlyons. A wedding date had been fixed for the third week in November, a time of year when Bhunapore's British residents would already be engaged in rounds of cold weather gaiety. Despairing of having everything finished in time, Mrs. Carlyon arranged to take Lydia on a shopping excursion to Delhi even though numerous trunks stuffed with the girl's trousseau had accompanied them from England.

The moment she heard of their plans, Maura pleaded for permission to remain behind. She had no desire to spend an entire week dancing attendance on Lydia at Whiteaway's, Hall & Anderson's, or any of the other large European stores in Delhi, preferring to wait until after the monsoon to visit the city, when the wedding would be behind them and there would be time to view the gardens, the

71

museums and mosques, and especially to make a stop in Lucknow to visit the graves of her parents and the home she had not seen in over ten years.

Aunt Daphne allowed that this was a fine idea. Privately she was relieved that Maura had elected to remain behind because now Mr. Carlyon would not be left alone at the Residency. This way, she and Lydia could concentrate on their shopping without worrying that dear Lawrence was lonely or that darling Maura was bored.

The following morning, amid a flurry of last-minute crises, the two of them finally departed. The weather was overcast and humid, and the wind sent stinging dust devils dancing down the cantonment road.

Watching the carriage rumble away beneath the tall, whitewashed gates, Maura and her uncle exchanged relieved smiles. How quiet and empty the house suddenly seemed! Discounting, of course, the presence of the thirty-odd servants making up the Residency staff, Maura thought wryly.

"Now don't tell me you wish you'd gone with them," Uncle Lawrence said upon hearing his niece's heartfelt sigh. "Afraid it's too late. And I hope you don't expect me to entertain you, either, m'girl! I've stacks of paperwork to see to."

"Oh, believe me, I don't mind," Maura said. Smiling, she kissed the top of his balding head.

Uncle Lawrence eyed her approvingly. "Made plans of your own, have you?"

"Yes."

"They wouldn't happen to include a certain young man living here at the station?" he asked meaningfully as she started for the door.

Maura's skirts rustled on the rush matting as she

turned to face him. "What do you mean, Uncle Lawrence?"

"Why, Burton-Pascal, of course." Her uncle's eyes twinkled. "Spoke to him yesterday at the club. Seemed damned pleased to hear you weren't traipsing off to Delhi with Daffy and Lydia. Now, why do you think he'd say that, hmm?"

Maura could feel her cheeks growing hot. It was clear from his tone that Uncle Lawrence believed Charles Burton-Pascal to be courting her. It was further obvious that he approved. The thought made her scowl. *Was* the man courting her? Discounting an occasionally meaningful glance or a somewhat inappropriate remark, Mr. Burton-Pascal's behavior had been impeccable toward her thus far. Maura found him tolerable enough, if a little too pleased with his own self, but as for thinking he actually meant to pursue her—!

"I can't imagine why Mr. Burton-Pascal would wish to single me out," she said stiffly.

"Egad! Then he's being too deuced cautious, I'd say! Why, when I first started courting your aunt—"

"I have no wish to be courted by Mr. Burton-Pascal," Maura interrupted, more forcibly this time.

Her uncle frowned. "I'd reconsider that carefully, gel. Bhunapore's a small place. You won't find another with better qualifications 'round here. Daffy likes him, too, y'know."

Maura's mutinous gaze slid from his. "Yes, Uncle, I know."

His manner brightened, for he hated confrontations. "You'll come to your senses, wait and see."

"I certainly hope one of us does, Uncle."

Back in her room, Maura announced grimly to

Meera that she wished to go riding. "Wouldst thou fetch my habit?"

She spoke in Hindustani because she and Meera were alone, although at all other times she was careful to speak only in English. Aunt Daphne had informed her tartly that it was considered shockingly improper for memsahibs of the British Raj to converse with their servants in their own language. An occasional smattering of "kitchen Hindustani" was permitted, but only enough to order the servants about.

"It is late," Meera protested now. "Thou hast not had tiffin."

"I'm not hungry," Maura countered, pulling her riding habit from the closet. She could not rid herself of a growing uneasiness. Surely Uncle Lawrence was mistaken about Charles Burton-Pascal! On the other hand, her uncle's manner had plainly indicated that he was expecting an offer soon; one which, as her guardian, he could quite legally accept on her behalf.

No one had to remind Maura that underage girls were married off all the time—usually without their consent—to any bridegroom deemed even remotely suitable by their anxious guardians. In fact, Uncle Lawrence had made it clear in no uncertain terms that he considered Charles Burton-Pascal more than a "suitable" catch.

Small wonder Maura's expression was thunderous by the time she cantered her mount through the Residency gates.

Although Lawrence Carlyon rarely rode himself, he took great pride in the blooded animals kept in his stables. Today Maura had appropriated a leggy colt whose burnished red coat had earned him the name of the Fox. Because the Fox was fresh, Maura let him have his head as he crossed the level ground beyond the cantonment streets. There was no sign of life save for a flock of rust-colored birds flitting among the tussocks of grass. A partridge gave a haunting call somewhere among the thorny *kikars* and it was answered, far in the distance, by a jackal.

As always, the unfolding beauty that was India brought a measure of calm to Maura's heart. Even the green fens of Norfolk, teeming with marshy wildlife, had never brought her this kind of comfort. How terrible to have wasted all those years in England! What a pity that all children born in India were sent home when they reached their seventh year, a rule championed by the British bible *Birch's Management and Medical Treatment of Children in India,* which preyed on every mother's unspoken fear that her offspring would not survive adolescence in this harsh Eastern land.

Smiling a little, Maura leaned low in the saddle and urged the colt to a gallop. There had never been any doubt in her mind that she had been sent back to England unnecessarily. Unlike Lydia or Aunt Daphne, she had never been afflicted by India's myriad native ailments: prickly rash, dysentery, the vomiting fever. And she had certainly never succumbed to the heat, although she had taken the precaution today of wearing a topi, the canvas pith helmet that was part and parcel of the uniform of the British Raj and which was intended to protect its wearer's brains from the scorching Eastern sun.

"I'm too tough to get sick or suffer heat stroke," Maura said aloud, laughing a little and feeling all the better for it.

The Fox slowed his pace to cross a rocky nullah, a narrow ravine littered with stones, before taking off at a smart trot down the road leading toward the town of Bhunapore. Up ahead, Maura could see the uneven rooftops and temple spires of the crowded inner city. She had not visited the bazaar since shopping with her aunt and cousin for Residency furniture, and all at once she welcomed the thought of spending several carefree hours among the crowded stalls of the market square.

The shopkeepers greeted her politely as she dismounted and wandered down the alleyways. They expressed open delight when she addressed them in their own tongue and showed them the proper deference for caste that most sahib-*log* did not.

The most vocal of these was the vendor of the fruit stand, who engaged Maura in a lengthy conversation when she paused to purchase and peel an orange. Mohammed Hadji was a placid little man whose numerous wives and children were constantly underfoot. Because they were devout Muslims, the women practiced purdah, the Eastern custom of seclusion in which women's faces were veiled in public and never revealed to any man who was not a close member of the family.

Nevertheless, Mohammed Hadji's four wives were all fat and merry, and their dark eyes danced behind the slits of their *bourkas* as they laughed and talked with Maura. Their shyness had evaporated the moment the English girl had addressed them in their native tongue, and they had been quick to accept her as a friend.

"Thou art being followed," remarked one of them unexpectedly. Her name was Hamada, and she was the youngest and most observant of the four. "Tell us. Dost thou have an admirer among the station sahibs?"

Maura looked mystified. "An admirer?"

The other wives pointed. Maura turned to peer

down the alley. The sahib was easy to spot. Not only was he wearing a topi exactly like hers, but he towered well above the crowd as he threaded his way purposefully toward them. As he came closer, Maura had no trouble recognizing the handsome features of Charles Burton-Pascal.

"Bloody hell!"

"What is it?" the women asked curiously.

"Thou art right, he has followed me here," Maura said quickly, "but he is not one I would wish to meet. Tell me, how might I best return to my horse without being seen?"

The women clucked their tongues and conferred with each other and with Mohammed Hadji. In the meantime Maura slipped behind a basket filled with tall rolls of tapestries. She didn't doubt that Charles had deliberately followed her into town. He had probably called at the Residency just as she was leaving and had decided to ride after her.

Maura's chin tipped. Well, she wasn't about to let him catch her, not when she had ridden out without a syce, a Residency groom. Aunt Daphne had already lectured her numerous times about the scandal she would cause were she ever to be discovered riding alone in the company of a bachelor!

"If thou wouldst leave by way of that gate," suggested Mohammed Hadji, pointing to an ornately carved doorway at the far corner of the market square, "thou wilt emerge near the temple where thou hast left thy horse."

"But the gate will be locked," Maura said doubtfully. "How will I get in?"

"Walid Ali, who owns the house, is a cousin of mine," Mohammed Hadji said complacently. "Tell his watchman I have given thee leave."

Maura thanked him prettily. Accompanied by the

77

giggling women who blocked her from view with their flowing *bourkas*, she hurried across the street to the gate. Upon hearing her predicament, the *chowkidar* obligingly let her in, and Maura hastened inside amid the whispered farewells of the four Mohammedan wives.

"Oh—!" she exclaimed, turning to look around her. The spectacular size and beauty of the garden had not been apparent from the street. Obviously Walid Ali was a merchant of considerable wealth, for a small fortune had been spent on the formal landscaping, which was graced by latticed pavilions and burbling fountains. The stucco house itself was a veritable palace, painted pink and white and soaring three stories and more into the sky. Numerous towers and balconies adorned the main structure, all of them covered by flaming creepers whose heady scent infused the air like perfume.

"This way," said the *chowkidar*, bowing.

Maura lifted the hem of her habit and followed him down a manicured walk strewn with white pebbles. The noisy market square might have been a thousand miles away. Nothing but the tinkling of the fountains and the droning of bees interrupted the golden stillness of the morning.

They passed the zenana, the women's quarter of the palace, its private terraces hidden from prying eyes by *shamianahs*—screens of gently rippling silk cloth—that served to protect the inhabitants' purdah.

Here, the insistent tinkling of a bell brought the watchman up short. Excusing himself, he slipped away between the flowering shrubs. A moment later he was back, bowing and explaining that Kushna Begum, the wife of Walid Ali, had been looking out of the window and, seeing Maura, had recognized her as an *Angrezi* memsahib by her Western riding dress. She had expressed an interest in meeting her. Would the memsahib please come this way?

Knowing it would be rude to refuse, Maura followed the *chowkidar* through an arching doorway. Here he stopped, prevented by custom from going any further. A veiled serving girl was there to escort her into the zenana, and Maura followed silently across the polished floor and up a narrow flight of steps.

The room they entered was very long and sparsely furnished. The walls, draped with dyed silk that rustled softly in the breeze, gave an appearance of cool, restful beauty. Sandalwood incense scented the air, and from somewhere deep within the palace walls came the sound of a sitar and a lovely voice accompanying it.

Kushna Begum was seated on a cushion near the arched windows that looked out on the garden. She was veiled in brilliant turquoise silk, but the upper part of her face was bare, revealing her fine, dark eyes, the deep widow's peak of her shining black hair, and the fact that she was not much older than Maura herself.

The two exchanged pleasantries, and Kushna Begum clapped her slim hands upon discovering how prettily the *Angrezi* girl could speak her language. News of the girl's appearance spread quickly through the zenana and soon the room was filled with curious maidens, staring children, and giggling, grey-haired aunts. Babies were held out for Maura to pat, her clothes were touched and unabashedly admired, and they were all delighted to learn that she had come into their midst while escaping the unwanted attentions of an ardent sahib. All too well, said Kushna Begum, did the women of

the zenana know the need to flee at times from over-
ly eager men!

All of them, including Maura, laughed merrily at
this. Refreshments were brought and Maura was
begged to describe *Belait*—far away England—and
her life in the gloomy environs of Carlyon Hall, a
place that was as incomprehensible to the women
of the zenana as the Eastern way of life was to the
British mem who arrived on India's shores.

After Maura finished with her tale, a disbelieving
hush fell over the room. How curious England and
its prudish customs must seem to these Mohammedan girls, Maura thought. From a very early age
they were taught the skills required of a courtesan,
and at a time when most British girls were still playing with dolls and wearing pantalettes, they were
entertaining men in the cool of the zenana halls.

The thought was rather disconcerting.

Turning her head, Maura was startled to see that
the shadows beyond the windows had shortened.
She came reluctantly to her feet, her wide skirts falling into place. "I must go."

"Wait, little sister," protested Kushna Begum. "We
must decide first how to rid thee of thy unwanted
suitor."

"Is he truly unwanted?" someone wished to know.

Maura didn't even pause to consider. "Yes."

"Then we must protect thee," Kushna Begum said
firmly. "Not only today, but for always."

"Poison him," suggested someone.

"That is not the *Angrezi* way," Maura replied,
laughing.

"Marry another," suggested Kushna Begum's matronly aunt.

"I have no wish to marry," Maura protested,
which shocked everyone greatly.

"But surely there must be someone who is promised to thee?" persisted Sita, the begum's younger sister.

For an instant Maura saw Ross Hamilton's face before her quite clearly; saw the deep raven's wing black of his hair, the rugged planes of his face, and that disturbing, sensuous mouth which could smile so endearingly whenever he was amused.

"No," she said stubbornly, "there is no one."

When the exclamations of disbelief had died away, Kushna Begum held up her hand. Her eyes glowed with excitement. "I know! I will give thee Ismail Khan!"

"Who is Ismail Khan?" Maura demanded over the delighted exclamations of the others.

By way of reply Kushna Begum clapped her hands. In a flash, a barefoot serving girl was kneeling before her. Words were exchanged and the girl hurried out. Smiling, Kushna Begum drew Maura onto the terrace. The pigeons were coming home to roost, and the smells of cooking fires drifted to them on the warm afternoon air.

"Look there," said Kushna Begum.

Maura followed her slim, pointing finger downward to the lotus garden, where a mountain of a man in white robes stood with his arms crossed over his chest glowering up at them. There was a puggaree, a turban, wound Afghan style about his head. He was heavily bearded and heavily armed, and Maura's jaw dropped disbelievingly.

"*That* is Ismail Khan?"

"It is, and I give him to thee," said Kushna Begum complacently, "for as long as is necessary. He is a Pathan of the border tribe of the *Usafzai*, and a man true to his salt. I have given orders that he is not to let thee out of his sight. Thou wilt be safe with him."

"Hai mai! I am sure of that," breathed Maura. How, she wondered, could she possibly accept this hulking creature as her bodyguard? But how on earth could she possibly refuse him without insulting her hostess?

"Do not look so," urged Kushna Begum. "In India bodyguards are common. I am told thou hast arrived here without a syce. Now thou wilt have one, and a faithful one at that."

Bemused, Maura thanked her gravely. The Indian girl held up a slim hand. "I would have thee do one thing in return."

"And that is—?"

The black eyes sparkled. "Come again. Often."

This Maura promised to do, not only because she felt she owed Kushna Begum as much, but because she genuinely wanted to. Indeed, she could have laughed aloud at the very thought. Oh, it felt wonderful to have made a friend!

"Come soon," urged Kushna Begum. "We are anxious to learn how thy unwanted sahib fares with Ismail Khan."

Laughing, Maura gave her word, and ten minutes later she was riding back toward the British cantonment with the big, bearded Pathan following a respectful distance behind.

The shadows had grown long amid the foothills, and the road was crowded with peasants and bullocks returning from the fields. Most of them did not bother hiding their interest in the slim memsahib and the glowering Pathan riding behind her. Maura wondered with growing trepidation what her uncle was going to say.

Casting a discreet glance over her shoulder, she saw that the burly Pathan had pulled a long knife from his belt and was busily cleaning his teeth with the blade. She bit her lip as the enormity of the situation dawned upon her. She knew nothing about Afghanis save for the fact that they were considered barbaric and unmanageable. Oh, God, what had she done?

The sun was beginning to set in a milky wash of apricot as the high walls of the cantonment came into view at last. A welcoming breeze rustled through the long elephant grass, and high overhead, skeins of waterfowl winged their way homeward toward the water of a distant *jheel*.

Behind her Ismail grunted, and Maura turned her head to see a pair of riders cantering toward them from the direction of Sundagunj, a prosperous village some six miles distant. Both men carried rifles slung over their saddles, and as they neared, Maura recognized Ross Hamilton and his bearer, Ghoda Lal.

Maura groaned. Her hands tightened about the Fox's reins, but there was no sense in trying to outrun them. Everyone in Bhunapore, including Ross, would learn soon enough about Ismail Khan.

Squaring her shoulders, she forced herself to greet him as calmly as she could when he neared. "Good afternoon, Captain Hamilton."

The roadway was so narrow that Ross was forced to draw rein beside her; so close, in fact, that his booted leg brushed hers. "Miss Adams," he responded politely. His questioning gaze traveled from her to Ismail Khan and back again. One slashing eyebrow rose skyward. "A new syce, Miss Adams? I don't believe I've seen him at the Residency."

Maura cleared her throat. "Yes, well, you see—"

At that same moment a python slithered without warning out of the rocks behind her. Tongue flicking, it crossed the rutted track directly beneath the

Fox's hooves. Startled, the colt shied violently and Maura, who had let her hold on the reins grow lax, went tumbling from his back.

Fortunately Ross was close enough to save her from a fall. With lightning speed he snatched her up by the arms and hauled her toward him. Maura was aware of a dizzying moment of weightlessness before she found herself deposited in front of him with her slim buttocks nestled intimately across his thighs.

"Are you hurt?" he demanded brusquely.

She shook her head, consumed by such an odd feeling of breathlessness that it was impossible to speak. Stealing a glance at him, she found his face so close to her own that their lips were very nearly touching. She became aware, too, that her hands were gripping the front of his shirt in a most undignified manner. Beneath them she could feel the steady drumming of his heart, and she snatched them away in panic only to find that she had no idea where to put them next. She and Ross were sitting so close together that unless she crossed her hands before her breasts or put them behind her, they would end up resting on his thighs. For goodness sake, what was she supposed to do?

With deep amusement Ross watched the bewildered emotions play across her face. For a moment he was tempted to take her pert chin in his palm, turn those lustrous eyes up to his, and assure her that there was nothing to be ashamed of. After all, it wasn't as though she had ended up sitting between his legs on purpose! Neither of them was remotely affected by this most intimate of positions.

Or were they? Maura was wearing the heavy riding skirts considered proper for a memsahib, but they were not so heavy that Ross could not feel the beguiling softness of her thighs pressed against his. And not until now had he noticed that the lovely curves of her breasts were hovering so close to his chest that he had only to lean forward a little to brush against them.

"I think—" he began harshly, but got no further than that. Ismail Khan, obviously thinking that his mistress had dallied long enough on the lap of this strange sahib, had urged his own horse forward and was now leaning between them with the tip of his knife grazing Ross's jaw.

For a moment no one spoke. Then Ross said lightly, "Miss Adams, would you mind calling off your syce?"

Her wide-eyed gaze clung to his. "I—I'm afraid I can't."

"Oh? Why not?"

"I-I don't know how. He doesn't speak English or Hindustani."

Ross uttered a crack of laughter. "Splendid! Do you happen to know what he *does* speak?"

"P-Pushtu, I think."

Fortunately this was a language Ross had mastered while serving on the Northwest Frontier. Explaining politely to Ismail Khan that he in no way intended to harm his mistress, he simultaneously used the pressure of his knees and a tight hand on the reins to back his horse safely out of reach of that ugly Afghan knife.

After a moment, and with obvious reluctance, Ismail Khan returned the weapon to the folds of his robes.

Dismounting, Ross lifted his arms and Maura slid gratefully into them. For all she knew they might both have ended up with their throats cut! She stole an anxious glance into Ross's face and was startled to see that he was laughing.

Fury overwhelmed her. "Would you mind telling me what's so funny?"

"Not until you tell me where your uncle found that hairy devil."

His laughter was so infectious that Maura couldn't help joining in. For a long moment the two of them stood laughing together while the nullah behind them seemed to throw back a chuckling echo.

Something very akin to joy bubbled in Maura's heart. She had never seen Ross look so relaxed, so pleasant, so utterly, devastatingly handsome.

The thought made her own laughter choke off abruptly. What on earth was that supposed to mean? She didn't prefer Ross Hamilton one way or the other! He was a member of her uncle's staff, nothing more, and to prove as much, she tipped her chin and eyed him with utterly quelling hauteur.

"I think I'd better go. My uncle will worry if I'm not home by dinner."

"By all means," Ross agreed, but Maura had the distinct impression that he was not only fully aware of her sudden change of mood, but of the reason behind it. Maddeningly enough, the reason seemed to amuse him, judging from the way his sensual lips kept on twitching as he signaled Ghoda Lal to fetch her horse.

Compressing her own lips into a thin line, Maura frostily accepted a leg up into the saddle. She sat stiffly, waiting for Ross to step away, pretending for all the world that she was quite alone.

Instead he stood there looking up at her intently, one hand on the strap of her stirrup. "How long have you had that fellow?"

"Since you went away on leave," Maura lied. It would be a mistake, she knew, to reveal where she had really come by him.

"I hope he doesn't prove too much for you."

Maura tossed her head. "Really, Captain Hamilton! Surely you know me well enough by now to realize that I'd never be afraid of my own syce?"

"Oh, trust me," Ross retorted, grinning, "I'm very well aware of it."

Eyes flashing, Maura wheeled her horse and cantered away. Even after she reached the cantonment gate and the Residency sprang into view, she fancied she could still hear Ross's laughter ringing through the air.

It made her want to turn around and ride right back to soundly box his ears.

Chapter Six

Just as Maura had feared, Ismail Khan's arrival caused an uproar at the Residency. Not only did Uncle Lawrence object strenuously to the Afghan's presence, but where on earth, he demanded of his niece, were they supposed to *put* the bloody savage?

Furthermore, he did not appreciate the fact that Maura had engaged the fellow out of hand and without permission (Maura had wisely refrained from revealing where, exactly, she had come by him), and surely she could have trusted her uncle to choose a syce for her from among the Residency staff? Why engage an utter stranger, an *Afghan* at that?

"He'll have to go back immediately," Uncle Lawrence pronounced, but in this both Maura and the burly Pathan proved inflexible. Maura was not about to send him away, and Ismail Khan had been given his orders and would stand by them to the end.

"Oh, very well," Uncle Lawrence said irritably when this fact became painfully obvious. "But keep him out of the house. We've enough servants as it is. I really have no idea what your aunt will say when she returns!"

"But where should he live?" Maura demanded, dismissing without a qualm of conscience the thought of her aunt's distress.

"In the stables."

"Uncle Lawrence, no!" Maura was genuinely shocked. Pathans were extraordinarily proud. She could not expect Ismail Khan to live with . . . with animals. A thought struck her. "What about the *bibigurh*?"

This was the small, two-room bungalow, detached from the Residency proper, which had served in former times to house the Indian mistresses of Bhunapore Residents. Since Lawrence Carlyon had emphatically refused to indulge in such a reprehensible custom, the bungalow had long stood empty.

"Oh, very well," he said resignedly. "But you'll have to get the servants to clean it first."

This was accomplished rather grudgingly, for the Residency Hindus did not welcome the idea of a surly Muslim from across the border living in their midst. Everyone knew that the land beyond the Hindu Kush was inhabited by Unbelievers, and that the Afghanis were, as a whole, uncivilized people. But they did not dare say as much aloud or even look the hairy fellow straight in the face. No telling what evil might be evoked if they did. *Hai mai!* How could the miss-sahib have done such a thing?

Ismail Khan, though aware of the talk, remained entirely unmoved. The *bibi-gurh* was to his liking and the horse he had been presented by Kushna Begum, worthy of respect. Guarding the poison-haired sahiba was going to be a simple bagatelle since it was already clear to him that he was expected to do little more than ride with her back and forth across the plains. He spoke no English and Maura no Pushtu, but they could converse well enough in the little Hindustani that he did understand.

Not that Ismail Khan was a talkative fellow. On his first full day at the Residency he proceeded to answer his mistress's questions with nothing more than grunts and shrugs. And because Maura could not adequately explain his duties to him, he followed her everywhere, including, in one horribly embarrassing instance later that evening, to the bathroom.

Maura, who had intended to wash her face and hands before supper, wasn't sure whether to scream or to laugh. Ismail Khan, unconcerned, flipped down the lid of the "thunderbox," that thoroughly primitive frontier version of a British toilet, and sat down on top of it. Taking out his knife, he began to clean his nails and hum an Afghan song beneath his breath.

"Wah!" exclaimed Meera, coming into the bathroom a moment later with clean towels for her mistress. Her shocked eyes met Maura's in the tarnished mirror.

"I cannot make him leave," Maura explained, laughing. "He speaks no Hindi."

"What foolishness!" Meera snorted, and proceeded to give the Pathan a tongue-lashing that left no doubt in Maura's mind that Ismail Khan understood considerably more Hindustani than he had led her to believe.

Maura was still smiling over the incident when she joined her uncle for supper not long afterward.

The punkah fan flapped lazily, setting the candles on the table to guttering. A pair of *khidmatgars* stood rigidly behind the British Resident's chair, horse hair whisks at the ready to flick away any offending insects. Both of them bowed as Maura came in and she smiled back at them, decorum relaxed what with her aunt away in Delhi.

Crossing to her chair, she drew up short. The smile died on her face. Ross Hamilton was sitting in the seat next to hers, the candlelight reflecting the darkness of his coal black hair. He was still dressed in work clothes, although he had taken the liberty of removing his vest and unbuttoning the collar of his shirt. A wide expanse of sunbrowned chest, covered with crisp black hair, was visible at the deep vee of his throat. Maura blushed and quickly looked away.

Uncle Lawrence motioned her to be seated. "Ev'ning, m'dear. Hope you don't mind Ross joining us. We've some business I'd like to clear up before morning."

Maura assured him that she didn't mind, although she certainly wouldn't have worn her oldest frock to dinner or left her hair in such disarray had she known that Ross would be present.

But apparently Ross didn't notice her disheveled appearance. In fact, he didn't seem to notice her at all, for he gave her no more than a brief nod before turning back to her uncle. Maura sipped her broth in silence as the two of them resumed discussing a local *talukdar*, a wealthy Hindu landowner, who had been severely injured during a heated dispute yesterday over the sale of a horse to the puppet ruler of Bhunapore, Nasir al-Mirza Shah.

Listening, Maura couldn't help feeling impressed with Ross's quiet yet forceful insistence that the

British Resident allow the two parties to resolve their differences without interference. In fact, Ross's approach to the problem was so very un-Western that Maura began to realize how well he understood the workings of the Indian mind. Small wonder he loved this turbulent, incomprehensible country as much as he did! His way of thinking was rare among men who served the British Raj—and very much the same as her father's had been: compassionate, level-headed and sympathetic to the Indian point of view.

The *khidmatgars* cleared away the soup bowls, and the roast was carried in. Maura's nose twitched hungrily, for the hour was late and the Residency employed a remarkably gifted cook. The enormous silver tureen was set on the table in front of her uncle and the lid removed with a flourish.

"Good God!" exploded the British Resident.

Maura's gaze followed her uncle's to the roast. She gasped when she saw that it had been garnished with a bed of mashed potatoes dyed a violent shade of blue.

"Lala Deen!" bellowed Lawrence Carlyon in halting Hindustani. "What is the meaning of this?"

"It is in celebration of the Padshah Victoria," babbled the *khidmatgar*, bowing and cringing. "News from *Belait*—from England—says she has been blessed with a new son."

Uncle Lawrence looked disapproving while Ross and Maura burst into helpless laughter. It was the same, unaffected laughter that they had shared together on the plains the day before. Both of them must have realized as much at the same time, because both of them turned in that same instant to look at one another. Maura was suddenly aware of an odd ache in her heart as she gazed into Ross's laughing eyes.

How foolish I feel, she thought. As though I've drunk too much wine—when in fact she'd had none at all. Confused and embarrassed, she looked away.

No sooner had the meat been cut than Ross's manner became brisk once again. Ignoring Maura completely, he resumed his discussion with her uncle about the hapless *talukdar*, a topic that was not abandoned even after the pudding and port had been consumed, or when Maura, yawning and bored, announced that she wished to retire.

The men rose obligingly, although it was clear that they were both distracted. Ross frowned as he bid Maura good night, behaving for all the world as though he were irritated by the interruption. Or as though he longed to ignore her completely.

I might just as well have eaten by myself, Maura thought grumpily. Men!

With a haughty toss of her head, she swept from the room.

The crowing of a cockerel awakened her some time before dawn. Padding barefoot through the silent parlor, she peered out of the verandah doors. The moon had not yet set, and its milky light laid great barred shadows across the grounds. The breeze was fresh and the air scented with flowers, a potent summons that, for Maura, proved impossible to resist.

Knowing she would sleep no more that night, she dressed quietly in her newest riding habit: a slim jacket and skirt of lightweight blue muslin trimmed with black braid. Drawing on her boots and collecting her topi and whip, she crossed the dark lawn to the stables.

The *chowkidar*, accustomed to the miss-sahib's early appearances, made a deep obeisance and hastily awakened one of the grooms. Ten minutes later Maura was riding the Fox through the cantonment gates with Ismail Khan following behind. Veils of mist were lifting from the hills, and already the promise of grinding heat could be felt in the warm wind that stirred the lion-colored grass.

Not far from the cantonment, where the dusty road forked between the village of Sundagunj and the city of Bhunapore, Maura encountered another rider wisely taking his exercise before the heat of the day; a tall, blond man in a superbly tailored jacket who trotted quickly forward to meet them.

On this particular morning, Charles Burton-Pascal found himself in an utterly foul frame of mind. Not only had he lost heavily at cards at the British Club last night, but he was still at a loss to explain how Maura Adams had managed to elude him after he had followed her into town two days before.

Word around the cantonment had it that she rode often before dawn, so he had risen early in the hope of intercepting her, stoically ignoring his hangover and the fact that he rarely left his bed before noon. He had been on his way back, saddlesore and angrily convinced that he had suffered for naught, when he had suddenly spotted the red-haired object of his dreams riding toward him through the graying light, her horse kicking up a finger of dust across the plain. Behind Maura rode Ismail Khan with a rifle slung frontier-fashion across his left shoulder. Thinking him an ordinary syce, Charles did not even glance his way.

"Good morning, Miss Adams," he called as she approached.

Maura returned his greeting warily. She had no idea how fetching she looked with her cheeks reddened from exertion and wisps of shining crimson hair clinging to her temples. The close fitting jacket showed off her slender figure to perfection, and Charles could scarcely contain himself at the sight. By God, she was a beauty! How could a man possibly resist her?

"You've been avoiding me," he charged emotionally, urging his horse to fall into step with hers.

Her dark eyes slanted up to his. "Have I?"

He gazed at her greedily. "You know you have. I followed you to the bazaar the other day, but somehow you managed to elude me. Were you avoiding me deliberately?"

"Why, no," Maura said sweetly. She couldn't help it; her eyes sparkled and she just had to laugh.

Poor Charles! He had never met such a mischievous imp before, and this, coupled with his bad temper and the agony of his unfulfilled desire for her, drove him to act unwisely. Reaching over, he wrenched savagely at the Fox's reins, bringing the animal to a sudden halt.

"Maura—" he breathed, longing vibrating in the utterance of her name.

She stared at him, startled, but even before Charles could make a move—before he even knew what he intended—he felt the cold steel of a gun barrel press against the side of his head.

"Good God! What the devil—?" Turning in the saddle, he found himself staring along the length of the rifle into a pair of very unsettling black eyes.

"What's the meaning of this?" he shrilled. "Miss Adams, call off your syce!"

"I can't," Maura said honestly. "Not unless you assure him you don't mean to do me harm."

95

"Harm you!" Charles spluttered. "How could I possibly harm you? This is an innocent enough encounter—!"

"Oh? Then you weren't out doe-hacking?" Maura demanded.

"Doe-hacking!" Burton-Pascal reddened. How the devil had the damnable girl come to know *that* expression, which very old India hands used when describing men who waylaid young ladies riding abroad without chaperones?

A wave of embarrassment washed over him, accompanied by outrage that her illiterate syce would dare treat a white man, a sahib, with such unheard of arrogance. He said between his teeth: "Tell him to leave off or I'll wring his filthy neck."

Ismail Khan said in halting Hindustani, "Does the man plague thee, sahiba? I could kill him if need be."

"Leave be," Maura answered quickly, aware that he meant it.

Casually, Ismail Khan slung the rifle back across his beefy shoulder.

Charles gave him a murderous look. "I won't forget this."

"I'm so sorry—" Maura began, but Charles ignored her. Wheeling his mount, he rode savagely away.

In the ensuing silence Maura sat chewing her lower lip and trying hard not to laugh. Oh, of course she felt sorry for Charles, but she was intensely grateful to Ismail Khan for having chased him off. Still, she knew better than to thank him aloud. That was not the Pathan way. Instead she grunted in Afghan fashion to show her approval and kicked her horse into flight. Grinning, Ismail Khan followed behind.

* * *

Two nights later, Maura was given the opportunity to relate this tale, with considerable embellishment, to a delighted Kushna Begum and her enraptured retinue. There was much laughter in the big reception room when she finished speaking. Outside the zenana, a pale new moon was rising in the velvet curtain of the sky. Insects shrilled in the garden and fruitbats whirred among the trees.

Earlier that evening, Maura's uncle had departed for a gentleman's soirée hosted by an elderly Eurasian merchant residing elsewhere in the cantonment. Maura had wasted no time in saddling her horse and slipping away to Walid Ali's lovely stucco palace. Ismail Khan had accompanied her, and both of them had been respectfully received by the gatekeeper who let them in. Maura had been brought immediately upstairs to the zenana, where a beaming Kushna Begum had clapped her hands when she was announced.

"Now tell us what thy *cha-cha*, thy uncle, said upon meeting Ismail Khan," she urged. "Or did the crows make off with his tongue?"

"A little of both," laughed Maura, and told the story of her uncle's first confrontation with the bearded Pathan.

"I think he has dampened the ardor of thy unwanted suitor," Kushna Begum concluded, obviously pleased. "Oh, how I wish I could have been there to see!"

"Perhaps one day—" began Maura, only to be interrupted by the sound of voices on the stairs.

All of the women looked up as the curtains covering the doorway quivered and a barefoot serving girl rushed over to whisper in Kushna Begum's ear. She spoke so quickly that Maura had difficulty understanding her, but it was obvious from her behavior that something was amiss.

Clapping her hands, Kushna Begum urged the older women to scoop up the crawling babies and hurry away. In the meantime, the younger ones adjusted the silk veils about their faces and whispered excitedly among themselves.

"What is it?" Maura asked.

"My husband has sent word that he wishes to pay me a visit," Kushna Begum explained happily while a pair of servants knelt to paint her palms with henna and put delicate slippers on her feet.

"Then I must leave," Maura said quickly.

"There is no need," Kushna Begum assured her. "I am permitted *Angrezi* friends. My husband has had *Angrezi* friends of his own since boyhood. One in particular is long known to him, and he is even welcome on occasion in our zenana."

"*Ohé!*" wailed an old crone who had been keeping watch by the door. "I fear that is happening now! The young sahib is with him!"

Kushna Begum's face paled beneath her exquisite veil. "Then thou must leave at once," she said urgently to Maura, "if thou dost not wish to be seen by one of thy countrymen."

"There is no time!" cried Sita, the Begum's younger sister, who had joined the old woman at the top of the stairs. "They are coming!"

Kushna Begum cursed. "What shall we do?"

"I must hide!" Maura exclaimed. "But where?"

"Nowhere, I fear. They will see thee on the balcony, and the other rooms all lead back to this one!"

"Hurry! Hurry! They are on the stairs!" wailed Sita.

Kushna Begum issued a rapid order. Immediately the servants ran to a trunk standing in the corner of the room and removed from inside a gold tunic and full trousers of gossamer green silk embroidered with gold threads. This was the traditional attire of any highborn Mohammedan lady, and while Maura unhooked her skirt with trembling fingers they dressed her quickly, wrapping a long veil deftly about her arms, shoulders, and face.

Although the color of her hair and the whiteness of her arms were now effectively hidden, Maura took the precaution of seating herself amid the shadows where the light of the oil lamps did not reach. Her heart was hammering—not so much from fear as with the unexpectedness of it all. An Englishman who had known Kushna Begum's husband long enough to be favored with a visit to the zenana was also a man who had lived in Bhunapore for a very long time. What if he was someone Maura recognized or, worse still, someone who knew her? Maura Adams might be a high-spirited girl, but she was well aware of how much damage she would cause her family's reputation were she to be caught consorting with native women in their home.

Aunt Daphne would never live down the scandal. Uncle Lawrence would be furious. Maura herself would be utterly disgraced, and probably placed under house arrest until her marriage, which would of course be arranged as speedily as possible. In all likelihood, Ismail Khan would be dismissed and Maura would never see him or Kushna Begum again.

Footsteps sounded on the stairs, the heavy tread characteristic of men. Quickly the women returned to their various tasks. At a word from Kushna Begum, a pair of serving girls seated themselves beside Maura and opened a game of *chartranj*. Maura bent her head over the board just as Walid Ali and his guests stepped inside.

Peeping at them curiously from behind her veil, Maura could tell which of the four men was the master of the house simply by the manner in which the women deferred to him. Walid Ali was much younger than she had expected, with dark, hawkish features that were extraordinarily handsome. She supposed that the two Indian gentlemen who had accompanied him inside were his uncles or brothers, for they would not have been permitted here otherwise. All three Mohammedan men were heavily bearded and dressed in the gorgeous embroidered coats and *salwar* trousers signifying wealth. A magnificent emerald winked in the elaborate turban worn by Walid Ali.

The Englishman came in last, and it was not until he stepped fully into the lamplight that Maura realized who he was. The shock of recognition hit her like a dash of ice water. There was no mistaking that coal black hair, the clean-shaven jaw and those rugged features.

Ross Hamilton! What on earth was he doing here? Surely he could not be a personal friend of Walid Ali's! Why, Uncle Lawrence had said that Ross hadn't been living in Bhunapore for more than a few months!

Maura watched, pulses pounding, as cushions were arranged in a half circle around the Kushna Begum. A particularly beautiful nautch-girl was selected to dance. The two fat uncles puffed contentedly on their hookahs and helped themselves to a pouch of betel nuts while they watched the girl move through the hypnotic steps of the *kathak*.

Walid Ali, meanwhile, squatted Indian fashion beside his wife, dandling his youngest daughter on his knee. Captain Hamilton lounged beside him with the negligent air of one who felt perfectly at home in the scented zenana of the pink stucco palace.

Maura continued to sit as though turned to stone amid the shadows. Not so much as by a single movement did she intend to betray her presence. If Ross recognized her and told her uncle. . . .

I will be sent back to England in disgrace, Maura thought. The prospect sickened her. Her heart pounded. Dear God, don't let him see me!

She could not know that Ross had noticed her almost from the moment he had stepped inside. Being well acquainted with the various family members and servants of the zenana, he had immediately recognized the girl as someone new. His interest had been further aroused by the fact that the slim creature in the gold-embroidered tunic kept peeping at him, and that she seemed uneasy, even afraid. Of what? Of him? Surely not. The womenfolk of Walid Ali were long accustomed to having sahibs in the house.

When the nautch-girl finished dancing, refreshments were carried in. Maura noticed that all three Mohammedan men ate in Ross's presence, a rare honor indeed since their caste usually forbade any such thing. In fact, all four of them talked so easily among themselves that they simply had to be acquaintances of long standing. Ross's Hindustani was as fluid, as broad with the vernacular, as their own.

The atmosphere in the shadowed room gradually became more relaxed, even salubrious. Maura was not at all surprised when the two uncles selected a pair of giggling handmaidens and vanished with them into another room. She had been seven years old when she had looked her last upon India, a child who had understood nothing of the ways of women and men. But in the short space of time since her return, she had listened to the whispered comments of the cantonment wives concerning the loose morals of Indian women, and had heard, too, the unvarnished gossip of Meera and the other servants at the Residency. She should have known that courtesans would be common in a harem as large as Walid Ali's, and she told herself now that there was no reason to be embarrassed by the fact that two of them had been selected to please the men of the family, or to believe for even a moment that—

Here Maura's thoughts checked abruptly and her heart started clamoring in her throat. Captain Hamilton had risen to his feet and was saying something to Kushna Begum. He was coming this way. . . .

Maura ducked her head and wrapped the end of her veil tightly about her face. She was careful not to let even her fingers show so that Ross wouldn't see that she did not possess the slim, brown hands of a kept Mohammedan woman.

But Ross was not speaking to her. In fact, he didn't even glance in her direction. Instead he was talking very amiably with the nautch-girl who had danced so hypnotically earlier that evening. The sloe-eyed creature was laughing back at him, and Maura had the sudden and unshakable impression that she and Ross Hamilton knew each other well.

Illogically, absurdly, she was infuriated by the thought. So *this* was the person Ross had gone to see on the night of Terence Shadwell's birthday party! She was sure of it! What lies had he told her just before she had watched him ride away from the Residency in the direction of town? Pressing work, indeed! Obviously he had quitted the party merely to dally with this brazen creature!

Fortunately the lower half of Maura's face was veiled so that Ross could not see the angry color that swept into her cheeks. But she could not prevent her eyes from blazing, or her head from lifting briefly in response to the sound of his deep laughter when the nautch–girl said something to amuse him.

This turned out to be a serious mistake, because at the same moment Ross turned his head to look at her. Across the room their glances met and locked—long enough for Ross to take note of the deep violet-blue of those flashing eyes.

A sudden stillness came over him. Quickly Maura lowered her head, but by then it was too late. There was a rustle of fabric and the sound of Ross's riding boots crossing the polished floor. His shadow loomed large as he bent over her, so close that his lean cheek very nearly brushed hers.

"If the Begum Sahiba would be so kind as to tell me where we have met before—"

He spoke in Hindustani, and Maura struggled to disguise her voice and inform him calmly in the same language that the sahib was mistaken, that she was a cousin of the Begum Kushna Dev and had only recently journeyed hither from Rajasthan. She had lived a very sheltered life in the home of her father and had never met a *feringhi*—a foreigner—before.

"My apologies, sahiba. The color of thine eyes—"

"My mother was a Circassian," Maura explained quickly, and named the tribe, which was known throughout northern India for the fairness of its people's skin and the uncharacteristic blue of their eyes. She sat with her head bowed and her hands folded in her lap as she spoke, for she was afraid to look at him again.

Fortunately, Ross took her behavior to be that of

someone raised in purdah; a woman clearly paralyzed with shyness in the presence of a sahib. Taking
pity on her, he apologized for having addressed her
so boldly. She had reminded him of someone, that
was all. He hoped she had taken no offense.

Maura shook her head demurely. Her heart
knocked and she felt dizzy with relief when Ross
straightened at last and went back across the room
to speak with Walid Ali. Shortly thereafter, both
men prepared to take their leave.

Watching them, the sloe-eyed nautch-girl
stamped her slim foot so that her ankle bracelets
jangled. It was obvious that she considered herself
rejected.

Ross did not seem to notice. "It is time," he told
Walid Ali.

The curtains covering the arched doorway fluttered behind them. Silence descended in the long,
lovely room. The men were gone.

"Wah!" exclaimed Kushna Begum at last. In the
next moment, all of them were talking at once.

Maura let out her breath in a shuddering rush.
Pushing aside the game board, she rose unsteadily
to her feet. "I think it's time I went home. I've had
about all the excitement I can stand."

She spoke in English without realizing. No one
understood her, but somehow it didn't matter. The
shaky smile that curved her lips as she unwrapped
her veil was explanation enough.

"*Hai mai!*" agreed Kushna Begum. "That was a
near thing!"

Abruptly it seemed to strike her as funny. She giggled, and the sound served to break the tension in
the room. Suddenly all of them were laughing together, including Maura, the sweet laughter of utter
relief.

Chapter Seven

"Good morning, Miss Adams."

Maura whirled at the sound of Ross Hamilton's deep voice, nearly upsetting the vase of lilies she was arranging on the drawing room table.

Reacting quickly, Ross caught the vase before it could topple. Setting it upright, he looked at her keenly. "Did I startle you?"

"No," lied Maura. But she had not expected to see him quite so soon. It was barely six in the morning and she had not yet recovered from the shock of encountering him in the zenana of the pink stucco palace the night before. She had hoped for more time to prepare herself before their first meeting.

"I've been summoned by your uncle," Ross explained, making no move to set down the vase and retreat. "The *chupprassi* suggested I wait for him here."

He was looking at her keenly as he spoke. He was

105

standing so close, in fact, that Maura could see the faint shadow of stubble darkening his jaw.

She wet her lips, which were suddenly dry. She disliked having him stand so close. With those disconcerting eyes upon her she could almost believe that he could look clear into her soul and know everything she was hiding from him there.

"Would you care for tea while you wait?" she inquired with admirable calm.

"Thank you, no. I've already had *chota hazri.*" Setting down the vase at last, he moved away. Maura immediately resumed arranging the lilies as though nothing were amiss.

"You understand what I mean by that, don't you?" he added from behind her.

She looked at him, perplexed.

"It's Hindustani for breakfast," he went on. "Little breakfast, to be precise. How much Hindustani do you understand?"

Maura turned away again quickly, not wanting him to see the wave of color flaring to her cheeks. Did he suspect?

She forced herself to utter a light laugh. "I'm afraid I'm limited to a mere smattering of kitchen Hindustani, Captain. The sort I used with that vendor in Bombay. You remember, don't you? I'm afraid the rest was forgotten during my years in England."

The lie fell glibly from her lips. She looked so innocent, so lovely, standing there in a gray-striped morning gown with the canna lilies in her arms that Ross must have believed her.

"I'm sorry," he said, turning away.

Sorry for what? Maura wondered. For having doubted her? For having realized that she couldn't possibly be the same girl he had met in the zenana the night before? But why should he regret that?

The cherrywood clock on the sideboard chimed the quarter hour. The *chupprassi* appeared to say that Carlyon-sahib was finally prepared to receive Captain Hamilton.

Maura waited until Ross left the room before tottering to a nearby chair and collapsing with a breathy sigh of relief. Thank goodness that was over! He hadn't recognized her after all. Or perhaps her unflustered replies to his questions had convinced him that he had been a fool to believe even for a moment that the Englishwoman Maura Adams was in any way related to the Muslim girl he had addressed the night before in the dim shadows of an Indian zenana.

I can't go there again, Maura thought. Not when the chance of another encounter existed, and especially not if it meant she would have to watch Ross take that sloe-eyed Indian beauty by the hand and lead her away to a secret, scented bedchamber the way Walid Ali's uncles had done!

"Bewakufi!" she exclaimed aloud. Nonsense!

"I'm sorry, Miss Adams?"

She turned quickly in the wide chair, horrified to see Ross standing in the doorway. "Captain Hamilton! I—I thought you'd gone."

"I forgot my portfolio." But instead of reaching for it there on the sideboard, he crossed to Maura's chair and stood looking down at her with a frown on his handsome face. Maura had to tilt back her head in order to meet his probing gaze, and she swallowed hard, feeling decidedly at a disadvantage.

"Are you certain," he said at last, "that your Hindustani is really so execrable?"

Her chin lifted. Wordlessly she nodded.

"Even if I were to tell you—"

"Oh," she exclaimed with utter relief, "there's Ismail Khan." Smiling prettily, she rose to her feet. "If you'll excuse me?"

But Ross wouldn't excuse her. He didn't even move aside as she rose, so that she found herself standing directly between his booted legs, the top of her head nearly brushing his chin.

Her cheeks flushed crimson and her heart began a wild tattoo. She forced herself to regard him calmly. "Is that all you wished to say to me, Captain?"

"Oh, no," Ross said darkly. "There's a great deal more I'd like to say, and far more that I'd care to know. But I've the feeling you're not going to tell me."

Maura's chin tipped. "I don't know what you mean."

"Don't you?"

She had no idea how to answer him. What on earth was he up to? Was he trying to catch her off guard? Did he suspect after all that she really was the one he had seen in the zenana last night?

Ross himself was having a hard time explaining his own behavior. Of late, nothing made sense where Maura Adams was concerned. The last time he'd dined here at the Residency he had ignored her to the point of rudeness, and still she had managed to get under his skin. Now, standing there frowning down at her, he tried to find a reason why her innocent replies to his questions should make him feel so completely, illogically angry.

But of course he knew. He was angry at himself, not her; angry for having been stupid enough to actually believe the fantastic thought that had hit him like a blow to the heart the night before after looking into the bewitching violet eyes of Kushna Dev's cousin.

Dressed in a muslin gown of gray and cherry stripes and with her glorious red hair glinting in the sunlight, Maura Adams looked bewitching indeed, but nothing at all like the shy Indian girl he had seen in the zenana last night.

Fantasy. Utter madness. He should withdraw immediately and forget the whole bloody thing rather than stand here like an idiot with this wide-eyed girl between his legs, looking up at him as though he'd lost his mind.

"Forgive me, Miss Adams," he said abruptly. "I'm not myself today."

Without another word he whirled on his heel and left her.

Once again Maura sank into the chair. Putting her face in her hands she waited for her racing heartbeat to slow.

I can't go there again, she thought. I mustn't.

Aunt Daphne and Lydia returned from Delhi the following day. Their shopping excursion must have been a great success judging from the number of parcels they brought home with them. Since Lydia was understandably eager to model her newest frocks for Terence, Mrs. Carlyon suggested a dinner party, just a small one, to provide the proper setting in which her darling could shine.

Maura, too, was to wear something new, which was why she stood fidgeting on this, the night of the party three days later, while Meera struggled with the numerous hooks and flounces of the ruffled green balldress that Mrs. Carlyon had bought for her in Delhi. The hoops of the ballgown's crinoline held up yards of shimmering emerald tafetta trimmed with blond, but above them Maura's slim shoulders and arms were bare. Meera had just finished brushing the girl's wayward hair and now she confined the heavy red mass in a netting of seed pearl.

"Thou art a princess," she murmured with pride.

By way of reply Maura hurled her fan across the room. She had had quite enough of Meera's poking and prodding. "There is no one I wish to impress tonight, so leave me be!" Collapsing onto the bed amid a pool of rustling green, she turned her face toward the wall.

"Thou art beset by demons tonight," Meera remarked, unperturbed. Calmly she smoothed out the wide skirts so that the dress wouldn't wrinkle. "What is it that plagues thee?"

"Nothing."

"Ismail Khan tells me you no longer ride."

"Ismail Khan should mind his own business."

"Thou art his business," Meera replied reasonably. "And mine. Now stand up, child, or assuredly thou wilt ruin—Oh, there is the memsahib calling. Quickly, now!"

Scowling, Maura picked up her fan and obeyed.

Outside, the sun was beginning to set in a brilliant wash of saffron, and the bearers were moving about lighting the paraffin lamps on the supper table. The British Resident and his wife, accompanied by their daughter, had already taken their places in the hall outside the drawing room to await the arrival of their guests.

Aunt Daphne was dressed in plum satin brocade while Uncle Lawrence looked surprisingly handsome in a dark suit bristling with orders. Lydia, breathtaking in silver-trimmed ivory damask, stood waiting impatiently for the arrival of her intended.

No more than a dozen guests had been invited, but she could scarcely conceal her annoyance as one after another of them was announced and still Terence failed to appear.

He came at last, disheveled and contrite, and towing Charles Burton–Pascal behind him. Maura had not seen Charles since their unfortunate encounter on the plains the week before, for he had been gone since then on a hunting trip to the foothills. She noticed that he looked sunburned and very fit as he came inside with Terence and, to her surprise, bowed quite agreeably over her hand. There was no mention of their last meeting or even any indication that he recalled the incident at all.

Smiling with relief, Maura watched him move off into the drawing room. Another guest was announced, and she turned back in time to find herself looking straight into the hard blue eyes of Ross Hamilton, who had just been shown in by the bowing *chupprassi*.

Maura felt as though she had been struck by a bolt of lightning. What on earth was *he* doing here? As far as she knew, he never mingled socially with anyone on the station! He was the last person on earth she had expected to see at Lydia's party, and yet here he was, crossing the floor to speak to her aunt and uncle, to kiss Lydia's hand, and to stop at last in front of her, his handsome face expressionless as he peered down at her from his great height.

"I wasn't expecting you tonight, Captain Hamilton," she said politely, offering her hand. "It's rare that you accept an invitation to the Residency."

But Ross appeared to be in no mood for small talk. He had stepped into the hall in time to catch the unguarded expression on Maura's face as she watched that puffed-up toady, Charles Burton-

Pascal, disappear into the drawing room. "I suppose I'll have to rectify that, won't I?" he said coldly.

Maura stiffened and resisted the impulse to snatch her hand away. She could tell that he was angry by the tight line of his mouth, but she could not understand why he chose to hold her responsible. Nor was she about to tolerate such treatment. Arrogant besom! Why hadn't he stayed away?

"Your cousin looks very fetching tonight," he added, deliberately neglecting to say the same about her.

"She always does. Now, if you please, Captain? You're holding up the line."

They glared at each other, refusing to acknowledge that each of them had scored a hit. Then Ross bowed and moved away, his eyes frosted with anger.

Good riddance, Maura thought furiously.

At least he didn't speak to her again after cocktails were served and the guests broke up into small groups to exchange gossip and hear the latest news from home. She noticed that he spent most of his time talking with Major Clapham from the Bhunapore garrison and did not once glance her way.

At nine o'clock, dinner was announced by the turbanned *chupprassi*. The guests lined up dutifully to enter the dining room in strict order of precedence as convention demanded. Earlier, Aunt Daphne had agonized over the seating arrangement, hounding her husband and poring endlessly over the official Warrant of Precedence, which was printed on the inside cover of her well-thumbed India Survival Manual. Her biggest dilemma had lain in deciding where to seat Captain Hamilton, who had never attended a Residency dinner before this. He was, after all, a military civilian, an officer seconded to the Government, and Daphne had had no idea if she ought to seat him according to his army or his civil service rank.

"Put him next to Maura," Uncle Lawrence had said at last, irritated by all the fuss.

Aunt Daphne had looked at him, bewildered. "Why?"

"Why not? He's a bloody unsociable fellow if I do say so myself, and she may be able to draw him out."

Aunt Daphne had reluctantly taken his advice, but her hopes of making a good pairing were immediately dashed by the fact that Maura insisted on snubbing Captain Hamilton from the moment they were seated. Captain Hamilton in turn only made matters worse by showing considerably more interest in Louisa Smythe, the attractive widow seated to his left.

At least the arrangement had not been a total disaster inasmuch as Daphne had placed Charles Burton-Pascal directly across the board from Maura. Her anxiety faded as she watched the two of them exchange numerous smiles as the meal progressed. Why, dear Maura was behaving positively kindly toward him tonight! Daphne's heart swelled with sudden hope. Perhaps Maura was growing up and becoming reasonable at last? Oh, wouldn't that be delightful!

The meal began with a clear gravy soup followed by tinned salmon. Though tasteless and greasy, it was hailed by all as a great delicacy considering that it had been imported to India directly from Great Britain. A haunch of mutton followed, accompanied by roasted partridge and the few vegetables that had not yet wilted in the Residency garden.

While the guests ate, the punkah fans flapped overhead, pulled by a pair of punkah-wallahs hidden from view behind a bamboo screen. No one seemed to notice the heat or the insects that had been attracted by the candlelight. It was enough that they had been provided with an excuse to put on their finery and dine together the way they always had back home in Mother England.

Throughout the meal Ross sat stonily watching Maura discuss Mughal art with Charles Burton-Pascal. He would never have guessed that she and Burton-Pascal were so well acquainted—or that she was even remotely interested in Mughal art. On the other hand, what did he really know about Maura Adams? Why should he be surprised that she would choose to favor a good-looking man like Burton-Pascal with her winsome smiles?

Furthermore, why should it annoy him so much? Was it because she continued despite everything to remind him of the enchanting creature in the gold silk tunic he had addressed in the zenana of his old friend, Walid Ali? Or had he been intrigued by the Indian girl in the first place merely because *she* had reminded him of Maura Adams?

Ross had no idea, and was angry with himself for not knowing. And angry with Maura, who should know better than to single out a male dinner guest with so much undivided attention. Surely she was aware that her behavior would arouse considerable speculation!

When the meal ended, the Residency *khidmatgars* brought in port for the gentlemen while the ladies withdrew to Mrs. Carlyon's bedroom to refresh themselves and await their turns in the commode. This affair was conducted in the same strict order of seniority that had marked their exit from the dining room, and Maura, as the youngest (Lydia had withdrawn to the verandah with Terence,) went in last.

When she came out again, she found herself alone. The ladies had departed for the parlor to sip tea and gossip until the menfolk joined them. Maura couldn't help uttering a sigh of relief. How good it felt to be away from those boring old matrons for a while!

Certain that she wouldn't be missed, she slipped outside by way of the bedroom door. The night was warm and very still. Starlight washed the sandy drive and the stretch of lawn that fronted the Residency. Maura could hear the dry cough of the *chowkidar* as he made his rounds, and the murmur of voices from the dining room where the men continued to sip their port and smoke cigars.

She wandered to the far side of the porch and sank down on the swing with a rustle of heavy skirts. Setting it rocking with a push of her slippered foot, she closed her eyes and uttered another weary sigh.

The smell of tobacco smoke made her sit up and look around her. Through the darkness she caught sight of the glowing tip of a cigarette. With a start she realized that she was not alone. Someone else was standing there by the railing, a tall man whose face was lost amid the shadows.

"Captain Hamilton," she said, sensing immediately who it was.

"Miss Adams." Though Ross could not see her either, he seemed to have recognized her as well. "I trust I'm not intruding."

"No," Maura lied.

"We always seem to be running into each other when we least expect it."

Maura stiffened. Was this some sort of veiled reference to that evening in the zenana? But, no, Captain Hamilton was leaning quite casually against the railing, not even looking at her.

115

"It's an odd thing," she agreed, relaxing a little.

Silence fell between them. After a while Ross flicked away his cigarette and straightened. Maura waited for him to leave, but he made no move to do so. Instead he continued to stand there gazing out into the darkness.

"It's a beautiful night," she remarked for lack of anything better to say.

She saw his lips twitch into a wry smile. "Is it? Most of your uncle's guests would disagree, I think. They've been vocal enough in their complaints tonight."

"You mean because of the heat?"

"That, and the lizards and insects and bats. And having the entire Indian subcontinent lurking in front of their doors, I suppose."

"Do you think people are still afraid of India?" Maura asked curiously.

"If you mean because of the Sepoy Mutiny, yes. It was a hard lesson, not easily forgotten."

"Or forgiven," Maura added, thinking of the harsh measures the British government had taken against any natives even remotely suspected of having supported the bloody rebellion. "Where were you when it happened?"

Ross uttered a harsh laugh. "I'm embarrassed to say that I was safely in England, studying at Addiscomb. My parents, who were here in India at the time, remained unharmed."

"Your father was with the East India Company?"

Ross smiled wryly. "What else? He spent years in Calcutta and later served as District Commissioner of Bulparaj."

"Bulparaj? I've never heard if it."

"Before the Mutiny it was a large royal state that happened to include our fair city of Bhunapore."

116

"Bhunapore! Then you're *not* a stranger to the area!"

"As a matter of fact, I spent most of my youth living not far from here. I've always had a fondness for the place, which is why I accepted the position of political adjutant to your uncle."

Which also explained how he had come to know Walid Ali, Maura thought. No doubt they had played together as boys in the village bazaar, or ridden their ponies across the plains, back in those early, glorious days of "John Company" rule when the English had mingled far more freely with the natives than they did today.

She thought of something else and turned to him with a frown. "You told me once that you loved India. Considered it your home. Does that mean you intend to stay here, in Bhunapore?"

"It's something of a backwater," Ross admitted, "but I like it well enough." He smiled ruefully. "Strange. I never thought I'd hear myself saying that. It must be that I've outgrown the rashness of youth. The lure of the border no longer calls me as it once did."

Was this true? Maura wondered doubtfully. Could a man the likes of Ross Hamilton really have had enough of the rough-and-tumble existence of frontier life? Had he served the British army long enough now to have a wish to settle down in a less demanding career? To someday take a wife and start a family, like most of the men who chose to remain in India after their time was up?

Maura didn't think so. There was a restlessness about Ross Hamilton that did not quite square with his complacent words. And she still didn't understand why he had willingly settled for the dull administrative post of Uncle Lawerence's adjutant.

Strange, but the thought that he would someday marry and have children filled her with an odd, lonely ache. In response she set the swing moving, hard. The hinges protested as the heavy skirts of her ballgown rustled back and forth, back and forth, across the wooden floor.

Ross reached into his breast pocket for another cigarette. It occurred to him that he ought to return to the dining room, where by now the absence of both himself and the Resident's niece was no doubt being noted by all the other ladies, who would be drawing their own inevitably tiresome conclusions.

But instead he lit the cigarette, inhaled deeply, and leaned back against the porch column. Without being aware of it, his gaze returned to Maura, who was staring off into the darkness, seemingly unaware of him. Ross noticed that her hair glinted like newly minted copper in the light falling from the window behind her. As well, the cut of her gown revealed the slimness of her bared shoulders and the silky whiteness of her throat. Below lay the lovely, rounded swell of her breasts.

Straightening abruptly, Ross ground the cigarette beneath his heel. "Come on," he said curtly. "It's time we joined the others, before they have reason to miss us."

His meaning was clear, and Maura rose swiftly. When she tried to step away from the swing, however, something held her back. Whirling, she saw that her skirts had caught on the rough wooden seat.

"Oh, bloody—" Muttering beneath her breath, she tugged hard, but the hem refused to come free.

"Miss Adams, wait." Reaching down, Ross dislodged the material quite easily. Straightening, he looked at her, a smile playing on his lips.

Maura glared back at him, her eyes sparkling with ill temper. Oh, but he was pleased with himself, wasn't he? And so sure that his nearness was flustering her completely!

Go on, she goaded herself, say something! Say something utterly quelling so that he'll know exactly how little he means to you!

But all she could do was stand there and look up into Ross's handsome face, watching the play of light and shadow across that very carnal mouth, and wonder suddenly if that same mouth had ever touched the lips of the sloe-eyed nautch-girl in the zenana. What would it feel like, she wondered illogically, unforgivably, if those same lips were to claim her own?

"Miss Adams—"

Lifting her eyes to his, she realized with a pang of dismay that he had seen exactly where her curious gaze had come to rest.

"Oh, no," she said quickly when Ross, his smile deepening, moved toward her. Frantically she searched for the words that would assure him that she had *not* been wondering what it would feel like to kiss him. But all she could do was put out her hands and try to push him away, although that turned out to be a grave mistake. Beneath her flattened palms she could feel the ridged muscles of his chest and the strong, steady beating of his heart.

"Oh, no," she said again, this time in a breathless little whisper.

"What's wrong?" he taunted softly. "Afraid?"

"No! I mean, of what?"

"That I might kiss you?"

He saw her pupils widen until those damnably purple eyes were nearly black.

"Y-you wouldn't!"

119

"Oh, no?" His big hands curved boldly over her hips. Still smiling, he drew her slowly toward him until they were standing center to center. Maura's heart seemed to stop beating as the crinkling taffeta of her ball dress was crushed between them. One of Ross's hands settled in the small of her back while the other cupped her chin, tipping it up so that he could look into her eyes. She tried to turn away but couldn't. So she twisted her fingers in the lapels of his coat, as though hanging on for dear life. Maybe she was.

"Still afraid?" he whispered.

"No."

"Don't you want me to kiss you?"

"I'd rather drink poison!"

But Ross only laughed and, bending his head, slanted his mouth across her own.

Maura went rigid in his arms. She knew that she should struggle, should cry out for help—but all she could think of was that she would die if anything were to stop this kiss.

Nothing did. Ross had only meant to tease her, to show her how easily he could disconcert her, and perhaps to prove to himself once and for all that this haughty young beauty meant nothing to him.

Too late. Too unwise. And utterly wrong. Maura gasped as the warm, seductive pressure of Ross's mouth closed over her own. His head tilted as he deepened the kiss, willing her lips to part.

For a moment, just for a moment, she resisted him. But then he dipped his head and cradled her nape with his hand to increase that wondrous pressure, and she had to give in. Her lips parted on a long, drawn-out sigh, and all at once both of them knew the sweetly forbidden taste of the other. Tongues touched while the breath caught in

120

Maura's throat and the very earth seemed to sigh. Fear and anticipation gave way to the magic pull of youthful yearning.

Breathless, she struggled to keep the tilting world solid beneath her feet. Up on her toes, she slipped her hands over Ross's shoulders and locked them around his neck. At last, at last, her slim body melted completely against him.

"Oh, God," he groaned in a half-despairing laugh. Quickly he grabbed her wrists and eased her away from him, away from his betraying, hardening self.

Maura looked up at him, her expression dazed, her heart tripping.

He stared back at her, fighting for breath.

The distant slamming of a door broke the taut silence. The floorboards shook. Someone was coming.

Maura stepped backward at the same moment that Ross released her wrists. Whirling, she found herself confronting the shocked faces of Terence Shadwell and her cousin Lydia. She had the mad urge to duck behind Ross's broad, reassuring back— an impulse that was instantly and completely squelched when she heard him utter a burst of impudent laughter.

Her temper flared. So he found the situation amusing, did he? Would he keep on laughing if she were to turn around and kick him right in the—?

"Good evening, Miss Carlyon, Shadwell," Ross said smoothly. "Pleasant night for admiring the moon, don't you think?"

Lydia managed to find her voice. "W-Why, Maura, Captain Hamilton! I had no idea—"

"Oh, we weren't looking at the moon ourselves," Ross went on, still sounding wretchedly uncaring. "Miss Adams caught her dress on a nail. Fortunately

I was nearby and came to the rescue." His eyes sparkled as he looked at her. "Isn't that right, Miss Adams?"

Maura gave him a look that would have felled a lesser man. Her tone, too, could have frozen water. "Believe me, I'm very grateful. Now, if you'll excuse me? I must see to my aunt's guests." Pressing back her crinolines, she brushed past him as though he did not exist.

Lydia, agog with curiosity, caught up with her in the hall. "Maura, wait!"

Maura paused with a long-suffering sigh. "What?"

Lydia put a finger to her lips and pulled her through the bedroom door. Shutting and locking it, she whirled. "Well?"

"Well, what?"

"Tell me! Captain Hamilton. Did he—?"

"Did he what?" Maura prodded as Lydia blushed and fell silent.

"Did he . . . Did he kiss you?"

She snorted. "Whatever gave you that idea?"

"When Terence and I saw you together on the verandah—"

"He told you what happened. My skirt got caught."

Lydia stamped her slippered foot. "Oh, don't be ridiculous! I know perfectly well he was kissing you!"

"Lydia, nothing happened."

"Oh, come, Maura! You were with him on the verandah *alone!*"

"That was my mistake," Maura said coolly. "Believe me, if I hadn't caught my gown I would have gone inside the moment he came out."

Lydia looked disappointed. "Do you really mean it? Nothing happened?"

Maura swore beneath her breath. She had no desire to go on discussing *that man*. She tried a different tack. "Would it matter so much if it had—which, I might emphatically add, it didn't? I thought courtship was encouraged here in India? Didn't your mother make certain that there was at least one unattached gentleman for each of us ladies tonight? Didn't she also rearrange the drawing room so that it contained a *kala jugga?*"

"A what?" Lydia asked with wide-eyed innocence.

Oh, really, Maura thought, exasperated. Every eligible girl on the continent, including Lydia, knew perfectly well that a *kala jugga* was a dark, secluded alcove where couples could sit out a dance if they wished—and where, as Lydia certainly knew from personal experience, they could indulge in far more than simple hand holding.

"Oh, come now, Lyddie, I saw you slipping in there on several occasions during Terence's birthday party."

Lydia said nothing, but her cheeks were scarlet.

"So why should it be so scandalous to find Ross Hamilton courting me out on the verandah?" Maura went on ruthlessly. "Which, I emphatically repeat once again, he was not!"

Lydia gave up. "All right, I won't say another word about it."

"Thank you."

"Besides, I always thought—I was so sure that you and Mr. Burton-Pascal . . ."

"Oh, for heaven's sake!" Maura's patience was finally at an end. "I'm tired, Lyddie. Can we talk about this tomorrow?"

An understanding smile curved Lydia's lips. "Yes. Yes, of course we can." She kissed her cousin's cheek, still smiling. "I'll see you back in the drawing room."

She thinks I'm interested in both of them, Maura thought, scowling after her. How utterly absurd! Just the thought of Charles Burton-Pascal made her skin crawl, and as for Ross Hamilton. . . .

Oh, no, you don't! She wasn't going to waste another moment thinking about him! Not even long enough to come up with a logical reason for the astounding emotions that had coursed through her when his demanding mouth had moved across her own.

Why hadn't anyone ever told her that kissing a man would prove to be so thoroughly vexing? Would she have responded the same way to some other man's kiss? Or had she felt that way only because it was Captain Hamilton who had kissed her? And what on earth had prompted him to do so in the first place?

Oooh! I'm not going to think about it anymore! I'm not!

Scowling, Maura peered through the bedroom door at the guests milling in the drawing room across the hall, wishing crossly that they'd all go home. At least she could be thankful that Ross hadn't returned from the verandah as yet. She wasn't ready to face him. As a matter of fact, she wasn't ready to face anyone.

So she sat on her bed, restless and irritable, and waited while the Residency guests played lengthy rounds of pontoon, gossiped and laughed, and drank up all of her uncle's whisky and soda. Long hours passed before they finally took their leave, and Maura was unutterably relieved when she heard the last of their carriages rolling away down the drive.

Tiptoeing to the door she ventured a peek outside.

Yawning servants were extinguishing the candles and clearing the cluttered tables. Thank God, the party was truly over. And thank God, too, that Ross had never returned from the verandah!

Only, where had he gone? Back to his bungalow? Or to that pink stucco palace in Bhunapore?

I won't think about it, Maura told herself fiercely, I won't! Even if Ross *had* gone to visit the nautch-girl Sinta Dai, she didn't care. The man meant nothing to her, nothing at all!

And to prove as much, she undressed for bed, extinguished the light, and fell asleep without giving him another thought.

Chapter Eight

To Maura's great relief, Lydia said nothing about Ross Hamilton the following morning. Lydia had her own problems to worry about, chief among them the fact that her mother had made up her mind over breakfast that Lydia's wedding dress was not, after all, suitable for the marriage of a British Resident's daughter to an up-and-coming civil service clerk, and oughtn't they return to Delhi to have the seed pearls and flounces replaced with silver basketwork?

Lydia firmly assured her mother that there was no need. Terence liked things simple, and she felt certain that a flounced skirt studded with silver embroidery would prove far too ostentatious for the subdued ceremony he envisioned. Besides, weren't the tiny seed-pearl chains and the stitched bodice lovely enough?

After some argument Aunt Daphne allowed that

perhaps they were, and added that it was just as well considering that she had just remembered an engagement that would prevent her from traveling to Delhi anyway.

"What is it?" Lydia asked, more polite than curious.

Aunt Daphne gestured vaguely. "Your father mentioned that we've been invited to some sort of darbar—dorbak—I forget what he called it."

"A durbar?" asked Maura, looking up from her breakfast.

Aunt Daphne's face cleared. "Yes, that's it."

"A what?" Lydia prodded.

Maura laid aside her knife. "It's a ceremony in which a head of state, usually a rajah or a prince, gathers together the men of his kingdom to hold court. Most of the time he does so mainly to dispense justice, but I think, seeing as the rajahs lost most of their power after the Mutiny, they're held more for show nowadays than anything else."

"Your uncle mentioned something about a festival," Aunt Daphne agreed, "welcoming the ruler of some foreign state to Bhunapore. The crown prince of someplace or other. They're holding it in the Peacock Palace."

Maura had seen the Peacock Palace, with its beautiful gold stucco towers and soaring elephant gates, situated amid the palm groves in the hills beyond the city gates. Meera had told her the palace was occupied by one Nasir al-Mirza Shah, a tired old ghost of a man who had once been the king of Bulparaj—before the East India Company had deposed him, annexed his land, and reduced the once prosperous kingdom to an insignificant little state known today as Bhunapore.

Bereft of his title and much of his wealth, Nasir

al-Mirza Shah nonetheless continued to hold court in his palace, though the dwelling was crumbling around him and his courtiers and faithful retainers were all aging or dead.

News that his young nephew, the ruler of a small kingdom in southern Rajasthan, intended to pay him a visit had apparently roused the old Mussulman from his lethargy. The nephew might only be a puppet ruler, installed by the British after the Mutiny to keep the kingdom of Kishangara loyal, but Nasir al-Mirza Shah did not care. He would hold a durbar in the prince's honor; a durbar filled with all the pomp and ceremony of bygone days; a showcase for his personal wealth and prestige despite the fact that both were sadly diminished.

As a mark of favor, Nasir al-Mirza Shah had decided to invite a number of prominent *Angrezis* to attend, among them the British Resident of Bhunapore and, at the prompting of his spiritual advisors, the Resident's memsahib, although she would be permitted to attend only those ceremonies to which the ladies of his own court had been asked. Not the durbar. Never the durbar. That would remain, as it had for centuries, the privilege of men.

"We'll only be gone one night," Mrs. Carlyon explained. "You'll be quite safe here in the Residency with Meera and Lala Deen to look after you. Louisa Smythe has also agreed to call on you in the event you should need anything. Oh, my dears, do you mind terribly?"

The girls exchanged swift glances.

"Why should we mind?" Lydia asked innocently.

Maura suppressed a smile, knowing that Lydia was already imagining herself driving *à deux* in Terence Shadwell's carriage through the golden dusk of the station streets, something her mother would never have permitted were she at home!

And I? thought Maura. What shall I do with this unexpected opportunity?

"Come to the festival with us," prodded Kushna Begum upon hearing the tale, her eyes dancing with mischief.

Maura's jaw dropped. "What?"

"Thou couldst dress again in the robes of a Mohammedan lady. My husband, too, shall attend the durbar, and I will accompany him to the festival. Thou couldst travel with my retinue."

"I couldn't possibly!" Maura exclaimed as Sita excitedly clapped her hands.

"Oh, say that thou wilt!" the younger girl pleaded. "Where can be the harm in this?"

"No one will know thee," Kushna Begum argued, "and surely there is some tale thou couldst tell at home so that thy absence will not be noticed?"

"There will be a royal procession," Sita put in excitedly. "That alone should not be missed!"

"I've never seen one," Maura agreed slowly. But she had heard of them; how grand they were, how gloriously they represented the long-lost age of the great Mughal empire, a spectacle that few sahib-*log* had ever witnessed and which she probably would never have the honor of viewing again. Her heart began a wild tattoo as she realized as much, knowing she was mad to think of going, knowing she would be an utter fool to stay behind.

"Surely thou couldst invent a tale to explain thy absence to thy cousin?" Kushna Begum prodded. "Thou wouldst not have to stay the night—only for the day, and Ismail Khan will bring thee back at nightfall."

"I could say that I am going to the bazaar," Maura

said slowly. "My cousin knows I am safe with Ismail Khan."

"Then it's settled!" Kushna Begum exclaimed, clapping her hands.

"But only for a few hours," Maura persisted. "Long enough to see the procession. Then Ismail Khan must bring me home. And if there is the slightest chance that I will be recognized—"

"*Hai mai!*" laughed Kushna Begum, "thou art worrying like an old wife! Who could possibly know thee?"

Lawrence and Daphne Carlyon took their leave long before the sun was up so as to spare themselves the journey during the hottest part of the day. Not long afterward, Lydia and Maura met at the breakfast table to exchange conspirational smiles. Lydia did not even bother hiding her delight when Maura informed her that she intended to spend the day shopping in the Bhunapore bazaar.

"I'd love to go with you," she said, blushing prettily, "but you see, I've . . . um . . . Terence has asked me . . ." Her words trailed away and her blush deepened.

Maura laughed. "Oh, I know what you intend. You needn't worry, your secret is safe with me. Besides, no one else will think it odd if you're seen driving alone with Terence Shadwell. The two of you *are* officially engaged."

"That's exactly what Terence said," Lydia agreed with relief. "We won't be gone long, Maura, I promise. We're taking a picnic lunch to the temple ruins and driving back over the Sindha Bhat road. His bearer and syce will be with us."

"It sounds wonderfully romantic."

"You could join us," Lydia added. "I'm certain Mr.

Burton-Pascal . . . or do you suppose Captain Hamilton—"

Making a face, Maura bent to kiss her cousin's cheek. "Go alone," she advised. "You'll enjoy yourselves so much more. And I," she added, grinning, "intend to have a wonderful time myself."

They parted company not long afterward on the Residency verandah, Lydia hurrying down to the gate to await Terence's arrival while Maura, dressed demurely in her topi and powder-blue habit, rode with Ismail Khan north toward town.

In the garden of Walid Ali's pink stucco house, confusion reigned. Turbanned bearers rushed about saddling horses, loading trunks and baskets, and readying the *ruths*, the closed bullock carts that would bear the womenfolk to the Peacock Palace. Maura was ushered into the zenana's audience chamber where she found Kushna Begum in the midst of a chattering crowd, issuing orders, while her palms and the soles of her feet were being painted with henna.

As Maura came in the Indian girl gave a glad cry and rose to embrace her. "I did not think thou wouldst come! I thought thy courage would fail."

"Mine?" Maura laughed, and the others joined in.

At a command from Kushna Begum, Maura was brought clothing to wear: a pair of salwar pajama trousers, loose and flowing at the waist and gathered slim at the ankles, of deep-blue silk embroidered with silver threads. The tunic that fitted over the top of them was of coral muslin, so fine that it clung to Maura's skin like insubstantial mist. Her hair was plaited into a single long braid which was then covered by an embroidered veil wrapped in a manner so as to conceal the lower half of her face.

The maidservants giggled as they worked, enjoying themselves hugely.

"If anyone asks, I will tell them at the Peacock Palace that thou art the daughter of a Circassian slave," explained Kushna Begum. "That will explain the purple of thine eyes. Here."

Maura stood patiently as rings were slipped onto her fingers and tiny slippers put on her feet. A gold-encrusted girdle was laid about her waist and then Kushna Begum cocked her head to one side to study the result. She clapped her hands and laughed in delight.

"Indeed thou art now one of us!"

Maura crossed over to the gilded mirror. During the last few weeks she had spent most of her time outdoors, and her cheeks and hands were browned by the sun. With her hair hidden beneath the veil, the blue salwars falling loosely about her hips, and with gemstones glittering on her fingers and about her waist, she did indeed look like a Mohammedan lady of family.

By now it was time to go, and the throng of women moved, laughing, toward the stairs. Not often were they permitted the luxury of leaving the zenana; rarer still were they allowed to go beyond the palace grounds. Spirits were high, and Maura was infected by the mood as she hurried with them toward the waiting bullock carts. With her face veiled and her head lowered, she climbed inside, and only Ismail Khan, standing at the end of the procession, knew that the slim girl in the blue trousers and coral tunic was in fact Maura Adams, English niece of the British Resident of Bhunapore.

The *ruth* in which Maura rode was enclosed to protect the women from the curious eyes of strangers. Out on the jolting road the temperature inside soared, but no one seemed to mind. There was much to talk about, to discuss and plan, and Kushna Begum entertained everyone with tales of Nasir al-Mirza Shah's colorful exploits, for she had known the former ruler since childhood.

Less than two hours later, the *ruth* began a tortuous uphill climb, and Maura dared to take a quick peek between the purdah curtains. Ahead of them loomed the Peacock Palace, standing on a barren hillside scored with nullahs and thorny *kikar* shrub.

Because the ancestors of Nasir al-Mirza Shah had come from Rajasthan, the builders of the Peacock Palace had adapted much of that architectural style. As a result, the dwelling was embellished with countless kiosks, fantastic ornamental towers, and crenellations that resembled nothing even remotely familiar to Western eyes. Mirrored tile and the brightly polished stucco known as *chunam* gleamed in the sun. The vivid colors of the walls and towers evoked the splendor of a peacock's tail. Sprawling courtyards and capacious durbar halls flanked the breathtaking gardens, which were dotted with temples and shrines.

The *ruth* passed beneath the *Hathi Pol*, the Elephant Gate, and halted on a drive of smoothed marble. The richly attired guards standing at attention averted their eyes as the ladies emerged and were escorted into the zenana. Maura kept her own gaze lowered so as not to attract attention, but still she managed to catch glimpses of glittering audience chambers as she hastened toward the stairs, the walls of marble and lapis, the fittings of thinly hammered gold.

Although there was an unmistakable air of decay which even the incense burning in brass lamps throughout the hall could not conceal, the palace itself was dazzling. What must it have looked like, Maura wondered, when the kingdom of Bulparaj had been in its heyday?

Attendants were on hand to receive the visitors, and Kushna Begum and Sita were escorted into the private audience chamber of Nasir al-Mirza Shah's senior wives to be introduced. Maura joined the others of her retinue who were chatting with the palace women and refreshing themselves with cooling drinks and delicate porcelain bowls filled with iced sherbet. Afterward, she secured her veil about her face and stepped out onto the balcony. Here, delicate *jali* screens carved with elephant and peacock motifs were strung across the balcony front to protect the purdah of those ladies who wished to view the gardens.

Looking down, Maura caught her breath. She had never seen anything so beautiful. The garden walkways were of polished white stones which were laid in exquisite patterns between lotus pools and pleasure pavilions whose marble domes and columns were lavished with hand-painted friezes and mirrored murals. The air was scented with the perfume of thousands of flowers; narcissi, frangipani and jasmine bloomed everywhere. Groves of tamarinds and cherry trees surrounded an artificial lake. Countless fountains burbled amid the flowerbeds, and there were numerous courtyards whose secretive alcoves offered cooling shade. Tame peacocks strutted across the lawns, and from a distant aviary came the lovely songs of exotic birds.

Enchanted, Maura stood and looked her fill, and wished with a sudden ache in her heart that she had someone to share with her the seductive beauty that was the garden of Nasir al-Mirza Shah's Peacock Palace. She wondered if her aunt and uncle had been permitted to see it, and a sudden shiver slithered down her spine as she thought of them, quenching her delight. If they should find out she was here . . .

I'm not going to think about that, she admonished herself sternly.

She had come to see the royal procession, which was scheduled to begin sometime toward sundown, when the air was cool and the crown prince of Kishangara arrived with his retainers. When it was over, she and Ismail Khan would ride home. Her aunt and uncle would never suspect that she had been here.

Neither, fortunately, would Ross Hamilton. Maura had made certain to ask his whereabouts before agreeing to come. How glad she had been to learn he was gone! It would seem he had been called away to a nearby village, where a *sadhu*, a Hindu holy man, was attempting to agitate the peasants into a rising against the Raj. Isolated instances such as these still occurred even now, years after the Mutiny, but they were always dealt with swiftly and decisively—which was why Uncle Lawrence had sent Ross to take the *sadhu* to task. Maura had no doubt that Ross would pursue the matter with his usual ruthless efficiency.

She had also told herself that it was utter nonsense to fear for his personal safety. Ross Hamilton was well known in the district, and he and his bearer could be counted on to handle any unforeseen trouble. How foolish of her to waste time worrying about him. Utterly ridiculous!

From somewhere deep within the zenana walls came the tinkling of brass bells. There was a rustle of fabric and the hushed voices of the women inside. Something was about to happen.

Thrusting the image of Ross aside, Maura left the balcony to take her place with the others. The women of Nasir al-Mirza Shah's harem had been granted permission to view the royal procession, but only from behind the *jali* screens lining the palace balcony. While the men of the court took their places along the parade route where hundreds of peasants already had gathered to witness the event, the ladies surged to the balconies, whispering excitedly.

Inasmuch as they could see only a portion of the road leading to the *Hathi Pol*, they would miss most of the procession, but no one seemed to mind. Already they could hear the throb of kettledrums and the cheers of the spectators as they waited for Crown Prince Omar Naini of Kishangara to make his appearance.

They did not have long to wait. The drums grew louder, heralding the arrival of the prince's bodyguards, who were dressed in purple and silver and carried silvered lances. Behind them came the flag bearers displaying the royal banners of Kishangara as well as the *aftadah*, the sun symbol, and numerous peacock fans. The elephants came next, half a dozen of them, draped in silken finery and bound together by ropes of flowers.

The last elephant carried the royal howdah on its back, and upon this heavy silver throne sat Prince Omar Naini himself, gorgeously attired in scarlet, his turban adorned with a huge, pigeon's blood ruby. Behind his elephant rode his wife, the *rajkumari*, in a silver conveyance draped with purdah screens of delicate silk. The palanquin was supported by twenty bearers in scarlet turbans and crimson overcoats gleaming with gold embroidery.

The women bearers came next, and behind them

the ladies-in-waiting, chanting the names and titles of the royal couple. Behind them, on another elephant, came the chief eunuch draped in cashmere shawls. He was followed by an endless stream of covered palanquins carrying the other, lesser ladies of the *rajkumari's* court.

Jugglers and magicians with trained monkeys moved among the crowd, and flower bearers tossed scented petals until the ground was littered as though with pink and yellow snow. A band played and the spectators cheered as the magnificent procession wound its way through the golden glow of the setting sun toward the elephant gate of the Peacock Palace.

From her vantage point behind the *jali*, Maura looked on with breathless wonder. The scene could have come straight from a fairy tale, a time out of mind, a different world. When the last of the palanquins had vanished through the gate, she hurried with the others back through the zenana and down a flight of steps to an inner courtyard screened by rustling palms.

From here, well secluded, the women could gaze down into the enormous marble courtyard while Crown Prince Omar Naini was officially received by his host. Already the court of Nasir al-Mirza Shah had gathered amid the columns and arches, and the priests had sprinkled the ground with rose water in anticipation of the prince's arrival.

Maura leaned against the parapet with her arms crossed, eagerly studying those below her. Eventually she spotted her aunt and uncle standing with numerous other European dignitaries in the shade of a fretted archway just behind the courtyard gate. Aunt Daphne was wearing her best gown of deep green *barège*. Gemstones glittered in her hair and on her fingers. She looked very imperious, although her magnificence paled in the presence of Nasir al-Mirza Shah's glittering courtiers. Uncle Lawrence, as drably neat and reassuring as always, was saying something into his wife's ear as the huge Rajasthani entourage surged into the courtyard.

"Is it not wonderful?" someone breathed behind Maura, but she did not notice. Her attention had been caught by a dark-headed man in the scarlet regimentals of an Indian cavalry regiment who had just stepped out of the shadows behind her uncle and now stood towering above him.

Ross Hamilton.

Maura's heart seemed to leap into her throat. She willed herself not to jerk back behind the balcony wall as though she had something to hide. Inwardly her thoughts were tumbling all over themselves. What was in the name of God was he doing here? Uncle Lawrence had said nothing of the fact that he would be back in time for the durbar!

I should never have come, Maura thought wildly. Supposing he sees me?

Breathing deeply, she forced herself to remain calm. After all, there was no way Ross could see beyond the pierced holes of the *jali* screen, and even if he could, he would certainly never recognize her. She was acting like a fool.

"Ohé, Little Pearl," whispered Kushna Begum from over her shoulder, using the nickname she had adopted for her English friend. "Wilt thou come with me?"

Wordlessly Maura followed the Indian girl back across the courtyard, but instead of returning to the audience chamber of the zenana, they descended a flight of narrow stairs tiled with polished mirrors.

Their colorful images flitted across the walls as they hurried downward.

"Where is it that we go?" Maura asked.

"The Begum Sahiba has invited us to join her outside the *Chitra Shala*. It is there that the menfolk will gather to refresh themselves before the durbar convenes." Kushna Begum giggled. "Since no one will see us, I thought at once to fetch thee."

Maura laughed, forgetting Ross in her excitement. "I am honored."

The *Chitra Shala*, or painted hall, was illuminated by dozens of bronze lamps running the length of the marble walls. The vaulted ceiling was lost in the gloom, but the magnificent motifs of tiled flowers, suns, and god-heads were still visible along the base of its flowing arches. The inlaid marble floor bore the colorful insignia of the royal house of Nasir al-Mirza Shah, and hand-painted miniatures of the ruler and his ancestors adorned the doors and walls. The hall was crowded with Indian men whose gorgeous attire made the few British representatives, modestly clothed in Western fashion, pale in comparison.

A gallery fronted by a pierced-marble screen ran along the length of the wall above their heads, and it was here that Kushna Begum led Maura. The senior begums of the household were already seated on gold-tasseled cushions, and Maura sketched a polite greeting when she was introduced to them as a distant cousin from Gwalior.

The senior begums made polite small talk as another cushion was carried in. Below them, the men of the court mingled in small groups. Refreshing sherbets sweetened with watermelon and passion fruit were brought in to appease their thirst, and the atmosphere gradually grew more relaxed.

The informal scene was a source of much fascination for the Indian ladies watching from above, but Maura, long-accustomed to sharing her world with men, soon grew bored. The gallery was too far removed for her to understand their talk, and she couldn't help feeling dishonest somehow for spying on her aunt and uncle when they had no idea she was here.

When the royal heralds began chanting in preparation for the commencement of the durbar, Maura said in an undertone to Kushan Begum, "I must go."

"Stay," the other girl pleaded.

"I cannot. Ismail Khan awaits me."

"The night is young, and thou hast not yet seen the dancing."

"I came only for the procession," Maura reminded her firmly.

"Ohé, thou art stubborn," the Mohammedan girl said with a sigh. "But go, if thou must."

"I shall visit thee soon," Maura promised and, rising, made her devotions to the senior begums before slipping quietly down the staircase.

By now the royal staff bearers were assembling below, and even the imposing eunuchs flanking the doorway did not spare Maura a glance, caught up as they were in viewing the event. Maura's thin slippers padded softly across the marble floor. There was no one about, and even the entrance to the women's quarters had been left unguarded.

Pulling open the heavy door, she slipped noiselessly outside and then halted, startled, upon finding herself not in the vast courtyard where Crown Prince Omar Naini had earlier been received by his host, but on the outskirts of the magnificent gardens

140

she had seen from the zenana roof. How had she managed to lose her way?

Somehow, it didn't matter. Not when she found herself standing in the midst of such seductive beauty. Up close, the gardens were even more breathtaking than she had thought. With the setting of the sun, the night-blooming flowers had opened their petals so that the air was perfumed with heady fragrance. From the balconies and courtyards above drifted the added scents of lemon, vetiver, and sandalwood; the incense of summer which was kept burning throughout the night by specially appointed attendants.

The moon was new, and only the stars cast their cool light upon the tinkling fountains and lotus pools. Candlelight glowed in distant arches, and now and again a faint burst of music drifted from the *Chitra Shala*. The gardens themselves remained deserted. No one dared step outside while the court was gathering for the durbar.

"I'll stay only a minute," Maura promised herself, but she ended up remaining a lot longer than that. She had no idea, in fact, how long she wandered the manicured paths, lost amid the fountains and the pavilions while crickets chirped and songbirds stirred sleepily in their aviaries.

Eventually she reached a pleasure pavilion that was surrounded on all sides by lotus ponds. Here, water lilies bloomed in profusion, and silver-bodied fish flashed in the shallows as Maura crossed above them by way of an arching bridge.

The pavilion was open on all sides to allow the cooling breezes to enter. Carved columns bore up the domed roof, and the floor was spread with thick tapestries. Brocade cushions were arranged to make a roomy divan, and Maura started toward them, delighted by the prospect of sitting tranquilly for a while.

The steps of the pavilion were flanked with potted roses, and as she ascended, she felt a sharp tug. Turning, she saw that the trailing end of her veil had caught on a thorn. She bent quickly to free herself.

"Allow me."

Maura froze as a tall shadow fell across her path. The dim starlight shone on broad shoulders encased in regimental scarlet. Carefully, Ross Hamilton reached down to untangle the veil before straightening and smiling at her.

Maura kept her gaze averted. Her heart hammered. "Thou art kind," she thanked him in breathless Hindustani.

Ross inclined his head to acknowledge this but did not speak. The girl reminded him of a frightened bird about to take flight, and he quickly searched his mind for the proper words to reassure her. He had, of course, recognized her the moment she had spoken as the beautiful cousin of the Begum Kushna Dev.

His shock at seeing her here was great, but he knew with a deep certainty that he did not want her to go. She was more of a mystery to him now than she had been on the night of their first meeting. And heart-stoppingly beautiful as well, her flowing veil and baggy salwars doing nothing to hide the seductive slimness of her shape. Even in the shadows of the pavilion, her eyes, darkened with antimony in the Indian fashion, were the most expressive Ross had ever seen.

But curiously enough, even dressed in the gossamer silks of an Indian lady and speaking the ancient language of Hindi, she was not able to dispel completely her remarkable resemblance to Maura Adams. Ross's coolly analytical brain told him that of course they could not possibly be one and the same. Still, it was hard not to draw a comparison between two women who possessed such unique, compelling beauty.

As the silence lengthened between them, Maura's heartbeat accelerated. Why didn't Ross say something? Why did he just stand there looking at her with that oddly tender smile on his face? Dear God, she'd not be able to keep her wits about her if he didn't stop being so . . . so damned disarming!

"Thou art not at the durbar," she ventured at last. Glancing up at him, she added with the suitable surprise of one who has just realized as much: "Why, thou art a sahib!"

"I am. And we have met before," Ross informed her in fluent Hindi.

Maura forced a lighthearted laugh. "Ohé, sahib! How can this be?"

"It was in the home of my friend, Walid Ali. Earlier this month, before the Hindu festival of Holi. At the time I was told thou wert a cousin of the Begum Kushna Dev. I assume thou art here with her?"

Maura nodded with downcast eyes. "The zenana rooms were too crowded. That is why I came into the garden."

Please, she thought, please let him be satisfied with that and go away.

"I was summoned here by the *burra*-sahib," Ross was saying. "We were to meet privately before the commencement of the durbar."

Maura threw a panic-stricken look over his shoulder. What "great man" did he mean by that? Surely not her uncle? Dear God, if Uncle Lawrence was on his way here—!

"The *burra*-sahib was detained," Ross added gently, assuming from her frightened look that she was shaken by the prospect of being seen by yet another white man.

Maura traced the toe of her slipper across the patterned rug beneath her feet. She knew better than to look at him again. She must make her excuses quickly, without arousing his suspicion.

Unfortunately, Ross seemed disinclined to make things easy for her. Propping his shoulder against a nearby column he crossed his arms over his chest and regarded her thoughtfully. There was no way she could flee down the steps without bumping into him.

Silence fell between them. The fountains tinkled and a perfumed breeze lifted the end of Maura's veil. She put out a slim hand to hold it fast, and Ross found himself wondering suddenly what she would look like if he were to remove that concealing piece of clothing. He had no doubt that her hair would be as black as night, and that her face, given its delicate bone structure, would be impossibly lovely to gaze upon. Would she still remind him of Maura Adams once he had seen it?

"The sahib is silent," Maura observed nervously.

"That is because I—"

"Wait!" said Maura in an electrified whisper. "Someone is coming!"

Ross turned quickly, for he, too, had heard the sound of footsteps on the path. Taking hold of Maura's arm, he drew her deeper into the shadows, grimly aware of the scandal that would erupt if a high-born Mohammedan lady were to be discovered fraternizing with a sahib in the pleasure pavilion of Nasir al-Mirza Shah's Peacock Palace. Even today, in the more remote reaches of India, women still died for such indiscretions.

The footsteps neared. Ross heard Maura catch her breath. In the dim starlight he could make out an elderly *chowkidar* shuffling toward the bridge. Despite his age his eyesight was obviously still keen, for he had not even set foot upon the bridge before he stopped and peered in their direction.

"Who is there?" he called in a raspy voice.

Maura laid a warning hand on Ross's sleeve. "It is I, the Begum Chota Moti," she said clearly, using the nickname Kushna Dev had given her. "I am a guest of the Padshah Begum of the Peacock Palace, and a cousin of the wife of Walid Ali. I am admiring the gardens with a . . . a friend."

Understanding her instantly, the elderly *chowkidar* uttered a stammered apology. He was merely making his rounds, he explained hastily, and had not expected to come across a pair of lovers meeting on the night of the durbar. Naturally he would leave them in peace. He prayed that he had caused no offense.

Maura assured him that he had not. But as the *chowkidar's* footsteps faded discreetly, the whole thing suddenly struck her as absurd. She bit her lip but was unable to prevent herself from uttering a strangled giggle.

"Be still!" Ross whispered.

She giggled again. Quickly he pressed her face into his coat, and she stood there with his arm about her shoulders, shaking with silent laughter.

"Ohé, but that was close!" she gasped when the *chowkidar* had gone and she could speak again. Tipping back her head she smiled at him.

"Art thou a fool to know no fear?" Ross inquired harshly.

Her smile grew broader; though she was veiled he could tell by the way her magnificent eyes began to sparkle. "No, sahib. Merely a quick thinker."

Ross's lips twitched despite himself. "Aye. And I am thankful for that."

They smiled at one another, and it was only then that Maura became aware of the fact that Ross's arm was still about her shoulders. There were other things to experience as well: the feel of his coat buttons pressing against her breasts and, beneath them, the rigid expanse of his wide chest. She was standing so close that she could hear the steady drumming of his heart.

Her laughter died abruptly and her own heart skipped a beat. Up swept her eyes to peer into Ross's smiling face and then to fall, quite of their own accord, to the full, carnal mouth hovering so close to her own.

"Oh . . ." she breathed without thinking, remembering how she had felt on the night that Ross had kissed her. What was wrong with her? Had she gone mad, wanting him to kiss her again?

For a glorious, aching moment she thought that he would. The arm about her shoulders tightened, drawing her closer against his body where Maura could feel the thundering of his heart beneath her flattened palms. His other hand reached up to brush back her veil—but then he turned away, releasing her abruptly from the crook of his arm. Without a word, he stepped to the edge of the pavilion and lifted his hand to the nearest column.

Maura's breath caught, aware all at once of what he intended. The pavilion was draped with *chik* blinds, held out of the way by tasseled pulls. By lowering them all around, any lovers meeting inside could assure their privacy completely. Now, beneath Ross's hands, they fell to the floor with a whisper of fabric.

Instantly the starlight was snuffed out and the pavilion was plunged into darkness. Ross came to stand before her. Maura couldn't see him, but she could sense his presence with every fiber of her being.

Ross said softly in Hindustani, "Chota Moti. Little Pearl. Is that really thy name?"

Maura tried to speak, but for some reason the words wouldn't come. Overwhelmed, she could only nod.

Gently, Ross lifted aside her veil. "It seems apt," he murmured. "Little Pearl, look at me."

Maura lifted her face to his, her heart so full that she could scarcely breathe. He cared for her, she exulted, cared enough that he had made an effort to spare her the need to reveal her features to him! What did it matter if he thought her someone else? For her, the distinction had blurred, become inconsequential. She was aware of nothing at the moment but the ache in her heart for him.

"Ross—" Her lips shaped his name, but fortunately the sound was lost as he bent his head and touched his mouth to hers.

It was a long, slow kiss filled with all the drugging wonder of that first one on the Residency verandah. Maura felt her senses reeling beneath the warm pressure of his mouth and the way his hands curved about her hips to fit her intimately against him. Her body, wrapped in nothing more than a layer of silk, was pressed tightly against his.

"Oh, God," Ross whispered raggedly. He lifted his head to look at her, but Maura's fingers slid through his thick hair, drawing his mouth back to hers.

This time when he kissed her, her lips parted beneath the pressure. She trembled as his tongue grazed hers. Her bones seemed to lose their very

147

substance and she melted against him, greedily absorbing his heat and hardness. Through the filmy silk she could feel every inch of him: the rigid muscles of his chest, the strength of his thighs, the heat of his rising maleness burning at the apex of her womanhood, an alien heat that made her shiver.

In the next moment she was lifted against the wall of his chest as Ross picked her up and carried her to the cushions. There he laid her down, touching her body with the heated length of his own. His hands were gentle and very sure as they stripped away her clothing.

The warm night air caressed her naked skin. The cushions sagged as Ross leaned over her. Propping one powerful arm on either side of her head, he bent closer.

"Little Pearl," he whispered, "kiss me."

It was the tone of his voice that undid her: the longing and the note of husky wonderment as if he, too, could not quite comprehend what was happening between them. That he burned for her was obvious; that he had not expected to do so was obvious as well.

Maura would never have thought Ross Hamilton a vulnerable man, but her heart soared at his ragged request. Slipping her arms around his neck, she sensed more than saw the hunger sparking in his black eyes.

Lifting her head to his, she let his hot mouth claim hers like a man starved. Cast adrift on a rising tide of want, she tightened her arms around him. Her body moved to the rhythm of his, hip to hip, thigh to thigh, even though the buttons of his uniform scraped her naked skin.

When finally he groaned and turned his face into her neck she slipped out from under him and eased off his coat. Her fingers were clumsy both with inexperience and need as she undid the buttons of his dress shirt, but it didn't matter. He seemed content to wait, threading his fingers through her hair, trailing his lips across her cheekbone to her jaw.

When he finally reared up before her, a white blur in the darkness, she sank back on her heels, her breath coming fast. Uttering an exultant laugh, he caught her in his arms and leaned her back into the cushions. His hair-roughened chest covered hers, their legs tangled. His hands were everywhere, caressing and arousing so that Maura knew no shame or fear when he touched her intimately at last, only a mounting excitement that gave way beneath his kisses and his touch to a slow-burning delight.

There was so much to learn, to savor and feel. She knew that Ross thought her experienced at lovemaking, and that she could not reveal the truth to him without letting him know who she really was. So she contented herself with following his lead, allowing him to reveal to her the wonders of love's mysteries without a telling word or whisper. Silently, accepting, she let him do as he wished, as he shaped her to his touch and showed her without knowing that he did how the hot, needful urgency at the core of her being could spread like fire through every weighted limb.

Instinct might not have taught her what a woman should know, but love and desire were lessons unto themselves. Ross sucked in his breath as Maura skimmed her hands down his rib cage to his hips, reveling in the difference between them, then kissing him back. Wanting to pleasure him as he had her, she closed her hand at last about the essence of his manhood.

"Oh," she whispered, unable to keep still at the wonder, the intimacy of discovery.

Ross's breath caught on a groan. "Thou art making me mad, *piari*." Sweetheart. "Wait—" His voice was raw. He could wait no longer. Splaying his hands across her hips he laid her back against the cushions and rolled her beneath him.

For the first time Maura felt the hugeness of him throbbing between her thighs. Her eyes closed while need and want rose within her, a clamorous demand.

"Little Pearl," he whispered, "this is how I've imagined you, dreamed of you . . ." He had no idea that he spoke in English as he slanted himself against her, wholly aroused.

In response Maura arched her hips while her hands lifted to clasp his upper arms. When he pressed against her she parted her thighs in silent invitation.

Drawing a shuddering breath he slipped his hands beneath her buttocks and positioned himself. She was warm and wet and waiting, for his touch had roused her to white-hot desire. Lifting her up, he surged forward and drove himself inside.

Maura had not expected the cruel stab that was the ending of her girlhood. But even as she pressed her face against his throat to hide her agonized groan, Ross came up on his elbows, bearing his weight to spare her further pain. With an unsteady hand he smoothed the hair from her brow.

"I'm sorry. Thou art unused to a man like me. I didn't think—" His whisper grew hoarse. "*Piari*, I'm sorry . . ."

She sensed the physical effort it was costing him to hold back, and a fierce tenderness welled inside her. When he dipped his head to trail encouraging kisses across her cheeks and brow she moved slowly, seductively beneath him. Ross's breath hitched as he jerked involuntarily, and Maura sighed in answer and wrapped her arms around him.

Only then did he resume his gentle assault, stroking slowly in and out of her in a timeless rhythm of love. The pain ebbed away into the glory of a touch Maura had never dreamed existed, a touch that seemed to burn its way through every fiber of her being.

Her fingers clasped the bunched muscles of Ross's upper arms as she strained to meet the powerful thrusts of his body. Within her rose an uncontrollable ache, an excitement that replaced her earlier pain and continued to build with Ross's every plunging stroke. She could not help crying out at the wonderful, quivering rapture that was bearing her aloft, carrying her higher and higher until she felt certain something within her would ignite and explode.

"Ohh—!" she gasped, writhing in helpless transport as it happened, as the ecstacy of her first climax burst upon her.

In that same moment Ross surged against her, his face pressed into the curve of her neck. His body bucked, fused to hers, as he groaned aloud with the force of release. Together they were hurled into the maelstorm and found themselves swept away.

It seemed a long time before Maura surfaced from sweet oblivion. But gradually the reeling world righted and she opened her eyes to find herself lying on the cushions with Ross's weight full upon her. Their sweat-slicked bodies were locked together. She stirred and sighed, and Ross slowly raised himself onto his elbows and cupped her face with his hands. The kisses he trailed across her mouth and cheeks were unbearably sweet.

"Mmmm," she murmured, and was about to say something else when all at once the sky above them exploded. Lights flashed, rockets whistled, fireworks flared. The darkened pavilion rocked beneath the blasts and set the birds in the aviaries shrieking. Flashes of gold, blue, and green lit the darkness.

Unnoticed, forgotten, time had slipped away from them. The durbar was over.

Terrified that Ross would recognize her in the light of the fireworks, Maura groped blindly for her veil. In the meantime, Ross eased himself away from her and crossed quickly to the edge of the pavilion. There was no need for him to lift the blinds. The flash of exploding powder turned the darkness into day.

"The durbar is over," he said in Hindustani, leaning against a column to watch. "They will be looking for us soon. Thou hadst better dress, my heart."

He expected a response, but there was none. Frowning, he turned his head. Bold flashes of light illuminated the scattered cushions behind him. He saw that they were empty. The girl was gone.

Chapter Nine

Maura bent over the kitchen table, hands dusty with flour. A bowl of eggs and a jar of precious sugar stood near her elbow. The Residency's assistant cook, a portly Muslim woman with an oily black braid, stood sullenly nearby cracking walnuts.

Indian servants tended to resent the intrusion of memsahibs into their domain, and Mumfaisal was no exception. She especially disliked handing over her prized baking utensils to this particular mem-sahib, who was well known among the Residency servants for her biting command of the vernacular and her lack of hesitation in using it. Adding insult to injury was the fact that the miss-sahib Maura had confiscated Mumfaisal's utensils for what could only be considered a heathen *Angrezi* ritual: the baking of a birthday cake for Carlyon-sahib.

"Art thou finished?" Maura inquired over her shoulder.

Mumfaisal nodded sullenly and brought over the nuts. Like the rest of the Residency servants, she spoke no English.

"Put them here."

Maura folded the nuts into the batter and then transferred the spicy mix to the baking pan. Mita Ram, the cook's boy, had already stoked the fire in the brick oven in the corner of the small, dark kitchen. Maura had wisely elected to begin her baking long before dawn, when the sun had not yet risen to unleash its furnace heat. Lydia was still abed and breakfast had yet to be served.

At that moment the cloth curtain covering the kitchen archway parted and Daphne Carlyon swept in. "Delicious!" she pronounced, licking batter off the mixing spoon. "Your uncle will be so delighted, dear. I don't believe he's had a cake for his birthday in the last fifteen years."

Maura wiped her hands on a dish towel. "I hope it won't taste too odd. The ingredients—"

Aunt Daphne licked more batter from the spoon. "Don't fret, darling. Lawrence will quite understand the shortcomings of trying to bake in this kitchen. Besides, whatever you make will taste far better than anything these pitiful Hindus can come up with."

"Muslims," Maura corrected automatically.

Aunt Daphne ignored that. "I never realized you had such a penchant for baking."

"I don't. Lydia and I drew straws. She's taking care of the gift."

Aunt Daphne regarded her niece with an affectionate eye. Who would have guessed that such a willful and exhausting child could grow into such a dutiful young woman? During the past few days, especially, Maura had shown herself so eager to

154

please, taking over a huge amount of the work involved in managing the servants and barely leaving the house at all.

"Do you plan to go riding?" she inquired now as Maura shook out her skirts and started for the door.

"Not today."

"Why not, dear? You used to ride every morning. Why, you haven't been out once since your uncle and I returned from the durbar, and that was nearly a week ago."

"It's been much too hot."

"I suppose it has. But don't fret, dear. We'll be leaving for Simla before too long and then all will be well."

How could it? Maura wondered hopelessly, leaving the kitchen via the covered walkway that connected the tiny building to the Residency bungalow. She was bored and hot and absolutely miserable and didn't know how much longer she could keep up this insufferable, self-enforced confinement. How long was she going to go on hiding from Ross Hamilton this way? Sooner or later he was bound to accept another of her uncle's invitations to dine at the Residency, and then all the emotions she had kept carefully under control ever since that night in the Peacock Palace would come crashing over her and he would know the truth merely by looking at her face. . . .

But I'm not in love with him, Maura told herself stubbornly. I'm not, I'm not! I hardly know him at all, and just because he . . . we . . .

"The sahiba wishes to ride today?"

Maura halted. "Oh, Ismail, I didn't see you." She glanced quickly over her shoulder, but the walkway was empty. Her aunt had remained in the kitchen.

She switched to Hindustani. "No, I don't believe I shall."

"The days have been long and the Fox grows impatient."

Maura considered this, then glanced thoughtfully into the Pathan's dark face. The bearded countenance was without expression and she had no idea why he had deliberately sought her out today rather than waiting as usual for her summons. Could it be that Ismail Khan was just as bored as she was after a week's confinement in the *bibi-gurh?*

"Oh, very well," she said suddenly. "Saddle my horse. I shall await thee on the *maidan.*"

Ismail Khan's expression brightened into something suspiciously like pleasure. "As the sahiba wishes." Bowing, he hurried across the lawn.

It was growing light by the time the burly Pathan and his young mistress met on the wide parade grounds below the cantonment gates. Birds were beginning to twitter in the trees and a breath of the terrible heat that was to come already weighted the air. Maura wore her trim blue habit and had donned a pith helmet. Slim and elegant, she touched her horse with her whip and took off at a canter toward the dew-veiled fields lying beyond the *kutcha* road. Ismail Khan, as usual, followed at a respectful distance.

Dawn glowed over the distant hills, washing the plains with gold. A flight of parrots rose, screeching, from the cane break, and the jungle-cocks awoke and joined in. A hot breeze sprang up to rustle through the lion grass, and Maura, inhaling the spicy air, drew a long, long breath of happiness.

How foolish she had been to chafe for so long under self-imposed house arrest! Nowadays Ross Hamilton was rarely to be seen around the settlement, for he was usually elsewhere in the district settling land disputes or meeting with some village *kotwal*, or headman, to discuss new methods of planting and drainage. Why should she hide from him? What was there to fear?

Hoofbeats pounded behind her, interrupting her thoughts. Turning quickly in the saddle she found Ismail Khan closing the distance between them at a gallop. Quickly she drew rein, causing the Fox to snort and toss his head.

"What is it?" she asked as the Pathan drew alongside. "Is aught amiss?"

"There are men ahead," he answered, his eyesight keener than hers. "Look there."

Maura followed his pointing finger to a thin trail of dust on the far side of the bamboo brake. The shadows were beginning to fade as the heavens grew pearlescent, and in the rising light she could make out a pair of horses heading their way. One of them carried a man who sat slumped forward in the saddle clutching at the reins as though to prevent himself from falling.

"Something's happened," she said breathlessly.

"It bodes no good," Ismail Khan agreed.

The horses drew nearer, and now Maura could recognize the injured rider as Ghoda Lal, Captain Hamilton's bearer. The man riding behind him was Amir Dass, Captain Hamilton's syce, who drew rein with visible reluctance as Maura waved him over.

"What has happened?" she asked in English, knowing he spoke the language well.

"Ghoda Lal has been attacked by a *mugger*," he responded through his teeth.

Maura's eyes widened. "An alligator?" She stared aghast at the wounded man and saw that his right arm was bound in a crude sling. The sleeve was stained with blood that even now continued to seep down his arm and drip into the dust. That, and the ashen color of his face, told its own terrible story.

"You must bring him to the Residency," she said urgently. "At once."

"We are on our way to the village," Amir Dass responded coolly.

"To see the *hakim?*" Maura tossed her head. "He will do nothing but sprinkle the wound with magic water to keep away the evil eye! Ghoda Lal's chances are better at the Residency. I will send for the *Angrezi* doctor."

Amir Dass looked doubtful. Station doctors did not usually attend to Indians, even if one of them happened to be the bearer of a sahib.

"Do as I say!" Maura urged. "It is three miles to the village, and only one to the Residency."

Ghoda Lal moaned, and the syce gave in. "Let us go."

They touched their whips to their mounts and pounded off across the iron-hard ground.

"Where is Captain Hamilton?" Maura asked, shouting to be heard over the thundering hoofbeats.

"Away in Sundagunj these last three days!"

"Look to thy companion!" shouted Ismail Khan, seeing Ghoda Lal sway in the saddle.

Amir Dass swerved his mount and, reaching over, took the other horse by the bridle. By the time they reached the wide, tree–lined road that led through the cantonment gates, his shirt was damp with sweat. The horses were breathing hard and Ghoda Lal had all but lost consciousness.

"We will put him in the *bibi-gurh*," Ismail Khan said darkly. "The Carlyon memsahib will not permit him in her house."

Maura did not argue, knowing this was true.

"Take him, then. I will fetch the doctor."

Although the Bhunapore cantonment was a small station with relatively few Europeans, it boasted the presence of a skilled—and surprisingly sober—university-trained physician. Franklin Moore had lost two children and a wife to India, but his love for the land and its people had never faltered.

When Maura explained the situation, he agreed to come at once. He had a fondness for Lawrence Carlyon's niece, thinking her a level–headed young woman with no nonsense about her. Besides, the wounded man was Ross Hamilton's bearer, and Dr. Moore had a strong liking for that young man as well.

Maura was breathless from the heat by the time she dismounted in the sandy yard fronting Ismail Khan's modest hut. Dr. Moore came bouncing along behind her in a high-wheeled *ekka*, his leather bag on the seat beside him.

"Tell me what you need and I'll fetch it from the house," she told him as he climbed down.

"Water, preferably boiled ten minutes or more. I've brought along everything else, except someone to help me."

"Ismail Khan can do so."

"Your Pathan syce? Will we be able to communicate?"

"He's learned a lot in the past few weeks, but—" Maura made a face. "I'm not sure yet how much he really understands."

"Oh, dear. I'm afraid that won't do."

"Then I'll help."

"Now, Miss Adams—" Dr. Moore protested.

"Would you rather depend on Captain Hamilton's syce?" Maura asked crisply. "His English is tolerable, but not *that* good."

159

There was no time to argue. Dr. Moore ran an agitated hand through his thinning hair. "Very well. Get the water and come as quickly as you can."

Maura herself carried the water to the *bibi-gurh*, for the servants were reluctant to expose themselves to the evil gods that they insisted were lurking within the vicinity of the badly wounded man. Maura was grateful for the fact that Aunt Daphne and Lydia were out making their morning calls and that her uncle was imprisoned in his office with his usual mountain of paperwork. No telling what they would do upon discovering that she had brought Captain Hamilton's wounded bearer home to the Residency!

She hadn't been inside the *bibi-gurh* at all since the day Ismail Khan had moved in. There were only two tiny rooms, but she saw that the Pathan kept them spare and very clean. The windows were covered with *khus-khus tatties*, blinds that were kept wet and so served to cut down on the terrible heat, but still the interior of the bungalow was sweltering. Amir Dass was patiently operating the punkah fan while Ismail Khan stood impassively beside the charpoy, the narrow string bed on which Ghoda Lal had been laid.

Dr. Moore had already removed the wounded man's torn shirt, and Maura gasped when she saw the ugly gash that ran in a ragged line from his shoulder to his elbow, laying the bone bare. Blood continued to seep onto the bed, and Dr. Moore was frantically removing instruments from his bag and spreading them out on a clean towel before him.

"Thank God for chloroform," he said, smiling encouragingly as he noticed Maura's pale face. "All right, girl?"

Maura nodded.

But Ghoda Lal refused to let the doctor touch him when he attempted to place the chloroform-soaked gauze upon his nose and mouth. "*Nahin!*" he protested weakly. "No!"

"Let be," Maura told him sharply in the vernacular. "Thy master would call thee a fool!"

Amir Dass grinned at her words and Ghoda Lal sheepishly quieted. No one spoke as the chloroform was administered. For the next few minutes nothing broke the stillness save the *creak-creak-creak* of the punkah overhead. At one point Maura glanced into Amir Dass's impassive face.

"What was Ghoda Lal doing at the river? Surely he knows enough to keep away from *muggers!*"

"The beast has killed two men in the village. Yesterday it attacked a child. It was Carlyon-sahib's order that it be destroyed."

"Perhaps he should have waited until Captain Hamilton returned," Dr. Moore put in grimly. "I understand he's a crack shot."

"I wonder why he left Ghoda Lal behind," Maura mused aloud. "It's not at all like him."

By now the wounded man was sufficiently sedated to begin. Following Dr. Moore's orders, Maura tied a towel, apronlike, about her waist and then washed and disinfected her hands. Meanwhile, Dr. Moore removed a stout needle from the tray and unraveled the length of horse hair that had been soaking in the boiled water.

"All right," he said calmly, "let's get started."

"Amir Dass," Maura said in Hindustani without turning her head. "Perhaps thou shouldst ride to Sundagunj with word for Hamilton–sahib as to the fate of his bearer. Let them know at his bungalow also. We will bring him there when the hakim has finished."

The syce sketched a brief salute and went out. His footsteps faded on the steps, and once again the hot silence closed in.

"Odd," said Dr. Moore thoughtfully.

Maura looked up from the bandages she was unrolling. "What, sir?"

"This wound. It's remarkably clean for an alligator mauling. Usually they snap. Leave ragged tears."

Maura moved closer. "Will he lose it? The arm, I mean?" She was well aware of what Ghoda Lal meant to Ross.

"I doubt it. Though he'll be lacking the use of it for quite a while. There. That's finished. Be a good girl and hand me that tincture bottle, will you?"

Now it was evening and Maura was sitting alone in the Residency drawing room. The brief Indian twilight had passed and the impenetrable darkness of night had closed in. The Residency lamps were lit. Behind her in the dining room the table glittered with china and newly polished wine glasses. Everything was ready for Uncle Lawrence's birthday supper. Only a few close friends had been invited inasmuch as he had insisted on keeping the affair private.

Lydia and Aunt Daphne were still in their rooms dressing. Maura, long finished with that, was sitting in an armchair trying to read the *Calcutta Review*. Tonight, for some reason, the words refused to make sense. She couldn't stop thinking about Ghoda Lal. Dr. Moore had assured her that his arm would heal, but she couldn't be so sure. Once out of a doctor's care, who knew how the Hindu would continue to treat it? Meera had once described for her some of the awful ways that the natives healed their injured and ill.

Don't! she told herself angrily. Ross will see to it that he gets proper care.

But still she fretted. She knew how much Ross depended on Ghoda Lal, and how close the two of them were. Furthermore, she had grown fond of the Hindu herself, though she'd sooner bite off her tongue than admit as much to either of them.

There was a dry cough behind her. Maura looked up. The Residency's head *chupprassi* bowed and straightened his freshly laundered turban. "Hamilton-sahib is here."

Maura's face went blank. Ross was back? Who had invited him to the party? Why hadn't anyone told her?

The *chupprassi* coughed again. She looked at him. "He has not come to dine with Carlyon-sahib. He asks to speak with you."

Maura rose and smoothed down her skirt. "Bring him here, Lala Deen."

She stood with her hands at her sides as voices sounded in the hall and Ross strode in. Although she had steeled herself for this moment, it was still a shock to see him. He must have just come in from riding because he was wearing breeches and dusty boots. His dark, windblown hair tumbled over his brow. His mouth, that hard, passionate mouth that had kissed hers so hotly, was turned down in a frown.

Maura, seeing it, straightened her shoulders. "Did you wish to see me, Captain Hamilton?"

As she spoke, her eyes, those huge, magnificent eyes, lifted to his. She could not know that they reminded Ross all too well of other eyes, equally dark, equally haunting . . .

"I've just returned," he said curtly. "My servants told me what you did for Ghoda Lal. I'm here to thank you. Few sahib-*log* would have done as much for a native. Your intervention saved his life."

Maura put her hands behind her back and willed herself to meet his hard gaze. She would rather die than let Ross know how much he was hurting her with his curtness. He might just as well have been offering his thanks to *anyone,* not the woman he had recently held in his arms and loved with such heart-stopping passion.

"You're welcome," she told him coolly. "It was nothing. Both your syce and Ismail Khan were there to help."

Ross's expression softened a fraction. "He's quite something, your Pathan bodyguard. How on earth did you manage to tame him? They're unpredictable devils, you know."

Maura studied the wall behind his broad shoulder, unable to look at him. She didn't know what she had expected when she saw him again, but now her throat ached with unshed tears and it was an effort merely to keep the tremor from her voice.

"Yes, I know. But we've reached an agreement of sorts. If I don't trouble him unnecessarily, he remains reasonably polite with me."

"I see."

Maura cast about for something else to say. "How is Ghoda Lal?"

"Resting comfortably. I'm sorry I couldn't come sooner, but I didn't hear about the accident until I got back from Bhunapore."

Maura's head came up. "Bhunapore? But I thought—Amir Dass said you'd gone to Sundagunj."

Now it was Ross's turn to avoid her gaze. His dark eyes slid restlessly to the wall behind her head. "I did. But I made a stop in Bhunapore on the way back."

The two towns were nowhere near one another. He must have made a considerable detour to stop there. Maura stared helplessly at his averted profile.

"Were you there on—on business?"

"No." Ross's tone was curt. "I was visiting a friend."

Maura felt the heat rising in a shameful tide to her cheeks. Without being told, she knew that Ross had gone to Walid Ali's pink stucco house in search of Chota Moti. Dizzily, she put out a groping hand and clutched the back of a nearby chair.

Why couldn't she simply accept the fact that it wasn't Maura Adams Ross had made love to that night in the pleasure pavilion of the Peacock Palace? It was the Mohammedan girl, Chota Moti, the visitor from Rajasthan, who had so enchanted him and whom he continued to seek even now!

Was that why he seemed so remote at the moment? Because he had been unable to find her? Had he lost his heart to her?

Maura swallowed hard against the bitter tears welling in her throat. "Excuse me," she said in a choked voice.

But Ross caught her wrist as she attempted to brush past him. Turning her around he saw that her eyes were bright with unshed tears. He felt his heart wrench in response.

"For God's sake, what is it?" he ground out.

I won't, Maura thought desperately. I won't let him see me cry! He would only think her totally mad.

But already the treacherous tears were sliding down her cheeks.

"Maura—"

He'd never said her name before. Sweet lord, how it flailed her heart! She mustn't let him know, mustn't let him guess that he was the cause of her pain. And why on earth was she weeping? Because he was in love with someone else? How absurd, when *she* was that someone else!

But I don't love him back. I don't! I don't!

Uttering a strangled sound, she pulled free of his grasp and fled through the door.

Chapter Ten

For a long while Ross stood where she had left him. Why on earth had he come here tonight? Why on earth had he subjected himself to the torment of seeing Maura Adams in a magnificent silk party dress, her upswept hair brilliant in the lamplight, standing before him in the drawing room of her uncle's house and weeping? He did not understand her tears or her pain, only that somehow he was the cause of them.

Women! Damn them all to hell and back! Never in his life had he known such frustrated anger, and that was only because he had wisely prevented himself from becoming entangled with any woman before this—although now he was, with two of them, no less!

Crossing to the sideboard where he knew Lawrence Carlyon kept his liquor, he splashed a healthy portion of brandy into a glass. His eyes narrowed as he drained it in one angry swallow.

Before, there had always been Sinta Dai, the sloe-eyed dancing girl with whom he had taken his ease in the early days of his posting to Bhunapore. But that had been long before Maura Adams, and long before the arrival of Kushna Dev's beautiful cousin from Rajasthan.

He grimaced. Two women so vastly different and yet somehow the same, and both—he must confess it now—growing annoyingly close to his heart: Maura Adams, the radiant half of the dark coin of his desires, for her conviction and courage, her love of India and her laughter, and the slender Chota Moti for a night of passion the likes of which he doubted he would ever experience again.

Damn, how the memory of that night continued to haunt him! As did the rage that had erupted within him after inquiring at the house of Walid Ali and receiving word from Kushna Dev that her cousin had returned to Rajasthan and would not be coming back!

Home again, his foul mood had only been worsened by the news of Ghoda Lal's injury, which would put the man out of commission for a week or more during a time when Ross could ill afford to lose him. *Mugger*, indeed! At least Amir Dass had assured him that neither Maura nor Dr. Moore had suspected that the Hindu's wound had, in point of fact, been made by the blade of a primitive knife.

Maura. The thought of her made him swear blackly. He had truly meant the words of thanks he had expressed to her, for few in the cantonment—in all India, probably!—would have done as much to save a Hindu bearer's life. She had acted courageously, and he had repaid her courage by making her cry. She had deserved his heartfelt gratitude and instead he had taken out all his frustrated anger upon her.

There was a sound of footsteps in the hall and Lawrence Carlyon came in. "Why, Ross, I didn't know you were back! Lala Deen didn't say a word, the black devil. Care to join us for supper? It's my birthday, you know."

The last thing Ross wanted was to participate in yet another Carlyon family festivity. On the other hand, he could not be so rude as to refuse to share in his own chief's birthday celebration. Still, he tried.

"Thank you, sir. I'd like that very much, but I'm afraid I'm not dressed for it."

"There's still time to change, man. Daffy will be delighted to wait on you."

Apparently there was no way out. Ross bowed woodenly and left.

Although Lydia and her mother acted overjoyed to see him when he returned, neither Maura nor Charles Burton–Pascal said anything more to him beyond terse greetings. Ross could see that Charles was seething inwardly at being forced to share the limelight, and the knowledge gave him a grim sort of satisfaction. Apparently his own instinctive dislike of the man was heartily reciprocated.

Fortunately, neither Terence Shadwell nor the Carlyons seemed aware of the tension simmering between the two men. The mood at the table remained festive throughout the lengthy meal.

"Now this," said Lawrence Carlyon, smiling at his niece when dessert arrived at last, "is the finest birthday *gâteau* I've ever had the pleasure of eating."

"It's wonderful," Lydia agreed.

"Delicious," added Terence Shadwell, swallowing with gusto.

Ellen Tanner Marsh

Aunt Daphne asked for another piece, and Maura smiled faintly. The flickering lamplight revealed the littered remains of a very successful birthday party. Only the cake was left, and now it, too, vanished. Aunt Daphne got to her feet, a signal that the three women were to leave the men to their port.

Ross took this opportunity to rise as well. "I'm afraid I must be off."

"Surely you can stay a bit longer!" Aunt Daphne protested.

"Let the man go," Lawrence urged. "He's ridden a long way today."

"And I'd like to look in on my bearer," Ross added.

Aunt Daphne's brows rose. "Has something happened to him?"

"An unfortunate accident, but I daresay he'll mend." Ross's gaze found Maura as he spoke, but she did not look up. His mouth thinned at that and, bidding them all a terse goodnight, he went quickly out the door.

"My goodness! He can be so prickly at times!" Aunt Daphne complained. "But you'll stay, won't you?" Her question was directed at Charles, whose eyes traveled first to Maura's bowed head before he turned to assure her that, indeed, nothing would give him more pleasure.

Out in the dark hallway Lydia caught her cousin's arm. "Oh, Maura! Isn't it exciting? Did you see the way Mr. Burton–Pascal kept looking at you tonight? I *know* he intends speaking to Papa! I can feel it in my bones!"

"Don't be silly."

"Terence thinks so, too."

"Terence could well be mistaken."

"Oh, really, Maura! Why do you think Mr. Burton-Pascal has remained in Bhunapore so long? Terence says he'd been planning to go to Delhi but that he keeps putting it off."

"Not because of me," Maura insisted stubbornly.

Lydia smiled lovingly. "How can you be sure? And do you know, I'd like very much to have Mr. Burton-Pascal—I mean Charles—for a cousin. Mama and Papa think highly of him, too." Her expression grew anxious. "You will consider it, won't you?"

"Consider what?"

"Why, marrying him, of course."

"Don't be ridiculous!" With a toss of her head Maura turned away, her skirts rustling as she swept out onto the verandah. The door slammed and the hot darkness surrounded her.

She was alone. Sighing, she leaned her aching head against a whitewashed column. Lydia's words were already forgotten. All she could think of was Ross; the way he had refused to look at her or say a word to her at dinner; the way he had fled the Residency as though he couldn't get away from her fast enough.

I hate him! Maura thought.

Movement among the shadows in the garden caught her eye. She straightened. "Who's there?"

Expecting to see the night watchman, she was startled when Ismail Khan stepped from behind the shadows of the plumbago bushes. She had rarely known him to leave the *bibi-gurh* after retiring for the night, and now she told him as much.

"Nay," he disagreed, coming to stand beneath her where the light from the house glinted on the dagger tucked in his belt. "As long as thou art about I will keep watch."

"That is the task of the *chowkidar*," Maura reminded him gently.

171

"Bah! An old man with half-blind eyes! What use is he, should there be trouble?"

"Art thou expecting any?" Maura demanded, startled.

"Ask Hamilton-sahib," the Pathan countered darkly.

"Captain Hamilton? Why? Has something happened, Ismail Khan?"

"His bearer has taken a knife through the arm. Is that not trouble enough?" Ismail Khan turned his head and spat disgustedly into the shrubs. "*Mugger* indeed! That Hindu is of thine uncle's household, is he not?"

"He is Hamilton-sahib's bearer," Maura agreed slowly, "and Hamilton-sahib is of my uncle's staff."

"Then assuredly I will keep watch as the *chowkidar* should." Bowing, the Pathan turned away, leaving Maura standing alone on the empty verandah.

"And that is why I came here," Maura finished quietly. "If there is something amiss in the city or the cantonment, then someone in thy household might have heard of it."

Kushna Begum leaned back against the silken cushions and thoughtfully chewed her lower lip. Neither she nor the other women of the zenana veiled themselves before Maura any longer, a mark of favor that had not gone unnoticed.

"*Hai mai,*" she sighed at last, "there is always trouble in the city, and elsewhere. The people are never content when the rains won't come and the crops die, or if the hunting is poor or one's wife fails to bear sons."

"Then this attack on Hamilton-sahib's bearer did not come because he serves a sahib?" Maura asked hopefully.

Kushna Begum smiled. "I do not think so. Our quarrel with the sahib-*log* ended with the Mutiny. Oh, there are still sadhus about who preach sedition on occasion, but they capture few ears. Bhunapore's menfolk did not rise against thine in the Mutiny, nor did those who served Nasir al–Mirza Shah. Thou art safe here, Little Pearl. Now let us forget these troubling thoughts and take refreshment together."

She clapped her slim hands and Maura wisely said nothing more. But she was not appeased by the Indian girl's careless dismissal of her fears. If Ismail Khan felt there was reason to worry. . . . Yet on the other hand, few of the natives living in the cantonment liked or trusted the bearded Pathan. Surely he would not be told any news to which Kushna Dev was herself not privy? The Mohammedan begum might live imprisoned in the zenana of her husband's house, but there was little that escaped her attention what with the legions of spies she employed, who reported the detailed comings and goings, the gossip and tales, of everyone in the city and beyond.

I'll ask Ross what he thinks, Maura decided, then instantly dismissed the thought. It was doubtful that Ross would tell her anything. Worse, he would probably laugh at her and treat her with that hateful indifference he had adopted toward her of late.

"I must go," she said after refreshments had been taken. Standing, she shook out the heavy skirts of her riding habit. "It is late, and my aunt and uncle will return soon from their visit to Clapham-sahib and his wife."

As would Lydia, who, like Maura, had taken advantage of the Carlyons' absence by slipping out to meet Terence Shadwell for a moonlit walk along the cantonment streets. Lydia had hinted that Charles

173

Burton-Pascal would be available should Maura wish to accompany them, but Maura had vigorously declined. She was not about to encourage Charles Burton-Pascal if he was truly planning to ask for her hand!

A turbanned servant was standing at the foot of the stairs when Maura left the zenana. Bowing, he opened the door for her. The night air was hot and sticky after the cool of the reception rooms.

Soon it will be May, Maura thought, and Aunt Daphne will remove her household to Simla, where we'll have to wait out the arrival of the cooler months before returning for Lydia's wedding.

Uncle Lawrence would not be accompanying them north. He was long accustomed to the grinding heat of India's summers, and the administrative headache of being British Resident of Bhunapore did not end with the coming of hot weather. Ross would not be leaving either, Maura knew. Once she left, it would be four months or more before she saw him again.

Her chin tipped stubbornly. So what? Let him find relief from the summer heat in the pink stucco palace with the willing Sinta Dai to soothe his hot brow and see to his every need! If she thought for even an instant that he—

"Have a care, brother! The *chowkidar* passed this way not a moment ago!"

Maura drew up short at the hissed warning that came from the shadows beneath the terrace steps. Alerted by the urgency of that whispered voice, she drew back among the shrubs lining the courtyard. As her eyes adjusted to the darkness, she saw two men standing together in the inky shadows. One of them she recognized as a member of Walid Ali's household. The other was a stranger. They spoke

quietly together and she had great difficulty understanding their rapid exchange until she heard them
utter a familiar name.

"—great foolishness! The bearer is worthless! It is
Hamilton-sahib we must kill!"

"But how? He is like a jungle cat, with eyes just
as sharp!"

"Perhaps an ambush?"

"Aye, that would be best. He rides to Sundagunj
again in two days' time, without his bearer. So says
the Mussulman employed at the Residency. If thou
art waiting for him at the nullah—"

"Hush, brother! Someone comes!"

The sound of hoofbeats rang on stone. A groom,
summoned by Kushna Begum, had arrived with
Maura's horse. Behind him came Ismail Khan, already astride his muscular stallion.

The two conspirators melted into the darkness as
though they had never been.

Taking a deep breath, Maura stepped calmly into
the lighted courtyard. Mounting the Fox, she nodded politely to the elderly syce and then cantered
through the gate.

As usual, the burly Pathan rode several paces behind her on the way back to the cantonment. For
once his deference suited Maura, whose obvious agitation would surely have alerted him to the fact that
something was amiss. She did not want to confide
in Ismail Khan. How could she be certain that she
could trust him? After all, someone in Walid Ali's
household was plotting intrigue against the British—
against Ross in particular. How could she be sure
that Ismail Khan wasn't involved?

What shall I do? she asked herself, urging her
mount faster and faster until they were fairly flying
across the ground. If only she could confide in Ross,

175

but how, without telling him where she had come by her information? She could *never* admit to him that she was acquainted with anyone in the pink stucco house! Ross was no fool. The moment she told him as much he would realize that she and the Indian girl Chota Moti were one and the same.

It was an admission that Maura would rather die than make. On the other hand, how could she not break her silence and spare Ross an ambush on the road to Sundagunj?

I'll have to tell him, she thought. I have no choice.

The Fox was badly lathered by the time Maura cantered him through the Residency gates. She ignored the *chowkidar's* obeisance and Ismail Khan's obvious anger at having pressed their mounts so hard. Tossing the reins to the syce who was waiting near the stable door, she marched across the dusty road toward Ross's bungalow, stripping off her gloves as she went and praying that her courage wouldn't fail.

He had already heard the sound of her booted feet on the verandah steps and was waiting for her at the door. He was dressed in his shirt sleeves, and his dark hair was tousled. The servants milling curiously behind him were dismissed with a curt word, but when Maura halted before him he made no move to step aside and let her in.

"Captain Hamilton—"

"Have you lost your mind?" The expression on his handsome face was black with anger.

Maura froze.

"What in hell do you think you're doing, coming here alone, at night, while your uncle and aunt are away?"

His tone was like the lash of a whip. The color

drained from her cheeks. "I—I'm sorry. I didn't think—"

"It's obvious you didn't! Half my household saw you come, and I daresay the same holds true for your uncle's staff! If you wish to retain what little of your reputation remains, you'd better leave immediately."

"But—"

"At once!"

"You don't understand! I have something important to—"

"Bagaleesh!" Ross bellowed in Hindustani to someone standing in the shadows of the hall, "take the sahiba home at once!"

A young boy emerged from behind the door. Maura ignored him. "I'm not going!" Her voice was sharp with fury.

"Oh, yes, you are. Or do you wish me to carry you over my shoulder?"

"You wouldn't dare!"

He took a threatening step toward her. "Try me."

Damn him! He would!

She turned and went without another word, her face burning.

There was no sleep for her that night or peace of mind the following morning. Ross did not appear at the Residency after breakfast, and Maura had no idea if he was avoiding her deliberately or just hadn't received his usual summons from her uncle. She was well aware of the furtive whispers of the Residency servants who had heard of her visit to his bungalow the night before, but she ignored them all and did not even try to defend herself when Meera clucked disapprovingly over her unseemly behavior.

"I have nothing to say," she insisted stubbornly.

"There are some who believe—" Meera began, then fell silent.

"What?"

"That Hamilton-sahib's heart softens whenever he looks at thee."

Maura uttered an unladylike snort. "Then why does he keep a mistress in the house of the merchantman Walid Ali?"

Meera was so shocked that she reverted to Hindustani. "How dost thou know this?"

"There is much I know. Too much! And if there is anything soft about Hamilton–sahib, then it is his brain!"

Fuming, she tossed her hairbrush across the room. What was she going to do about that insufferable man? She had tried to warn him, but not only had the self-righteous prig refused to listen, he had all but kicked her off his front porch, with half his household there to witness her humiliation! Worrying about *her* reputation, was he? What about his own?

A slipper followed the hairbrush into the corner.

"Thou art impossible," Meera cried, throwing up her hands. "I will return when thy foul temper has burned itself to ashes."

As soon as she was gone, Maura slumped onto the bed with her head in her hands. She wasn't really angry at Ross, not at the moment anyway. At the moment she was afraid, desperately afraid for his life, and she had no idea how to go about letting him know.

If he refused to receive her at his bungalow or to make an appearance at the Residency, how was she to warn him about avoiding the nullah? She didn't dare write a note that might be intercepted, or confide in Ismail Khan when she wasn't entirely sure that she could trust him. She could not summon Ross to the Residency herself without arousing suspicion, either. All she could do was hope that he would come of his own accord or, failing that, allow himself to be encountered in a place that would appear to any outside observer as coincidental.

But that entailed waiting, and waiting had never come easy for Maura.

Later that afternoon, when Terence Shadwell paid his usual call at the Residency, Charles Burton-Pascal was with him. By then Maura was far too distracted to pay him much mind.

Poor Charles! Handsome, unmarried and wealthy in his own right, he was not accustomed to being so thoroughly snubbed by a member of the fairer sex. On the contrary; he had rarely failed in his well-traveled youth to make feminine hearts flutter wherever he went. Understandably, he was at a loss to explain Maura Adams's continued refusal to warm to him. Hadn't he tempered his behavior toward her of late, become restrained, reassuring and unfailingly polite? How could he get her to notice him today when she seemed hardly able to sit still? While Miss Carlyon poured tea for himself and her affianced, Maura paced the drawing room scarcely acknowledging a word that was said.

Nevertheless, Charles could not help thinking how fetching she looked dressed in blue brocade damask so pale as to appear almost gray, which made her hair shimmer a rich gold-red and gave her violet eyes a lustrous darkness that made them seem more expressive than ever.

But while it was true that she had welcomed them politely enough and once or twice even smiled at his jests, why in blazes did she keep staring out the window? Who the devil was she expecting?

There was the sound of brisk footsteps on the porch outside. The front door opened in response to a loud knock.

"Good afternoon, Lala Deen. Is the *burra*-sahib in?"

Ross Hamilton's voice. Charles saw Maura's head jerk up and those magnificent eyes of hers widen. Jealousy—unexpected and entirely unpleasant—grabbed him by the throat. His resentment deepened as Hamilton was shown in, looking windblown and devil-may-care in nonregulation riding breeches and a lawn shirt. He was a damnably good-looking devil, Charles conceded darkly, but at least he could soothe himself with the fact that the fellow scarcely gave Maura a glance. Instead he turned to Lydia, sketching her an insultingly brief bow.

"Good afternoon, Miss Carlyon. I was looking for your father. The *chupprassi* indicated that he was here."

Lydia smiled, looking sweetly girlish in an apple-green frock trimmed with lavender ribbons and a fichu of Belgian lace. "He was here earlier, when Terence and Mr. Burton-Pascal first arrived. I think you'll find him in his office."

"Thank you. I'm off to Sundagunj and wanted to—"

"But—but I thought you weren't leaving until tomorrow!"

The outburst was Maura's. When all of them turned to look at her, she drew herself erect and tilted her chin. Color stained her cheeks but she managed to speak calmly. "At least that's what Amir Dass said. I spoke to him in the stable yard this morning."

Ross ran an agitated hand through his hair. It was obvious to everyone that he was impatient to be off.

"Yes, well, plans have changed. I'm leaving in a matter of hours."

A matter of hours. No time to warn him about the ambush without revealing how she knew. On the other hand, was there any cause for worry now that he had changed his plans? Perhaps no one would be lying in wait for him in the nullah since he was leaving a day earlier than scheduled. But how could she be certain?

"If you'll excuse me," Ross added coldly. Turning on his heel he left the room. The door closed roughly behind him.

"Well!" said Lydia with an embarrassed laugh.

"What a rude fellow," Terence agreed. "Is he always like that?"

"No," said Lydia.

"Yes," said Maura.

They looked at each other and then everyone burst out laughing.

No one seemed to notice how false Maura's gaiety sounded.

"Who'd like more tea?" Lydia inquired brightly. Abruptly the smile froze on her face. "Why, Maura, what's the matter? You look so strange all of a sudden. Frightfully pale. Are you unwell?"

"I think I've got a headache coming on. Would you mind very much if I excused myself?"

They all assured her that they would not. Lydia offered to escort her to her room while Charles manfully volunteered to ride for the doctor. Maura thanked them both politely, but insisted that she would be fine in no time if left alone. Clutching at her head and sighing delicately for extra effect, she tottered from the room.

The moment she was outside she picked up her skirts and flew across the lawn to her uncle's office.

181

Ross was just coming through the door and she nearly ran him down in her haste to intercept him.

"Steady." He had to grab her arms to keep her from barreling into him. "Is there something you wished to say to me, Miss Adams?"

She nodded, fighting for breath.

"Perhaps we should step into your uncle's office?"

"No! That is—"

"I have a pressing engagement, Miss Adams."

"In Sundagunj, I know. But you can't go there!"

His brows rose. "I can't?"

"No. At least not today! Or tomorrow, for that matter."

He frowned at her and she willed herself to calm down. "I'm sorry. I know I'm not making sense. But you mustn't go."

"Why not?"

"I've heard there may be trouble there."

Ross's offhand manner vanished. "What sort of trouble? Who told you?"

"One of—of the Residency servants. He . . . he says there is talk of resurrecting the old days, to return things to the way they were before the Mutiny. He hinted that it may not be safe for white men in the village."

"There's always talk like that in Indian villages. You know as well as I do that most of it is harmless."

He didn't believe her, Maura thought frantically. "But if your bearer has already taken a knife through the arm—"

Ross's manner was suddenly menacing. "Who told you that?"

"I . . . um . . . No one. It's just a rumor."

"Utter nonsense! I would have thought you too intelligent to listen to such idle gossip, let alone believe it!"

It wasn't gossip, but Maura saw that there was no sense in convincing him that she knew that. How could she let him know that he could safely take her into his confidence? If only she could tell him where she had really heard such talk, and that she believed it, and feared for his life, because she truly cared for him!

Only, where was the sense in that? He certainly didn't care for her in turn. His brusqueness, his impatience, his scowl told her as much. Why did she keep fooling herself? If he cared for anyone, it was the Mohammedan cousin of Kushna Dev's, a woman who didn't even exist. . . .

"Is that all you wished to say to me, Miss Adams?"

Defeated, Maura nodded, her eyes downcast.

Above her bowed head his mouth twisted. After a moment he said very softly, almost wonderingly, "Don't worry about me. I know how to take care of myself." And she felt a touch on her cheek, so light that she thought she must have imagined it. She looked up quickly, but Ross had rounded the corner of the bungalow and was gone.

Chapter Eleven

The sun was already descending toward the distant hills when Maura cantered the Fox through the Residency gate with Ismail Khan following behind. The Pathan had been startled when the miss-sahib had sent word that she wished to ride, for she normally preferred taking exercise early in the morning. Nevertheless he said nothing, for that was not his way, and was only glad that she had resumed her daily rides after the last week of frustrating inactivity.

Perhaps the miss-sahib wishes to hunt, Ismail Khan thought. She was not wearing her usual powder-blue habit, but had donned a far less cumbersome thing of sensible cotton in a pale khaki color that blended with the landscape and matched the topi on her head. As well, she had requested that Ismail Khan bring his rifle, which he had done, although she had insisted on carrying it herself tucked into the breech of her saddle. Ismail Khan had grunted skeptically at this. He had never known the miss-sahib to hunt before and doubted she knew how.

But Maura knew very well how to shoot. As a child she had been an apt pupil of her father's, who had taught her the rudiments of military marksmanship in his precise, no-nonsense style. Later, growing up in England, she had often hunted waterfowl on the watery fens of Norfolk in the company of Carlyon gamekeepers. And she had rarely missed.

Thinking about this as she turned the Fox down the dusty road leading to Sundagunj, she realized that she was probably out of practice, but told herself fiercely that it wouldn't matter. No one was going to attack Ross tonight. After all, he wasn't expected in Sundagunj until tomorrow, and only after word of his appearance had gotten round the village would his enemies know that they must change their plans. They would be waiting for Ross, if they waited at all, when he started back to the Residency.

And just in case, Maura intended to be there, too. Not that she had any illusions as to what she was capable of doing. She just wanted to warn Ross, not interfere. But she had asked Ismail Khan to bring a gun nonetheless, and had taken the precaution of keeping it herself since she still wasn't entirely certain that he could be trusted.

After Ross had walked away from her outside her uncle's office that afternoon, Maura had gone inside and casually asked where he had gone. Uncle Lawrence had obligingly told her that Ross was investigating some sort of land dispute in Sundagunj and that he had just received an urgent summons from the parties involved, which had also explained his impatience when he had interrupted Lydia's tea party.

Exiting her uncle's office, Maura had promptly bribed one of the servants to keep an eye on Ross's bungalow and let her know the moment he left. She didn't care what sort of talk the request would arouse. Ross's safety was far more important.

Word had come an hour ago that Hamilton-sahib had ridden away at last, without Ghoda Lal, just as the assassins in the garden at Walid Ali's had predicted. For appearance's sake Maura had waited out that agonizingly slow hour in her bedroom before summoning Ismail Khan and leaving for Sundagunj herself.

Now she prayed that she had not misjudged the delay, and that she would have time to catch up. Surely the landowners who had summoned Ross could be counted on to keep him waiting before airing their grievances in a meeting under the neem tree in the center of the village, which was the usual way of conducting business in rural India. Anyone who cared to could stop and voice his opinion, and Maura was hoping that Ross would be occupied for several hours at least.

If all went as expected, she intended to intercept him on his way back from the village at the bridge that had been built by British engineers shortly after the annexation of Bulparaj. An encounter there would not seem unlikely; Maura and Ismail Khan rode that way often enough, and she was not unknown to the peasants living nearby. She would pretend surprise at their meeting and then warn Ross discreetly, before it was too late.

Please, please, let everything work out!

The air was uncomfortably hot despite the fact that the sun was already drawing long shadows across the plains. In the distance, blackbuck stood unmoving in the shade of the thorn trees. There were few people on the road, and the driver of the occasional bullock cart they passed did not spare the Pathan or his English mistress more than a glance.

As the road brought them closer to the deep ravine that separated the border of the village from the plains, Maura felt her heartbeat quicken. With her eyes she searched every rocky crevice and heat-stunted scrub capable of hiding a man.

She saw no one. Her breathing slowed a little. Perhaps the killers had not had time to alter their plans after all. Feeling more hopeful, she left the nullah behind.

The sun was slipping behind the hills when they reached the river at last. The sky was awash with apricot clouds that were reflected in the water. Lights twinkled in the dwellings beyond the bridge, and the smoke of cooking fires hung in the air. A conch brayed in a distant temple, and Maura, rising in the stirrups, searched the roadway and the bridge ahead of her.

Both were empty. No sign of Ross as yet. Was he still holding forth in the village square?

"Let's ride a little further," she suggested.

Ismail Khan shifted uneasily in the saddle. "It will be dark before we return to the Residency."

Maura acknowledged his concern with a nod but started across the bridge anyway. She had visited Sundagunj several times before and knew that it resembled countless other Indian villages with its baked-mud huts and filthy streets. Indeed, there was not much to be seen save for the few folk who lingered at the well in the center of the square, folk who were accustomed to memsahibs in their midst and so ignored her as they went about their gossip.

A quick search showed Maura that Ross was not among them. His tall figure would have set him instantly apart from the dhoti-clad village men. Relief and worry nagged at her in turn. He had probably finished his business sooner than expected and returned safely home.

Why, then, hadn't they passed him on the road?

Behind her Ismail Khan cleared his throat. The daylight was fading and Maura understood why he was reluctant to linger. She, too, did not care to be abroad after dark. Nor did she wish to alarm her aunt and uncle by returning too late. Sighing, she touched her horse with her heels and set him trotting toward the bridge and home. Ismail Khan followed with undisguised relief.

The swift Indian darkness fell upon them as the gates of the cantonment appeared up ahead. There had been no sign of Ross anywhere on the road. Maura was filled with ever-increasing worry. Where in God's name was he? She hadn't quitted the Residency more than an hour after he did. He could not have concluded his business in Sundagunj and gotten home even before she left!

She turned in the saddle. "Ismail, wouldst thou ride ahead and see—"

Hoofbeats interrupted her, approaching at a gallop through the darkness from the direction of the cantonment. Cursing, Ismail Khan drew his dagger from its sheath. Maura swallowed hard. Decent people knew better than to leave the safety of their settlements at night.

The drumming grew louder. Ismail Khan's stallion pricked its ears and snorted. Instantly the hoofbeats slowed, and Maura heard the telltale click of the safety being removed from a service revolver.

Ismail Khan coughed a warning.

"Who's there?" came a curt demand in Hindu-stani.

Maura exhaled a relieved breath. Though she couldn't see him in the inky darkness, she knew Ross's voice. "It's me, Maura."

Ross spurred his mount forward. In the dim starlight Maura could see his windblown hair and familiar, broad-shouldered form.

Unharmed, completely unharmed.

The glad smile on her face froze as he crowded his mount against hers. Leaning from the saddle he snatched at the Fox's bridle. His fingers closed around hers in a grip so bruising that she had to cry out.

"You little fool!" he lashed at her. "What are you doing out here? Are you deliberately trying to get yourself robbed or killed? Or worse?"

"No! That is, R-Ross, I—"

He didn't even hear the breathless utterance of his name. His head whipped around as he confronted Ismail Khan. "Thou art a fool to let thy mistress ride at night! Is her safety not in thy hands?"

The Pathan's brow darkened, but he could say nothing in his defense. Despite the sahib's unjustified fury, he spoke the truth.

"Come on," Ross ground out, whirling back to Maura. "I'm taking you home. Bloody night, this! I ride all the way into Bhunapore and what do I find when I return? That you've left the Residency without even—"

Maura gasped. "Bhunapore! You said Sunda-gunj—"

"My plans changed," he snapped, then shook her as he saw the color draining from her cheeks. "What is it now?"

189

Ellen Tanner Marsh

Maura wrenched herself free without speaking. No wonder he looked so disheveled, so wild-eyed and ferociously male! If she got any closer to him she would no doubt catch the scent of perfume on his clothing! Here she'd ridden to his rescue, making herself frantic with worry over his safety, while he chucked his responsibilities and rode to Bhunapore! Bhunapore, not Sundagunj, and for what? To take his ease with that nautch-whore Sinta Dai!

Burning with the need to howl her rage at him, she cracked her whip down on the unsuspecting Fox's hindquarters. The big horse squealed in pain, then exploded away, tearing the bridle out of Ross's hands.

"Maura!"

He was after her like a shot. Neck and neck their horses pounded across the hard ground until Ross succeeded in reaching over and catching the bridle. Wrenching it hard, he brought the Fox to a savage halt. Grabbing Maura's upper arms he dragged her onto the saddle in front of him, his face black with fury.

"Have you lost your mind? What in hell was that all about?"

"Let me go!"

"Not until I get some answers!"

"Why should I tell you anything?"

"Because it seems to me you have plenty to hide! Riding after dark with no more than a syce, and carrying arms, no less!" Ross's eyes blazed into hers. "Just what are you up to, woman?"

"It's none of your business!"

Oh, but it was. And she was trying hard to choke back the bitter tears of knowing that her fear for him had been in vain.

"Maura." He must have sensed as much, because

his voice was suddenly far less fierce. And he actually let her go, although he made no move to put any distance between them. "Your ayah brought word to my bungalow that you'd left the Residency. She said she feared for your safety. Now I find you miles from home with only your syce and a rifle. Would you please tell me what's going on?"

Damn him! Why did he have to sound so bloody . . . kind? Didn't he know she fell to pieces whenever he was? She couldn't stop sniffling to save her life, much less her ravaged pride. Worse was the fact that, despite the concealing darkness, he was fully aware of her tears. Producing a handkerchief from his breast pocket, he waited while she blew her nose and tried to bring some order to her windblown hair and dusty attire.

"I went to S-Sundagunj looking for you."

Though her voice was thick with tears and muffled by the wadded handkerchief, he heard her nonetheless. A startled frown darkened his brow.

"Me? Why?"

"They—they were going to ambush you. In the nullah. Only no one was there because you'd changed your p-plans. I was worried that they'd be waiting for you when you started b-back to the Residency."

Bless him, he didn't laugh. Or act the least bit scornful. He just sat there on his horse waiting while she hiccupped and blew her nose again.

"Who?" he said at last.

She shook her head. Sniffled. Tried to ignore the fact that her heart was all but broken. "I don't know who they were. I heard them talking outside the Residency. There were two of them. They said that since your bearer wouldn't be with you when you

191

rode to Sundagunj, they would lie in wait for you there."

"So you rode out yourself, with only a rifle and your syce, to stop them. Two bloodthirsty assassins."

"I didn't know what else to do!"

"You could have come to me."

Up swept her eyes, scorching him with blame. "I tried! Last night at your bungalow! And then this afternoon, but you said—"

"I know what I said." His voice was harsh, like his expression. For a moment he said nothing, only looked off into the darkness while the horses blew and Ismail Khan shifted restlessly in the saddle.

"I told you once before, a long time ago, that in India it's wisest to leave the heroics to the men. Do you remember that?"

She couldn't help flinching at his tone, even though she should have known that he'd go back to hiding behind that arrogance of his. Her battered heart just couldn't take any more. She tossed her head if only to conceal the return of her tears.

"And if the menfolk are taking their ease with nautch-girls in the meantime, Captain? What then?"

"What?" He stared at her. "What do you—"

She didn't allow him to finish. Taking up the Fox's reins she slid into the saddle and sent him galloping away.

This time he let her go.

Lights were blazing in the Residency dining room when she clattered into the stable yard. Wonderful. Now she was late for supper as well.

Panting, cursing, dashing away the hot tears, she dismounted and crossed the yard at a run. Skirting the front door, she slipped through the kitchen and into her room. There she found Meera hanging the mosquito netting around her bed and readying the room for the night.

Taking one look at her mistress, the Hindu woman inquired sharply, "Art thou ill?"

Maura tossed her topi and whip onto the bed and did not answer.

"Come," Meera said encouragingly, "get changed. The meal has begun and the memsahib has been asking for thee. I am glad thou hast returned. Shadwell-sahib is here, as is the other one, whose eyes are always upon thee. I have laid out the white dress with the dark green ribbons. It is thy prettiest."

"You went to Hamilton-sahib." Maura spoke in English, her voice throbbing. There was no need to translate.

"*Hai mai!* What else could I do? I feared for thee."

"Then why go to him?"

"As I've said before, his heart is not untouched by thee."

Maura switched to Hindustani. "And as I have said before, thou art sorely mistaken in that!"

"It is also said that he can be trusted."

"Bah! He is as bad as all others. A sahib who uses your women for pleasure alone!"

Meera's eyes narrowed. "He has hurt thee, tonight on the road."

Maura snorted. "Thine eyesight is failing."

"Perhaps. But love, too, can be blind."

"Art thou suggesting that I am in love with him? With Hamilton-sahib?" Maura laughed, loudly and incredulously. "Now I know thy mind has gone!"

"Come, put on thy gown," Meera said sharply. "The hour is late. Thy uncle is waiting."

* * *

"Here you are at last," Aunt Daphne exclaimed in relief when Maura appeared in the dining room. "We were beginning to worry. Lydia said you weren't feeling well earlier."

Maura slipped quickly into the empty seat next to Charles. "I'm fine now. Sorry I'm late."

"No matter," said Uncle Lawrence and signalled the bearer to begin serving.

Maura drank greedily of her wine. Charles immediately refilled the glass. She drained this, too, and was relieved when no one thought to ask her why she'd been delayed. No one seemed aware that she'd left the house at all. Good.

Swallowing still more wine, she finally felt buoyed enough to join in the conversation, to flirt outrageously with both Charles and Terence and laugh gaily at her uncle's execrable jokes. Inwardly she struggled to overcome her hurt, to accept the futility of her ride to Sundagunj, and above all to dismiss the utterly ridiculous things Meera had said to her.

In love with Ross Hamilton! She'd sooner love a toad!

But the wine could lift her spirits for only so long. A broken heart was not so easily ignored. Ross did not love her, had never loved her, and never would.

I am the fool, not Meera, she thought wretchedly during dessert.

And if Meera already knew what Maura herself had tried to deny, then it wouldn't take long before others began to suspect. Her aunt and uncle. Lydia—who had already hinted that she knew. The Residency servants. Ross's servants. Ross himself.

The thought was intolerable. She would have to do something, fast. Her heart was already ground into dust. She couldn't stand being utterly humiliated as well.

When the meal was over, she accompanied her family and guests onto the verandah. It was a beautiful night, as all nights in India are beautiful, but for once Maura found no pleasure in it. She stood at the railing as pale and silent as a wraith.

Under cover of the general noise of leave-taking someone said her name. Reluctantly she turned her head to find Charles at her elbow.

"Are you feeling unwell, Miss Adams?"

"Why would you think so?"

"You seemed distracted tonight."

Maura assured him that he was mistaken. She had risen long before dawn yesterday to bake her uncle's cake and had taken an imprudently long ride before supper today. "So you can see why I'm tired. I hope I haven't been a boring addition to the party."

"On the contrary." Moved by the weariness in her unguarded face, Charles took her hand in his and pressed a surprisingly tender kiss into her palm. Then he smiled down at her, his expression for once wiped free of aloofness. "I'll call on you tomorrow."

Maura looked bewildered. "Tomorrow?"

"Yes." He took a deep breath. "Miss Adams— Maura—if you will permit me, I'd like to speak to your uncle. I've been thinking about nothing else for days—weeks! I don't believe we should wait any longer. Certainly you must agree?"

Looking up at him, she realized with a pang of surprise how handsome he was—and how approachable and very kind. *He* would never ride off to make love with a nautch-girl when she expected him to be elsewhere! *He* would never say cutting things or toss her out of his house on her rear or shout at her that she was a fool when all she wanted was to warn him of imminent danger!

"Miss Adams? Maura?"

"I'll think about it," she promised.

195

Chapter Twelve

Maura and Charles Burton-Pascal's engagement was announced during a formal afternoon reception at the British Residency three days later. Maura wore a balldress of ivory brocade, its foaming skirts caught up with ruffled flounces and embroidered silver ribands. She wore seed-pearl combs in her magnificent hair and a huge diamond betrothal ring on her slim left hand.

A beaming Charles stood beside her as Lawrence Carlyon made the announcement to those gathered in the Residency drawing room and pronounced himself delighted with the arrangement. Theirs would be a double wedding, Uncle Lawrence said, with his darling Lydia and her affianced marrying simultaneously at the end of the hot weather. Afterwards both couples would honeymoon in Delhi and then, monsoons notwithstanding, travel south to Poona and Calcutta.

Everyone applauded and then moved out into the garden to take refreshment under the gaily striped tent that had been donated for the occasion by the Bhunapore Tennis Club. The regimental band played and gorgeously attired bearers moved among the crowd serving champagne and caviar.

"It's from tins, of course," Daphne Carlyon confessed, "but fresh off the steamer from home."

Games were played and dances danced, and the station matrons agreed among themselves that young Maura Adams would make a most fetching bride. It didn't matter that she had become engaged with unseemly haste. After all, the groom was an admirable catch and no one could blame the girl for reeling him in.

"She was never the sort you'd expect to go back to England unmarried anyway," pronounced Mrs. Campbell-Smythe. "There's a word for those kind of girls, Daphne. I can't remember what it is. Can you?"

Mrs. Carlyon could not.

" 'Returned Empty,'" someone in the know supplied with a snicker.

The other women tittered. None of the mothers present expected their own daughters to be labeled so unkindly, of course, though they were all admittedly disappointed that Maura Adams had made off with one of the station's most eligible prizes. At least they could console themselves with the fact that there was still Captain Hamilton. . . .

But Ross was not present that afternoon. He was away in the Punjab; had been gone ever since the morning following his furious encounter with Maura on the road to Sundagunj. While Maura had attributed his abrupt departure to his caustic dislike of her, the actual reason had been in the nature of a personal emergency: An old friend from Ross's years with the Punjab Light Cavalry had met with an accident while handling munitions in the Faisalabad garrison and had requested Ross's presence at his deathbed.

The vigil had lasted considerably longer than the doctors expected. Ross had stubbornly remained until the end. Sirdar Awal Singh had fought at his side during the bloody border skirmish that had earned young Hamilton his first brevet, and until Ross's promotion to the civil service and his subsequent posting to Bhunapore, the two men had been as close as brothers.

Amir Dass had accompanied Ross to Faisalabad while Ghoda Lal had remained behind recovering from his wound. Fortunately he was no longer bedridden, and by the time Ross and his syce returned home a fortnight later, he had managed to make several excursions to the village of Sundagunj on Ross's behalf.

Dismounting outside his bungalow that evening, Ross drank long and thirstily from the goatskin flask that Ghoda Lal handed him, then tossed the rest to the waiting syce. "I'm in dire need of a bath," he announced, starting up the path. "Bring me hot water for shaving as well."

"At once, *Huzoor*," Ghoda Lal responded in English.

"What news of the cantonment?" Ross inquired, yawning.

"The usual gossip, *Huzoor*. Births and sickness and letters from Belait. Ohé, and the miss-sahiba has become engaged, *Huzoor*. Last week at the Residency."

Ross laughed. "I thought the girl was engaged already. Poor Shadwell! What made him want to go through the same torture twice?"

"*Nahin, Huzoor*. It was not the daughter of Carlyon-sahib. It was the other, the one with the poison hair."

Ross froze in his tracks. Turning, he said slowly in English, "You don't mean Maura Adams?"

"Yes, *Huzoor*."

For a long moment there was silence. Amir Dass, who had gone on ahead, waited with bated breath on the bungalow steps. He, too, had been halted in midstride by the unexpected news.

"Art thou certain, Ghoda Lal?" Ross asked, this time in Hindustani.

The Hindu nodded.

"Well," said Ross softly. "Well, well." He looked up. "What about that water, Amir Dass? I'd better shave before I present myself at the Residency."

"Carlyon-sahib is not there," Ghoda Lal informed him.

"Oh?"

"He has taken his family to Delhi."

"In this heat? Good God, is he mad?"

The bearer shrugged. "The memsahib wished to celebrate her niece's engagement."

"Tweak the noses of her Delhi friends, you mean," Ross grated in English.

"*Huzoor?*"

"The memsahib is proud that she has arranged the *shadi*, the wedding, of two in her family," Ross explained darkly. "It is considered an auspicious thing among the mem."

"Ah." The Hindu nodded knowingly. He cleared his throat. "The *Huzoor* will wish a full report concerning Sundagunj?"

"I'm afraid it will have to wait."

"But *Huzoor*, surely—"

Ross's expression was hard. "You mistake me, brother. Pack your gear. We leave for Delhi upon the hour."

Above the rose-tinted walls of the city soared the minarets and turnip-shaped domes of Shah Jehan's Grand Mosque. The rising sun painted its gleaming silverwork and drew soft fingers of light through the mist. Other domes filled the crowded skyline, their curved moon symbols of Islam a lasting reminder of the Mughal invaders who had laid the first cornerstones of this ancient city of the plains. The trade roads they had carved into the desert existed still, and despite the early hour and the rising heat, they were crowded with pilgrims and beggars, bullock carts and camels, and the elegant carriages of the memsahibs.

Wearing a pith helmet and a veil to protect her from the choking dust, Maura Adams drew on the reins of her high-wheeled *ekka* and steered it safely around a sacred Brahmini cow grazing in the center of the road.

The Chandni Chawk, Delhi's Avenue of Moonlight, was shaded by great trees and cooled by a channel of water flowing down its length. Maura would have preferred riding on horseback between the crowded vendor stalls, but this was Delhi, and young ladies were simply not permitted to ride abroad at this hour. That pleasure was reserved for the cool of the evening, when convention was relaxed and one could hack down the avenues or walk with one's beau along the walls of the great city gates, or picnic in the moonlight or dance at the Governor's Palace.

In the daylight, convention was strictly upheld;

appearances were all that mattered. For that reason, and in lieu of the company of her uncle and aunt, no fewer than two household servants and a trio of uniformed syces had accompanied Maura on her outing. Ismail Khan was not among those riding three abreast behind the *ekka*. Mrs. Carlyon had been extremely vocal in her insistence that they leave him behind.

Maura, for once, had offered no protest. But she had refused to allow Ismail Khan to wait out her return in the cramped *bibi-gurh* at the Residency. Much to his relief—and Aunt Daphne's—she had dismissed him temporarily from her services, sending him back with a note for Kushna Dev to the pink stucco palace of Walid Ali. Neither her aunt nor uncle had known about that part, of course, but seeing as Maura was extremely untalkative nowadays, they had been disinclined to ask her where the Pathan had gone.

Next to the cloth shop, with its bolts of fine Tibetan brocades and Chinese silks and muslins, stood a tiny fruit stand. Setting the brake, Maura descended from the *ekka* to purchase an orange. Letting the juice trickle down her parched throat, she wandered amid the brightly colored bolts with the bowing vendor dogging her heels. Stoic and unblinking, her five escorts waited by the carriage.

In all honesty Maura couldn't say that she was enjoying her stay in Delhi. She should have talked her aunt and uncle out of making the trip, or at the very last minute feigned an illness in order to remain home. But she had wanted so much to get away from Bhunapore—from Charles—that she had eagerly accepted Aunt Daphne's suggestion.

What a fool! She should have known that Charles would follow her here! Furthermore, Delhi was hot and crowded and dull beyond belief. Because everyone wanted to host a party in honor of her and Lydia's engagements, Maura literally hadn't had a moment to herself since their arrival. Even the enormous mansion in which they were staying as guests of Uncle Lawrence's oldest friends afforded no escape, for their hosts kept a veritable army of servants. Thirty-nine of them to be exact, and Maura had been dismayed to discover that she could not communicate with a single one of them. Half were Mughs from the Burmese border while the rest came from southern India and spoke only Bengali.

If only she had a friend, someone she could confide in! But even Meera had remained behind in Bhunapore, tending a sick relation.

At least Lydia and her parents seemed happy to be on holiday. Terence was staying with mutual acquaintances nearby and Lydia saw him often. Charles, too, had taken rooms somewhere in the city. There were parties and picnics and balls, and Uncle Lawrence went often to the Governor's residence to debate politics and the like with other members of the Foreign and Civil Service.

Oh, yes. All of them were happy. Happy to be in Delhi, happy for Charles, happy for her. No one seemed to notice that she was completely, utterly miserable.

At first she had tried convincing herself that the strict rules of etiquette governing Delhi society were responsible for her unhappiness. And why not? Every morning at precisely ten o'clock, Maura and her cousin and aunt were expected to meet their hostess in the morning room for breakfast. Afterward they received visitors for exactly an hour and then withdrew to their rooms to write letters, although Maura was never sure to whom, before reading until lunch.

After the meal they were sent back upstairs to take a nap whether they were tired or not. Upon arising, they were bathed by attendants and then readied for the evening's festivities, which might include a drive, a promenade, or a visit with friends.

Small wonder Maura felt confined and constrained and intensely unhappy! Her only pleasure lay in escaping into the city, where she could lose herself for a little while amid the shops and bustling bazaars. But even this had to be accomplished in the early dawn hours with the requisite number of escorts in tow, and of course she had to make certain to be home in time for breakfast. To show up late was considered an unpardonable breach of etiquette.

Etiquette! How Maura hated that word! And how she longed for the cool reception rooms of Kushna Dev's palace, knowing she could have visited as often as she liked had she remained behind in Bhunapore!

But Ross was in Bhunapore and he was the last one on earth, discounting Charles, she wished to see. . . .

Directly in front of the fruit vendor's stall sat an ancient astrologer, spindly legs crossed, his blind eyes staring sightlessly ahead of him. Hearing the rustle of Western skirts on the rush matting, he reached out to grab Maura's hem.

"Thy fate is cast in the stars at birth, memsahib. For the price of a rupee I will reveal it to thee."

Maura gave a bitter laugh. "Some things are best left hidden, my father." A coin was placed in his outstretched hand nonetheless and the sound of her footsteps faded into the noisy din of the bazaar. The morning's shopping was over. It was time to go home.

Nevertheless she got back much too early. Idling in her room until the summons came for breakfast, she sifted without interest through the calling cards that had been delivered in her absence. It was up to Aunt Daphne and their hostess, Mrs. Carrington, to decide which of the invitations they should accept. Both Maura and Lydia were considered too young and socially insignificant to express desires of their own.

She glanced irritably at the clock. Half an hour until she was permitted to leave her room. What on earth was she to do with herself until then? Fulfill her gentle obligations by reading a book or writing letters? But to whom should she write? Kushna Dev? To tell her what? That she had made a great mistake in agreeing to marry Charles Burton-Pascal? That she had been wrong, so terribly wrong, to accept his offer only to spite Ross Hamilton?

"Oh, God." Slumping onto the bed, Maura buried her face in her hands. How much longer could she go on hiding from the truth? Pretending it was the boredom of being here in Delhi that was making her so wretched?

Once again her stupid, impulsive temper had plunged her into a hopeless fix!

I only wanted to make Ross jealous. To show everyone he didn't matter a whit to me. I didn't know they would all make such a fuss, drag us to Delhi to celebrate, make it impossible for me to say I've reconsidered. . . .

Despair washed over her. She must have taken leave of her senses on the day a beaming Uncle Lawrence had told her he had accepted Charles's offer for her hand and that Aunt Daphne had already rushed out into the cantonment to tell everyone the news. Rooted to the spot, miserably in love with Ross, she had not thought to contradict him, to refuse outright, or later, when it began to dawn on her how effectively she was trapped, to run away and never come back.

Now she could not bear to think that she might truly have to marry Charles. Why, she couldn't even stand to let him touch her!

She remembered with a shudder the first time he had kissed her, not long after their engagement was announced. Uncle Lawrence and Aunt Daphne had squired Lydia to a moonlight dance somewhere in the cantonment. Maura, pleading a headache, had remained behind. Lonely for Ross, who was gone somewhere in the Punjab, she had spent the evening wandering aimlessly through the quiet Residency, and then, at Meera's insistence, bathing and washing her hair. Despite the ayah's protests, she hadn't bothered pinning it up again after it dried. What for? She had no intention of going out, and no one was expected at the Residency, what with her uncle away.

Darkness had fallen by the time she settled in the parlor to read. Moths batted against the lamp on the nearby table. She was sitting in the armchair thinking about Ross, the book forgotten in her lap, when Charles was shown in.

Maura hadn't heard him because the *chuprrassi* hadn't had the chance to announce him as yet. That was because Charles had stopped short in the doorway at the sight of her sitting there with her red-gold curls tumbling down her shoulders and back. He'd never seen her with her hair unpinned. How sweetly innocent she looked curled up in the armchair, her cool muslin gown revealing the slimness of her tiny waist! Cut low at the shoulders, it exposed the creamy expanse of her white throat and the shadowed hollow of her curving breasts.

Dismissing the *chupprassi* with a savage gesture, Charles had approached soundlessly and leaned over the back of the chair. Pushing aside the gleaming red tresses he had pressed his lips to the curve of her neck.

Gasping, Maura had slipped out from under him and taken refuge behind the end table. Charles had straightened with a scowl.

"Is that any way to greet your future husband?"

"I—I'm sorry." She struggled to compose herself. "You startled me, that's all."

Charles watched as she gathered the waist-length mass of reddish hair and attempted to roll it neatly into place. "Don't do that."

Her hands stilled and she looked at him questioningly.

He came to stand before her, wrapping a shining strand around his fingers. "I've never seen you with your hair down. I like it that way." His voice was hoarse. "Leave it for me."

Tightening his hold on her hair he pulled her closer and slipped his hand about her waist. When his mouth came down to claim hers she lifted her face dutifully enough, feeling a perverse sense of satisfaction in knowing that now Ross would no longer be the only man who had ever kissed her.

Groaning softly, Charles pressed his lips to hers. How sweet they were, parted and warm and waiting!

But after a moment he raised his head. His breathing was labored, his pupils dilated with passion, but his expression was no longer languid. "I may not know you very well, my dear, but I can certainly tell when you're not enjoying yourself. Relax a little, will you?"

He kissed her again, his arms tightening around her so that he could press her fully against him. Her hair spilled into his hands, a sweet-smelling cloud that made his senses reel. But although she was trying hard to respond, he could feel the rigid unwillingness within her.

"Come, Maura," he murmured, drawing back so that he could gaze deeply into her eyes. "Kiss me."

Come, Little Pearl, whispered a rough echo from her past, *kiss me . . .*

Uttering a strangled oath, she broke free of his hold. "I can't!" she whispered, more to herself than him. "I just can't!"

Charles had stared at her, his mouth falling open. Never in his life had he been rebuffed like this—and by his own bride-to-be, no less! His temper flared. God above, he'd been burning for the redheaded witch almost from the moment he'd laid eyes on her! How long had he been dreaming of bedding her, and coming to the reluctant conclusion that he'd not be able to do so unless they were rightfully wed? How dare she behave as though his very nearness disgusted her!

"Very well," he had told her through clenched teeth, "keep your maidenly virtue for now, if it means so bloody much to you!"

Turning heel he stalked out of the house, slamming the outer door behind him.

When Aunt Daphne suggested the next morning that they spend a few weeks in Delhi, Maura had accepted almost desperately. Perhaps time and distance would cool Charles's ardor and bring her some relief from the pain of her love for Ross. And surely she would find a way out of this ludicrous engagement, which she had no intention of seeing through!

She hadn't known at the time that her aunt had encouraged Charles to come to Delhi as well. Fortunately he hadn't mentioned that awful meeting in the Residency parlor when Maura saw him again. In fact, he had been unfailingly polite as he patiently escorted her from one social outing to another. But his mere presence only served to drive home to Maura how much she disliked him, how ill-suited they were, how miserably the future as his wife stretched before her should she be forced to go through with the wedding.

Which she wouldn't! She'd sooner be dead! But until now she hadn't come up with the perfect plan for getting rid of him. If only there was someone she could confide in, who could help her think things through at a time when she wasn't thinking clearly at all.

But everyone thought her so happy, so much in love—only because she was making sure they had no reason to believe otherwise. Once she'd decided on her course of action she intended to take all of them by surprise.

I don't love him, she thought now, agonized. I never have and I never shall. And he doesn't love me. He desires me and, for now, he's playing at being the indulgent affianced. But how long will that last? And how on earth will I find a way out of this mess?

She pounded the pillows with her fists as the hot tears slid down her cheeks. How easily they fell these days, even though she had always despised them!

I'm not the same person I was when I came to India, she thought despairingly. A month ago she would have known instantly how to rid herself of

GET YOUR 4 FREE BOOKS NOW — A $21.96 Value!

Mail the Free Book Certificate Today!

Get Four Books Totally FREE — A $21.96 Value!

▼ Tear Here and Mail Your FREE Book Card Today! ▼

PLEASE RUSH
MY FOUR FREE
BOOKS TO ME
RIGHT AWAY!

Leisure Romance Book Club
P.O. Box 6613
Edison, NJ 08818-6613

AFFIX
STAMP
HERE

Charles and this unwanted engagement. But here she sat weeping like a helpless babe, paralyzed by indecision, and furious because of it.

I hate you, Ross Hamilton! It's all your fault! Whatever have you done to me?

Chapter Thirteen

At breakfast Mrs. Carrington announced with delight that all of them had been invited to a garden party at the Williamson Peters House the following afternoon. Yes, she knew it was sudden, but Amanda Peters was one of Delhi's senior memsahibs, and because she had personally requested Lydia and Maura's presence, it was terribly important that both girls attend, looking their very best.

"But I have nothing to wear!" Lydia protested.

"What do you mean?" her mother demanded.

"I gave my things to the *dhobi* to wash!"

"When?"

"Yesterday."

"Including your afternoon frocks?"

"All of them!" Lydia wailed.

Mrs. Carrington and Aunt Daphne exchanged looks of alarm. The unwritten laws governing the stiff formality of Indian garden parties dictated that every lady present wear an appropriate afternoon frock with elbow-length gloves and a matching hat. Nothing else was acceptable.

Maura said soothingly, "Summon the *dhobi* and have him bring one back. He must have finished a few of them by now, don't you think?"

Lydia looked as though she wanted to cry. "But I gave him so many! Yours, too, Maura."

"Oh dear," said Mrs. Carrington. "He's such an unreliable man."

Poor Lydia looked so miserable that Maura sighed and came to her feet. "Tell you what. I'll go right now and fetch them for you."

"Oh, would you?" Aunt Daphne asked gratefully. Turning to their hostess she added proudly, "Our Maura has quite a way with the natives, you know."

Mrs. Carrington looked relieved. Like most British memsahibs, she was thoroughly intimidated by her dark-skinned servants.

Glad for an excuse to leave the breakfast room early, Maura swept into the hall calling for the *chupprassi*. A servant was dispatched to fetch the *dhobi*, who arrived shortly thereafter out of breath and begging to know how he could serve the much-blessed miss-sahib. Maura wasted no time in explaining the problem.

"But most honored miss-sahib!" he exclaimed in horror, "I no longer have the gowns!"

"What do you mean?" Maura demanded. "Where are they?"

Herewith the *dhobi* pretended not to understand another word of English, but when Maura threatened him in fluent Hindustani with all manner of hideous punishments, he shamefacedly admitted that he had rented both her and Lydia's wardrobes to other patrons for the weekend.

"I do not understand, Bappa Singh. Rented them? What does that mean? To whom?"

"To the *mem* in the Delhi garrison. They will be returned to me on Tuesday."

Maura's mouth fell open as understanding dawned. "Thou hast given them to the soldiers' wives to *wear*? *My* dresses?"

"There is to be a party tonight on the garrison *maidan*," the dhobi squeaked. "The soldiers' memsahibs are poor, but of course they desire pretty clothing—"

"So you gave them mine and my cousin's?" Maura demanded, incredulous. "In exchange for money?"

"It is done often, by others, too," he replied defensively.

God, his arrogance was too much. For a moment Maura was tempted to fly at him and claw his face to shreds. She'd had more than enough of these incompetent city servants and their greedy, grasping ways! No sense in expecting him to get her clothing back, either! She'd have to ride to the fort and do that herself.

Scribbling a hasty note to her aunt and Mrs. Carrington, she left the house without bothering to summon her syces. Ten minutes later she was riding hell-for-leather up Delhi Ridge amid a cloud of swirling dust, the sunlight burning her back and shoulders, for she hadn't stopped to fetch her topi and veil. Behind her the city fell away in a shimmering heat wave while the great curve of the Jumna River glared like molten silver in the midday sun.

Though she was already uncomfortably hot and thirsty, Maura was aware of a welcome stirring of contentment in her heart. Could it be that she had at last managed to shake off the lethargy of the last few weeks? Why hadn't she realized before that simply breaking the stifling rules of etiquette that governed her life in Delhi was all it took?

She could have laughed aloud at the thought.

And she did.

"I don't know where you've been, Maura darlin'," she said aloud in the lilting, long-forgotten Irish accent of her father, "but welcome back, colleen, welcome back!"

Though her horse was already lathered, she urged him ever faster so that the wind whistled in her ears and sent dust devils dancing beneath his hooves.

Ahead of her the countless tombs and great ruins of the Seven Cities came into view. Beyond them rose the tower of the Kutab Minar, lifting high into the humid sky. The military garrison lay sprawled to the west of it, the huts and headquarters erected in front of the parade grounds, the officers' bungalows in a tidy row behind. Humming beneath her breath, Maura guided her mount toward the gate.

The sentry there, taking one look at her disheveled hair and wild eyes, moved quickly to bar her way. "Sorry, ma'am. Fort's closed to visitors this time o' day."

She halted her blowing mount directly in front of him so that he had to back up to avoid being kicked. "I should like to see your commanding officer," she informed him now that she had him at a disadvantage. "At once, if you please."

"Colonel Bradley be down in the lines, ma'am."

"Will you summon him, please?" she repeated.

"Beggin' your pardon, ma'am, that's impossible."

"Then I shall wait here for him."

"It may take hours, ma'am."

Maura tossed her head. "Then I insist that you

send someone to fetch him. It's a matter of utmost importance."

The sentry's patience was wearing thin. "Sorry, ma'am, I've got my orders."

Maura, too, was beginning to lose her temper. Her earlier elation had been replaced by a raging thirst and now her head was starting to ache. She longed to take her whip to the insolent fellow's hide. Why, for all she knew, he could well be one of those soldiers whose wives had shamelessly paid for the privilege of wearing *her* gowns to a dance tonight!

The thought made her furious. Patience gone, she spurred her mount forward in an attempt to ride roughshod over him. To her surprise he refused to budge. Reaching up he grabbed the off-side rein, and a scuffle ensued as both of them tried to wrest control of the snorting, frightened horse.

Maura raised her whip. "Let him go!"

"Back off! Back off, I say! Oww!" he howled as she leaned over to whack him.

In the next moment she was grabbed from behind and yanked bodily out of the saddle. Enraged, she swung on her captor only to have the whip jerked from her grasp.

"Give me that!" she cried.

"Leave off!"

The barked command was accompanied by a rough shake that nearly rattled her brains from her head. Whipping around, she found herself staring into Ross Hamilton's furious face.

"R-Ross! W-What—How did you—"

"I don't believe this! Have you completely lost your mind?"

"I was—"

He shook her savagely. "Be quiet! I've had enough of your bloody misadventures! Don't tell me you rode bareheaded all the way from Delhi? No wonder you're going around attacking the sentries! You're lucky you didn't die of sunstroke! On the other hand, maybe that would have been best for us all!"

Oh, it was too much: her infuriating exchange with the sentry, the humiliating whereabouts of her gowns, the hot ride from the city, and especially the way Ross was shouting at her. She'd never seen him so angry, when all she wanted at the moment was to crawl into his lap and lay her aching head against him.

"Let me go," she said tiredly.

But he wasn't through with her yet. "No, I won't. You're going back where you came from. This minute!"

"I'm not."

"Yes, damn it, you are."

Maura couldn't help it; she burst into tears.

Above her bowed head Ross's face twisted. "Oh, for God's sake—" Awkwardly he put his arms around her and held her while she wept. She had grown thinner since the last time he'd touched her, he thought, and the memory of the wrenching kiss they'd shared on the Residency porch hit him like a blow to the heart. His mouth thinned and his face was suddenly scored with harsh lines.

"Maura, don't," he growled. "I'm sorry I shouted. I didn't mean it."

"Of c-course you did."

Becoming aware of the gaping sentry, Ross swore softly and produced a handkerchief. While Maura did her best to dry her eyes and set her appearance to rights, he escorted her into the relative cool of the dispensary. She declined the services of the army doctor, but did accept the drink he brought her. Revived by both the water and the cooling breeze from

215

the punkah flapping overhead, she gave him a shaky smile.

"Thank you." She glanced meekly at Ross, who was leaning against the dispensary door with his arms crossed before him, the expression on his handsome face thunderous as he watched. "I can't imagine what came over me."

"I can," he retorted. "You were lucky you didn't succumb to the heat any worse than you did. Now, would you care to tell me why you're here?"

Quietly she told him about her gowns. Ross said nothing as he listened, and it was impossible to guess his thoughts from the look on his face. The doctor, however, was aghast, and immediately withdrew to dispatch an orderly to summon Colonel Bradley.

"I suppose I overreacted," Maura said in a small voice when she and Ross were alone.

"No," he said, his gruffness gone, "that isn't true." He doubted there was another woman in all India who would have taken the matter into her own hands so promptly and ruthlessly.

She smiled wryly. "I was being impulsive, though."

"That you were."

She found she had to look away from his piercing blue eyes. She looked instead at the glass-fronted cabinets with their tidy rows of bottles and tinctures. "What are you doing here?"

Ross shrugged. "Meeting an old friend. He's a staff sergeant at the garrison."

"Uncle Lawrence said nothing about it. I wasn't aware you had leave coming."

Ross shook his head. "I'm here officially. The fellow happens to hail from Sundagunj and there are a number of things I need to ask him."

It was the same lie he had told Ghoda Lal.

Maura's eyes widened. "Oh! Does it have to do with what nearly happened in the nullah last month? Were you able to find out—"

"No," Ross said shortly. "But I will."

She clasped her hands together. "Then—then you do believe me."

She thought for a moment that something flickered in his eyes, a twinge of pain, even anguish, but it passed so quickly that she doubted she had really seen it.

"Perhaps. Neither of the *talukdars* involved in that land dispute are willing to accept my proposals, though of course both insist that they will and that the other is to blame. Seeing me permanently out of the way would please both of them mightily, I imagine."

"How can you talk like that?"

"Come, Miss Adams, no need to look so stricken! You know perfectly well that this is the way things are done here."

"And if they do to you what they did to Ghoda Lal?"

His tone was sharp. "Would it matter to you if I were hurt? Or killed?"

She tried desperately to make her answer flippant, but the words stuck in her throat. All she could do was look at him, her heart in her eyes.

Ross had gone still. Now he straightened and came toward her, looking down at her with his mouth a thin, tight line. "Well?"

She shook her head.

He took hold of her chin, lifting her face to his. He said her name, and what was there in his voice made her tremble. Tears welled in her eyes.

"Oh, Ross, I—"

217

Ellen Tanner Marsh

"Well, then, here we are!"

The door burst open and the doctor strode in followed by the agitated Colonel Bradley. Not only did he apologize profusely for the embarrassment and inconvenience Maura and her cousin had suffered in the matter of their gowns, but he had already arranged to have them retrieved. He assured her that those responsible would be brought up for immediate discipline. In the meantime would Miss Adams consent to dine with him and his wife before returning to the city?

"I'll send an orderly to notify your people, of course. Won't do to have 'em worrying."

Maura nodded, rather overwhelmed.

"What about you, Hamilton?" boomed the colonel, turning to Ross, who had retreated once again, arms folded across his chest, his expression black. "Will you dine with us?"

Ross frowned. "I'm afraid, sir—"

"Come, boy! Won't take no for an answer!"

"But I've business in—"

"—the officers' quarters. I know, I know. But the men won't be back from the lines 'til after tea so you might as well sit out the hottest part of the day with Miss Adams and m'wife. Caro will take offense if you don't."

Ross's smile held very little humor. "Then I certainly can't refuse, can I?"

Caroline Bradley, small, gray-haired and wrinkled like a prune after years and years in the scorching Indian sun, professed herself delighted with the prospect of having young people in her house once again.

"And the two of you are so extremely well-suited," she added as she ushered them happily into her parlor. "I know Isabelle Carrington, and I understand there's to be a wedding come the cold season?"

Maura lowered her eyes and Ross said curtly, "I'm afraid you're mistaken, ma'am. Miss Adams is not my affianced."

"Oh? But I thought— How odd. You seemed so—" She broke off, blushing deeply.

Maura cleared her throat. "I'm engaged to marry Mr. Charles Burton-Pascal."

"I see. Never mind me. George always says I prattle too much, don't you, dear?"

"Nonsense," said Colonel Bradley, and smoothed over the awkward moment by sending the *khidmatgar* for drinks.

They dined on cold fowl and clear vegetable soup. Maura downed a glass of wine and immediately wished she hadn't. She felt drowsy and giddy and found herself unable to do anything but sit there and ache for Ross, who sat so close to her at the Bradleys' small table that she could have reached over to caress his cheek had she wished.

She was glad that Mrs. Bradley talked as much as she did, although normally she would have chafed with impatience at being forced to sit through such a lengthy meal. But she had no wish to ride back to Delhi during the hottest part of the day, and she had already taken a strong liking to Colonel Bradley, a career soldier who reminded her in no small measure of her father. A few hours in the Bradleys' company was infinitely preferable to the dull afternoon awaiting her with the Carringtons!

And, oh, to be with Ross again, even though he barely spoke to her and constantly glowered at her the way he always did back home! Just knowing he was here in Delhi made all the difference in the world.

He can help me, Maura thought fuzzily. Surely he can talk to Uncle Lawrence? Explain that I was never serious about marrying Charles?

She had to subdue a tipsy snort recalling the first time she had tried telling her uncle as much herself, because both he and Aunt Daphne had instantly, albeit fondly, put down her remarks to prenuptial nerves.

"It happens all the time," Aunt Daphne had said, kissing her cheek.

"Nothing to be scared of, m'dear," Uncle Lawrence had added with a wink. And after he had thought Maura out of earshot he had whispered to his wife, "Better have that . . . you know, talk with her soon."

As though Maura didn't already know exactly what to expect!

Her amusement faded at the thought. She'd rather die than lie with Charles Burton-Pascal, let alone marry him! Surely Ross could convince her guardians of that? Uncle Lawrence thought the world of him, and Maura knew firsthand how forceful Ross could be if he wished. Only, how to broach the matter when she was almost too drunk to mention it? When she was desperately afraid that she'd only end up revealing to him where her heart truly lay? And when to speak to him? Perhaps she might get the chance to do so privately, before she returned to the Carringtons'?

Ross didn't make matters any easier for her. She might not have been there at all for all the attention he paid her during luncheon. After a while she began to suspect that he was ignoring her deliberately, and it only made her want to burst into tears all over again. Or turn the soup tureen over onto his darkly handsome head.

Was this what being in love was all about? Feeling so completely, utterly miserable? If so, she wanted nothing more of it, thank you very much.

She felt drained by the time the meal ended at last, and only too glad to leave for the city, even if it meant having to endure that much more of Ross's hurtful company. A trunk containing her rescued wardrobe accompanied them in a cart which, along with a driver, had been graciously provided by the colonel.

"Least I could do," he said in response to Maura's thanks.

"You'll come again, won't you, dear?" Caroline Bradley added.

"Certainly." No longer fuzzy from the wine, only infinitely weary, Maura kissed the older woman's wrinkled cheek.

Neither she nor Ross spoke as they rode away down the drive. The sentry at the gate saluted them smartly, and then they were out in the waning daylight, headed home. A faint breeze rustled the long grass. Overhead a pair of kites rode the simmering thermals.

No doubt aware of Maura's fatigue, Ross made certain that they kept the pace slow, and rested their mounts often in the shade of the roadside trees. Given a choice, he would have preferred leaving the fort later that evening, after the sun had set completely, but that would have meant traveling with Maura after dark, an unconscionable breach of etiquette that would have scandalized her hosts and her family.

So they pressed on through the hot, still twilight, the tall sahib and the silent lady garnering curious looks from the passersby. What was it that stirred their interest? Perhaps the look of sadness on the

221

lady's lovely face? Or the lingering anger on the handsome sahib's?

Near the ancient walls flanking the Water Bastion, Ross drew rein at last.

"Can you find your way back alone?"

Maura looked at him, surprised.

"It wouldn't do for me to be seen escorting you all the way into the city. Your fiancé would find it unacceptable, and I can't say as I'd blame him."

Color rose in Maura's cheeks. "Yes, of course."

There followed a moment of silence in which their horses stamped restlessly and the cart driver waited with impatience a little further down the road.

"Thank you for your help," Maura said stiffly, not looking at him. "It—it was kind of you."

Ross made no reply.

She took up the reins and prepared to wheel her mount. When he said her name she drew up short, gazing at him inquiringly.

"Why did you agree to marry him?"

Now it was Maura's turn not to answer.

"You're not in love with him, are you?"

She shook her head.

"Did your uncle—"

"No," she said quickly. "It was my decision." She smiled into his scowling eyes, glad that she was thinking clearly now, no longer befuddled by the wine. She would not humiliate herself by begging for his help after all. She would find her own way out of this dilemma.

She said a little breathlessly, because she was afraid her voice might falter and so alert him to the fact that something was amiss after all, "If you'll excuse me? I'd like to get back before dark."

Urging her horse onward, she disappeared down the road, the cart trundling behind her.

Ross watched for a long time without moving, even after the cart had vanished around the bend.

There was a rustle in the canebreak and another horse appeared beside him. "Wah!" said Ghoda Lal. "Now I know why we came to Delhi."

Ross said nothing.

"Clearly it has little to do with Sundagunj."

Still Ross remained silent.

Ghoda Lal glanced sharply into his hard face. "Thou art beset by demons, brother."

"Am I?"

"Assuredly! And hast been from the moment thou laid eyes on her."

"Thou art a fool to believe such," Ross said curtly.

"Nay, I am not the one," Ghoda Lal replied, but Ross had wheeled his mount and set off at a canter in the direction of the fort and so did not hear him. Cursing roundly beneath his breath, Ghoda Lal followed behind.

Chapter Fourteen

The Peters's garden party was every bit as dull as Maura had feared. A regimental band played endless patriotic marches while liveried servants offered guests trays of dainty hors d'oeuvres with white-gloved hands. The ladies promenaded up and down the lawn in their frilly frocks and matching hats. Compliments were exchanged. Gossip repeated. Fluted voices tittered. The gentlemen discussed polo and the latest cricket scores from Poona.

Maura walked beneath the palm trees with Charles, her fingers resting lightly on his arm as convention demanded. He looked classically handsome in a cutaway coat and high collar, and everyone who came to speak to them assured her that she would be deliriously happy from the moment she became Mrs. Charles Burton-Pascal.

It all made her want to scream.

"You'll be such a marvelous addition to our set," Amanda Peters remarked at one point. It was a high compliment; a sign that Charles and his intended would be officially welcomed into Delhi society as soon as they were wed.

Everyone within earshot murmured approvingly. Aunt Daphne beamed. Earlier, the same honor had been bestowed upon Lydia.

"Where do you intend to live?" Mrs. Peters went on kindly. "Here in Delhi, I hope?"

"I'm afraid not." Charles put his arm familiarly about Maura's waist. "We'll be returning to England soon after the honeymoon."

There were gasps from the bystanders.

"Maura! Is this true?"

But Maura couldn't answer her aunt. She could only stare at Charles, as shocked as everyone else.

"You're not going to live here?" Lydia demanded at last.

Charles uttered a crack of derisive laughter. "In India?"

Maura couldn't bear to stay another moment after that. Seeking a private audience with her aunt, she pleaded for permission to be excused. She had a pounding headache. Might she be allowed to go home?

Alarmed by her appearance, Aunt Daphne readily agreed. If Maura could wait just one moment while she rounded up Lawrence and Lydia—

"Oh, there's no need for you to ruin your afternoon! Why don't I go home with Major and Mrs. Bottisham? I understand they're leaving early. Surely you could ask them to drop me off at the Carringtons'?"

This was quickly accomplished and Maura, ignoring Charles's offer to drive her home himself, was spirited away in the Bottishams' carriage. Everyone agreed that the dear thing was not in her looks. What had come over her?

What indeed?

Maura was literally shaking with rage by the time the Carringtons' *chupprassi* admitted her into the silent house. Upstairs in the cool of her bedroom she laid her aching head on the pillow. At this moment she was glad Meera was not there, for she needed desperately to be alone. She wanted to scream and scream and scream. Kill herself. Kill Charles. Cut out his heart and grind it into dust.

Instead she wept noisily into her pillow as she had not wept for years. When her tears were exhausted at last, she washed her face and repaired her ravaged appearance as best she could in front of the bathroom mirror.

She felt somewhat calmer when she went downstairs. Accepting an iced drink from the *chupprassi*, she settled herself in Mr. Carrington's library and began to plan how best to deal with this latest nightmare. It was one thing to marry a man she didn't love. It was altogether another to let him take her away from India!

She'd sooner be dead.

Unless she killed him first.

She didn't know how long she sat there scheming and plotting before she was interrupted by the sound of hasty footsteps in the hall. Looking up, she was startled to see the *khansamah*, the Carringtons' cook, appear in the library doorway.

"What is it?" she asked, hurrying to her feet. She had never known him to leave the kitchen before.

He spoke no English, but there was no mistaking his urgent gestures as he frantically exhorted Maura to come, come quickly.

Her first thought was that the kitchen was on fire. It happened a lot in stately homes like this one. Why else would he look so frightened?

She followed him at a run into the dark, oily smelling kitchen. In the doorway she halted in utter bewilderment. There was no sign of a fire, but the servants were nonetheless in a panic, waving their arms and banging pot lids together. The din they created was deafening.

After a moment Maura saw what all the fuss was about. A jackal that had somehow found its way in from the garden was standing in a corner bolting down the water buffalo haunch that had been roasting on the range for the sahibs' supper.

Maura couldn't help it. She burst into laughter. After the last miserable hour it felt wonderful to laugh. Pushing her way past the gibbering womenfolk, she opened the back door, which had fallen shut in all the confusion. Grabbing a broom she tried to shoo the animal outside.

"Go on!" she ordered, jabbing him.

Still holding the roast in its jaws, the jackal began trotting in circles, searching for a way out.

She couldn't stop laughing. "Go on! Get out! Shoo!"

Seeing that the miss-sahib was not in the least bit alarmed, the servants resumed their banging and shouting with renewed enthusiasm.

Back and forth the jackal paced while Maura did her best to herd him toward the door. There was no sense in trying to explain to the servants that they were confusing him. They were enjoying themselves too much and, besides, the noise was deafening.

Finally the jackal spotted the open door. Bolting outside, it vanished amid the plumbago shrubs, leaving the haunch behind. A cheer arose. Pot lids and dish towels were waved in triumph. Maura joined in with her broom.

In the midst of the celebration she became aware of someone standing in the doorway leading into the hall. Someone who wasn't taking part in the merriment but was watching her with his arms crossed before his wide chest. Turning her head, she saw that it was Ross.

"No one answered the door," he explained when their eyes met. "I heard the noise and let myself in."

Maura could barely speak through her laughter. "You always seem to show up during times of utter chaos, Captain Hamilton!"

But the servants had fallen silent at the sound of Ross's deep voice. None of them had ever seen a strange sahib in the kitchen before.

In the ensuing silence his voice sounded decidedly harsh. "You need to remind them to keep the doors and windows closed. The next jackal or *pi* dog to find its way in may be a good deal more dangerous."

Maura's merriment faded at his tone. Now what was *he* so bloody angry about? A scant second ago she'd been giddy with delight at seeing him again. Now she wished he'd go away. Turning her back on him, she busied herself with putting away the broom. "What brings you to the Carringtons' house, Captain Hamilton?" Her voice had grown cool. "I'm afraid I'm the only one at home."

"So I gathered. I've letters for your aunt and uncle. They arrived in Bhunapore the day I left. Most of them are from England. I thought they would want them as soon as possible."

"You could have given them to me yesterday."

"I didn't expect to see you yesterday."

She shot back with: "Well, then, you should have had your bearer deliver them."

Which had been his own thought exactly, except for the annoying fact that he hadn't been able to talk himself out of coming, to make certain she'd recovered from yesterday's heatstroke, to see her again . . .

Scowling, he drew a packet from his breast pocket. Their fingers touched as he handed it to her and Maura snatched her hand away as though she'd been burned. Putting the letters behind her back she lifted her chin.

"That was very kind of you. Thank you. How is everything back at the Residency? I confess I've missed it even though we've only been away three weeks."

"Everything's the same," Ross said shortly. "I wasn't there very long myself before coming on to Delhi. Oh, but I did happen to see your Pathan syce. We ran into each other on the Sinda Bhat Road. Did you know he's moved back to the city during your absence?"

Maura nodded, her expression softening. "How is he?"

"Uncouth as ever." Now Ross, too, was smiling a little. "Demanded to know when you intend to return. Said his horse wasn't getting enough exercise. I daresay he's the one chafing at the bit, wanting to get back to the Residency and his *bibi-gurh*."

Maura was shaken by the homesickness she felt at his words. She had never realized before how fond she had grown of Ismail Khan and placid little Bhunapore until she'd left both of them for the hot, hectic environs of Delhi. And to think that Charles intended to take her away from Bhunapore for good!

For an awful, awful moment she was tempted to confess her troubles to Ross. But how could she say one word to him when he was standing there glowering at her as though the very sight of her filled him with annoyance and dislike?

Much to her disgust, her throat began to ache. Not again! She'd shed enough tears already. To hide the need to cry from him, she sorted through the mail he had given her. An envelope with numerous forwarding addresses caught her attention.

"Why, this is for Mr. Burton-Pascal!"

"I know." Ross's voice was cold. "His bearer brought it to the Residency the morning I left. That's how I learned he was here in Delhi. I thought you might like to give it to him yourself."

Turning the envelope over, Maura saw that it was not a letter but a telegram, and that it had been opened. This was not unusual in India since the natives often read their masters' mail—provided they knew how.

A wildly improbable thought seized her. Supposing, just supposing, that Charles had left someone—a lover, perhaps, or even a betrothed—behind at home? Someone he had never told her about and who, being most unwilling to let Maura have him, had sent a wire decrying their engagement the moment news of it had reached English shores?

Impossible. Daft.

But as such a way out . . .

Swallowing her pride, she unfolded the paper and read it right there with Ross and the servants looking on. She gasped as she did so, then looked up at him with wide eyes.

"Oh, Ross, it's terrible news! Charles's mother has died!"

"Then you'd better see that he gets it at once. It seems to have been considerably delayed in getting here."

Without a word, Maura hurried into the hall to retrieve her topi and gloves.

"You're not going now?" he demanded, following her.

Oh, yes, she was. The sooner the better. Though she felt terribly sorry for him, she knew that Charles would have to leave India immediately. His father was long dead, and as an only child, Charles would have to personally oversee the settling of the estate. Why, he might be gone for weeks. Months. Perhaps as long as a year.

Long enough for Maura to break their engagement without anyone considering her unfair . . .

"You can't really be thinking of going yourself!" Ross was saying angrily.

"He isn't home right now," she countered, pulling on her gloves. "He's attending a garden party at the Williamson Peters House. I'll leave it with his bearer so he'll get it the moment he comes in."

"You could send a servant to do that."

"Since when can they be trusted?"

He looked at her keenly for a moment, then said curtly, "At least let me drive you."

She sat beside him on the narrow seat of the Carringtons' *ekka,* glad that it was midday and far too hot for the majority of people to be about. They drove in the direction of the Kashmir Gate, a section of the city with wide, palm-fringed avenues flanked by huge villas. Maura had no idea where Charles lived; she knew only that he had rented a set of rooms from a wealthy British nabob by the name of Esmond Tolliver.

"I know him," Ross had said grimly.

They made good time, for the thoroughfares were nearly deserted. An occasional beggar or a mud-smeared sadhu made their ablutions in the filthy gutter, but that was all.

Ross was silent as they wheeled down the empty streets. Maura, who hadn't been this close to him for a while, was shaken by a rush of longing every time she looked at him. How well she knew every angle and plane of that handsome face, and the way his mouth turned down at the corners as he sat there trying hard to shut his thoughts away from her.

What was he thinking? What would he say if he knew she had become engaged to Charles because of him?

Charles.

Maura fingered the telegram in her lap. Harsh experience had taught her never to hope for too much. But if this was truly the way out of her dilemma . . .

Please, oh, please, she prayed. Let it be so.

She looked again at Ross. "You're angry with me, aren't you?"

"What makes you say that?"

Her shoulders lifted. "You always look that way when you're angry with me."

"It's easy to be angry with you. You're an impossible woman."

Maura resisted the urge to smack him. "You can let me off right here if you're going to be rude."

"And let you walk the rest of the way? Like yesterday?"

She tossed her head in a huff. "Very well, I admit your appearance at the fort was . . . helpful. But that doesn't mean you have to treat me like a . . . a . . ."

"Tiresome child?"

She glared at him, but saw that he was smiling. Her heart seemed to squeeze in response. "I've said it before, Captain Hamilton. You are no gentleman."

"Only because you bring out the worst in me."

232

Now they were both smiling, and Maura's heart wasn't hurting anymore but swelling so much that she thought it might burst. Ross had never teased her openly before. Could it be that he, too, was looking forward to the very real possibility of Charles's departure for England? That he had been angry with her all along because he objected to her engagement for reasons of his own?

Oh, but she knew better than to hope for that much! Knew better than to take anything he said too personally. Past hurts had taught her far too well, and yet she couldn't shake a feeling of growing happiness, the first in weeks.

She was still fired with renewed courage when Ross drew rein at last before a tall, stuccoed house at the end of a crowded cul de sac. Lilies bloomed in the untidy garden and palm fronds rustled in the breeze. There was no one about. The blinds were drawn over the windows and the entire house appeared dark.

A servant with a crumpled turban and sleep-swollen eyes rose yawning and scratching from his resting place near the door as Maura and Ross ascended the outer steps. His expression as he looked Maura up and down was so insolent that Ross closed his hands into fists.

"We have a letter for Burton-Pascal-sahib," he said through clenched teeth.

At his tone the servant quickly straightened his turban. Yes, yes, the sahib was at home, he informed Ross very politely. He had returned perhaps half an hour ago and was resting upstairs in his personal chambers. "I will fetch him for you," he concluded, bowing and backing toward the door.

But Ross knew better than to entrust the task to this slovenly fellow. More likely than not he'd bolt for the back of the house and never return.

No, Ross would have to go himself, and he'd have to take Maura with him. No way in bloody hell was he going to leave her alone out here on the stoop with this leering *chupprassi*.

Inwardly he cursed her, not for the first time, for her stubborn insistence on coming along.

Taking her arm in a hard grip, he led her into the house. They went together up the stairs, where Ross released her on the landing.

"Wait here."

But Charles must have heard them coming, because the bedroom door opened before Ross had the chance to knock.

"Well, well. Captain Hamilton. Whatever brings you to m'humble abode?" His bleary eyes slid past him to the landing. "And Maura, my own affianced! To what do I owe this unexpected pleasure?"

Uttering an oath, Ross moved quickly to block him from view. Too late. Even from the landing Maura could see into the darkness of a bedroom that reeked of brandy and the acrid remains of hashish. Charles, clearly drunk, was standing stark naked in the doorway while behind him a plump Hindu woman with sloe eyes and a wide, red mouth sprawled on the rumpled bed. The hookah they had been smoking had overturned, and now she drew the soiled sheets carelessly over her ample breasts.

"Decided t' have a party of my own," Charles explained, slurring his words. "Amanda Peters's little social got too dull after you left, m'dear. Actually, now you're here, why not join us? Yasmin, here—" He bent to pinch a dark nipple, which made the woman squeal and slap his hand away, "—prefers women over men, or so she keeps tellin' me."

He laughed, belched, backhanded his mouth and

turned a bleary eye on his betrothed. "Never too late to join us." Apparently the thought of having Maura in bed with him and his mistress aroused him, for his member began to thicken as he leered at her. "Well?"

Maura made a small, gasping noise and backed toward the stairs. Ross was already stepping over the threshold and, before Charles could react, hit him. Hard.

Yasmin screamed. Charles crumpled to the floor without a sound, blood spurting from his nose and mouth.

"Come on." Stepping over him, Ross took Maura's arm and pulled her down the stairs, past the staring *chupprassi* and out into the glaring heat of the day.

In utter silence he drove the *ekka* away. Maura, her head bowed, sat rigidly beside him.

Not until they were turning down the main road did Ross turn to her, scowling. He said harshly, "Do you want—"

"Please," Maura gasped, "don't say a word. Just take me home."

He did so, his expression rigid.

When the *ekka* halted in the Carringtons' drive, Maura sprang up before Ross could even set the brake.

"Maura, wait—"

Shaking her head she held aside her skirts and jumped to the ground. Without another word she disappeared up the path.

Ross made no attempt to follow her. After a long moment he turned the *ekka* around. Though he rarely used his whip, he did so now, startling the horse and setting it cantering away in a cloud of dust.

Evening found him pacing his room at the Delhi

garrison with all the restless fury of a caged tiger. He had spoken to no one since returning from the city, and even Ghoda Lal, recognizing his mood, had wisely kept out of his way. Later, when Colonel Bradley's bearer arrived with an invitation for supper, Ross ignored it. It was left to Ghoda Lal to send his master's regrets.

Evening wore on and midnight approached and still Ross showed no inclination to set aside the brandy bottle and retire. He was in the process of pouring himself yet another drink, in fact, when a knock sounded on his door. Scowling a warning at Ghoda Lal he went to open it himself. On the threshold stood a native he recognized as one of the Carringtons' servants.

"Please, sahib," the man squeaked, nailed by Ross's glowering gaze, "Carlyon-sahib sends for thee."

Ross glanced at the clock and saw that it was nearly one o'clock. What the devil did Lawrence Carlyon want with him at this hour? Unless—

"Ghoda Lal, fetch my horse!"

Earlier that evening he had stripped down to shirtsleeves. Now he didn't even bother to put on the coat his bearer held out to him. Striding out of the bungalow, he rode hell-for-leather into the city.

Lawrence Carlyon was waiting in the hallway just inside the Carringtons' front door, a breach of courtesy that could only spell trouble. At the sight of Ross he ran a shaking hand through his hair. "Thank God you're here."

Ross crossed over to him, disheveled and dusty, his expression black. "What is it, sir? Your family—"

"I'm afraid it's my niece."

A brief pause.

"What's happened?"

The British Resident waved a crumpled piece of paper in the air. To Ross he seemed to have aged ten years and more in the space of a single evening. "She's disappeared! Daffy found this on the dressing table when we got back from the Peters's party. Said she was leaving and that we weren't to worry about her." He regarded Ross with baffled anxiety. "What the devil's she up to? What does it mean?"

"Have you tried looking for her?" Ross demanded.

"Good God, everywhere! Carrington himself is still out with the staff, and I've only just returned. Daffy was beside herself, as you can imagine. Dr. Lockley put her to bed with a sedative. Lydia, too."

Lawrence looked as close to panic as Ross had ever seen him. "What do *you* think is going on, sir?"

"Hell, I don't know! Daffy's convinced the girl's eloped. I told her Charles'd never hold for it, but I'm afraid he ain't to be found neither. You don't honestly think—"

"I very much doubt it."

"Well, thank God for that." The British Resident mopped his brow with a wadded handkerchief. Putting it back in his vest pocket he cleared his throat. "Ahem."

Ross looked up. "Sir?"

"Some of the servants claim you left the house with her this afternoon." Lawrence reddened. "I've always thought highly of you, m'boy, but under the circumstances, and considering that the two of you were alone—"

"I assure you there was nothing improper about our outing," Ross said smoothly. "Miss Adams wished to run an errand and as the servants were inconvenienced with some sort of emergency—a jackal in the kitchen as I understood it—and all of you were away, I took her myself. Considering it was broad daylight and my ties to your family are not unknown in Delhi—"

"That's what I told Daffy." Lawrence looked relieved. "And we did hear about that jackal."

Ross held out his hand. "May I see the note?"

Just as he had expected, the hastily penned missive told him nothing, only that Maura was leaving Delhi and that her guardians were not to worry.

Not that it mattered. He knew perfectly well why she'd gone, and could even guess where.

"I'll find her, sir," he promised between clenched teeth.

Chapter Fifteen

Dawn had barely crept over Bhunapore when Ross rode through the silent gates of the British cantonment. He had not slept all night and his mood was foul as he pounded on the door of the Carlyons' house to summon the *chupprassi* from his bed.

No, yawned Lala Deen, scratching at his backside, there was no one home. His master, Carlyon-sahib, was still in Delhi. The entire family had gone with him. Surely the *huzoor* knew that?

"Yes, of course, but where is the miss-sahiba Maura?"

The *chupprassi* blinked. "Why, she is in Delhi too, *Huzoor*. Where else would she be?"

"Fetch her ayah," Ross ordered, stepping past him into the hall.

Meera came a moment later, pale and out of breath. "What is it, Sahib? What has happened to the child?"

"I came to ask the same of you. Where is she?"

Meera shook her head. Ross switched to Hindustani. "Thy mistress. I believe she returned to the Residency last night?"

"*Nahin*, Sahib. There is no one here. Only the servants."

Behind her the *chupprassi* nodded vigorously. "As I said, *Huzoor*, we are alone. The family is still in Delhi."

Meera motioned him to be quiet. "What has happened, Sahib?"

Ross rubbed a hand wearily across his eyes. "I'm not certain now. She left Delhi sometime yesterday. I thought she was headed here."

He explained briefly while Meera wrung her hands and implored the gods for mercy. "Lala Deen speaks the truth," she assured him. "We have seen nothing of her since she left with her family."

"Bloody hell!" Ross cracked his riding whip against his gloved hand. "Then where on earth am I to start looking?"

Slamming out of the house, he swung himself onto the back of his exhausted horse.

"Sahib!"

Ross turned impatiently. Meera came running across the lawn, the end of her sari flapping. Breathless, she caught at his stirrup. "There is a place where thou couldst begin thy search. Dost thou know Mohammed Hadji?"

"That fat merchantman? What could he possibly tell me?"

"I am not certain." Meera looked troubled. "But I know that Maura-sahiba has visited him from time to time. Always alone."

Ross's face darkened. "She went alone into the city?"

"Many times, before Ismail Khan became her syce. And after."

"And always to see Mohammed Hadji?"

"I asked her once if she went elsewhere, but she refused to say. She is close to my heart, Sahib, but there are many things she will not tell me. Secrets she keeps for my sake, she says, not hers."

"Now why doesn't that surprise me?" Ross muttered in English.

"I have a cousin who sells trinkets in the bazaar. He has seen her visiting with Mohammed Hadji's wives. Not so often now as in the beginning, but perhaps it will be enough?"

"It's a start," Ross agreed, although he didn't look too hopeful.

Without bothering to stop at his bungalow, although he would have dearly liked to eat and change his dusty clothes, he rode the distance to Bhunapore at a punishing pace. The sun was up by the time he reached the outer gates of the city, and in the bazaar the merchants were busy setting up their wares. Mohammed Hadji was not among them.

"He has gone to Rajasthan," someone said, "to attend the wedding of a favored nephew."

"How long ago?" Ross demanded.

No one could quite agree, though the consensus seemed to hover around a week.

Ross's increasingly black expression prompted someone to suggest that he inquire at the house of Walid Ali, who was a distant cousin of the Mohammedan merchant. Perhaps he would know more.

Until that point Ross had completely forgotten about the family connection between the two men. Now he left his horse tethered near the trinket seller's stall and crossed quickly to the alley where

241

the garden of the pink stucco palace flanked the square.

Someone was just exiting through the gate as Ross approached and he stepped aside to await him. "Ohé, Father," he said in Hindustani, expecting the *chowkidar*, "thou art abroad early."

But it was not the elderly gatekeeper employed by Walid Ali. Moving out of the shadows of the overhanging vines at the sound of Ross's voice, the fellow revealed himself to be considerably younger and larger, a beefy man sporting a dark, grizzled beard which complemented his swarthy complexion.

"What in bloody hell are *you* doing here?" Ross exploded.

Ismail Khan cocked his turbanned head and grinned. "We meet again, *Huzoor*."

The last time had been a chance encounter on the Sinda Bhat road, Ross recalled. But what was the Pathan doing here in Walid Ali's garden?

"This is where I come from," Ismail Khan explained, sounding surprised that Ross didn't know.

"I don't understand." Ross, too, had switched to Hindustani. "What does this mean: where thou art from?"

"Assuredly the matter is simple, *Huzoor*. Before I went to work for the sahib-*log* I earned my salt at the table of the Begum. Now that the Carlyons have gone to Delhi, I have returned here."

"How can that be? I've known the master of this house for years. I've never seen thee here."

Ismail Khan laughed. "Is that so strange? Surely the sahib knows that the Begum maintains a household separate from her husband's?"

This was true, and such were the ways of intrigue in large Indian households that one member of a family didn't always know what the others were up to. But still . . .

"My services were a gift to the Begum, presented by my former master in Gwalior shortly before the Adams-sahiba's arrival in India," Ismail Khan added helpfully.

"And how didst thou find thy way into the services of the Adams-sahiba?"

The big shoulders lifted. "The Begum made a gift of me to her in turn."

There was a long moment of silence. Then Ross said slowly, "Dost thou mean to say that the Begum knows thy mistress? That the two of them are acquainted?"

Ismail Khan nodded impatiently, as though this was the most obvious thing in the world.

"And the Begum was the one who placed thee in the service of the *Angrezi* miss?"

The big Pathan nodded.

"But why?"

"Hai mai!" exclaimed Ismail Khan, throwing up his hands. "This I cannot understand! To protect her from the attentions of the very sahib she now sees fit to wed! *Beshak!*" He added almost mournfully, "assuredly the ways of the sahib-*log* are strange!"

"I will speak to the sahib now, Ismail," a soft voice said from behind the gate. "Bring him hither."

Ismail Khan salaamed deeply to the woman framed in the doorway of the garden. She was covered from head to toe in a flowing bourka and only her dark eyes were visible through a slit made especially for that purpose.

"I was taking the morning air on the upper terrace," she explained to Ross, her soft voice muffled by the heavy folds, "and heard thee below. Is it thy wish to speak with me?"

"If the Begum Sahiba would so honor me, yes."

"Come," she said, and motioned him into the garden. "Ismail Khan will see to thy horse." She led him down a neatly raked path and through a painted gate overhung with vines, which she motioned him to lock behind them.

Ross did so, then turned to find himself in a private bower encircled by flowering shrubs that gave off a heady perfume. Kushna Dev had seated herself on a bench but did not draw back the hood of the bourka. Though she often bared her face to this man, her husband's oldest friend, in the privacy of the zenana, she was not about to do so here, where there was a chance that one of the gardeners or other male attendants might see her.

"Thou hast been speaking with Ismail Khan," she said as Ross began pacing the length of the bower, his manner distracted and angry.

He stared at her hard. "Who told me something I find impossible to believe. Is it true that he was a gift from thee to the niece of the British Resident?"

Kushna Begum gave a low laugh. "Is this so unusual, Hamilton-sahib?"

"Yes," he said curtly, "it is."

"Why, when we are friends?"

"Friends?"

Ross looked so astonished that she went on in a rush, "Aye, and as such I confess I have worried for her these three weeks past. Perhaps I was wrong in not sending Ismail Khan onward to Delhi when she returned him to me, but I did not wish to interfere. Not in the lives of Carlyon-sahib's family." She stared down at her hands, the slim tips of which were visible beneath the bourka's flowing sleeves. "It is said she will wear white for her *shadi*."

"British *mem* always wear white when they marry."

"But white is the color of death!"

"I do not think she will marry Burton-Pascal-sahib now," Ross said quietly.

Kushna Dev gave him a probing look. "How dost thou know this?"

"Because she fled Delhi last night exactly for that reason."

"*Shabash!*" the Indian girl exclaimed, clapping her hands and laughing as though a great weight had been lifted from her shoulders. "I had so hoped—"

"What dost thou know of her engagement?" Ross asked sharply.

"Only that she had no wish to marry that sahib from the very first."

"And how didst thou discover this?" Ross asked slowly.

Kushna Dev obligingly related the tale of how she had first met Maura after the English girl had fled Burton-Pascal-sahib in the Bhunapore bazaar. She told him how insistent Maura had been in not wanting to encourage the man's attentions, and that she had never had any intention of allowing him—or anyone else—to press his suit.

"Then why in God's name did she see fit to accept his offer in the end?" Ross demanded, tight-lipped.

"Perhaps she changed her mind," said Kushna Dev, though it was obvious that she herself did not believe this. "But now at least the tale of Ismail Khan is known to thee. This is his home. When the wife of Carlyon-sahib did not wish him to accompany the family to Delhi, of course he came here."

"Maura never told me this tale."

"Is that so strange?"

"No," Ross said softly. Not when one considered that he had never done anything to encourage Maura's confidence. Quite the opposite! In denying his own feelings for her he had kept her at arm's length, been brusque and unkind, and treated her with constant anger and impatience. Small wonder she had refused to tell him anything at all!

Turning his back on the Begum, he thrust his hands into his pockets and said nothing for a very long time, watching the petals fall at his feet and dust the floor of the bower in fragrant white. There was much he would have given to know, and much he would have liked to ask, but he did not.

"I gave her the protection of Ismail Khan because I knew he could be trusted to watch over her," Kushna Dev said at last, addressing Ross's broad back. "But her family saw fit to send him away. I do not like it, Hamilton-sahib. Who will watch over her now?"

Ross said nothing.

"Thou art searching for her." Kushna Dev spoke carefully, stepping nearer so that she could peer into his stony face. "For Carlyon-sahib's sake, or thine own?"

"Her people are afraid for her."

"And thee?"

"It is not my place," Ross said woodenly.

"I see."

Silence. From above them came the droning of bees. The clatter of pots and pans and women's voices drifted from the kitchens. A baby wailed. The household was stirring.

"I must go," Ross said at last.

"Where?"

"I do not know yet."

His tone made Kushna Dev look away. When she

sketched him a wordless farewell with her hands,
Ross thought he saw the glimmer of tears in her
dark eyes. Then she slipped through the unlocked
gate and he heard the soft slap of her slippers fading
on the path.

Ismail Khan was still waiting where Ross had left
him. Taking one look at Ross's face the Pathan did
not speak, only stepped aside, salaaming.

"Thou wilt tell me if word of her reaches thee?"
Ross demanded.

Ismail Khan's eyes slid past him, but Ross was
pulling on his gloves and so didn't notice. "Assuredly."

"I will ask again at the bazaar, and then in Sundagunj. If I have no luck there I shall return to Delhi.
Thou canst leave word at my bungalow until then."

Ismail Khan made another deep obeisance, then
stood watching, motionless, as Ross strode away.

Barely two hours earlier, the crowing of a cock
had heralded the arrival of morning in Walid Ali's
pink stucco palace. From the bed in which she lay
Maura had turned her head and seen the paling of
the light beyond the arching windows. Soon the
smell of cooking and the chatter of women would
drift from the courtyards below, she knew, but for
now there was only silence.

She had lain there for a long time without moving. The zenana was cool and still. She had slept
deeply, in utter exhaustion, during the few hours
that had remained of the previous night. How kind
Kushna Dev had been to take her in! Weary, dusty,
and reeling from thirst, Maura had been whisked
away upon her arrival to be bathed and fed and put
quickly to bed. Kushna Dev had asked no questions,
only murmured soothingly as she personally led

Maura to a private bedchamber close to her own and promised that she would not be disturbed until morning.

Maura had slept and slept, awakening only briefly to the crowing of that cockerel. Now, as Ross Hamilton rode away from the house, and with the smell of cooking fires filling the air, she awoke for a second time.

I can stay here as long as I wish, was the first thought that occurred to her, and she smiled, filled with a sense of comfort and well-being. Kushna Dev had promised her as much the night before, and it was wonderful to dream of hiding away forever in the perfumed zenana, surrounded by friendly women and cooing babies, with no demands placed upon her by anyone.

I could read books, Maura thought, and play chess and study Pushtu, which is Ismail Khan's native tongue. I could raise exotic birds, as does Kushna Dev's mother-in-law, and forget I ever heard of anyone named Charles Burton-Pascal.

She shuddered as she thought of him, wondering if she would ever be able to banish his hated image from her mind. Would she ever forget the way he had appeared before her when she and Ross had arrived unannounced at his house, reeling from alcohol and the effects of drugs, aroused at the thought of sharing his bed with both his betrothed and his Indian whore?

Her eyes filled with furious tears. How could she have been so ignorant? Not realized from the very first what sort of man he really was? Then again, no one, not even his close friend Terence Shadwell, had suspected that Charles partook of hashish and kept a slatternly mistress in such dissipated Indian fashion!

Nobody knows even now, she thought. No one except Ross.

Ross. She closed her eyes and swallowed convulsively. She'd seen Ross angry before, of course, but not as angry as he'd been yesterday afternoon. Why, the heat of it had nearly flailed her as he drove her home, and she had taken one look into his face and known better than to speak. . . .

I mustn't think of him either, she thought desperately. Never again.

She was simply too humiliated, too hurt and ashamed.

Self-pitying tears stung her eyes but she dashed them fiercely away. She would have to let her aunt and uncle know where she was, of course, but not yet. Not until she stopped hurting like this. Though she regretted the worry and pain she must be causing them, she couldn't bear to face them just yet.

"Not now," she whispered aloud. "Not yet."

At the sound of her voice there was a stirring beyond her bed and the two maids who had assisted her the night before were there, smiling and salaaming and asking what she required.

"Tiffin," Maura responded, smiling back. "Breakfast, and water to drink, please. Lots of it."

Later, dressed in a pair of pyjama pants, an embroidered *choli* and a pale blue veil with silver trim, she joined Kushna Dev and the others in the great reception hall. Everyone was delighted to see her. No one posed questions or seemed to expect an explanation as to why she had appeared on their doorstep in the middle of the night.

Maura knew better than to tell them the truth, even if she had been willing to talk about it, which she wasn't. Last night she had merely told Kushna Dev that she had left Delhi in order to flee her be-

249

trothed, whom she could no longer abide. Kushna Dev had accepted this, and so apparently had the others. Maura knew that none of them, not even Kushna Dev, would have understood her horror and disgust at Charles's behavior yesterday, for it was not uncommon among the menfolk of some Indian households to behave in similar fashion. From infancy, the zenana women had been raised to ignore, and even tolerate and accept, the dissolute ways of their men.

But I am English, Maura thought. I don't have to put up with it. And I won't.

Not that it mattered. No one seemed to care what, exactly, had driven her to run away. It was clear to everyone that the Little Pearl had suffered some sort of heartache in connection with her betrothal, and that was enough. She was welcome to stay until she recovered, however long her heartache lasted. All agreed that she had been right to come to them.

It was only later in the day, when most of the women were occupied with other tasks, that Kushna Dev sought a private audience with Maura and informed her of Ross's visit early that morning.

"Do not look so!" she added hastily. "I did not tell him thou wast here, nor did Ismail Khan. We both behaved as if we had only just learned of thy disappearance. After all, I did not know then exactly what had driven thee from Delhi, and so could not be sure that he himself was not responsible."

"No," said Maura in a small voice. "He has done naught." She looked up. "Did my uncle send him here?"

"He did not say. But I am thinking he came of his own volition. That someone in the bazaar sent him hither."

"He didn't ask if I was here?"

"I think he expected me to tell him if that had been the case. When I did not, he said only that Ismail Khan should bring any word of thee to his bungalow."

"He'll be back," Maura said with certainty. "You know how stubborn he can be."

"Hai mai! So many times he came here asking for the little pearl who was my cousin from Rajasthan," Kushna Dev agreed. Her expression softened as she looked into her friend's unhappy face. "Thou hast never told him?"

"No."

"I believe he suffers," Kushna Dev said, toying with her veil.

"Not because of me."

"Art thou certain?"

Maura's chin tipped.

Kushna Dev added carefully, "Today in the garden, he was as a tiger caged. I think his duty is not to thy *cha-cha*, thy uncle, alone."

"He is always gruff and impatient." Maura's voice dropped to a whisper. "Especially with me."

"Sinta Dai never claimed so."

Maura sprang to her feet, but Kushna Dev pulled her back with surprising strength. *"Ohé*, perhaps that was the wrong thing to say! But know that he has not chosen her, not once in many months!"

Maura went still. "He—he hasn't?"

"Nahin, Little Pearl. When he comes, it is thee he asks for."

"Not me." Maura scowled fiercely. "Thy Rajasthan cousin, who does not even exist! And while I am grateful for thy silence with him today, is there reason now to discuss him further?"

Kushna Dev sighed and rose to her feet. "We will speak of him no more. Thou art weary still. Rest now. The soothsayer is expected tonight. Thou wilt, I think, enjoy the diversion."

She kissed Maura's cheek and withdrew, though she lingered in the doorway long enough to see the English girl scrub a furtive hand over her eyes. Biting her lip, she wandered down the corridor, scowling as if undecided about something. Then all at once she clapped her hands. Instantly a serving girl knelt at her feet.

"Summon Ismail Khan. I wish to speak with him at once."

.

Chapter Sixteen

"Pull!"

A clay pigeon hurtled into the sky. Gunfire erupted as it shattered into dust. Applause rippled through the audience of brightly attired women watching from the zenana balcony. Down in the garden Kushna Dev's young sister Sita squealed with delight. "Again, again!"

Smiling, Maura handed the musket to Ismail Khan for reloading. Then, settling the weapon onto her shoulder, she sighted carefully.

"Pull!"

The servant obeyed and again the clay pigeon fragmented with a puff of exploding powder. Ismail Khan grunted his approval while Sita hurried off to gather the remnants as souvenirs.

"A strange sport," Kushna Dev remarked as the women withdrew to their rooms for refreshment now that the exhibition was over.

"Very popular in Britain." Maura handed the musket to Ismail Khan and dusted off her clothing. The skeet shooter and box of clay pigeons had been purchased in the bazaar several days ago by one of Walid Ali's nephews, who had not known at the time what it was for. Since no one else in the household had been able to clear up the mystery, the box had been shown to Maura. Upon learning that these were the implements of a strange *Angrezi* sport, the women had hounded Maura with requests for a demonstration.

Maura had been only too happy to oblige, for the last time she had shot skeet—an admittedly unladylike pursuit—had been on the Norfolk fens with Lawrence Carlyon's gamekeepers. She wasn't sure now who had enjoyed the exhibition more: the servants who loaded and launched the skeets, the women watching from the balconies, or Maura herself.

At any rate, everyone had benefited from the diversion. Walid Ali was away on an extended visit to the south along with his uncles and brothers, and his household always tended to languish whenever he was gone. Thanks to the *Angrezi* sport, they had all managed to fill another long, hot evening, Maura's fifth in their company.

"Perhaps thou wilt teach me this?" Sita asked now, joining them with her arms filled with clay fragments. Dropping them onto the bench, she took the Brown Bess musket from Ismail Khan and experimentally sighted down the barrel.

Maura laughed, for the slim Indian girl could barely lift the heavy weapon to her shoulder. Lord knows where Walid Ali had come by the rusty old thing. "Perhaps."

"In return I will take thee to the palace of Nasir

al-Mirza Shah and teach thee to ride an elephant," Sita offered grandly.

"Hast thou ridden elephants?" Maura asked indulgently.

Sita nodded proudly. "I am better with them than any mahout."

"Thou wilt be married in two months' time," Kushna Dev reminded her gently. "There will be too much to do preparing for thy wedding."

Sita made a face. Even though she was nearly thirteen she was not in the least bit interested in marriage. "That aged princeling! I'd sooner wed a monkey!"

Kushna Dev shook her head as her sister ran off down the path. "I have allowed her too much freedom since our mother died. Come, we will dine and lament as we do over the ingratitude of the young."

"Very well," Maura agreed, smiling.

Arm in arm they strolled back to the house.

After dinner and a bath, Maura allowed herself to be annointed with fragrant oils and sat quietly while her hair was braided before dressing in the gossamer silks that had become part and parcel of her Indian wardrobe. A long, leisurely evening of gossip, games and tapestry needlework awaited her, but for the first time since her arrival she felt a twinge of rebellion at the thought.

Could this mean that she was beginning to feel a little like her old self once again?

"I hope so," Kushna Dev said when Maura confessed as much when they met in the reception hall a few minutes later.

"I hope not," Maura countered at the very same time.

They both laughed, lightly and affectionately.

"One game of *shatranj*," Kushna Dev wheedled,

Ellen Tanner Marsh

"then thou art free. Perhaps this . . . skeet? Yes, this skeet shooting has set thy British blood flowing once again."

"Heaven forbid," Maura said with a rueful laugh.

In the capacious reception hall of the zenana the oil lamps glowed. Darkness had fallen outside and a hot breeze stirred the silken hangings. In a few more weeks the heat of summer would close fully upon the land and life would grow intolerable for those living in Bhunapore.

Aunt Daphne and Lydia were probably on their way back from Delhi by now. Soon they would start making plans to withdraw to Simla along with the other ladies of the cantonment.

Maura's heart squeezed at the thought. She had managed until now to push the image of her family completely from her mind. After all, Kushna Dev had dispatched a servant to Delhi the morning after her arrival with a note handwritten by Maura assuring her uncle that she was well. There was no need to start worrying about them now.

Nevertheless, she lost badly at *shartranj*. Couldn't seem to take her usual pleasure in dandling a black-eyed, gurgling infant on her lap. The astrologer who came to perform magic tricks and predict the future did not delight her as he did the others.

Kushna Dev took pity on her at last. "I will send to Delhi for news tomorrow. Then we will hear how thy family fares. Perhaps they are preparing a return to the Residency."

Yes, Maura thought. News from Delhi would be welcome. Surely it would help to calm her growing restlessness.

"In the meantime, take a turn in the garden. Always thou art in far more need of movement than we. And tomorrow, before daylight, I will lend thee a horse from my husband's stable. Surely a ride across the plains will settle thee as well."

Maura rose and kissed her cheek. "Thou art kind, and wise."

No, Kushna Dev thought, watching her leave the room. Only young enough to remember how my heart, too, quailed with misery until Walid Ali finally assured me of his love.

She sighed and bent her head over the text she was reading. Two days had passed since she had dispatched Ismail Khan to Hamilton-sahib's bungalow with a carefully worded missive. Why had he not come? Had she perhaps misjudged him? Done wrong in summoning him?

Hai mai, the Begum thought, assuredly the path of love is strewn with many stones.

A bone white moon was rising in the sky, silvering the exotic flowers in Walid Ali's garden. The hot wind brought with it the distant beating of tom-toms. Maura was glad for the loose, flowing, silk pyjama pants she wore, for the warmth of the night would have been uncomfortable otherwise. She wondered how she would ever tolerate heavy Western attire again once she returned to her uncle's house.

Provided her aunt and uncle would welcome her back.

The thought struck her quite without warning.

"I did not think . . ." Maura whispered aloud. "I always assumed they would . . ."

More restless now than ever, she paced the tended walks with her hands clasped, her face pale. No one would dream of blaming the Carlyons if they were to cast their niece from their house in disgrace. After all, look how she had chosen to repay their kindness! Indeed, they might never forgive her for causing such a scandal by disappearing the way she had!

"I can't bear it," she whispered. "I have to go back. I must!"

Up ahead she saw the *chowkidar* opening the gate that lead to Bhunapore's now-deserted market square. She moved closer, curious. There was the sound of voices and then the *chowkidar* stepped aside to let someone in, a tall man who turned his head as the *chowkidar* gestured in Maura's direction.

Ross.

Maura gasped and turned to flee, but it was too late. Ross had already made a polite obeisance to the elderly watchman and was crossing toward her with a purposeful stride. He was dressed for riding and his breeches and boots were dusty, as though he had ridden in haste. His dark curls were windblown, and she watched as he raked his hands impatiently through them. The gesture was so familiar, so dear, that the will to flee simply drained from her heart.

"Forgive me," he said in rueful Hindustani. "I am not exactly prepared to be received. I was on my way back from the Peacock Palace when I was told that someone had been shooting weapons here in this garden earlier today. *Angrezi* weapons, no less. Naturally it is my duty as the Resident's adjutant to investigate. The *chowkidar* told me there was a lady in the garden and would not let me in, but I insisted. I had no idea it would be thee, that thou wert back from Rajasthan."

Those stupid skeets! Maura could have screamed aloud. She should have realized that they would draw the attention of the British population! Oh, why hadn't she left the bloody things alone?

Too late, too late!

With supreme effort she willed her racing heart-beat to slow. This wasn't the time to panic. The damage was done. Ross's presence was far more pressing than anything else.

At least she could take comfort in the fact that he hadn't recognized her; that nothing in his demeanor suggested he didn't still believe her to be Kushna Dev's cousin from Rajasthan.

Realizing as much, Maura unclasped her hands and breathed a little easier. Maybe, just maybe, she would survive this awful turn of events. If she could lure Ross into the reception hall she might be able to hand him over to Kushna Dev, who would know how to get rid of him quickly.

Taking a deep, steadying breath she touched his arm. "Thou art weary, Sahib, and in need of refreshment. Come, I will take thee to the Begum."

"If I may speak with thee privately first?"

The urge to refuse screamed through her. She forced herself to speak calmly. "The hour is late, Sahib."

"It will take but a moment."

She could think of no reason to refuse. Silently, unwillingly, she seated herself on a nearby bench. She must not let him know how wildly her heart was hammering. She had been this man's lover once. He would think her behavior odd if she showed signs of fear or nervousness now.

To her dismay Ross didn't seem to be in any hurry.

Seating himself beside her he fumbled in his breast pocket for a cigarette, then grimaced when he realized he had none. Leaning back, he studied her averted face in what seemed to Maura a far too leisurely fashion.

"I came often to inquire after thee following the durbar at the Peacock Palace," he said at last.

She inclined her head to acknowledge this. The less she spoke, the less chance that he would recognize her, she hoped.

"What brings thee back to Rajasthan?"

Maura thought quickly. "Sita's wedding."

"Ah, yes. But that is two months hence, and will take place far from here. I had thought . . . nay, I had hoped, that thy return to Bhunapore might have something to do with me."

Maura caught her lower lip between her teeth. What on earth was she supposed to say in response to that? At any other time her heart would have rejoiced to find Ross flirting with her, showing interest in her, speaking to her gently. But all she wanted to do at the moment was flee into the darkness, even though she knew that a well-reared Indian lady simply did not turn heel and run from a man.

Besides, she didn't think she'd get very far. For a man his size, Ross was damnably fast and she couldn't risk having him catch her by snatching at the trailing end of her veil and perhaps pulling it from her face.

That appalling thought alone kept her rooted to the bench. "I have . . . thought of thee on occasion," she confessed in an offhand tone.

"And I of thee. More than occasionally."

Maura remained silent, her face averted. The *chowkidar* had left the garden and now all was silent around them. Only the palm fronds rustled softly in the breeze.

"Little Pearl, canst thou not look at me?"

She shook her head.

"Dost thou regret what happened between us on the night of the durbar?"

Oh, how desperately she longed to lie, but she could not. By all that was holy, she could not. Instead she gave a small, sad shake of her head.

Ross shifted on the bench and before she knew what he intended he had taken her face in his hands. Tipping her chin he looked deeply into her eyes. "I want thee to know that I have thought of little else since then."

Her heart swelled with a joy that was sharpened by pain. No one had to tell her that the depth of emotion that lay behind this man's voice, that burned in his eyes, was genuine. He cared, cared deeply.

But not for her. For the Indian girl, Chota Moti.

She would have wrenched herself away, but found that she could not move. Her bones had turned to water.

"Little Pearl," he whispered, leaning closer. His nearness overwhelmed her, his rough voice made the world no longer solid beneath her feet. "Wilt thou not kiss me as thou didst once before?"

Where was the harm in it? her heart cried out. One last time. Only once. Surely she would never see Ross again once her uncle banished her from his home, from Bhunapore, perhaps from India!

He was still holding her face in his hands. With her own hands not quite steady, she reached up to clasp his wrists.

"One kiss," she whispered, "but then I must go. And thine eyes must not look upon me."

His thumbs stroked her cheeks through the filmy veil. "Very well. I give thee my word."

Only when his eyes were closed did she lift the veil aside.

One kiss. Only one.

Their lips touched, gently at first, as though nei-

261

ther was certain what to expect. Then Ross's head dipped and the contours of his mouth changed.

Instantly the kiss changed too. Pain and anger slid away as his tongue grazed hers. Maura gasped, then sighed while memory ignited like a clamorous rush in their hearts.

Without lifting his mouth from hers, Ross dragged her onto his lap. Cradling her head in the crook of his arm he bent her back like a flower. The kiss deepened as his mouth moved in a hot demand of lips and tongue and teeth.

"I have thought of naught but this." His voice grated, raw with need.

"Nor have I."

He groaned at that and his hand dropped to her ribcage, his fingers splaying to cup the fullness of her breast. When his thumb grazed the sensitive nipple through its thin layer of silk, Maura gasped and jerked against him.

"Oh, God—" Dragging his mouth from hers, he trailed a heated path of kisses to her collarbone. His dark head dipped and his hands moved again. No stranger to the intricacies of Eastern attire, he skillfully parted the trailing ends of her veil and pushed aside her embroidered vest.

Maura's head fell back as he found and laved the bared, budding nipple with his tongue. Her fingers threaded through his hair as she arched against him, her heart clamoring.

With tongue and teeth he savored the other breast, branding her with heat. Then he lifted his head and claimed her mouth again with an urgency that told her he was starved for its taste and sweetness.

"Little Pearl, surely thou must know—"

But he didn't finish what he meant to say. Instead

he swallowed hard and rose to his feet, still holding her in his arms. When she opened her eyes to look at him he let her slip slowly, oh so slowly, to the ground. Her body cleaved to his on the way down, her lovely, silk-clad curves fusing to muscles of steel, until she was standing on her toes between his thighs, the heat of his maleness straining against her very center.

Her head tipped back and her breasts rose and fell to the heated rhythm of her breathing. With feral eyes Ross watched desire transform her features as he cupped her buttocks and kept her joined to him, moving his hips to let her know how much he wanted her, ached for her.

But simply to mimic the act of mating pushed him dangerously close to the breaking point. He shuddered, aware that he could wait no longer.

Looking deeply into her eyes, he lifted her against him and lowered her to the ground. Leaning over her, he stripped away her clothing so that the warm night air caressed her burning skin and the grass made a lush bed beneath her.

"Little Pearl," he whispered again, his voice ragged. He could not seem to say her name enough, as though the endearment held a magic all its own.

Her smile was dazzling as she reached up to ease his shirt from his shoulders and press her lips to his chest, entranced by the difference in his hard man's body and her own. Ross shuddered in response and she felt the heady joy of knowing how vulnerable she could make him with just a kiss, a touch. And touch him she did, removing the rest of his clothes while he turned obligingly, always with his mouth fused to hers, telling her in a raw whisper what it meant to have her touch him here, caress him there.

When he was naked and holding himself above

her with strong arms propped on either side of her head, she took him at last into her hand. Shuddering in response he turned his face into the curve of her neck while she stroked and worshipped and learned once again the power of being a woman.

"Little Pearl, thou hast enslaved me." His voice was rough with arousal.

"Because thou hast taught me so well, Sahib." Her lips left a trail of fire down his chest while he shifted above her to accommodate.

"Have a care," he warned as she paused and lifted her face to his, "lest I gaze upon thy features. Or might I hope that this is no longer forbidden?"

"It is still forbidden," she said quickly, though she wondered why he sounded so amused.

He didn't give her the chance to ask. Hooking his heel around her leg he brought her back beneath him. Now it was his turn to show her how the touch of a man's mouth and lips and hands could make a woman ache, could bring her hard and fast to that breathless edge where pain and pleasure meet.

He brought her there swiftly, and knew exactly when to leave her, gasping and writhing at that poignant point of fulfillment. Even as her eyelids grew heavy and her hands fell away from him he reared up and placed himself against her.

"Oh—" Her eyes opened wide.

Trembling, he laced his fingers through hers and pressed the backs of her hands into the grass. Then slowly, silkily, he slipped inside to fill her completely. His mouth fitted to hers while his body did the same, stroking in and out in a slow, seductive rhythm.

"Ross," she whispered, "oh, Ross," and did not know that she spoke his name in English.

Nor did he. And even if he had he would not have

cared. Already the first shudders of fullfillment were wracking him, pushing him to the breaking point. Clenching his teeth he moved against her, taking her savagely now, and swiftly.

Maura clung to him, and in the very moment of breathless gathering before he came, he felt her arch beneath him and sob out in bliss.

With a hoarse cry he surged against her, his eyes closed, feeling her tighten around him. Joined together, he spilled himself inside her.

Sweet, sweet recompense. The balm of every heartache. How could she possibly be unhappy after this? How could life seem wretched any longer? If there was any hope, any promise of an unclouded future, then surely she would find it after what had happened here.

I will go home to the Residency tomorrow, she thought, and face whatever it is that Uncle Lawrence sees fit to do with me.

Gladly, after this.

With renewed hope, after this.

Beyond tomorrow loomed an uncertain future, but not as darkly as before. She would think of it later, for it was far, far sweeter to dwell on the here and now, with Ross's weight resting heavy upon her and lingering pleasure pulsing through both their veins.

After a long moment she stirred and sighed. In response his fingers threaded through her hair.

"Thou hast bewitched me, Little Pearl."

She smiled against the curve of his neck. "It is thy spell, Sahib, not mine."

Levering himself onto one elbow, he shook out her veil and gently arranged it about her face. Her heart turned over at the thoughtful gesture. Not until her features were covered did he peer into the dreamy violet of her eyes. "I think not. In my world, there is naught that compares with thee."

She stroked his jaw, deliberately following the path of her fingers with her eyes. "There is no one who has claimed the sahib's heart in this world of thine?"

He caught her hand and held it against his chest. "Other than thee? Nay, there is not."

Even as she tried to pull her hand away he tightened his grip, almost as though he had known that she would react with anger. "I cannot lie, *piari.*" Not while he lay above her, still joined to her in the aftermath of such soaring pleasure. "Thy world or mine, it is all the same."

Up swept her eyes to lock with his, snapping. "The sahib plays games." Her breath came harshly.

He released her at once. "Forgive me. I did not mean to cause pain."

No, he never did. But somehow it always ended up that way. He had made it clear just now that he cared nothing for the Englishwoman Maura Adams.

A lump as large as all India seemed to form in Maura's throat. Lifting her hands to push him away, she saw the spark of rebellion in his eyes. Oh, so he didn't want her to leave yet, did he? Well, he didn't have much of a choice. Because if he didn't get off of her this instant, she was going to blacken both of his eyes.

Fortunately the *chowkidar* announced his return at that moment with an audible cough and a great deal of rustling of the shrubs lining the path. Quickly Ross eased himself away from her. Maura had learned the intricate ways of Eastern dressing well by now, and she was on her feet and stepping into her slippers even as Ross was still tugging on his breeches.

"Hamilton-sahib."

Her voice was cold. He turned to her questioningly.

"It is perhaps wisest that we do not meet again."

He rose before her, shrugging into his shirt and fastening his belt. His eyes smoldered as he looked at her. "Certainly that cannot be thy wish."

"It is."

"Nay, that I will not believe."

Her chin tipped. "Then thou art a fool."

His voice was like a lash. "And if there should be a child from this coupling?"

Not too long ago the bluntness of such a question would have made her reel with shock. But she had lived among the women of the zenana long enough to take such matters in stride. Besides, she had worried enough about that the last time, after the durbar, when her monthly flux had been late and for several nightmarish days afterward she had been forced to confront that exact same likelihood.

Fortunately her fears had been unfounded then, and while there was always the chance she had conceived now, she refused to allow herself to succumb to worry. Surely Kushna Dev would take care of her should it be true?

"That is not unusual among the women of my people," she said with a very un-Eastern toss of her head. "I will manage."

"The child would be half-caste," Ross ground out. "Unacceptable to both our worlds."

"This, too, can be overcome."

He said nothing to that, only looked at her for a long moment with his mouth a thin, hard line. How well Maura knew that look by now! He was feeling

267

a great deal, inside, and doing his best to hide it.

"This is truly my wish," she repeated coldly.

To her surprise he didn't say anything hurtful or unkind. Instead he laid a very gentle hand upon her cheek. "Thou hast grown up quite a bit since last I saw thee."

Bitter tears misted Maura's eyes. How he must care for this woman, she thought, to speak to her so tenderly. Never, never had he used that tone with her.

The *chowkidar* was coming. They could hear him shuffling up the path.

"I must go!" Maura choked, but Ross's hand did not drop away from her cheek. Instead he lifted the other hand so that he could cup her face and turn it to his.

"Very well, I will heed thy wish. We will meet no more. But in one thing I stand firm. If anything should happen, if there should be a child, then thou must come to me."

"Sahib—"

"Beshak! Thy word on this."

She was shaken by his urgency and the way he was looking at her. As though he were commanding her to understand the import of his words simply by willing as much with the burning intensity of his eyes.

"Promise," he grated, holding her chin in his hand. "No matter where thou art, no matter in whose household. If there should be a child, my child, thou wilt come to me."

The *chowkidar* stepped into the moonlight behind them.

"Thy word!" Ross commanded. "No matter the circumstances! Little Pearl, dost thou understand this?"

She nodded mutely.

Almost growling, Ross released her. Bending to gather his riding gloves and whip, he made a low obeisance in her direction as was considered proper. Then, as Maura stood frozen, her heart trampled to ashes, he nodded likewise to the *chowk-idar* and vanished in the dark.

Chapter Seventeen

The following evening was hot, the sunset hazy with humidity. Dismounting in front of his bungalow after a scheduled tour of the district, Ross Hamilton found a messenger from the Residency waiting on the steps.

"He has been here an hour or more," said Ghoda Lal, appearing with the water flask.

Ross drank deeply, then stripped off his gloves. "Does Carlyon-sahib wish to see me?"

The messenger bobbed his head. "At once, *Huzoor*."

"I've just returned from Sundagunj. Tell him I shall need to bathe and dine first."

"But *Huzoor*, the summons are immediate. I was requested to stay until—"

"The miss-sahiba has returned," Ghoda Lal interrupted in an undertone.

Ross's head came up. "When?"

"Early this afternoon."

"Oh, for God's sake."

Dusty, weary, scowling, Ross presented himself immediately at the Residency. Without waiting for Lala Deen to announce him, he strode down the hall and into the parlor, and stood in the doorway for a moment looking at those within.

Whatever furor Maura's return had caused during his absence seemed to have given way to calm. In fact, the scene before him appeared as one of untroubled domestic harmony. Lawrence Carlyon sat in his favorite armchair sipping a rajah's peg while his wife read aloud to him from the *Calcutta Review*. Lydia was sitting beneath the window with her hand in Terence Shadwell's, their heads bent close together.

There was no sign of Maura.

Ross cleared his throat.

Immediately the calm shattered and all of them leapt to their feet.

"Ross!" Lawrence came forward, his tubby face reddened with pleasure.

"I've already heard, sir. She's all right, then?"

"Couldn't be better. A little tearful, of course, but under the circumstances—"

"We're ever so grateful to have her back," Daphne added, dabbing emotionally at her eyes.

"Tried to catch you earlier," Larwence went on, "but your bearer said you'd gone on inspection once again."

"I left early this morning." Ross looked from one smiling face to the other. "So where has she been all this time?"

"Lucknow," said Lydia.

"Lucknow!"

"Come, come." Lawrence thumped him on the

shoulder. "No need to look so startled, Ross. That's where she's from originally, right? I only wish I'd remembered it m'self, thought to send you there in search of her. We understand she stayed with old friends of her parents who kindly took her in."

"And all because she simply *had* to leave Delhi," Daphne quavered.

"There, there, Daffy." Lawrence went to her and patted her hand. "No need to cry."

"But I feel just awful for the poor dear!"

"We all do, Mama," Lydia added tearfully.

Ross couldn't help it; he lost his temper. "Will one of you please tell me what the devil happened? You're all acting as though someone has died!"

No one seemed at all shocked by his rudeness. Apparently emotional upheaval was the order of the day.

"But that's because someone did die," Aunt Daphne explained tremulously. "Charles's mother."

Ross feigned credible surprise. "Charles Burton-Pascal? Miss Adams's affianced?"

Aunt Daphne nodded. "Isn't it awful? Naturally he had to leave India immediately to settle the estate. It's quite involved, we understand, which means he won't be returning for at least a year, if at all. Do you know, he left so quickly that he didn't even bother telling anyone goodbye? Not even his own fiancée! Maura was devastated, and who can blame her?"

"She was s-so looking forward to our d-double wedding," Lydia added, crying openly by now. Immediately Terence was there to offer a manful arm for her to lean on while Ross whirled and paced to the window.

With his back to the assembly, as though overcome by emotion, he asked brusquely, "But why did she run away to Lucknow?"

"Come, boy, it's obvious, ain't it? Too upset to face the lot of us. Broken-hearted. Had to be alone. You know how temperamental the gel can be."

"Yes, sir, I do."

Daphne sniffled loudly. "I feel terrible for not being there to help her get over this dreadful turn."

"I daresay she'll mend," Ross said bracingly. He turned at last to face the British Resident, his expression collected, calm. "What will you do with her now?"

"Do? I—harrumph, well, to be honest, we haven't really discussed it."

"Nor will we," Daphne said firmly. "The girls and I are leaving for Simla next week as originally scheduled. Dear Maura will have all the time she needs to recover from her heartache there."

Lawrence nodded approvingly. "A few months in the mountains will do her a world of good."

They had no clue, Ross realized, as to the real reason why Maura had fled Delhi. Apparently they had accepted everything she had told them at face value, without digging into the matter. Perhaps that was just as well. Let their memories of Burton-Pascal be free from the horror of the truth.

The man had actually done them a favor by disappearing without a word. And since the Carlyons obviously bore their niece no ill will for having caused them so much worry, then it should prove easy enough for the family to put the episode in the past.

A fitting ending for everyone's sake. Truly the girl had the luck of the Irish!

And yet . . .

Lala Deen appeared in the doorway. The British

Residence's eyes lit. "Ah! Supper, is it? You'll join us, Ross?"

"I'm afraid not, sir. I'm not exactly dressed for the occasion."

"But Maura will be so disappointed!" Daphne protested.

"Where is she, by the way?"

"Resting. And perhaps we should let—"

"It's all right, Aunt Daphne, I'm here."

There was a stir as Maura appeared behind the *chupprassi.* No one could have been more solicitous than her family as they crowded around to receive her. Scowling, Ross had to admit that she did look unwell, with shadows beneath her magnificent eyes and the usual bloom gone from her cheeks.

As always, however, she looked heart-stoppingly beautiful. Her ayah had rolled her hair into a chignon appropriate for dining en famille and its glossy red color glowed in the lamplight. Even though the style lent touching dignity to her youthful features, Ross had to admit that he preferred her hair plaited, the way she had worn it at the zenana, with the thick red braid swinging well past her curving hips.

Oh, yes, he knew perfectly well how she had worn it beneath the veil she had adopted while living in the zenana of the pink stucco palace. And that was because he had known her identity even before he had seen her standing in Walid Ali's garden last night.

Although, to be honest, he never would have guessed her identity or found her on his own without the help of Kushna Dev . . .

After his meeting with the Begum in the garden that morning, Ross had ridden through the length and breadth of the city in a fruitless search for Maura. Aferward, when a similar search of Sundagunj had yielded naught, he had ridden all the way back to Delhi without bothering to eat or rest. Small wonder that his mood had been foul when he had arrived there; small wonder it had only worsened after learning from the now-frantic Lawrence Carlyon that Maura was still missing.

Unable to tolerate the tears of the women and the gloom that had settled over the Carrington household, he had quitted Delhi in a temper and ridden all the way back to his bungalow in Bhunapore only to find that Ismail Khan had been waiting there for him for well over twenty-four hours. Ghoda Lal had been waiting as well, vastly insulted that the Pathan had refused to entrust him with the note Kushna Dev had written, but Ross had understood why Ismail Khan had preferred to deliver it into his own hand the moment he had read it.

The fact that Maura had been present in the zenana all along had filled him with raging fury. Small wonder both the Begum and Ismail Khan had seemed so distracted that morning! In fact, a great many things had suddenly become clear to Ross that had bewildered him before.

In her letter, Kushna Dev had urged him to show restraint, to wait until he had gotten his anger under control before returning to the zenana to confront Maura. Her request had further fanned Ross's simmering temper, but after he had sent Ismail Khan on his way, after he had bathed, shaved and eaten, he had calmed himself sufficiently to see the wisdom of her plea.

It would not do for a sahib to cause a scene in the home of a Mohammedan lady, especially when the menfolk were not in residence. Ross had heard that Walid Ali was away, and he had spent the better part of the night that followed wondering how best to gain admission to the pink stucco palace while he was gone.

When reports of gunshots in the palace garden had reached the Residency not long afterward, he had gone immediately to investigate, this time with the authority of the British Raj behind him.

It bore repeating that he would have recognized Maura regardless of Kushna Dev's letter the moment he encountered the veiled beauty in Walid Ali's garden. Over the last few weeks he had come to know Maura well, and he would not have been guilty of mistaking her identity again. He had been livid with her at first, but by the time the *chowkidar* had left them and he had become aware of her own unhappiness, his heart had calmed considerably.

Obviously too much! By all that was holy, he had truly not intended to make love to her last night— or ever again! A willing Indian courtesan was one thing; the niece of the British Resident of Bhunapore, no matter her disguise, was another!

Only one kiss. They had given their word, he and Maura both. But desire and need had swept away their best intentions the moment their lips had met.

And in the end Maura had given herself to him, as sweetly, as trustingly, as that first, magical time.

Did she love him?

Looking at her closely as he bowed over her hand, Ross could detect nothing save calm in those lovely, shadowed eyes. But Maura had always been a consummate actress; he knew that now. On the other hand, why should she feel the least bit tender toward him? He had certainly gone out of his way to fight his own feelings for her by being rude, distant and cold, and convincing himself that it was the mysterious Indian lady from Rajasthan who held him in her sway.

Did she love him?

Ross would have been surprised if she did. But he would have given much to know. Someday he would allow himself to go back over every smile, every word, every look she had ever exchanged with him, and interpret them in light of his awakened knowledge of her deception, but now was not the time.

Still, he brooded over the likelihood. He knew now, of course, that she had come to him a virgin that first time in the pleasure pavilion of the Peacock Palace. But not the last time . . .

Looking into her pale face, he was struck with the sudden, wrenching realization of what her wan and listless appearance might mean.

"Thou must come to me," he had commanded the silent Chota Moti, "no matter where thou art, no matter the circumstance."

Had she understood the actual meaning behind his words? That should she find herself in a family way, she must put aside her masquerade and come to him with the truth?

Of course she had. She must have!

Only, would she?

Perhaps if he were to tell her that he himself now knew the truth concerning her identity? But Kushna Dev had begged him not to, and he had heeded her wishes and been endlessly glad that he had . . .

"I understand you spent the last week in Lucknow, Miss Adams?"

He was not toying with her. For once in his life he honestly had no idea what to say.

Maura nodded without looking at him. "My family tells me you did much in the way of trying to find me, Captain. I am grateful. And very sorry for the inconvenience I caused you."

Ellen Tanner Marsh

"Grist in the mill of the service," he reminded her casually.

Where once those old, familiar words would have brought a smile, or at the very least a haughty toss of the head, she only withdrew her hand from his and moved away. Ross looked after her, frowning.

"She is not herself," Aunt Daphne whispered. "What do you think we should do with her?"

"Ross certainly ain't the one to ask," Lawrence protested, overhearing them.

"I confess I know little about the workings of a young lady's mind," Ross agreed curtly.

Or her heart . . .

Recalling that the family had been summoned to supper, he excused himself with a brief bow and did not wait for Lala Deen to show him out.

"Some things never change, do they?" Aunt Daphne asked, looking after him. "Come, dear." She took Maura by the arm. "Let's go in to supper. I confess you've grown thin as a rail."

And so began a difficult week for Maura despite the fact that her friends and family could not have been more supportive or kind. Even those matrons in the cantonment who might have been inclined to gloat over the disintegration of her engagement to wealthy Charles Burton-Pascal were genuinely moved by the girl's pale, listless appearance.

"Took the wind right out of her sails," Dr. Moore's sister pronounced, discussing the affair at tea several days later.

"I hadn't realized she was so deeply attached to him," murmured Mrs. Carrington-Smythe.

"Breaking off an engagement would floor anyone, especially a proud girl like Lawrence's niece," her husband guessed.

278

But as scandals went, this one was not particularly tragic. Because the Carlyons refused to make a fuss over the fact that their niece had run away to Lucknow without telling them, no one else thought to do so either. Calling at the Residency to express their sympathy and to welcome Daphne and her niece and daughter back into their midst was a sufficient gesture for the ladies of the cantonment. Memories faded quickly and by the end of the week Charles Burton-Pascal's name was rarely mentioned.

At any rate, the social season was winding down as the warmth of late May gave way to the breathless heat of June. Thoughts turned to the cool hills of Simla. Maura was no longer the center of everyone's attention, and for this she was intensely grateful.

It wasn't so much the questions and commiserations that had left her on the constant verge of screaming, it was the misery of returning home from the pink stucco palace to discover that nothing had changed in terms of her love for Ross Hamilton. She saw him almost daily at some function or another, or encountered him now and then going into or coming out of her uncle's office. Sometimes they spoke, more often they did not, and although he was always unfailingly polite, she could sense the distance he was deliberately keeping between them.

She had hoped, in her secret heart of hearts, that Ross might show some sign of awakened interest in her now that her engagement to Charles Burton-Pascal was officially ended. The fact that he was privy to the truth concerning her flight from Delhi should have brought them closer; instead, Ross saw fit never to mention that episode on those rare occasions when they did find themselves alone.

Maura eventually came to the agonized conclusion that Ross simply didn't care for her one way or the other. If he was in love with anyone, it was the fictitious cousin of the Begum Kushna Dev. No man who had held a woman, kissed her, murmured words of endearment as Ross had done that night could possibly be indifferent!

Every sleepless night Maura had spent since then (and there had been many) had been given over to fighting the desire to tell him the truth. But she was too proud for that. After all, had she truly been the woman Ross loved, he would have recognized her immediately from her voice, her touch, even—despite the darkness—the color of her eyes. He would not have been blinded by the allure of the mysterious "Little Pearl."

Bah! How Maura had come to hate that name! And how it galled her to realize that she was jealous of a woman who didn't exist, a woman who was, in actuality, her own self!

Confused, miserable, wretchedly in love, she found it difficult to sleep or eat or show a return of the spirit her family had once considered tiresome but now would gladly have welcomed back. At least she didn't have to worry that there was a baby on the way. That fear had been removed not a week after her return to the Residency, but this, too, only served to keep her pale and languishing, and made her aunt and uncle agree that a rapid removal to the hill country was in everyone's best interest.

And so it was that Ross, riding past the Residency gate a little after dawn one morning, came across a number of carts and wagons crowding the drive in front of the house. Bearers were scurrying about carrying bundles and boxes under the direction of Lala Deen, who stood importantly on the verandah consulting a sheaf of copious notes.

Reining in, Ross dismounted and clattered up the steps. "What's going on, Lala Deen?"

"The memsahib has decided to send her belongings to Simla today. The weather is considered auspicious for traveling."

"And the memsahib herself?"

"The family follows tomorrow."

They would be gone at least three months, if not more. Up in the shadows of the great Hindu Kush—the Himalayas—the weather would be cool, the society of fellow Englishmen gay, Ross knew. Lawrence Carlyon would not be going, nor would he. Pressures of work prevented as much, in particular the matter in Sundagunj, which was currently coming to a head.

Watching the stream of servants exiting the Residency with furniture and clothing and boxes of housewares, Ross scowled and fumbled in his breast pocket for a cigarette. He was tired and cross, for he had been up all night meeting with certain villagers and then, just before dawn, riding into Bhunapore to confer with Mohammed Hadji, the fat, placid merchantman who was a cousin of Walid Ali.

Unfortunately, the meeting had availed Ross nothing. The discussion had not involved Maura Adams; her name had not even been mentioned. Rather, Ross had hoped to come away with legitimate proof of a planned insurrection against the British residents of Bhunapore, for Mohammed Hadji could be counted on to know such things.

Instead the merchantman had merely repeated a string of bazaar gossip, harmless talk that Ross himself already knew. He had paid the fellow nonetheless and Mohammed Hadji had bowed and slunk away, and now Ross stood on the front steps of the

Residency thinking unpleasant thoughts and watching Lawrence Carlyon's servants loading the carts.

Damn these furtive Indians to hell! Why didn't one of the hundreds he'd confronted give him the information he sought? Surely there were plenty in the village who knew of the threats being whispered against the British Raj here in Bhunapore! Even the lowliest Untouchable had to know that that oily old scoundrel, Nasir al-Mirza Shah, was secretly conspiring to wrest control of his kingdom back from the British!

Not that the fellow stood a bloody chance in hell. His doddering army was ragtag and ancient, its weapons consisting of broken lances and rusty *jezails* left over from a former day and age. Furthermore, Ross knew perfectly well that few people in Bhunapore cared to see that thoroughly corrupt old despot return to power.

Nevertheless, those henchmen still loyal to Nasir al-Mirza Shah continued to harbor long-standing resentment toward the British and would drive them out of Bhunapore at all costs; never mind that their numbers were few and their cause virtually hopeless. They were fanatics, every last one of them, and Ross and Lawrence Carlyon had been working hard for the past six months to flush the discontented lot of vipers from their pits.

Ross's involvement in the land dispute between two of Sundagunj's powerful *talukdars* had been a cover, a tale that had been given out while he and Ghoda Lal worked secretly to search out and arrest the men responsible for preaching sedition. Only their intent was secret no longer, for Ghoda Lal would not have taken a knife through the arm otherwise, and Ross would not have been targeted for an ambush in the nullah below the Sundagunj bridge.

The threat of an insurrection had started several months before Maura's arrival in India with her cousin and aunt, when a Hindu holy man by the name of Lala Ram Mahim had begun campaigning aloud against the British Raj in the villages and exhorting others to join him in revolution. He had not succeeded in rousing many to his cause, but those few who had joined his ranks had been bazaar scum, thieves and murderers, dangerous radicals whom Lawrence Carlyon had wished to bring speedily to trial.

Ross had already succeeded in having one or two of them arrested, most notably the hot-headed son of a wealthy Sundagunj landowner considered loyal to the Raj. But Lala Ram Mahim himself had eluded him, and Ross was grimly certain that it was he who had given the order to ambush Ghoda Lal as his bearer sat alone on a deserted stretch of the river waiting to shoot a man-eating *mugger*.

Now, weeks later, a reliable source had finally revealed that someone in the house of Walid Ali was linked to the planned uprising. But Ross had been unable as yet to come up with specific names. Walid Ali, affable and uncaring, had promptly dismissed his English friend's concerns, which was why Ross had reluctantly gone to his foolish cousin Mohammed Hadji in the hopes that the man might know something more.

Fat lot of good that had done him! Scowling, Ross ground out the cigarette beneath his heel. At least he could be heartened by the fact that Maura and her aunt and cousin were leaving for Simla tomorrow. Neither he nor Lawrence Carlyon considered the women in any danger, but still it would be a relief to have them out of the way.

No more distractions, Ross thought gratefully. And as for the immediate future, he might as well return home and sleep away what was left of the few hours before he was expected to appear at the Residency office.

"Captain Hamilton."

Maura, dressed for riding in her powder-blue habit, had stepped out onto the verandah behind him. She looked fresh and lovely, a soothing contrast to the dust and heat of the approaching morning.

Ross scowled at her as was his usual way. "Good morning, Miss Adams. Going riding?"

"Yes. I'm a little late today. Ismail Khan is indisposed."

"Oh?"

"A minor illness, he assures me, but I would rather he remain behind."

Ross's scowl deepened. "Were you planning to ride alone?"

Her face was averted for she had yet to meet his eyes, but he saw the swift rise of color to her cheeks. He swore softly. "Surely you've learned your lesson by now?"

She shrugged. "Everyone's busy."

"Packing for Simla, I know."

"We leave tomorrow." She glanced at him as she said this, looking so stricken that Ross's heart turned over.

"Come on," he growled. "I'll take you."

He might just as well have suggested that he was going to chop her into little pieces and eat her for tiffin. Before she could utter a word of protest, however, he took her elbow and marched her to the stable yard, where the Fox stood waiting. Boosting her unceremoniously into the saddle, he took another mount from its stall, for his own was exhausted.

Ten minutes later they were heading through the cantonment gates and out into the heat of the day. The sunrise was golden, the plains an unfolding vista of purple, green and brown. Kites rode the thermals and in the distance a herd of galloping blackbuck drew a finger of dust across the horizon.

"It's going to be hot today," Ross observed as they trotted side by side down the track. "Good thing you're leaving for the mountains."

"I don't want to go to Simla," Maura said, not looking at him.

"My dear girl, everyone wants to go to Simla. The cool of the mountain air, the beauty of the Hindu Kush, make it extremely popular with our countrymen. There may even be snow while you're there."

"Oh, snow! We had plenty of that in England. Too much."

He raised an eyebrow. "Am I to understand that you prefer this?" He gestured across the plains, which were lovely in their own way but certainly nothing compared to the mighty Himalayas or the verdant green of the British Isles.

Maura sighed. "I've gotten used to it."

His lips twitched. "You don't think much of parties and dances, do you?"

She glared a challenge. "Do you?"

"Touché," he said softly, and realized all at once how much he would miss her. The social whirl in Simla would be in full swing by the time she arrived. British citizens from all over India would be converging there to spend the summer playing cricket and cards, to hunt and dance and flirt, and perhaps fall in love and become engaged . . .

Ellen Tanner Marsh

Ross's mouth thinned. Surely Daphne Carlyon would keep a tight rein on the girl in view of what had happened in Delhi!

He realized Maura had asked him a question. "What?"

Damn him! It had been hard enough asking the first time! Maura looked down at her hands. "Will you be coming to Simla at all?"

"I don't have leave until September."

"Is it extended leave?"

Ross nodded. Once this affair with Lala Ram Mahim was settled to everyone's satisfaction, Lawrence Carlyon had assured him as much. "I was thinking of going back to England for a time."

"Oh." Her hands tightened about the reins. "Oh."

Ross's eyes narrowed, but after a moment she lifted her head and smiled at him brightly. "Would you care to gallop, Captain Hamilton?"

He followed at a respectful distance, alert for any danger that might cause her mount to stumble or spook. A good syce would have done the same, but a syce would not have scowled as Ross did and immediately reach for his weapon when a pair of riders converged on the road ahead of them from behind a dense stand of bamboo.

They were bearded Muslims riding horses of better breeding than those normally owned by locals, and Maura drew in her breath as she recognized them. They were brothers, both high-ranking servants in the house of Walid Ali. The younger one, Attock, was darkly handsome and had in recent weeks taken a keen interest in the nautch-girl, Sinta Dai. Maura had seen him loitering about the anterooms of the zenana, and walking with the girl on occasion in the garden.

The other was of the same age as Walid Ali and

was described by those in the household as one of his more trusted advisors. Kushna Dev had given him the nickname "the Eagle" because of his hawkish features and overblown pride. Maura had never come face to face with the man while living in the zenana, and she did not think he or Attock would recognize her now.

Or so she could only pray.

The four horses met in the center of the road and the Muslims, drawing rein, greeted Ross affably. They took scant notice of Maura, since the women of sahibs were of no interest to them. A curious glance at her hair, which was of a color unknown to most, was all she received, and she took advantage of that to withdraw down the road and wait discreetly while they exchanged pleasantries with Ross.

"They are on their way to a festival," he reported when he rejoined her.

"Oh? Where?"

"In Punjore, just across the border."

"Will you be going?" she asked.

"I haven't decided. It may prove advantagous."

"Because you're still trying to find out who wanted to ambush you in the nullah?"

He frowned. "You've not forgotten that."

"How could I?"

"You're much too meddlesome for your own good, lass."

Maura bristled even though Ross had spoken without his usual curtness. "I have a right to know!"

"Do you? Why?"

He had asked the question casually, but for some reason Maura felt a warning prickle down her spine. She cautioned herself to choose her words carefully. "I was the one who overheard the plot, wasn't I?"

287

Ellen Tanner Marsh

"In the Residency garden," Ross remembered, though he had recently come to the conclusion that the encounter had taken place in the garden of Walid Ali's stucco palace even though Maura had never admitted as much. "There's something else I've been meaning to ask you. How did you know my bearer had taken a knife through the arm?"

"Ismail Khan said it was so."

"Your Pathan is no fool," Ross said quietly.

"Then it *is* true!"

He looked at her thoughtfully. "Perhaps it's a good thing you're leaving for Simla."

Her chin lifted with a jerk. "Why? Do you think I'll interfere?"

"The way you did last time? I certainly hope not." Grinning, he leaned forward and laid a finger to her lips. "No, don't speak. I know why you went, and I promise I'll listen the next time you have anything else of import to say to me."

Her mouth trembled and she jerked her head away. What would he say if she were to tell him that she was in love with him, that she loved him so much it hurt? Would he consider that of import or would he merely laugh, the way he had laughed at her all too often in the past?

"We'd better go back," she said tightly.

"I think so, too. In a moment we'll be quarreling."

A fine way to behave on the verge of a three-month separation, Maura thought despairingly, taking up the reins.

"Miss Adams."

She arched an eyebrow at him.

"You'll have a care in Simla?"

"Why? What do you think might happen to me?"

"A high-spirited girl like you? Too much."

She tossed her head, beginning to feel a little better now that she realized he was teasing her. "I don't intend to go tiger hunting, if that's what you mean."

"Or husband hunting?"

Her eyes spit fire. "That was uncalled for, Captain."

"Not interested in matrimony anymore?"

She snorted, very unladylike, very Maura-like, and he had to concentrate hard to keep from smiling. "Believe me, I wasn't the first time."

He was truly startled. "Then why on earth did you accept his offer?"

"I'm not yet of age," she reminded him tartly. There, let him be satisfied with that.

"Your uncle?"

"And my aunt. Lydia, too. All of them approved."

"But you didn't."

She shrugged.

"And here I thought—"

"What?" she pressed when abruptly he fell silent.

"Does it matter? In view of what happened?"

They both thought back to that scene on the landing of Charles's Delhi townhouse. But perhaps the memory of that awful scene was fading, or perhaps her grief at leaving overshadowed all else, for Maura suddenly found that the image no longer evoked the horror and disgust it once had. She shook her head and smiled. "All grist in the mill of a fishing-fleet girl."

Their eyes met and they smiled at each other, for the first time in a long time freely and without pretense.

"You'll have a care in Simla," Ross repeated.

It was the nearest he had ever come to expressing concern for her.

"I will," she promised, and rode with him homeward, her heart curiously full.

Chapter Eighteen

Maura had promised herself that she would go no more to Walid Ali's pink stucco palace, at least while Ross was in Bhunapore. Ismail Khan had delivered word to Kushna Dev that Maura had returned to the Residency safely and that all was well between herself and her family. In her missive Maura had expressed regret that they would not be able to meet again until her return from Simla, but she had promised to call on the zenana the moment she did.

Indeed, her intentions had truly been the best, but she had not counted on the summons that was waiting for her when she returned to her room after luncheon on the day of her outing with Ross.

Meera had taken delivery of the letter in the Residency hallway, and although she had not opened it, she had recognized the young boy who brought it as one of the servants of the wealthy Bhunapore merchantman, Walid Ali. She had sent him away with a coin and the admonition not to tarry in the streets, and her expression was disapproving now as she turned the letter over to her mistress.

"It is whispered that thou hast friends in the house of that Mussulman," she said tartly, "and that thy hairy Pathan once ate from the table of the Begum."

"That may be," Maura said distractedly, untying the gilt string that held the letter.

Meera busied herself straightening the wardrobe but kept a watchful eye on her mistress. The moment Maura laid the letter aside she whirled. "I know that look."

"Indeed?"

"Indeed! When thy face wears that look it means thou wilt be leaving the house shortly, telling no one thy destination. Thou hast done it often enough and always, always there follows trouble!"

"*Bewakufi!*" Maura scoffed. "Utter nonsense!" She gestured for her habit, but Meera shook her head. "Thou hast already ridden once today. It is too hot now."

"On the contrary, it is the best time."

"While thy guardians are napping, eh?"

Maura considered a moment, then sighed. "Very well, the truth: The younger sister of my friend, the Begum Kushna Dev, was to have been wed in the cold season, but from this letter I have just learned that she has been summoned early to the home of her intended. She leaves in four hours' time and travels first to the Peacock Palace to bid official farewell to Nasir al-Mirza Shah. The bridal procession will depart directly from the Peacock Palace for Gwalior. She asks that I visit with her one last time so that I, too, may bid her farewell."

Meera scowled. "Is this necessary?"

"It is probably the last time I will ever see her."

Actually this was true, as Meera well knew. Once an Indian woman married, she became the property of her new husband and his family. Visits home were few and far between, if they were permitted at all. And besides, tomorrow Maura and the Carlyons were leaving for Simla.

The look on Maura's face was one of genuine sadness and the ayah, relenting, took down the habit. "Very well, but go quickly, whilst thy family rests. Remember that Ismail Khan is indisposed, so thou must take a syce from the Residency. Do as I say!" she added at Maura's mutinous expression. "Thou wilt ride with escort or I will summon thine uncle!"

"And thou wouldst! Truly thou art a martinet!"

"Bah," said Meera, but without heat.

"Thy concern is misplaced," Maura said, smiling fondly at the older woman. "I will not be gone above an hour or two. What could possibly go wrong?"

"Do not ask," Meera grumbled.

Laughing, Maura slipped into her habit, then quietly left the house carrying her topi and whip and a water canteen. Meera had been right; the heat was appalling, but the advantage to this was that everyone else in the Residency was resting behind drawn blinds and would not see her leave.

The cantonment streets also were deserted, as was Ross's bungalow, thank goodness. Mounting the Fox, Maura took off at a brisk trot with a Residency syce following behind.

At the house of Walid Ali, chaos reigned. As Maura was ushered up the stairwell, the serving girl explained the situation. It would seem that Sita's prospective mother-in-law had fallen ill unexpectedly and had demanded to see her son wed before her death. Poor Sita now had only hours to prepare for a departure that should have taken weeks or even months. She had been crying all morning, and had balked at the thought of leaving without bidding farewell to her dear *Angrezi* friend.

"Surely thou canst make it bearable?" the serving girl pleaded.

"I will try," Maura said, though she was doubtful.

The moment she stepped into the huge reception room she was caught up in the tumult. Servants rushed here and there packing the bride's belongings, preparing the gifts and trousseau, locking the casks with Sita's jewels and other valuables, while the household priests who had access to the zenana chanted endless prayers.

The nervous excitement in the air was palpable, but underneath it Maura sensed a growing sadness. No one regretted the fine match that had been arranged for little Sita, but she would be sorely missed.

Kushna Dev, looking weary and harrassed, embraced Maura with undisguised relief. "Sita has said that she will not leave without thee. Canst thou come with us to the Peacock Palace?"

Maura shook her head. "I must return to the Residency before dark. But I am here now."

"Then that will have to do." Kushna Dev lowered her voice. "Couldst thou stay at least long enough to entertain the child?"

"Oh, please," an elderly aunt agreed. "She clings to us all, delaying the preparations, weeping unseemly tears. It is provident thou hast come."

"I will tell her tales from Belait," Maura suggested.

Both women looked relieved. "Indeed, she will sit quietly for that!"

And Sita did, while Maura wracked her brains for stories about England that the girl had not heard before. Everyone breathed a sigh of relief as she began to talk and Sita listened with a rapt expression.

For nearly an hour Maura told tales of her childhood in England, embellishing a number of them and inventing others so as to keep Sita from succumbing to hysterics. When those stories ran dry she turned to classic literature, with herself cast in the role of the heroine.

Sita did not know the difference, nor would she have cared. It was enough to be distracted from the chaos around her and the fear of leaving all she had known for a distant land and an elderly husband and all that marriage entailed.

"Allah be praised," whispered Kushna Dev's elderly aunt. "This will end well after all."

But she had spoken too soon. No sooner did the time approach to depart for the Peacock Palace and receive the blessings of Bhunapore's glorious ruler, than Sita stamped her foot and burst into fresh tears. She would not, she announced wildly, go to the palace without Chota Moti.

Maura had no intention of delaying her return to the Residency. Already the sun had passed its highest point in the sky and was descending toward the plains. In an hour, perhaps less, the Residency household would be stirring and she herself would be summoned from her nap. No one must know that she hadn't been abed all along!

"I cannot," she said firmly, but when she caught sight of Kushna Dev's pleading expression she relented a little. In the end a compromise was reached: Maura would travel with the bridal procession as far as the palace gates, then take her horse and syce and return home from there.

"We will leave now," Kushna Dev said quickly lest

Sita change her mind, "even though all is not yet prepared."

"But it is daylight still," a serving girl pointed out. "The sahiba will be recognized."

Maura bit her lip. "If I am seen then word will surely reach my uncle."

"This cannot happen," Kushna Dev agreed. For a moment she was silent, considering. "I know! Thou wilt travel with us as far as the palace in the bridal *ruth*, as thou didst the first time. We will carry thy clothing with us."

Maura consented, and again there were sighs of relief all around. Though the procession had been planned for evening when the weather cooled, all of them now scurried to finish their tasks, and messengers were sent to Walid Ali with the news that the bride would be ready within the hour.

Maura changed out of her habit into the now-familiar *salwars* and *choli*, and wrapped a veil about her face. She would be riding in the first *ruth*, the one that was carrying the bride, her sister and ayah, and it would be too hot and cramped if she were wearing her cumbersome Western habit.

This will be the last time, she soothed herself.

Just one last time, to help poor little Sita through the difficult leave-taking. After that she would never don the *salwars* and *choli* again. Too much danger lay in doing so, and too many painful memories were wrapped in their use. In the fall, when she returned from Simla, she would carry on her friendship with Kushna Dev openly, no matter how much her aunt and uncle might disapprove.

Let Chota Moti die a quick and painless death, Maura thought acidly. And if Ross Hamilton missed her then he would just have to suffer.

* * *

The male retainers of the household politely averted their eyes when the heavily veiled women stepped into the courtyard and entered the resplendently appointed vehicle. No one thought it odd that a strange pair of horses and a syce known to be in the employ of the British Resident of Bhunapore were attached to the retinue. Walid Ali had always indulged his wife's many desires, for he understood that life in the zenana could be dull at times. If she cared to invite someone not of the household, then no one had objections. As for Sita's histrionics, these, too, were expected, and if the child sought the comfort of some unknown guest, then the household would indulge her in that as well.

By now the market square was filled with spectators, for everyone was eager to see the bridal procession pass. Flowers were tossed at the *ruth* and well–wishers ran alongside hoping to catch a glimpse of the bride through the drawn curtains. Beggars, too, wove in and out of the oxen's path and Walid Ali gave the command that they be showered with coins.

Once through the city gates the crowds thinned and the carts, horses and marching retainers that made up the procession were soon on their own. The road turned uphill and the plains spread out below. Away to the west, across the molten river, lay the British cantonment, but the curtains were drawn and so Maura could not see it. Sighing, she leaned back against the cushions. The sun glared down and the dust rose, and the women quickly grew thirsty and hot.

"Oof," said the elderly ayah who rode with them. "I wouldst that I had remained behind."

"We left early for Sita's sake," Kushna Dev reminded her sharply.

"But we must stop for refreshment soon," Sita gasped, "or assuredly I will die!"

"I see a *jheel* a short distance ahead," the ayah reported, peeking through the curtains. "And shade for all."

"Oh, please," Sita cried, "let us stop there!"

Kushna Dev made a sign to the ayah, who beckoned through the curtains to one of the mounted retainers.

"At once," he replied upon hearing the bride's wish, and the shouted command was sent down the line.

"We will be there shortly," Kushna Dev soothed as Sita groaned and fanned herself with the end of her veil.

I wish I hadn't come, Maura thought crossly. She had had enough of the stifling *ruth* and Sita's temper tantrums. Granted, the girl was upset about leaving home, but why did she have to make things so difficult for everyone else, especially her sister?

Perhaps when we reach the *jheel* I shall make my farewells. Surely Sita will not begrudge—

Maura jerked upright as a trumpet blast shattered the stillness.

"What was that?" Sita cried in alarm.

"It sounded like a bugle," Maura replied, frowning.

"A bugle?"

"Yes, a fanfare from the army of the Raj. But that is impossible. There is no—"

Maura's words were drowned out by the thunder of approaching hooves. The very road seemed to tremble. Frightened, Kushna Dev leaned forward to part the curtains but before she could do so a crackle of gunshots filled the air.

Maura caught at her arm. "Get down! Get down!"

"What is it? What is happening?"

"I do not know! But stay where thou art! Stay!"

More gunshots crackled. Choking dust streamed into the *ruth* as the horses reared in panic. Outside, men shouted in confusion. Sita began to scream while the ayah moaned in fear.

"Be still!" Maura hissed. Cautiously she peered through the curtains. The *ruth* had halted in a curve of the roadway where the hills rose sharply on both sides. Maura gasped as she saw a band of horsemen come pouring down into the narrow valley, firing their rifles as they came.

As incredible as it might seem, the bridal procession was under attack.

"I don't believe it!"

"What?" Sita cried. "What is it?"

Maura did not answer. In a panic, Kushna Dev crawled to her side. "Why, they—they are English!"

It was true. The riders spilling onto the roadway were dressed in the scarlet regimentals of a British calvary unit.

More gunshots rang through the air. An awful scream sounded from somewhere in the procession. Taken completely by surprise, Walid Ali's men did not have the chance to fight back. Horses neighed and reared. More wounded men began screaming. The noise and confusion were appalling.

Maura whirled in panic to confront her companions. "Have you no weapons?"

The three women could only stare. In the next moment the curtains were jerked apart and Sita screamed as a mounted horseman thrust his arm inside. Screeching, the ayah flung herself upon him, biting and scratching.

"No!" Kushna Dev shrieked.

Sita screamed again and Maura whirled to see a

soldier framed in the doorway. She struck frantically at the hairy hand that had fastened around the girl's *choli*. "Leave her be!"

"Attok! Here!" a voice roared in Maura's ear, and a dizzying moment later she found herself being pulled through the air and flung onto the back of a wheeling, plunging horse.

Dust stung her eyes and her veil tangled about her face, making it impossible to breathe. Gasping, she struggled with the man who held her across the horse's neck.

"Let me go!"

A rough hand pushed her down, but she twisted and bit hard into flesh. Her captor screamed. Maura didn't see the other man who crowded close on his mount and lifted his rifle butt high in the air. She felt only the sharp crack of pain at her temple before everything around her faded to black.

"Kind of you to agree to dine with us tonight, Ross," Lawrence Carlyon said, smiling. "Always too busy, never at home, not dressed for the occasion . . . Have you run out of excuses at last?"

Smiling wryly in return, Ross accepted the drink his superior handed him. "It *is* the ladies' last night in Bhunapore."

"Certainly a reason to celebrate," Lawrence agreed. Abruptly his manner became serious. "Just between us I'm deuced glad to see 'em go."

"I quite agree, sir."

"Trouble's coming," Lawrence added glumly. "Don't know when or from where. I just feel it in m'bones."

"I certainly hope you're mistaken, sir."

"So do I." Lawrence lifted his drink. "Cheers."

The two men were seated in the Residency drawing room waiting for the womenfolk to join them before going in to supper. Terence Shadwell was expected as well, for Lydia had pleaded with her mother to invite him one last time before their departure for Simla. Daphne had agreed and sent an invitation to Ross as well, if only to make an even number at the table. They had all been astonished when Ross had accepted.

Had Daphne thought to ask him why, he could not have explained. Perhaps it was the fact that he had spent the entire afternoon shut up in his office with a mountain of paperwork. I'm paying for it now, he thought irritably. Inactivity certainly had a way of dulling one's senses.

There was the sound of masculine voices in the hall and Lawrence looked up, brightening. "That'll be Terence. I'd better let Daffy know he's here."

But the strident voice was not that of Lydia's affianced, and Lawrence drew back, astonished, as the drawing room door burst open and a bloodied apparition strode in unannounced.

"What hast thou done with my wife? Where hast thou taken her?" The wounded man spoke in Hindustani, jabbing a threatening finger into Lawrence Carlyon's startled face.

Although taken aback, Lawrence was no coward. "Lala Deen! My service revolver!"

But by then Ross had recognized Walid Ali through all the blood and dust and moved quickly to intervene. "It's all right, sir. The man is known to me."

To Lala Deen, who had halted, stunned, in the doorway he barked, "Fetch the hakim! At once!"

The *chupprassi* hastened out while Ross eased Walid Ali into a chair and handed him his own brandy.

"Nahin!"

"Drink! Thou art near collapse and will do thy wife no good this way. Where are thy servants?"

"I came alone."

Hiding his astonishment, Ross reached for the Muslim's blood-spattered coat, but Walid Ali struck his hand away. "Leave be, it is but a scratch!"

"That I do not believe."

"Believe!" Walid Ali snapped. "Although it could have been worse, far more so! We could not defend ourselves, we had no weapons! Why should we? Why would anyone—why would they—" and here he cast a murderous look at Lawrence Carlyon, "—dare ambush a bridal procession?"

"Who is this fellow? What the devil's he talking about?" Lawrence demanded.

"I'm almost afraid to find out," Ross answered grimly. In Hindustani he said gently, "Tell me, brother."

The news Walid Ali related was nothing short of appalling. Not only had his retinue been overrun by a score of British soldiers while on its way to the Peacock Palace, but his own wife, his sister-in-law and two other women sharing their *ruth* had been carried off into the hills. Without weapons Walid Ali and his men had not been able to fight back, and the casualties had been many.

"I want them returned unharmed," he concluded savagely, "and then this *Angrezi* offal will tell me why my women were seized in the first place!"

There was a faint scream from the doorway, where Daphne and Lydia had just managed to push their way through the crowd of staring servants.

"Papa!" Lydia was standing on tiptoe peering over her mother's shoulder. "Why is that man all bloody?"

"Get them out of here!" Lawrence bellowed, but Ross was already striding toward them.

Before she could utter a word of protest Daphne found herself herded out into the hall along with her daughter and the servants. The drawing room door was closed none too gently in their faces.

"Sahib, wait!" At the last moment Maura's ayah ducked beneath Ross's arm. "I could not hear all that was said . . . I thought . . . Did someone say that a Muslim bridal procession has been attacked?"

"It is so!" Walid Ali staggered to his feet, shouting. "And the *Angrezis* are the ones who have done this!"

"We don't know that for certain," Ross said sharply.

"Do you accuse me of lying?" the Mulsim asked savagely. "With my own eyes I saw them! And by all that is holy I will kill them all if they do not—"

"*Hai mai!* It cannot be!" Meera caught at Ross's arm. "Indeed, Sahib! Thou must go after them!"

Ross shook her off. "Thou art too hasty. We have no reason yet to believe anyone from the cantonment was responsible."

By now tears were running down the ayah's cheeks. "But sahib! I fear my mistress may be with them!"

For a moment there was silence. Then Ross whirled. "By God, is this true?"

"I know not!" bellowed Walid Ali. "And indeed I do not care! Now I will ask this man—through thee—one last time where my wife has been taken. Tell him if he does not answer that I will choke the life from him with my bare hands."

"That will avail thee naught," Ross said, his voice like a lash. "Cool reason, not hot heads, will return thy wife to thee this night."

He was right, of course, and after a wild moment

Walid Ali cursed violently and sank back into his chair. By then Dr. Moore had managed to push his way through the crowd still gathered outside the door. While he saw to the young Muslim's wounds, Ross took Lawrence Carylon aside and explained tersely what had happened, omitting the likelihood that his own niece might be involved.

"Preposterous!" Lawrence bellowed. "I gave no such orders! Does he think me mad?"

"Most likely, sir."

"Then what'll we do? I don't care to mess about in native affairs, but if he thinks the British are at the bottom of this . . ."

"I've known him for years. He has no reason to lie. And fantastic as it may seem, what if he is speaking the truth?"

Lawrence cursed roundly. "How the devil d'we find out?"

"I suggest the first thing we do is find those women, sir."

"Yes, yes, of course." Lawrence's face seemed to sag. "Damned volatile thing. If word gets out, we'll have another mutiny on our hands! You know the trouble we've been having! You'll take care of it, Ross?"

"Of course, sir." Ross was already drawing on his gloves. "If you'll send a bearer to my bungalow for my pistols?"

Walid Ali rose too, shaking off the doctor. He understood no English, but Ross's expression was explanation enough. "I will go with thee. As will those of my household who are not injured . . . or dead."

"Thou art unwell—"

"*Beshak!* Dost thou think I would remain here in this house when thine own people have done this?"

"They have done this to the *burra*-sahib's niece as

well," Ross countered sharply. "Deny what thou wilt, but I believe it was with thine own permission that she accompanied thy wife."

"Does it matter now?"

To Ross it did, and they looked at each other for the first time in their lives with cold animosity.

At last Walid Ali jerked his head in Lawrence Carlyon's direction. "He knows not?"

"No. And I would keep it that way." Turning heel, Ross strode through the door.

Outside on the lawn, Walid Ali's motley collection of servants waited. Ghoda Lal had just arrived with Ross's horse in tow. Amir Dass was with him, as were several others of Ross's staff who had refused to allow their master to ride without them.

"I will come too, *Huzoor*."

Ross whirled, then shook his head. "Thou art too ill to be of use."

"My bowels are afflicted," Ismail Khan said blackly, "not my shooting arm. And I am still in the miss-sahiba's service."

Ross stiffened. "Who told you she is gone?"

"The ayah brought word to the *bibi-gurh*. Rest easy. Carlyon-sahib still knows naught."

Walid Ali forced his way between them. "We waste time on words. Come!"

Those gathered on the Residency verandah watched in silence as the group of heavily armed men rode away. Down at the gate a crowd had gathered, most of them natives who had rushed outside the moment word of a British attack on highborn Mohammedan ladies had reached them.

Hindu and Muslim alike, they now stood jeering and shouting as Ross led the mounted procession at a canter through the gate. A stone whistled past his head, then another. Leaning low in the saddle, he urged his mount to a flat-out gallop.

On the verandah Lawrence Carlyon turned to his *chuprrassi*. "Send for the guards! I want that rabble dispersed before they cause more trouble. And summon Major Clapham. I want the garrison put on alert. Do you understand? Clapham-sahib!"

"At once, *Huzoor!*" Pale with fright, Lala Deen hurried away.

"Daphne," Lawrence continued authoritatively, "go back to your room. Take Lydia and Maura with you. Lock the door and don't open it for anyone but me."

"Lawrence, what on earth—"

"Do as I say, woman! I'll explain when there's time!"

"But Papa," Lydia squeaked, "Maura's not with us!"

"What!" Lawrence's expression was suddenly black. "Where in the name of Beelzebub is she?"

"In—in her room, I think."

"Then leave her there! Tell her ayah to lock her door. Better yet, tie the tiresome chit to her bed! I've got to get down to my office. Baga Leesh, send Clapham-sahib to me the moment he comes!"

Chapter Nineteen

Not once in all her life had Maura ever been afraid of the dark. Certainly not of the soft Indian darkness with its whispery sounds and the familiar, far-off braying of conches. But hurrying through the moonless night, stumbling over rocks and catching her clothing on thorns, she felt her heart leap with terror at every sound.

She had no idea how long she had been gone before her captors had noticed her absence, but there was no doubt that they had, for she knew that she was being followed. Every now and again the wind brought to her a snatch of whispered voices or the faint, metallic ring of horseshoes on stone.

The thought of being caught filled her with panic. If only she had a mount of her own, or at the very least sensible shoes rather than these thin-soled slippers! Her feet ached, her throat was parched and her head still throbbed where the kidnapper had hit her with his rifle butt.

Those must have been terrifying hours. According to Kushna Dev, Maura had lain unconscious for most of the afternoon, for they had had no way of reviving her.

The Muslim girl had actually burst into tears when Maura had finally opened her eyes. "We had thought thee dead to this world!"

"It would take more than a blow to kill me," Maura had answered with the ghost of a smile. But pain and nausea had kept her unmoving for a long time afterward. When at last she did find the strength to sit up, she found that the four of them had been locked away in a sweltering, mud-baked hut. There were no windows, and the door was made of sturdy wood, barred from the other side.

Sita and the elderly ayah were dozing on the hard-packed floor and Maura had summoned Kushna Dev closer with a finger to her lips. "Where are we?"

"I know not."

"Has anyone made demands of thee?"

"Not yet." Kushna Dev's voice faltered. "I believe they seek to ransom us. My husband is a wealthy man. Why else would they hold us here?"

Maura had no idea. "Hast thou no clue of their identities?"

Kushna Dev shook her head. "I have heard naught that might be useful. No one has come, and the guard outside will not speak. But surely thou couldst reason with them? They are thine own people, after all."

But this Maura had refused to believe. No British soldiers, especially those under her uncle's command, would dare undertake a daylight ambush and make off with the wife and sister-in-law of a prominent Indian merchant! To do so would be risking grave reprisals—a serious incident in a land where the last mutiny was by no means forgotten.

On the other hand she, too, had seen the scarlet uniforms and regulation rifles of their attackers . . .

"I cannot think about it anymore," she had whispered, clutching her throbbing head.

"Be still, then," Kushna Dev had answered quickly. "Thou art unwell. Surely my husband will come for us soon."

But afternoon had waned and the hut grew shadowed, and still no one approached their prison. Deep in her heart Kushna Dev began to suspect that perhaps Walid Ali might be dead. Why else would they not have been rescued?

The terrible thought must have occurred to Sita as well, for as thirst and fear and inactivity began to take their toll she started weeping hysterically, then throwing herself repeatedly against the barred door. Bruised and bleeding, she was pulled away by the ayah.

"Be still, be still," the ayah hissed, "or they will surely beat us!"

But no one came to investigate the cause of the tumult, and Maura wondered about this. Was the hut not as closely guarded as they had assumed?

She investigated this possibility by pounding on the door herself with a rock dug from the floor. It made considerably more noise than had Sita's fists but still no one came to investigate.

Taking a deep breath, Maura used the rock to smash the bracings on the door.

A horrified silence fell. She hit the door again, harder.

"*Nahin!*" Sita shrieked. "Oh, thou must not—"

"There is no one guarding us," Maura interrupted fiercely. "I am sure of it!"

She hammered again and again, and at long last the rusty bracings fell away. Sita moaned with fear. Ignoring her, Maura eased open the door. To her astonishment she saw that twilight had fallen. The camp was silent, although here and there a cooking fire flickered and the hobbled horses stamped and blew.

"I will go and seek help," Maura whispered to her companions.

Aghast, they pleaded with her not to leave, yet she would not be swayed. Neither water nor supper had been brought to them and Sita's condition had deteriorated throughout that long, awful day. The ayah, too, was pallid and weak. Without water they could not think clearly much longer.

Perhaps Kushna Dev had been harboring similar fears, for when she saw that Maura truly meant to leave, she begged the others for silence. With tears in her eyes she embraced the English girl and tremulously gave her her blessing.

"I will send help as quickly as I can," Maura promised.

Tears welled and trickled down Kushna Dev's cheek. "If Allah wishes."

Maura's escape had been ridiculously easy. The nearest campfire burned quite a distance from the hut, and there was no longer a sentry stationed by the door. Why should there be, when their captors believed the prisoners sheltered zenana women who would never dream of slipping away into the darkened desert?

But that was exactly what Maura did, slithering on her hands and knees toward the nearest thorn scrubs and then taking off at a run once the camp fell away behind her.

At first she had been elated by the ease of her escape, but since then many long, wearying hours had passed and she found herself still miles from the Residency. And now there were horsemen on her trail . . .

The first time she had heard the telltale sounds of pursuit she had been gripped by the wild hope that it was someone coming to rescue her. But the hope had died almost instantly. No true friend would stalk her in this way.

So she had wisely kept away from the main road and struck out across the plains. But there were untold dangers there, too, such as snakes and scorpions and uneven terrain over which she constantly stumbled and fell.

How long had she been walking? How far did she still have to go? Thirst tormented her and all at once weary tears stung her eyes.

Don't! Don't panic. Just find Ross.

Ross. The thought of him had been foremost in her mind from the first. Ross always knew exactly what to do in any situation. Surely he would come to rescue her and the others?

Somewhere out in the darkness a horse whinnied. Maura's throat closed in fear. Crouching behind an outcropping of stone, she peered through the dim starlight. There was nothing to see but murky plains. A ghostly *kikar* tree loomed ahead.

In the silence she could hear the slithering of night creatures underfoot, but she paid them no heed. Every muscle taut, she strained to hear from which direction the sound had come.

There it was again. A whicker, then a faint cough. A human one.

Maura cowered lower. Whoever it was was coming nearer. There was more than one, too, for now she could hear a number of saddle trappings chinking softly. Hoofbeats thudded and then stopped, not ten feet from where she hid.

Silence.

Maura could almost feel the unseen pairs of eyes trying to penetrate the darkness. Her scalp prickled. Pressing her hand to her mouth she tried to still the thundering of her heart. Oh, God, what if they should hear it?

"It is of no use, Sahib. Assuredly no one has come this way."

But that . . . that was Ismail Khan!

"Thou art right." Another voice, resigned, almost weary. "Let us rejoin the others. Perhaps they have discovered the trail."

Maura closed her eyes, wondering if she was dreaming, if thirst and fatigue and the pounding of her heart hadn't made her prey to hallucinations.

"Ross—"

He could not possibly have heard that tortured whisper and yet, unbelievably, he must have, for seconds later a horse came crashing through the scrub, its rider standing up in the stirrups, eyes burning in a thin, lined face.

"Maura!"

She no longer had the strength to stand up. She could only wait as he dismounted and went down on one knee beside her. She felt the solid warmth of his arms closing around her and with a blissful sigh she turned her face into his shoulder.

"Thank God," he managed. "We had thought—" But he did not finish. Lifting his head, he gestured impatiently for the water flask.

Maura protested weakly as he held it to her lips.

"Drink!"

Too weak to argue she let the sweet liquid pour down her throat.

"Better?"

She nodded without opening her eyes. Ross scowled as he looked at her. She had lost her veil somewhere out in the darkness and her face was scratched and bleeding. One of her slippers was gone. Beneath his hands he could feel the butterfly beating of her heart.

He gestured again for the flask, and this time it was Ghoda Lal who brought it. The young Hindu uttered a muffled oath when he saw what Maura was wearing as she lay half unconscious in Ross's arms. Her hair, plaited in a native-style braid, dangled against his thigh.

"*Huzoor!*" Ghoda Lal was genuinely scandalized.

Ross glared a warning, then turned back to Maura. Shaking her slightly he demanded, "Are you all right? Did they hurt you?"

"N-No."

The tension in his face eased a little. "How long have you been walking?"

"I don't know. Hours." She spoke in a difficult whisper.

"From which direction?"

"The north. Beyond . . . beyond the Sindha Bhat road. They took us—"

"That's enough for now. Save your strength."

"But Ross—"

"Hush. Rest a moment, then tell me."

She struggled weakly to sit up. "But—"

"You never listen, do you?"

"Ross, please. You've got to g-go after them."

He could tell that she was close to tears. Leaning down, he brushed his lips against her hair. Surely the others would not notice. "Are you talking about Kushna Dev and her sister?"

She nodded, unable to summon the strength to speak. Her eyes closed and her head fell against him as she breathed a deep sigh of relief. She was safe, safe from all harm, and Ross would surely rescue the others.

"Who kidnapped them?"

"Was it the *Angrezis?*" demanded Ismail Khan, kneeling down beside her.

"N-no," Maura whispered, rallying herself with difficulty. "At least I d-don't think so."

Over her head Ross and Ismail Khan exchanged startled glances.

"How do you know?" Ross demanded. "Walid Ali described their uniforms and said they carried regulation weapons."

"Walid Ali? Then—then he isn't dead?"

"No, *piari.*"

She did not even hear him utter the term of endearment. She was trying hard to drag up an image of the ragtag band of scarlet-clad soldiers who had stormed the bridal procession, but the memory remained elusive. Her head hurt too much.

"Think, my love. Think hard. It's terribly important."

"I-I never got a good look at them. It was dusty, and there was so much c-confusion."

"Where did this happen?" Ismail Khan rasped.

"On—on the northerly road toward Sinda Bhat, just below the . . . the *jheel*. Sita wished to rest and the Begum said that we would stop there for water." She frowned, straining to remember, to muster her strength. "That's when a bugle sounded and the horses came down from the hill and . . . and . . . Ross!" She clutched weakly at his arm. "They

313

couldn't have been English. I remember now! Their bugler didn't sound the charge, he blew reveille!"

"What does this mean?" demanded Ismail Khan, for in her agitation Maura had reverted to English.

"I think she means that they were trying to make the attack seem real," Ross said slowly, "by charging in the manner of *Angrezi* troops. But a true *Angrezi* bugler would have known the proper charge."

"Is this true, little one?"

Maura nodded despite her throbbing head.

"What else can you remember?" Ross asked gently.

She thought a moment. "Their uniforms. They didn't—they weren't quite right."

"In what way?"

"I'm not sure. But they were . . . were piecemeal. An infantry coat here, cavalry breeches there. Do you know what I mean?"

Ross did, and his expression grew black. "Then—"

"Wait," Maura interrupted. "I remember now. The most important thing. The one—the one who pulled me out of the *ruth*. He—It was Attock, Ross. I didn't see his f-face, but the other—I heard him say his name."

Attock, who with his brother, the Muslim known in the pink stucco palace as The Eagle, had told them just the day before that they were on their way to a festival in Punjar . . .

Without another word Ross came to his feet and carefully set Maura down beside him. "All right?"

She wouldn't dream of telling him how much her head ached, how the world spun simply with the effort to stand, but that she didn't mind in the least as long as he was holding her. "I'm fine."

"Then tell me where they are, as best you can."

"Some of them are following me," she remembered with a sudden catch in her breath.

Ismail Khan's eyes narrowed. That much English he had understood. "I will meet them," he said darkly, reaching for his rifle. Taking up his horse's reins he vaulted into the saddle.

"Wait," Ross said sharply. "I will go with thee. Ghoda Lal, take the miss-sahib back to the Residency."

"No!" Maura caught at the lapels of his coat.

"And I would rather—" Ghoda Lal began.

"Do as I say!" Ross's furious command was aimed at both of them.

Maura was suddenly too weak to argue. Besides, she was too woefully familiar with the lash of Ross's voice, the impatience and irritation he always seemed unable to hide whenever he was with her . . .

Tears stung her eyes and she turned dejectedly away. Ghoda Lal was already astride his horse and because she couldn't tolerate the thought of Ross touching her again, she slipped her foot into the stirrup and caught his outstretched hand herself.

In one easy motion the young Hindu pulled her onto the crupper behind him. Without another word or a glance at Ross, he whirled his mount and cantered away.

Chapter Twenty

Maura's return to the Residency caused an uproar which surpassed by far the one that had followed her disappearance from Delhi. At least on that occasion her family's outrage and concern had been tempered with understanding given the heartbreak she had suffered at the dissolution of her engagement.

Not this time. This was different. Because of the turmoil that had followed on the heels of Walid Ali's bloodied appearance at the Residency, Maura's absence had not gone unnoticed very long. And no sooner had her empty bed been discovered than her ayah had been confronted by the irate Lawrence Carlyon.

Under his intense questioning Meera had tearfully revealed that her mistress had gone secretly to the home of Walid Ali to visit with his wives; and that she had probably gotten herself involved in the kidnapping.

Aunt Daphne had promptly fainted away, and Lawrence had immediately dispatched Major Clapham and a contingent of soldiers to Bhunapore to investigate the matter. Their return an hour later with news that the Resident's niece had indeed been part of the ill-fated bridal procession had caused Aunt Daphne to faint a second time and Lydia to succumb to hysterics.

At that time none of the rescue party under Captain Hamilton's command had as yet returned, and so a number of anxious hours had passed while Maura's fate remained unknown.

Lawrence Carlyon, who seemed to age as the night progressed, had paced the withdrawing room like a man possessed. Concern for his niece and shock at her behavior tormented him equally as much as the thought that soldiers from his own garrison had allegedly kidnapped a highborn Muslim bride and her wedding entourage. Unfortunately the rumor could not be categorically dismissed, for many in the garrison had been granted leave that night and a complete head count was impossible.

Tension rose throughout the cantonment as word of the attack spread. Doors were barred and sleeping children placed under the watchful eyes of trusted servants. When those servants whose loyalties had sometimes been questioned were seen whispering among themselves or casting furtive glances at their masters, tension turned to outright alarm.

Slowly, slowly the night progressed, and when no further word came from either Captain Hamilton or Major Clapham a terrible hush fell over the cantonment. To Lawrence Carlyon, standing watch on the Residency verandah, it was as though the darkened streets themselves awaited news with bated breath. Something had to happen, and soon.

Regrettably, Maura's return to the Residency brought no one a sense of relief. She came alone, riding astride behind Ross Hamilton's bearer in a breach of etiquette that was no less shocking than her attire.

Aunt Daphne took one look at her as she stumbled, bloodied and bedraggled in her torn trousers and vest, up the verandah steps, and fainted away for the third time. It was left to Meera to whisk the girl past the owl-eyed servants and into her room.

Dr. Moore was summoned, and Meera saw to it that her young charge was duly bathed and dressed in a simple cotton frock before he arrived. By the time he was shown in Maura was sitting in the dining room staring unseeingly at a plate of cold fowl that Aunt Daphne had placed before her.

Taking one look at the girl's wan features he insisted that she be put straight to bed. No sense in trying to feed her at this point.

"That's a jolly good blow to the head," he added, examining it, "and I wouldn't be surprised if there was a bit of a fracture."

"A fracture!" Aunt Daphne, who had rallied herself sufficiently to lend her presence to the good doctor's examination, steadied herself on the back of a nearby chair.

"Nothing serious, ma'am, though I daresay it must hurt. Now, off to bed with you, missy, and you, too, ma'am. I'll leave a sedative for you both, and one for Miss Lydia."

Maura waited until her aunt had left and her uncle had shown the doctor to the door before pouring the laudanum out of her bedroom window. Did they think that they could fob her off with a sleeping potion while Ross and Ismail Khan were out there in the wilds and Kushna Dev and Sita remained in the hands of kidnappers?

I should never have left them, she thought in a fit of helpless anger. They were sheltered women, not used to harsh treatment. Supposing their abductors tried to . . . to do them harm? How would they defend themselves?

The thought of gentle Kushna Dev and fragile little Sita suffering the attentions of those rough, uncaring men filled her with agonized fear. Surely that wouldn't happen! Surely they had been seized for ransom alone, since it was well known that Walid Ali was a wealthy man. Or perhaps the bridal portion, the dowery, that Sita had been carrying with her had been the thieves' goal.

Nevertheless, she could not bear sitting safely here in her room while her friends were still in the hands of their captors. She would have crept out of the house immediately and gone after them had she not been so weary and her head throbbing still from that earlier blow. For once in her life she admitted honestly to herself that she would be of no help to anyone were she to interfere now.

Ross would save them. She had to believe that. And believe, too, that he himself would come to no harm. . . .

She must have fallen asleep there in the chair beneath her window, for it was hours later that a sound from the hall made her open her eyes and struggle unsteadily to her feet.

Cautiously she peered through her door. Nothing stirred from the direction of her uncle's study. Aunt Daphne and Lydia had retired long ago. Although

Lala Deen had been ordered to stand guard he, too, had fallen asleep on the cushions in the hall.

The sound came again; a knock on the front door, quiet yet unmistakably urgent. Maura lifted her skirts and hurried barefoot across the tiles to draw back the bolts.

When Ross stumbled in she uttered a muffled scream at the blood that smeared the front of his shirt.

"Not mine," he managed, and collapsed in the nearest chair.

Maura hastened to poured him brandy. When Lala Deen appeared in the doorway, she whirled on him. "Fetch Carlyon-sahib!"

"It's done," Ross told her when they were alone. "They're back home safe and sound."

"Oh, thank God! And Ismail Khan?"

"I sent him to the *bibi-gurh*. He was completely done in."

Maura's skirts swirled around her as she knelt beside him. "As are you! Why couldn't you wait until morning before coming to report to my uncle?"

Ross sat with his eyes closed, his head thrown back against the chair rest. "I c-came to give you news. Knew you'd probably ride after me if you didn't hear." His words were slurred, as though he was drunk with exhaustion.

Scowling, Maura took the drink from his lifeless fingers. "Come."

"Where?"

"To bed."

He offered no resistance as she tugged him to his feet. Stumbling a little he let her lead him to her bedchamber, leaning heavily against her as they went.

Meera sprang up from her cot in the anteroom,

wide-eyed with disbelief at the sight of them, but one look at the sahib's face was enough. Wordlessly she helped lay him on the bed and remove his boots and coat.

Uncle Lawrence appeared in the doorway. "What the devil's going on? Lala Deen says—"

Maura put a finger to her lips and shook her head. Closing the door softly behind her, she joined him in the hall. "He's done in."

"Harrumph! I can see that. But I still need—"

"From what he said I believe everything's been settled. The Mohammedan ladies are safely at home. Please don't question him until tomorrow, Uncle. Let him sleep."

Though Lawrence was clearly unwilling, he merely sighed and nodded. "Mayhap I'll send for his syce, question him instead. No doubt he's back too. Where will you sleep, gel?"

"In the parlor, I suppose."

For once he did not object to her unconventional behavior. He merely nodded and shuffled out, looking so old and harassed that Maura's heart ached for him. Still, she let him go without a word, and because she had no strength left herself, she curled up on the divan and closed her eyes. Despite everything her heart was at rest. Nothing mattered anymore but the fact that Ross was safe.

In her bed Ross slept the sleep of utter exhaustion, not stirring once, not even when the darkness began to gray and the room brightened slowly around him. Even the crowing of the Residency cockerel failed to awaken him, although it did Maura, who rose stiffly from the uncomfortable divan and crossed to the mirror where she did her best to repair her wayward hair. Shaking the creases out of her frock, she tiptoed into the morning room.

Uncle Lawrence sat breakfasting alone, and he nodded distantly when she joined him. He, too, had been awake for much of the night and the strain showed. Maura had to resist the urge to put her arms around him, for she knew that he was furious with her. No doubt her punishment would be coming as soon as the more pressing matters of the night had been resolved.

While they breakfasted together Major Clapham called to make his report. It was a sign of her uncle's distracted state that Maura was permitted to remain at the table as the major described the rescue of the Mohammedan ladies by Captain Hamilton and a contingent of his own troops. Thanks to the information supplied by Maura, Captain Hamilton had known exactly where to look for them.

"And you were right, Miss Adams," he concluded, turning to Maura. "Those devils weren't ours! They was natives wearing stolen uniforms, and God alone knows where they'd come by those weapons! Scattered like hares when the lot of us charged into camp, but that Pathan syce of yours rode 'em down, him and Hamilton and that fellow, Walid Ali. Left us with nothing more to do than round 'em up, and I daresay they'll be swinging afore long."

"And the ladies were unharmed?" Maura breathed.

"Shaken up, as you can expect, but otherwise all right."

"Why the uniforms, the deception?" Lawrence demanded, for this had been weighing on him more heavily than anything else.

"Hamilton said they pulled the stunt to make it seem as if we were responsible."

"Good God! What for?"

"To stir up ill will against the Raj, he said. I'm inclined to agree with him."

"Good God!" Lawrence said again.

"They almost succeeded," Major Clapham added grimly. "We spent the rest o' the night trying to restore order in Bhunapore and elsewhere, and convincing people to go back to their beds. Thanks to Hamilton, they did. Except for the ones he clapped in irons."

Maura looked up, her eyes wide.

"How do you mean?" her uncle demanded.

"After we'd rescued the ladies, he and that big Pathan fellow rode off to Sundagunj. I lent him a detachment of my best, and damned if he didn't ferret out another cobra's nest of bloody plotters and bring 'em in, if you'll pardon my language, Miss Adams. Then off he goes to Bhunapore to that Walid Ali's and arrests two or three more! Some of 'em put up quite a fight, I'm told. There were casualties." Major Clapham didn't look particularly happy about this. "I'll file a full report later and so will young Ross, I'm sure."

"He mentioned nothing about this," Lawrence said disbelievingly, eyeing his niece. "Did he?"

She shook her head. "He was barely coherent when he returned."

Major Clapham snorted. "Small wonder! He did the work of half a dozen single-handedly last night. My guess is there'll be another brevet in it for him. The Pathan, too. He's quite something, your syce," he added to Maura.

"Yes, he is," she said distractedly. Oh, God, she'd had no idea that Ross and Ismail Khan had placed themselves in so much danger last night! The thought of what might have happened to them made her head spin.

"You all right, gel?" her uncle barked.

She took a deep, calming breath. "I am. Please, Major Clapham, forgive us. We've forgotten our manners. Won't you stay and take tiffin?"

The major's ruddy features softened. "Kind of you, Miss Adams, but I'm off. Too much left to do as I'm sure you can appreciate."

Lawrence rose to walk him to the door, where the two men spoke in subdued voices a while longer. By then Aunt Daphne had appeared from the back hall, and of course that meant that Major Clapham had to repeat his story all over again.

Maura was still sitting as though turned to stone at the table when her aunt and uncle returned. No one spoke for a very long time, and the clink of silverware against china and the quiet comings and goings of the servants were the only sounds in the room.

"There's no way you can leave for Simla today, Daffy," Lawrence said at last, sounding deeply harassed. "Much as I'd love to keep that part of it private, Maura will have to give a deposition."

"Lawrence, no!"

" 'Fraid so. She was there. Eyewitness. Her word's important."

"But if she tells—If that happens, then everyone will know—"

"Can't help that, I'm afraid."

"Oh, dear Lord. Whatever shall we do?"

Tears stung Maura's eyes. The last thing she'd wanted was to bring heartache and shame to these two decent people, whom she loved so dearly. Biting her lip she wondered what she should say when it was obvious that this time an apology would be nowhere near good enough.

"How will we ever live down the scandal?" Aunt

Daphne continued, sounding close to tears herself. "Especially on top of the last one?"

"More important, what are we to do with you, gel?" To Maura's deep shame Uncle Lawrence didn't sound angry. He sounded baffled and defeated, which was worse, so much worse. "Sneaking out of the house dressed like a native to attend some heathen ritual! I've known all along you were difficult; always thought Archie'd made a big mistake keeping you here in India so long, but I never dreamed. . . . I always thought—"

He seemed unable to continue. Muttering beneath his breath, he sipped his tea while Aunt Daphne pressed a napkin to her eyes.

Maura's cheeks heated. Bowing her head she clasped her hands tightly in her lap.

"I have a solution."

All of them whirled.

Ross was standing in the doorway, looking gaunt and exhausted. The shadow of a beard darkened his jaw and he still wore the filthy, bloodstained clothing of the night before. Aunt Daphne squealed faintly at the sight of him.

He grimaced. "My apologies, ma'am. I tried making myself presentable, but I'm afraid the results are less than pleasing."

"Sit down, Ross," Lawrence commanded.

"I'd rather stand, if you don't mind, sir. I've always been able to think best on my feet." Ross propped his shoulder against the door and frowned at his superior. "Now, where were we?"

"We were discussing Maura." Lawrence aimed a scowl at his niece. "I'm sure you can appreciate what'll happen the moment word of her . . . adventures gets round."

"Indeed I do, sir. That's why I suggest you let me

take care of the matter. You've enough on your plate as it is."

"Don't I know it!"

"But what . . . what will you do?" Aunt Daphne quavered.

"Take her off your hands."

"H-how?"

"Isn't it obvious? Marry her. By the time we get back from our honeymoon, the entire cantonment will be removed to Simla. All should be forgotten come the cold season."

He might have suggested that he take the girl outside, behead her with a cutlass and toss her down the well. For a moment the room was so silent that the scurrying of the lizards in the shrubbery beneath the window could be heard quite clearly.

"But—but—" That was all Aunt Daphne could manage.

"Hasty marriages aren't exactly seemly," Ross agreed smoothly, "but in view of the fact that Miss Adams's reputation will be salvaged in the end, I'm certain we can all weather the immediate storm."

"It may work," Lawrence said slowly.

"Mr. Carlyon!" Daphne was shocked that he should think so. Her bosom heaved as she struggled to regain her composure. "Captain Hamilton, while I appreciate this great sacrifice on your behalf—"

"Believe me, it is," Ross murmured, looking intently at Maura's bowed head.

"—we can't possibly expect you to take on a responsibility like this!"

"Oh, I assure you, ma'am, that I'm quite up to it." As he spoke he moved to stand behind Maura's chair, propping his hands on her shoulders as though expecting her to bolt at any moment. "I realize I've been rather abrupt, and of course you'll need time to get used to the idea. Why don't you discuss it while I have a few words with my intended?"

The hand he clamped about Maura's arm was not in the least gentle. She went with him calmly, aware of the silent warning, but the moment they were alone in the drawing room and Ross had shut the door she flew at him.

Fortunately he had expected as much and trapped her wrists neatly before she could deliver so much as a single blow. "I see you've recovered quite well from last night's escapades."

"How could you? How could you fool them that way!"

"Fool them? My dear Miss Adams, I have every intention of going through with this."

"Is that so?"

"Indeed."

"And if I should feel differently?"

"I'm afraid you have no say in the matter. Not after last night."

She struggled to free herself and hit him, because she knew he spoke the truth.

"Why are you so angry?" he went on, sounding not the least bit breathless, even though it wasn't an easy thing to subdue her. "This is the best way out for you, and I don't think your feelings for me are entirely uncaring."

"Well, you're wrong. I hate you!"

"No, you don't."

"Yes, I do! You knew—you knew all along, and yet still you—we—"

His face changed even though his voice remained cool. "Ah, so that's what this is all about."

"You had no right," Maura choked. "No right, in

the garden that night—" She turned away and tears rolled down her cheeks.

Above her bowed head Ross's face twisted.

"And that time at the durbar—"

"I didn't know then," he said harshly. "I swear it."

"But in the garden—"

"Yes, I knew."

"And still you let me go on thinking—"

Abruptly he released her wrists. Turning his back on her he went to the window. Arms crossed before him, he said darkly, "That was a mistake."

She caught her breath as the pain of that hit home. So, it had been easier, more convenient, for him to go on pretending she was an Indian native so that he could use her simply for pleasure, as though she were no different from the whore Sinta Dai! No doubt he'd even laughed about it afterward, and boasted to his Indian friends about how easily he had taken his ease with the unsuspecting niece of his own employer!

She would have hit him again, or smashed a chair over his head, if she hadn't felt so utterly, desperately defeated. And hurt. Hurt beyond words, beyond caring. That she could have fancied herself in love with a man like this, who had used her, lied to her, made sport of her feelings, and carelessly taken her gift of innocence . . . !

"I hate you." Her voice was drained of emotion.

"No, you don't."

"You flatter yourself, Captain Hamilton."

"Do I?"

"Absolutely."

They looked at each other in silence. Maura's chin was tipped at that old, stubborn angle. Never again would she shed a tear because of him.

Ross's face was devoid of all expression. His dark,

cool look hid his thoughts as completely as ever.

Neither of them spoke for another long moment, then Maura took a deep breath. Her voice was calm. "I'd sooner kill myself than marry you."

"I told your uncle the truth. You've no say in the matter. Not anymore."

"Really? Than I suppose I shall have to accept the inevitable—and make your life a living hell."

"I've no doubt that you will."

She bit her tongue, hard, to still the sob welling inside.

"Maura—"

Oh, God, why did he have to say her name like that? Her throat ached so that she could scarcely breathe. As she lifted haunted eyes to his he came toward her and stood looking down at her, his mouth a thin, hard line. Then slowly, gently, he took her face in his hands.

"Maura, it isn't the end of the world."

"How can you say that?"

A muscle twitched in his cheek. "I suppose I deserved that. But I don't want you to think—"

"Maura!" The door burst open and a jubilant Lydia danced inside. "Can it be true? Are you really going to marry Captain Hamilton?"

"No," said Maura.

"Yes," said Ross.

Scowling at each other they stepped apart. The tender moment had passed. She twisted her hands in the folds of her skirts while Ross turned his back to her.

"Your father seems very much in favor of a match, Miss Carlyon."

Lydia squealed and clapped her hands. "Then it *is* true! At first I couldn't believe it! I thought perhaps Mama and Papa were teasing me!" She laughed

329

again with sheer delight. "Terence! Oh, goodness, I've got to tell Terence!"

Pausing to kiss Maura's cheek and then shyly embrace Captain Hamilton, she danced from the room.

"Lydia, wait!" Maura, her eyes spitting fire, swept after her.

Silently Ross let her go.

Chapter Twenty-one

The wedding took place three days later in the military chapel of the garrison. There were few guests because by then most of the residents had already departed for Simla. Since the cantonment's minister and his family were also making plans to leave, Aunt Daphne reluctantly had agreed to the hasty ceremony.

"We'll celebrate again in the cold season," she'd promised her niece. "A beautiful reception to coincide with Lydia's wedding. It will be ever so grand, wait and see."

Maura had said nothing in response. By then she was beyond caring. She hadn't seen Ross at all since her stormy departure from the drawing room three endless days ago. He was away on official matters relating to what everyone was now referring to, rather grandly, as the Bhunapore Uprising.

There had been a number of arrests in Sundagunj

as a result of the attack on young Sita's bridal procession, and several servants in the house of Walid Ali had already been arrested or dismissed—or worse.

At the Residency, the nephew of the elderly gardener as well as a kitchen boy had mysteriously vanished. Aunt Daphne had complained bitterly about the unreliable nature of native servants who simply up and ran away, but when Maura asked Ismail Khan what had really happened to them he had merely shaken his head and refused to answer.

The burly Pathan was abroad much in the aftermath of the uprising, and Maura had heard that he and Captain Hamilton were often to be seen together entering the palace of Nasir al-Mirza Shah or conferring with Walid Ali for hours on end.

Maura had also heard that Kushna Dev had been returned to the pink stucco palace unharmed but that her sister had been confined to bed because of the heatstroke and hysterics she had suffered during their ordeal. Her wedding had been postponed, perhaps indefinitely, but Maura could not help thinking that in this, at least, the ambush had wrought some positive results.

And she herself? How had the events of that awful night affected her? To be honest, the days had passed as little more than a blur. There was no doubt that her aunt and uncle were delighted to be placing her permanently in Ross Hamilton's more-than-capable hands, and if they noticed her silence and wan appearance, they made no mention of it.

One matter had given Lawrence and Daphne cause for vast relief, and that was the fact that word of Maura's involvement in the ambush seemed not to have leaked beyond the Residency walls. While both had braced themselves for an unpleasant scandal, they had been baffled and surprised when none had materialized.

Friends and acquaintances departing for Simla said only that they regretted missing Maura's wedding. In view of the heartache caused the girl because of Charles Burton-Pascal's unseemly defection, they could well understand her desire to make an immediate match with her new intended.

"She always was an impulsive thing," the station matrons agreed among themselves. "Small wonder she doesn't have the patience to wait until the cold weather. Poor Daphne!"

Fortunately for Maura, no one, not even Ross, had foreseen to what extent the Residency servants would close ranks to protect her reputation. The Muslims had chosen to repay her kindness toward the Begum Kushna Dev by refusing to gossip, and the Hindus of the household, who had never forgotten what Maura had once done for the injured Ghoda Lal, did the same.

Naturally Major Clapham and his men had remained discreet as well; the major out of respect for the British Resident, the soldiers because they knew better than to cross Captain Hamilton, whose warnings in the matter had been most explicit.

And so it was Maura who ended up suffering the most in the "mutiny's" aftermath. The fact that Ross had offered to marry her simply to save her from scandal rankled horribly, and her bitterness only increased when the anticipated scandal never materialized.

She had no wish to marry Ross. Not when he wasn't the least bit in love with her. Not when he had burdened himself with her only to spare her uncle the need of having to do so ever again.

But here she was on this hot and hazy afternoon,

leaving the tiny cantonment chapel in an *ekka* festooned with ribbons and flowers. Ross sat beside her looking impossibly handsome in his scarlet regimentals, but as hard and remote as ever.

A reception had been planned at the Residency, but the heat was appalling, and after one or two halfhearted dances, the few guests took their leave. By then Aunt Daphne and Lydia were also anxious to depart, and there followed an emotional moment—at least for Daphne and her daughter—on the verandah as they bid farewell to Lawrence and the newlyweds.

"Are you sure you won't consider joining us in Simla?" Aunt Daphne's wistful inquiry was directed at Ross since he was now Maura's husband and as such in charge of all decisions.

"We'll try our best, ma'am."

Tears welled in Aunt Daphne's eyes. "My dears, I feel so dreadful deserting you like this."

"Now, now." Ross bent swiftly to kiss her cheek, smiling in that indulgent way he'd always reserved just for her.

Why, he's truly fond of her, Maura thought, and her heart contracted. If only he possessed the barest of similar feelings for me . . .

Lydia embraced her tearfully. "Maura, if you don't come, we shan't see you for months!"

The stiff skirts of Maura's wedding dress rustled as she hugged her cousin back. "I know. But I suspect you'll be far too busy to miss me."

"Never!"

"Come, my dear." That was Terence, who had volunteered to accompany the womenfolk to Simla. "I'd like to take advantage of whatever daylight's left."

"Too true," Lawrence agreed. While Ross went

down the steps to help the ladies into the carriage, he cleared his throat and turned to his niece. "Harrumph! Almost forgot to tell you. Daffy's arranged for your things to be brought to Ross's bungalow."

Maura looked at him blankly.

Lawrence reddened. "Can't live at the Residency now that you're wed, can you?"

Fire crept into her own cheeks. Oh, Lord, in her misery she hadn't even thought of that!

With a crack of the whip the driver sent the carriage bouncing away. Aunt Daphne sat dabbing her eyes while Lydia and Terence waved madly until they disappeared around the bend.

Coming back up the stairs, Ross held out his hand to Lawrence. "We'll be going, too, sir. I'll report back in the morning."

"Yes, yes, of course." Lawrence pumped his hand enthusiastically, slapped him fondly on the back, then kissed his niece's cheek. With every evidence of relief he left them alone on the verandah.

"Come on," said Ross, "I'll walk you over."

In silence they crossed the lawn. The air was hot and still. The entire cantonment seemed eerily deserted. It had been a strange, unreal day, and for the first time in a very long time Maura had no idea what to say. She stole a glance at Ross as they went up the sandy walk, but he wasn't looking at her. Nor did he speak until they had climbed the steps of his bungalow and a bowing Amir Dass held open the door for them.

"Your ayah insisted on moving in with you. I trust she's made the place a little less austere. I've asked Ismail Khan to keep watch tonight. Not that I expect any trouble, but it's always wise to take precautions."

She lifted startled eyes to his. "Are you going away, then?"

"For tonight, yes."

"But where? Why?"

He frowned at her. "My dear girl, obviously you must realize that it took some doing on your uncle's part to spare you a hearing before the authorities in Delhi. But that doesn't mean the matter's settled. I'm expected at the Foreign Office with a copy of your deposition. Colonel Armbruster requested it personally."

"The Foreign Office? In Delhi?"

He looked at her sharply. "You'll be all right here alone, won't you?"

She realized that she had to pull herself together. "Of course. Why shouldn't I?"

He didn't answer that question either. He just stood there looking down at her, frowning still, wondering how anyone could appear so heart-stoppingly beautiful and so forlorn at the same time. Her white wedding dress was dusty, and locks of her magnificent red hair had worked themselves loose in the heat. She was not the Maura he knew so well: feisty, tart-tongued, undefeated.

His mouth twisted. God, what he wouldn't give to stay here with her tonight! To hold her and soothe away the worried lines from her sweet, troubled brow! But she had made it clear that she wanted none of him, and that the only thing he could do for her now was to respect her wishes and quit her sight.

Perhaps in time . . .

But that was foolish, too, and with tightly reined self-control he lifted her hand to his lips and bowed over it very formally. Then he was gone, his boots clattering down the steps and his shadow falling long on the grass as he crossed to the pepper trees where Ghoda Lal awaited him.

Maura had never set foot inside Ross's bungalow before. Oh, she had tried, once, only to be humiliatingly dismissed from his sight in front of all his servants. Now she wandered through the cool, dark rooms looking at the possessions of the man who was now her husband and who remained every bit the stranger he had always been.

There was surprisingly little to look at. No personal mementos crowded the desk in the small study, only paperwork and a bottle of brandy. Ross's ceremonial sword, his pistols and orders were stored away with the same casual disregard as everything else.

The servants followed her about, wide-eyed with curiosity, until Amir Dass angrily dispersed them. In the bedroom Maura found Meera unpacking the few belongings Daphne had sent over for her. Admittedly the ayah had done her best to brighten the masculine room with cloth blinds and a vase of summer blooms, but Ross's presence remained overpowering.

She looked up, scowling, as Maura appeared. "Where is thy husband?"

"Gone." Maura sank onto the bed amid a pool of white satin damask. "To Delhi."

"On the night of thy *shadi,* thy wedding?"

Maura nodded, her face averted.

"Hai mai! This is an inauspicious beginning!"

Maura snorted, but without much spirit. "Didst thou expect another?"

"No," said Meera after a moment.

Maura's head came up. "What art thou thinking? I know that look."

"Dost thou?"

"Aye! It means there are too many thoughts in thy head, and none of them wise! Thou wilt not interfere when he returns. If one word passes thy lips—"

"I will not speak to him." Meera busied herself folding garments away. "But if thou didst truly love him, it would not have been hard to convince him to stay."

Maura made no reply to this and Meera looked at her sharply. "Dost thou?"

Maura put a hand over her eyes. Her slim shoulders shook. "From the very beginning," she whispered. "So much so that it hurts."

Meera's triumphant smile faded. "Then why not tell him?"

"I cannot."

Meera snorted. "Because thou art too proud—as is he! *Hai mai*, thou art a pair! I would have thought that after all this time, and all that has gone before—"

She broke off because she saw all at once that Maura was crying. Not noisily, like the miss-sahiba Lydia cried, or dramatically, like Carlyon-sahib's lady, but silently, the tears rolling down her cheeks to plop onto her wedding dress.

Ismail Khan brought Maura to the pink stucco palace the very next day. The suggestion had been Meera's, who had sought out the Pathan shortly after dawn, complaining that Hamilton-sahib's little bungalow had been sweltering and that neither she nor her mistress had slept all night. Surely the mem-sahib would be more comfortable in the shadowed rooms of the Begum's zenana?

"I know now that she has friends among these Muslims," Meera had concluded reluctantly, "and perhaps with her aunt and the mem of the cantonment gone, no one will know if she stays with them."

Ismail Khan scowled. "And Carlyon-sahib?"

"I will tell him that all is well, should he ask. But he is much diverted with paperwork and will assuredly not think of her until Hamilton-sahib returns from Delhi."

Ismail Khan had grunted his agreement. Surely the zenana of the Begum Kushna Dev would prove far more restful for his mistress than the sahib's dark little bungalow! The *bibi-gurh*, too, was uncomfortably hot these days and he saw no harm in returning to his own cool rooms in the house of Walid Ali.

"I will take her," he promised. "But only while the sahib is away. She must be returned before he hears of it. Think of his temper."

Meera bowed her head in agreement. "I will send word."

It was Maura's first visit to the pink stucco palace since the ambush of the bridal procession. Her appearance brought much rejoicing, and everyone rushed over to embrace her and inquire eagerly how long she intended to stay.

Only Kushna Dev noticed how weary she appeared, and quickly issued orders that she be brought to bed. A pair of serving girls led the way to her old, familiar bedchamber with its arching windows and cooing doves, and even though the sun was still high above the horizon, Maura fell asleep the moment she lay down amid the scented silk cushions.

And slept and slept as she had not done since the terror of that night out on the plains and the heartache of her marriage to Ross. Nor did she awaken until well into the afternoon of the following day—

feeling surprisingly refreshed and ravenously hungry.

"Rest has helped thee," Kushna Dev said approvingly as Maura joined her in the reception room following tiffin and a long, leisurely bath.

"I feel a hundred times better," Maura agreed, popping a piece of honeyed fruit in her mouth. "Nay, a thousand." Indeed, she did look well, her cheeks rosy and her violet eyes bright.

"I am pleased that thou hast recovered from thy travails."

"And thou?" Maura looked searchingly at her friend. "All is well?"

"Sita recovers slowly from the ordeal, but all will be well in the end. There is talk of another match for her, one far more to her liking. And I confess my husband is pleased to have cleared the cobras from his house."

"My uncle, too." Maura leaned back against the tassled cushions. "I had not known there was so much unrest in the countryside."

"Nor I! There were those who suspected that plans were afoot to intrigue against the British. But few were willing to aid Hamilton-sahib in finding them, for it would not have been seemly to betray our own countrymen."

Maura thought back to Ghoda Lal's slashed arm and the foiled attempt on Ross's life. Seeing her shiver, Kushna Dev added quickly, "But those feelings have changed since it became known that some of our kind were intriguing against *us*. This will do much, I think, to mend the differences between my people and thine."

"Let us hope so."

They smiled at each other fondly. Kushna Dev poured tea and waited while Maura helped herself to a sugar cube. Then she said carefully, "Perhaps now is also the proper time to make peace in thine own life."

Maura eyed her blankly. "How so?"

Kushna Dev shrugged, as though the subject was of little import. "Thou art newly wed, yet never have I seen thee more joyless." She put a finger to her lips. "Nay, do not look so! Let me speak my piece and then I will say no more on the matter."

"Allah be praised," Maura muttered.

The Begum was gracious enough to overlook that. And if anything, her friendship with the English girl had taught her to be stubborn. "I have known Hamilton-sahib since the day I came here as a bride. I was barely more than a child then, and very much afraid of *Angrezis*. But my husband had a wish for me to mix with thy kind, and so the sahib came often to the zenana."

"I'm well aware that he made a habit of that," Maura said darkly.

"Beshak! He is a man, and all men have needs! Surely thou art not so entirely Western of mind as to condemn—"

"I cannot change what passed before my return to India," Maura interrupted, although she was thinking bitterly of Sinta Dai. "But after? Did he not continue to come here and take his ease with the nautch-girl and . . . and later, with thy cousin from Rajasthan?"

"Surely thou art not jealous of thine own self!"

Maura's chin jutted. "What if I am?"

"And the time he came to thee in the garden after he knew the truth? Surely his feelings were obvious then!"

Maura gave a mocking laugh. "They were not! I can only assume that he was playing an unkind joke on me—perhaps so that he could boast to his friends how he took his leisure with the unwitting niece of Carlyon-sahib!"

"He is not that way!" Kushna Dev said sharply.

"Then how dost thou explain it?"

"I cannot. I know only that after the durbar at the Peacock Palace he never again took his pleasure with the nautch-girl, though tempt him she did! As I have said, I have known him many years, and always, always, his look softened and his manner changed when he spoke of thee. Not of my 'cousin' from Rajasthan, but of thee as the niece of Carlyon-sahib!"

Maura tossed her head. "That I will not believe!"

"Then thou art a fool. Because I am not the only one who thinks this. His feelings were always well hidden, perhaps even from himself, but there are those in my household who saw. My husband's mother, for one, and even my husband's uncles, though they are not, Allah preserve them, the most imaginative of men. Even Ismail Khan once said—" She broke off, her expression loving. "What is it, *piari*? Canst thou not believe what I say?"

"Thy words are never spoken lightly," Maura assured her tremulously, "but why then did he not stay? Why did he leave for Delhi on the night of our *shadi*?"

"Perhaps because he had no reason to believe he was welcome."

"That is untrue! He never once said—I did not—I mean, I never—" Maura broke off, recalling Meera's accusing words the day Ross left. Her chin tipped defiantly. "He never made it clear that he wished to stay! He told me from the very first that he had no choice but to go. And—and not too long ago I overheard him say to my uncle that he was marrying me only to keep me from further trouble!"

Kushna Dev's lips twitched. "Now that I will believe."

But Maura saw no humor in the situation. Not when her heart was filled with so much misery. To love like this was hard enough, but to know that she must spend the rest of her life hiding her feelings from Ross was too much to bear. Tears stung her eyes, but she stubbrnly refused to dash them away.

Kushna Dev must have noticed nonetheless, because all at once her tone became brisk. "We will speak no more on this matter. Thy time here will no doubt be brief. Perhaps we should spend it—"

Without warning a serving girl appeared and threw herself down at her mistress's feet. "I am sent to warn thee that Hamilton-sahib is below in the garden! He seeks the mem-sahib!"

Maura gasped.

"I do not understand this," Kushna Dev said in alarm. "Thy ayah promised to send word of his return!"

"And how did he know I was here?"

"I will speak to him."

"Nay, let me." Sighing, Maura got to her feet. No sense in delaying the inevitable. She would have preferred confronting Ross in a proper morning dress, but suspected from the serving girl's fearful manner that he wouldn't have the patience to wait while she changed out of her *choli* and veil. No doubt he was furious with her and spoiling for a fight. The least she could do was spare the women of the zenana an unpleasant scene.

"Stay," Kushna Dev urged, catching at the trailing end of her veil. "We can both—"

Maura shook her head. "I will meet him in the

courtyard. It is more private, and the garden will be far too hot."

Kushna Dev motioned for another serving girl to bring henna and perfumes, but Maura shook her head again. "There is no reason. *That* will be the last thing on his mind!"

The Begum pursed her lips. "Perhaps thou art right. I will say a prayer instead."

"I'll probably need it," Maura muttered in English.

The courtyard was shaded and cool. Beyond the marble arches palm fronds rustled in the breeze. Ross was standing with his back to the doorway watching the play of sunshine on the water in the fountain. He must have just returned from Delhi and ridden into the city without bothering to bathe and change, for he was dusty, sweat-stained and disheveled.

Maura's slippers made no sound on the smooth stone, but he turned nonetheless. The whip he had been tapping restlessly against his thigh stilled, and his dark eyes narrowed at the sight of her. He said nothing for a long moment, but Maura saw a muscle twitch in his unshaven cheek.

She had already steeled herself for his anger, but she was not prepared for the impact his dark, wind-blown looks had upon her. A rush of desperate longing overcame her and it was all she could do to stand there calmly instead of running to him.

Speak, she willed herself furiously. Say something to defend yourself! Let him know you don't care what he thinks or that he's caught you out. Make sure he realizes that you're not in the least bit happy to see him! Oh, but she was. Shaken to the core of her being with the joy of it, in fact. Wanting nothing more than to run to him, stand on tiptoe and lock her arms about his neck while he crushed her to him and lowered his hungry mouth to hers.

Thrusting her hands behind her back, she closed her eyes to temptation. For an endless moment the only movement between them was the breeze lifting the end of Maura's veil and fanning it out behind her.

"I know you're angry with me—" she whispered at last.

He pounced on that with all the ferocity of a preying tiger. "And why shouldn't I be? The moment my back is turned off you go, running away from home to play dress-up once again. For God's sake, Mrs. Hamilton, you're a married woman now! Too respectable for such games!"

Tears stung her eyes. Her throat ached. She had never been able to bear it when he was hateful. For a moment she was tempted to run back up the stairs, she who had never in all her life run away from anything. She reminded herself sternly that she was a cavalry colonel's daughter and now a captain's wife. She had more backbone than to shame herself like that!

Still, her lower lip thrust out childishly. "It was hot in your bungalow—"

"So your ayah told me. Why could you not have returned to your uncle's?"

"I prefer being here."

His smoldering gaze raked her gauzy attire with seeming contempt. "I can see that."

"And I have friends here."

"I know that too. And, believe me, I'm grateful to them. But it's still time you faced the facts."

She eyed him haughtily. "Is this to be another lecture, Ross? God knows you've given me enough since we met."

"And a hell of a lot of good they've done me—and

you! One would have thought, what with all the trouble you've caused, that you might have adopted some decorum by now! Obviously you haven't, and it's no wonder your guardians have aged twenty years since your return from England!"

Her chin tipped bravely. "Is there a reason for this, sir, or are you merely being insulting for sport?"

His lips tightened. "No, ma'am. I'm attempting to stave off gray hairs of my own for as long as I can."

"And the best way to do that is to take me firmly in hand, isn't it?" Maura snapped. "That's what you promised my uncle."

"I like to think I'm up to the challenge."

Up went her chin another notch. "And are you?"

Striding closer, he glared into her eyes. Better that than to drop his gaze to her mouth, which all this time and despite her bitter words he ached to kiss. Better to maintain this facade of anger than to let her know that he really didn't object at all to her being here; that seeing her dressed in those gossamer silks had wiped away all thoughts save one: how much he desired her.

Oh, God, how he wanted her! Beyond all imagining! But more than that he wanted her to desire him as well. To see her for once hurrying toward him with those magnificent eyes alive with welcome. To have her look at him with longing and love.

"You're a worthy adversary, Mrs. Hamilton," he said instead.

But despite his harsh words, despite everything, he didn't want her to be his adversary any longer. In fact, he hadn't thought of her in that way for a very long time now. Since that night they had slept side by side beneath the *ekka* in the jungle. Perhaps even before that: on the Delhi train, when she had accosted him, blazing-eyed and beautiful, with an umbrella.

Aye, he'd wanted her then, with a growing desperation as time went by that had tormented his soul. God knows he'd nearly done himself in trying to hide it!

Yet what was the point in hiding it any longer? One had only to look at the slim gold band Maura wore about her finger to see that she was his.

He had made a mistake, Ross thought with sudden clarity. He had been wrong when he'd boasted to Lawrence Carlyon that he could tame his niece simply by marrying her. He knew now that he would have to subdue her fiery Irish temper and stubborn will as well. Only not with unkindness . . .

But how to do so without revealing what lay in his heart? Lord above, she'd grind him into dust if she knew the truth!

He closed his eyes, then opened them again.

"Get dressed," he said curtly. "I'm taking you to Simla."

Chapter Twenty-two

"He cannot mean to take her away!" Kushna Dev pushed back from the balustrade where she had been listening shamelessly to the exchange below. Although she understood no English, she had recognized the word "Simla," and the stony look on Ross's face and the answering anger in Maura's had told their own story.

She stamped her slippered foot. "Why must the sahib-*log* play such stupid games?"

A smile touched the lips of the elderly attendant standing beside her. "Calm thy heart, *piari*. It is always so between women and men who love, no matter their origins. Dost thou not recall thy first weeks here in this house?"

Kushna Dev blushed prettily. "My husband was kind. It was easy for me to fall in love. But Hamilton-sahib—"

"Is stubborn and proud. As is his sahiba. Both will keep close guard on their hearts."

"Bah! That is foolish, and I intend to show them how much so!"

"They walk a different path from thine," the elderly ayah warned.

"That I will not believe! The path of all love is the same. I merely wish to remove the stones that litter theirs."

"Thy interference may not be ordained."

"How canst thou believe that? Was it not a lucky star that put Maura-sahiba in our path on the day of Sita's bridal procession?"

Shuddering at the memory, the attendant murmured a quick prayer. She said no more as she followed the Begum back to her private rooms, where servants were dispatched with messages for both Hamilton-sahib and Walid Ali.

Ross had already given orders that Maura's horse was to be saddled and brought round when one of the servants appeared before him. Would Hamilton-sahib please pay a call upon the master of the house before he left?

"Assuredly," Ross said at once. Inwardly he cursed the delay. The last thing he wanted at the moment was to trade pleasantries with Walid Ali. For the first time in his life he was tempted to be rude to his old friend and simply ignore the invitation. But as Maura would probably be some time changing into her habit and gathering her belongings, he followed the waiting attendant up the stairs.

His exchange with Walid Ali was blessedly brief. Instead of wasting time on greetings, the young merchantman came directly to the point. He needed to ask a favor of his old friend. Would Ross be willing to stop briefly on his journey to Simla to inspect a house that Walid Ali owned? The detour was not great and it had been a month or more since anyone of his household had been there. He was concerned that it might have been vandalized during the recent unpleasantries involving the abduction of his wife and sister-in-law.

The favor was by no means difficult and Ross readily agreed. Besides, he and Maura would reach the house sometime during the hottest part of the day, and there was no reason that they couldn't break their journey there until nightfall.

"Then it is settled," said Walid Ali complacently, and the two men shook hands in Western fashion.

Fortunately their exchange had been conducted in Hindustani so that the serving girl listening shamelessly at the door was able to slip away and report in full to her mistress.

Kushna Dev accepted the news with a satisfied smile. Walid Ali had played his role well, and she was convinced that Maura and Ross would now have another chance to mend their differences.

"What is written, is written," the elderly ayah muttered disapprovingly.

"Thou art a poisoned old woman," Kushna Dev responded gaily. "Now leave me be so that I may bid my friend farewell."

But Maura was not at all happy to take her leave. She had no wish to quit the pink stucco palace, and no desire to go to Simla. The thought of the endless rounds of teas, garden parties, tennis, polo matches, and fancy dress balls awaiting her filled her with angry despair. Surely Ross couldn't mean for her to endure such mind-numbing boredom! And surely he didn't mean to send her out of his sight for the next few months?

How he must dislike her, she thought with a painful catch of her heart.

They met in the courtyard where a servant stood waiting with their mounts. Ross had brought along one of his syces, who held a pack mare by the lead.

"The rest of your things will be sent later," he told Maura curtly. "Your ayah will follow then, too."

"Do you mean to say we are leaving for Simla now?" Maura demanded, startled. "From here?"

"Your aunt has probably taken along everything you need. Can you think of any reason to return to the Residency?"

"No." Her expression was stony. Obviously he couldn't wait to be rid of her.

"Walid Ali has offered us the use of a house not far from Kishnagar. That's about three hours from here. We can break our journey there. I've made arrangements for us to travel the rest of the way by carriage. That way you won't have to ride so far."

"Thank you. That's very kind." Ignoring his outstretched hand, Maura climbed into the saddle herself.

His mouth a tight line, Ross did the same.

She turned to him. "What of Ismail Khan?"

"He'll be staying here until you return. I doubt very much that he'll fit in well in Simla."

The thought of the surly Pathan trying to get along with the Hindu servants who would be crammed into the back quarters of the small house Aunt Daphne had let for the summer made Maura laugh unexpectedly. Looking up, she met Ross's answering smile. In this, at least, they could agree.

Some of the tension had eased out of Ross's face at the sound of her laughter. Now, spurring his horse closer, he laid his hand over hers.

"I hope you'll give me no reason to regret not sending him?"

She tossed her head. "Don't worry. I'll behave with the utmost decorum."

"That, I think, is impossible for you." But he was smiling as he spoke, an unexpectedly tender smile that caught at her heart and made her wonder if perhaps he was worried about her after all, just a little.

"I won't get involved in any intrigue or kidnappings, if that's what you mean."

"I certainly hope not." Ross didn't add that he wouldn't be letting her go if there was the least chance of that.

His smile faded abruptly. There was another, more compelling reason for sending her away. If she had given him the slightest hint that she would miss him or that she wished him to accompany her, then he would have done so at once. But Maura had made it clear by her silence and her coolness that she preferred going alone. Which was why he musn't give her any indication of his concern for her, or let her suspect how much he would miss her.

Now, looking into her upturned face upon which the trace of a smile still lingered, he ached to caress the soft curve of her cheek, to lean closer and lose himself in the violet wonder of her eyes. Their mounts stood side by side and he had only to lift his hand to run his fingers through her silky, upswept hair.

Hiding his regret behind a sudden frown he picked up the reins. "The morning's wasting. Let's go."

* * *

They rode side by side, not speaking, the pack mare and the syce following behind. It had been a stroke of good luck, Ross thought, that Walid Ali had asked him to make an inspection of his house in Kishnagar. While normally a three-hour ride was nothing to him—or to Maura from what he knew of her—the day's heat would soon be bad enough to pose a serious risk to their health.

Having spent the last four summers riding tours of inspection along the Northwest Frontier, Ross had forgotten how truly hot the plains around Bhunapore could become. It was barely noon when they saw the first mud-baked huts of Kishnagar shimmering in the distance, and already the temperature had soared. The horses were lathered and walked with a shuffling gait, and the metal barrel of the rifle Ross carried before him on the saddle was almost too hot to touch.

Maura rode with her head bowed, the reins slack between her gloved hands. The tendrils of hair that had worked themselves loose from beneath her topi were damp, and Ross felt certain that her heavy riding habit was clinging uncomfortably to her shoulders and back.

But so far she had not uttered a word of complaint. Thinking back, he doubted that he had ever heard her do so. In fact, she had never said one unkind thing about India.

He wondered now if her love for the country had dimmed in the face of such appalling heat. Because his certainly had.

Next year I'll apply for extended leave and take her to Kashmir, he thought. No place in all India was as remote and wildly beautiful. The thought of seeing Maura running through the mountain snows made him smile. And then frown, wondering if he had taken leave of his senses.

Here he was planning extended leave with a wife who didn't love him, who was willful and disobedient and fled to the home of her Muslim friends every chance she got. What on earth would they be doing a year from now? Would she be willing to go *anywhere* with him? Had he ever stopped to wonder what he and Maura were supposed to do with themselves for the rest of their lives?

He'd certainly never stopped to ask himself these questions when he'd first informed Lawrence Carlyon that he intended to marry her! The proposal itself—if one could even call it that—had been a moment of utter madness, the first impulsive thing he'd ever done in his life. The fear for her that had driven him throughout the nightmare of that long and awful night had apparently banished reason.

In his own defense he could argue that he hadn't been the only one afraid that night. The Sepoy Mutiny was still very much alive in the minds of many Britons who resided in India.

On the other hand, the Bhunapore insurrection had been put down with surprisingly few casualties, and Maura, though she didn't know it, had earned herself the gratitude of countless Muslims—and quite a few Hindus as well. Ross doubted very much that he'd ever be called upon to protect her again.

So why on earth had he married her? For all intents and purposes he was a free man now. Technically his tenure in Bhunapore was over. Now that he'd discharged his final duties by presenting a full report of the uprising to the Foreign Office in Delhi he could do as he wished with his life: quit his post as Lawrence Carlyon's adjutant, take the brevet that had been offered him, and return to the army.

Or join the prestigous ranks of the Indian Political Service, which was responsible for looking after all princely India and the Northern Frontier. Lord Seabrook at the Foreign Office had assured him that the IPS had plenty of room at the top for men of his experience. There was no doubt that he would be handed a plum assignment simply by asking.

Should he take it? Ross wondered. Quit his comfortable life in Bhunapore even though he now had a wife to look after? Maura would probably thrive on the rough-and-tumble existence of frontier life.

But would she thrive with him?

Once again Ross found himself cursing inwardly. He had told her once, on that glorious night on the Residency verandah when he'd kissed her for the first time, that he intended to settle down someday. Marry and start a family. Of course, back then he had merely been goading her, feeling quarrelsome and ill-tempered because he'd been annoyed with himself for finding her so desirable.

But now?

His lips twitched despite himself. Lord, how Ghoda Lal would mock him for such womanish fretting! He could almost see the contempt on his bearer's face, hear it in his derisive laughter.

But Ghoda Lal had never been in love . . .

"Ross?"

He started, then took a moment to collect himself by removing his topi and mopping his brow. Only after tucking the handkerchief back in his pocket did he turn his attention to his wife.

"You said something about inspecting a house here in Kishnagar. Where?"

He realized that they had reached the outskirts of the town without his having been aware of it. The cart trail had given way to a surprisingly level road.

Up ahead a few European-style houses surrounded the empty market square. Some long-forgotten British district officer must have arranged to plant trees, for the square was shady and cool.

Although they were barely three hours out of Bhunapore the air seemed fresher, the plains more hilly and green. Ahead lay Simla and the foothills of the mighty Hindu Kush. The proximity of the mountains could be felt in the crisp air and seen in the water of the market square, which flowed in a clear stream, not the color of mud from a well.

All at once Ross felt his spirits lifting. Turning in the saddle, he smiled at his wife. "The house isn't far beyond town. We're welcome to break our journey until evening, when the traveling will be cooler. Walid Ali has sent some of his servants ahead. They'll be expecting us."

Maura could barely hide her relief. "I should like to stop for a while."

"Tired, are you?"

She was surprised by the concern in his voice. "A little."

"I'll tell the syce. He knows the way."

Maura had half expected the Kishnagar house to resemble Walid Ali's pink stucco palace, only not quite so grand. To her surprise the syce halted in front of a European-style bungalow replete with a wide verandah and shutters. Flower beds had been laid out with proper British precision, their borders lined with smooth river rocks no doubt brought down from the hills. Though most of the beds were wildly unkempt and wilted in the heat, a few verbena and a rambling rose clung stubbornly to life.

Maura lifted questioning eyes to Ross's face. "What is this place?"

"Originally a British station. The District Commissioner and his family lived here in this house. Another half dozen families or so lived across the maidan." He pointed with his whip at the browned lawn that had once been the parade grounds. "I came here a few times over the years and liked it quite well. You'd almost never know you were in India. There was a proper milliner's shop and book-store in town, and a Portuguese baker who made all sorts of English breads and tarts."

"Where are they now?"

"The station was abandoned during the Mutiny."

Maura's eyes were wide. "Does that mean—Do you know—Did they—?"

Ross's mouth thinned. "The women and children were sent to Lucknow for safety, although most of them perished in the siege. The menfolk were mas-sacred en route."

"Were there no survivors?"

"If there were, they chose not to return. This house stood empty for years until the Foreign Office presented it as a sop to Nasir al–Mirza Shah. If memory serves me right, he in turn gave it to Walid Ali in recognition of some minor favor. I think the old fellow was glad to be rid of it, and Walid Ali has never quite known what to do with it either."

Maura drew rein at the edge of the untidy flow-erbed. Shading her eyes she scanned the sagging ve-randah. "Have you ever been inside?"

"Honestly, no. Though I've certainly passed this way often enough."

A turbaned servant appeared at the door to wel-come them. The interior was dark and cool thanks to the cane blinds that had been lowered over the windows and outer walls to protect the house from the full glare of the sun.

After the heat and the brightness of the open road

it felt like a blessing to step inside. With a sigh Maura swept off her topi and tossed it onto the nearest chair. Pulling off her gloves, she wandered into the salon with its high ceiling and heavy supporting beams. Hunting trophies lined the whitewashed walls.

The servants had obviously been busy, for the floor was swept and spread with rugs. The tarnished mirrors had been polished and the furniture dusted and aired. A platter of peeled and quartered fruit stood on the low table and Maura happily helped herself to a succulent fig.

"The bed chambers have been prepared," said the turbanned servant in Hindustani, bowing deeply. "If the memsahib wishes to retreat?"

Maura laughed. "I couldn't possibly sleep in the middle of the day!"

"I thought you were tired?" Ross asked.

"Bone tired, but I certainly don't want to rest."

"Why not? Everything's clean. Savaji has seen to that."

The *chupprassi* swelled visibly at the praise. "I have prepared water, memsahib. For bathing."

Maura's eyes widened. "You mean there's a bath?"

Ross's lips twitched. "Quite modern, so Walid Ali told me."

Maura eagerly followed the *chupprassi* through a cool room with a very comfortable looking bed, and hurried past him when he gestured grandly toward a second door.

"There, memsahib."

The bath was completely tiled, right down to the raised platform for the water closet, a real one, not like the hated "thunderbox" at the Residency. A gleaming copper bath, no doubt brought over from England at great expense, took up most of the space beneath the window. And wonder of wonders, a bottle of lavender water and a real sea sponge—a rare luxury in Bhunapore, where such objects were likely to conceal scorpions—had been placed nearby.

Maura turned accusingly to Ross, who had come to stand behind her. "I thought you said the British who lived here were long gone?"

"They are." He, too, was frowning. "I've no idea where Walid Ali came by such things."

The *chupprassi* remarked quickly that his mistress, the Begum Kushna Dev, had sent the gifts for the memsahib, certain that she would feel more at home surrounded by familiar things.

"For such a short stay," Maura marveled. "How kind of her! Of course I must use them!"

The menfolk obligingly withdrew, and a pair of maidservants were sent to assist her. They were local girls, hired for the afternoon, and much too shy to answer Maura's questions with more than a nod or a shake of the head.

But they could not resist fingering the fabric of her riding habit or exclaiming over the color of her hair after Maura had washed the heavy red mass and then brushed it out to dry.

Maura chatted with them easily, and after a while they lost their fear and began to giggle and ask questions of their own. She learned that their village had languished since the abandonment of the station by the British, but that their fathers and uncles, who had lived through the Mutiny, held out hope of their return.

"Perhaps thy sahib and thee—" one of them began timidly.

"Oh, no! We are but passing through." But Maura had to admit that the thought of staying was surprisingly tempting. She found she liked the idea of having a house of her own, with no Aunt Daphne peering over her shoulder and admonishing her to behave. A house of her own meant that she would have the right to entertain whomever she pleased, whether British or native.

And Ross would be there . . .

"The memsahib is sad?"

"No."

But her expression was wistful as she finished dressing and joined Ross in the dining room.

He, too, had changed for dinner, and stood with his back to her in breeches and shirtsleeves, a drink in one sun-browned hand. He seemed lost in thought, and from the tension in his wide shoulders she knew that he was frowning.

Was he thinking of her?

I've been a bother to him since the first time we met, she thought unhappily. Oh, Ross, if only I'd not been so horrid! Maybe then you'd not have married me out of a sense of duty.

He turned then, and their eyes met across the room. Though Maura had often seen him dressed so casually, the sheer force of his masculinity brought a quickening to her heart. He was, as one of the cantonment matrons had once said, as handsome as the devil. And they were alone in this house but for a handful of servants . . .

She pushed the thought from her head. He was taking her to Simla. He wanted to be rid of her.

"Hungry?" he asked. His tone was cool, his expression unreadable.

"Yes."

"Come, then."

"Thank you."

If he noticed that her voice was shaking a little he gave no sign. Setting aside his drink he led her silently to the table.

Chapter Twenty-three

Their meal together was a silent one. For all that they had been through together, Maura had never once dined with Ross alone, and she found herself now at an uncharacteristic loss for words. For once even her infamous temper deserted her and she could not draw on it for the courage to behave uncaringly. She could only bow her head and eat, and try to ignore the awkward silence between them as it grew into a yawning void that could not be filled.

Thank God, Ross was thinking, that we're not spending the night here! The privacy of the empty house and now a meal shared by just the two of them was wreaking havoc on his senses. That, and the fact that sitting across the table from Maura afforded him the chance to study her at leisure, a forbidden luxury he found himself unable to resist.

She was beautiful, wildly so. After bathing she had donned a modest green frock from the few in her luggage, and the unadorned neckline was cut low enough to reveal the tempting swell of her breasts. In the lamplight her hair gleamed with a coppery fire.

He watched her sample a piece of fruit, her mouth like a ripe berry itself. With an effort he tore his gaze away.

"What will you do with yourself in Simla?" It was all he could think of to say.

She shrugged. "Go to parties. Play croquet. Chaperone Terence and Lydia about. Now that I'm married I suppose I'm respectable."

Married, yes, but only in name, Ross thought. Even prim and proper Daphne Carlyon would have been aghast to learn that he and Maura had not yet shared their wedding bed.

Children are a requisite of Empire, he could almost hear her saying in her most disapproving tone. That's why certain duties are expected of all newlyweds living abroad.

But the thought of *doing his duty* wasn't the reason Ross was finding it difficult to keep his eyes off his bride today. Damn it, why did the chit have to come to the table looking so bloody desirable? Why did their first meal alone together as husband and wife have to take place here in these very British surroundings, which were throwing him thoroughly off balance?

It wasn't just the fact that he found her desirable, though Lord knows he'd been aching for her for days—weeks! It was the way she made him feel when they were alone like this. Absurd as it might seem he was reminded of the comfortable domesticity of an elderly colonel with his regimental days behind him, sitting in his cozy parlor with slippers on his feet and a Rajah's peg at his elbow. Damn!

When had he himself ever felt so completely at ease, so bloody content?

After Maura's abduction, he remembered with a sudden cramping of his heart. When he had stumbled, exhausted, into the Residency following a night of killing, for there had been those among the sadhu's followers who had not taken the failure of their plans lightly and had refused to surrender to a sahib.

He remembered now, clearly, though at the time he had been reeling with fatigue, how he had allowed Maura to lead him to bed, scarcely aware of what she did, knowing only that her arms about him were the only things keeping him from falling. He remembered how she had undressed him, calmly and efficiently, but with a tenderness he had not known since he'd felt the loving touch of his mother's hands.

Fool, he thought savagely. That's why you told Lawrence Carlyon you were going to marry her!

Because he'd realized upon waking in her bed that he could no longer live without her. That she appeased a loneliness inside him that had never bothered him before, but which had been driving him mad all those long, restless weeks since her arrival in India.

Of course, he'd hidden his feelings behind aloofness, making sure that the Carlyons—and Maura—knew the enormity of the sacrifice he was making by volunteering to take her off their hands.

Bloody idiot! He'd managed to convince even himself that it was true!

Which was why he had fled to Delhi the moment she had started working her way past his defenses and into his heart. And now here he was, still acting the coward by packing her off to Simla!

Only, how was he supposed to maintain his sanity in the intimacy of these surroundings? Maura's mere presence here humbled him, nay, tormented him, and made him long for the impossible.

Without warning he pushed back his chair and stood. "It's still far too hot for traveling. Why don't you rest?"

His voice was so harsh that Maura's heart skittered to a halt. Oh, God, what had she done? Why did he want her out of his sight so unexpectedly?

"Rest?" she echoed faintly.

"Why not? I'd like to make it as far as the border tonight. That means at least five more hours in the saddle."

She said nothing, not daring to look at him.

Striding around the table he held out his hand to her. "Come on."

She kept her head bowed so he wouldn't see the tears in her eyes. She'd rather die than let him know that he had the power to make her weep. And all the while she could feel him staring down at her, smoldering with impatience. For an awful moment she wondered if he was going to yank her bodily out of her chair if she didn't obey.

"Well?" he rapped.

Swallowing hard she laid aside her fork and put her hand in his.

Expelling a long breath, Ross helped her to her feet. "Thank you."

For what? her heart cried out.

The servants had withdrawn and the house was utterly still. The silence throbbed around them as Ross nudged open the bedroom door. Letting go of her hand he retreated across the threshold and bowed formally.

"I'll have Savaji wake you in an hour. Will that be

long enough?" He cocked his head when she made no answer. "Maura?"

Up swept her violet eyes, and he saw with a blow to the heart that they were luminous with tears.

Oh, God. He could bear anything, anything but that.

Groaning, unable to help himself, he gave in to madness and drew her hard against his shirtfront. Her willowy body bent to his like a blade of grass. Her trailing skirts, unimpeded by a corset and hoops, pooled around his feet.

And then he was kissing her, tormented kisses that nonetheless burned with relief. And they were lush, lush beyond all imagining with desire. His mouth drank greedily, and oh, the wild sweetness of the moment when her lips finally opened to his!

"Oh, God," he groaned again, gathering her closer. Cradling her head with his hand he molded her to him, center to center, his other arm wrapped tightly about her waist.

She couldn't help it. Lifting her arms, she locked them around his neck and let the tautness of his man's body take the full weight of hers, for by now her bones had turned to water.

In response he uttered a half-despairing laugh and eased her away. His hands clasped her arms as though to keep her—or him—from falling.

"Bloody hell!" His chest heaved. "I'm sorry."

"Are you?"

"Maura, don't."

"Don't what?"

"Maura, please." His breathing was tortured.

"Don't what, Ross? I've not done a thing."

"I know. It's—I'm sorry. I didn't intend to frighten you."

She uttered a soft, incredulous laugh. "Frighten

me? You've done all sorts of horrible things to me since we met, Ross Hamilton, but frightening me hasn't been one of them!"

He glared at her. "What sorts of things?"

She thrust a hand beneath his nose and proceeded to count on the tips of her fingers. "You've frustrated me, insulted me, annoyed and ignored me, made me feel murderously angry at times. . . . Shall I go on?"

He expelled a long, defeated breath. "No."

"In fact," she added tartly, "it's probably lucky for you that you never made me angry when there were weapons about."

He had been massaging the bridge of his nose as she spoke, but now he looked at her sharply. She was glaring at him, arms akimbo, her chin tipped at that old, stubborn angle. No doubt about it, she was spoiling for a fight.

"Is that so?" His voice was rough. "It seems I remember a time or two when you accosted me with an umbrella and . . . what else? A riding whip, your uncle's pistol, oh, and your syce's rifle."

"That's not true!"

"And let's not forget your fists and slashing tongue . . ."

Which had wounded him most of all, although he'd never tell her that.

She scowled at him. "You make me sound like a barbarian!"

Which she was. A maddening, enchanting, thoroughly charming little savage. And all at once his heart was throbbing painfully in his chest because he sensed suddenly that she wasn't really as angry as she seemed. He didn't dare hope that she was teasing him, that she had actually welcomed those hungry kisses and perhaps . . . perhaps longed for something more.

"I'm not afraid of you," Maura went on, her dark eyes locking with his. "Not of you, Ross. Never of you."

For a moment he was still, so still that suddenly she *was* afraid. Had she made a mistake? Misunderstood the reason for his seeming anger? Oh, God, if that were true . . .

But then he uttered a strangled laugh and, in one fluid motion, bent and hooked his arm around her knees. Sweeping her upright he crushed her against him and kissed her, lavishly, almost desperately, and she responded with her arms locked tight around his neck. Their heads dipped and swayed with the intensity of that kiss, and Ross could feel her heart tripping to the same wild rhythm as his.

"Piari," he whispered. "Little Pearl, I can't pretend any longer. You've enslaved me so that I've no more wish to run."

"Oh, Ross . . ." His name was no more than a sigh against his lips. "I know. But don't talk now. Just kiss me. Kiss me, please."

Throbbing with need and a desire that was almost pain he laid her across the bed. Levering his weight on one arm he leaned into her, keeping their bodies fused, the kiss unbroken. Tongues mated and danced, lips sought succor after what seemed to them an endless thirst.

Slipping his hand inside her bodice, he cupped her naked breast. Maura's breath caught and she arched to his touch.

"Sweet," he whispered. "So sweet."

His thumb grazed her nipple and the rosebud peak strained against his palm. Groaning, he lifted his mouth from hers and followed the heated path of his hand. Once again she sighed his name.

Gently he caressed her, his touch rough magic.

And always his lips followed to finish what his hands had begun.

She moaned, a whispery sound, while his pulse pounded and his body clamored for hers.

"Ross . . ."

A plea or a benedicton? Elated, uncaring, he reared up and covered her mouth with his once again. Skillfully, without breaking that heated touch, he managed to ease off her gown.

She shifted and turned to his bidding until she lay naked beneath him. His eyes glowed as he ran his hands down the slim lines of her hips and murmured the name he so loved.

"Maura, beautiful Maura. Do you know how long I've imagined seeing you like this?"

She opened heavy-lidded eyes, confused all of a sudden. "But we—you—"

"It was dark those other times," he reminded her softly, his breath stirring the silky curls at her temple.

He felt her smile against his throat. Then she rolled out from under him.

"What—?" he began.

"Hush." Kneeling before him, she eased off his shirt. "Now it's my turn."

Laughter rumbled in his chest. "You're a minx, Mrs. Hamilton."

Smiling, she clasped her fingers around the tightly corded muscles of his upper arms. "You're just as I remember."

"Am I?"

"Oh, yes," she whispered, stroking him lightly.

He smiled into her hair and arched himself boldly against her. "Do you remember this?"

"How could I possibly forget?"

"Thou art far too brazen," he murmured in Hindustani.

"Because thou hast taught me so well," she murmured back.

His being throbbed. His body demanded. Lord, how much longer could he resist her?

To buy himself time he rolled over and stripped off what remained of his clothing. She watched him through the dim light coming from the blinds, one arm cradled beneath her head.

When he lay down beside her again, face to face, his arm, too, beneath his head, she pressed her palm to his naked chest.

"It feels so different." Her voice was filled with wonder.

"What does?"

"This. Everything. As though you're really mine now."

He found he had to swallow before he could speak. When he did, his voice was rough. "That's because I am. Didn't I just say you've enslaved me?" And to prove it, he took her hand and brought it down to that part of him that clamored for her the most.

Her eyes went wide at the heated size of him, but she did not draw away. Instead she let him mold her hand to his hugeness before he removed his own. His breath stilled as she began to caress him.

"I've dreamed of this, so many times," he murmured. "Being with you, touching you, letting you touch me . . ."

"How long? After the last time you had Chota Moti?" Her breath tickled the dark hair curling across his chest.

He shuddered in response. "No. Long before that."

369

She gazed at him, surprised. "When?"

"Since we slept together beneath the *ekka*, on the road to Delhi."

"But that was before—we barely knew each other then!"

"Believe me, I wasn't the least bit happy about it. Much as I tried, I couldn't keep myself from wanting you. It would have been easier to stop breathing."

"I—I thought it was Chota Moti, not me, that you . . . you desired." Her voice trembled with remembered anguish.

"Oh, I did." He was kneeling before her now, her face cupped in his hands, his fiercely earnest eyes holding hers. "I won't deny that she was a true seductress, this Rajasthani pearl who bewitched me in the prince's garden. But it was the stubborn, damnable niece of Lawrence Carlyon who taught me that there's more to a woman, so much more, than the means of finding pleasure."

He sensed more than saw the tears that glimmered in her eyes, and suddenly understood some of the hurt that he had caused her. How she must have suffered thinking him infatuated with another while knowing all along that that other woman was her own self!

Yes, she had despaired, but so had he, and there was much to be revealed and explained and forgiven before the matter could finally be laid to rest.

But because this was not the time nor the place, he showed her with his mouth and his hands all that he felt inside. To still any lingering doubts that she was the one he desired, the one he loved . . .

She responded with a fervor that sent his spirit soaring. She knew, ah, she knew, his clever, fiery enchantress!

His fingers cupped her thighs and his lips traced

370

a heated path along the taut skin of her belly. Heady triumph mingled with passion. There was no need to hurry now, no reason to fear exposing the deception between them—or worry that the night watchman might discover them! For once he could take his time to worship and adore that for which he had yearned so long. To openly make love to Maura, his wife, and not hide behind the pretense that he thought her another.

Maura's head fell back as she surrendered to his loving. His touch was magic, her response a building fire. She moaned and writhed as the pleasure mounted. Flames licked through her blood to center at last at the core of her womanhood, a budding flower, ready to burst.

"Ross, oh, Ross—"

But he already knew what she wanted. Even as she arched her hips and shuddered he moved quickly away.

"Wait, love, wait."

Propping his arms on either side of her head he lowered himself, ever so slowly, until all his great, wonderful weight settled upon her. As he reached between them to ease her thighs apart she opened herself willingly beneath him.

His heart caught at the silent invitation, this piercing moment of trust. "Maura," he whispered raggedly, "Maura—"

The earth seemed to hold itself still as he placed himself against her. Then slowly, slowly, he thrust inside.

"Oh—!"

Quivering, she wrapped herself around him and held him tight with her legs and her arms. Her body arched to take him deep.

With an answering groan he surrendered. Drawing back, he waited for an electrified moment, then surged forward to fill her again.

Only once, twice, then barely again before passion unfurled like a white hot flower, burning its way to the core of their beings. They clung together, joined in that most intimate of moments, as the fire roared and the explosion came, shattering them completely.

Chapter Twenty-four

"We'll have to leave soon. It's late."

Maura opened her eyes to find Ross standing naked before the window. The blinds had been raised and a thread of silvery light showed on the horizon. The dawn was coming.

She stretched and yawned and smiled almost shyly when he turned to look at her.

His answering smile made her heart miss a beat. She had wondered, before drifting off to sleep last night, what it would be like to awaken in the presence of this man, after he had loved her beyond all imagining the night before.

The moment was far more passionate than she had thought. Crossing to the bed, he leaned over her, arms propped on either side of her head, and she became aware again of his hard man's body, his feral touch.

"You're blushing." His breath tickled her ear.

"I'm not. I never blush."

He leaned closer. The rough hair on his chest brushed her naked skin. "Contrary as always, my beautiful Maura. What will it take to bend your will to mine?"

She would have purred like a cat when he dropped his weight fully upon her and let her feel the extent of his arousal, how much he wanted her. But even as longing began to burn through her veins she lifted solemn eyes to his.

"Tell me that you love me."

Startled, he drew back a little.

She took his face in her hands, trapping him gently. "It isn't hard, Ross. The world won't end if you do."

He cleared his throat. Adorable man. Any moment now he'd actually start squirming. "I've never said those . . . um . . . words to a woman before."

She bit her lip to hide her smile. Never through all their hair-raising adventures together had she seen him so unsure of himself. Would Ghoda Lal and Amir Dass recognize their courageous sahib if they could see him now?

"It's easy." With her thumbs she stroked the strong line of his jaw. "I love you." Now her eyes clung to his and her voice trembled with emotion—and dawning surprise. "I love you more than I thought I could possibly love anyone. From the moment you laughed at me in the Bombay train station, I think. At the time I thought it was anger."

"Maura." Leaning down, he took her hands in his. Raising her up from the pillows so that their faces were close, their lips nearly touching, he looked deeply into her eyes. "I thought it was anger, too."

For a moment she stared at him. Then she burst into laughter. Her smile was as dazzling as sunshine. "Oh, Ross, no one's ever said 'I love you' to me quite like that before!"

His lips twitched. "I certainly hope not."

He laid her back against the linens, aggressively male now that he was on safe ground once again. Leaning over her he kissed her, and the searing touch of his mouth told her more than words ever could how much she was loved, cherished . . . desired.

Her breath was a sigh against his lips. Surrendering, she let him lead her back into that world of intimate delights wrought by a touch, a caress, a murmured word of endearment.

"Oh, Ross—"

Then, abruptly, she sat up.

"What is it, love?"

"I don't know. I felt—I thought for a moment that I might be ill."

He kissed the palm of her hand, his expression concerned, but she relaxed against the pillows, the twinge of pain gone.

"No, I'm all right."

His worried frown softened and he reached for her again. But to his surprise, Maura drew away a second time. "What is it, love?"

"I don't know. I feel . . . strange." Gasping, she swung her bare legs over the side of the bed and hurried into the bathroom. A moment later he heard her lose what remained of last night's supper.

When he appeared in the doorway she was rinsing her face. "All right?" he asked gently.

She gave him a shaky smile and nodded.

"I don't think I've ever had a woman react that way to my kisses," he teased. He helped her back to the bed, hiding his concern. She was far too pale for his liking.

"Oh, Ross, I'm s-sorry. I feel so utterly awful."

His guts wrenched with sudden fear until he reminded himself sternly that this was not the season for cholera or any of the myriad illnesses that left the Indian soil littered with fresh graves every year.

"It'll pass, love. Perhaps some breakfast—"

"No, I-I can't. I think I'm going to be sick again."

"Come lie down, then. It's all right. Here." He brought her water to drink, but the moment she sipped from the cup she scrambled back to the bathroom.

"It must be the food I ate last night," she murmured weakly as Ross carried her to bed a second time. "I'm truly s-sorry."

"Don't be. Tainted meat's not uncommon in India, as you well know."

"Did you have to say that word?" she groaned, attempting a shaky smile. But it was the last time for quite a while that she was able to tease him.

Ross tended her unfailingly during the difficult hours that followed. An old India hand, he had seen his share of such agony and experienced enough himself, but his heart ached for her every time Maura tossed and moaned. Though she seemed unaware of him as her wretchedness mounted he did not once leave her side.

There was no use sending for a doctor, he knew. No hakim in the village could be trusted to look after her properly, and there was little enough anyone could do to ease her suffering.

So he bathed her brow while her fever burned, and when the chills came he covered her warmly and talked to her soothingly as though she were a fretful child.

Luckily by nightfall Maura was resting easier. The

nausea passed and at long last her eyelids fluttered shut.

The moment he had assured himself that she was truly asleep, Ross summoned one of the serving girls. His eyes blazed in his weary face as he admitted her inside.

"Watch over her."

"Assuredly, sahib."

Out in the hall the *chupprassi* waited. "I have sent for thy horse, sahib. But it is late and—"

"Then bolt the doors and go to bed," Ross said curtly. And despite his fatigue, he leaped into the saddle and cantered down the deserted road.

It was the sound of angry words in Hindustani that awakened Maura many hours later, long after the dawn had chased away the stars. Weak but free from pain, she struggled to sit up just as the bedroom door burst open and a middle-aged Indian woman in a bright red sari stormed inside.

"Meera!"

"Wah!" the ayah exclaimed, hands on her hips in a manner eerily reminiscent of a very annoyed Daphne Carlyon. "I have traveled through the night because I heard thou wert ailing, and what do I find when I arrive? This silly monkey of a girl will not let me in!"

"Memsahib, please!" The girl's hands were clasped in appeal. "I had orders from the sahib before he left that I was not to let anyone disturb thee!"

Startled, Maura turned to the ayah. "Did Ross fetch thee from Simla?"

"He did not. I had already left with summons from the Begum Kushna Dev, who wrote that thou hadst broken thy journey here. Then came word of thy illness—"

"Bad news travels fast," Maura muttered resignedly, though secretly she was glad that Meera had come. How kind of Kushna Dev to think of it! She turned to the serving girl. "Where is the sahib?"

"Gone for many an hour." But the girl did not know where.

Although she felt absurdly weak, Maura insisted on dressing. Meera was none too pleased. "But thou hast been ill!"

"I am better now."

Meera snorted. "That I will not believe! Thou art like a newborn foal on thy feet! What plagued thee?"

"Tainted meat, I think."

"I thought as much. Thou hast the look of one who has been poisoned."

"Ahh. Does this mean thou hast become a hakim in my absence?"

Meera ignored the barb. "It would explain why thy husband is not here. May he find the merchant who would dare sell spoiled meat to a sahib!"

"Can we talk of other things, please?" Maura asked with a shudder.

Meera relented, and fussed over her while Maura bathed and dressed and drank a bowl of weak broth. Afterward the ayah demanded to be shown through the house and hear the tale of how Walid Ali had come by it.

Although she was glad for Meera's company, Maura could not help growing impatient as the afternoon waned and Ross did not return. At her request the *chupprassi* made inquiries in the village, although he returned almost immediately to report that the sahib had not been seen there all day.

"Then where has he gone?" Maura demanded fretfully. "How can he stay away so long and not send word?"

"Perhaps because he does not wish to disturb thy rest," Meera soothed.

"Wouldn't he at least wish to know how I am faring?"

The ayah patted her hand and did not reply.

She wants me to sit here doing nothing while I await his return, Maura thought angrily. But I won't! I've never been the least bit patient and I don't like it when he plays these games!

God knows he'd done it often enough before they were married!

"Where art thou going?" Meera demanded a moment later.

"Out."

"To search for the sahib when all in the village could not find him? To run about in the darkness without a syce?"

"Why not?"

"*Hai mai!*" Meera was genuinely angry. "Because thou art a memsahib now, no longer a willful girl! Thou must behave once and for all in a manner befitting thy station and bring no more shame to thy husband's name!"

Meera had never spoken so sharply before and Maura could not argue with the wisdom of her words. With an angry swish of her skirts she threw herself down in a nearby chair.

But only for a moment. The sound of heavy footsteps on the verandah had her bounding for the door. The *chupprassi* had not even appeared in the hall before she had thrown it open.

"Ross, thank God! Where in heaven's name have you—"

But it was not Ross who stood there on the threshold, dusty and travel weary. Maura's hand flew to her lips.

"Ismail Khan! What on earth—"

The Pathan bowed deeply. "I bring a letter from the Begum."

Maura turned her back on him as she broke the seal. The message was brief, the words written with obvious haste. Ross, it said, had appeared unannounced at the pink stucco palace late yesterday evening and requested a private bedchamber for the night. He had sent immediately for his former lover, the nautch-girl Sinta Dai. Did Maura know of this? Had she given them her blessing?

"What is it?" Meera asked sharply. "Where art thou going?"

Maura ignored her and whirled on the *chupprassi*. "Send for my horse."

Meera ran after her, plucking at her sleeve. "Thou wouldst not dare ride at this hour! Thy health—"

Maura shook her off. "Ismail Khan, wilt though accompany me back to Bhunapore? Thou hast already ridden the distance once this day, and I would spare thee and take a syce—"

But Ismail Khan had no intention of leaving his mistress in the hands of a lowly groom. Allah alone knew what could happen when the memsahib's eyes glittered that way. Ohé, she was like an angry tigress! Besides, he already knew what awaited her at the home of Walid Ali. Her reunion with the sahib would not be pleasant.

"I will accompany thee."

"Thou wilt not leave until the sahib returns!"

Maura scarcely heard either of them. I will kill him, she was thinking wildly as she hurried to her room. Or her, or both! Cut out their hearts and grind them into dust at my feet!

Slamming the bedroom door, she tore off the dress she had chosen to wear for Ross when he returned. Some of the pearl buttons popped off and rolled beneath the bed. She didn't even notice.

Was it all lies? Everything he had said to her the night before, and had shown her with his passionate kisses and his touch?

No! She knew in her heart that it couldn't be.

But she had been ill. Violently so. And Ross had stayed with her until the worst of it had passed.

There was a tearing sound as she stepped on the hem of her skirt. "Leave be!" Slapping away Meera's hands she kicked herself free.

I am a fool! A fool!

It was obvious that her illness had offended him, that it had turned his dawning affection for her into disgust.

"Oh, why didn't I send him out of the room?" she howled. "Why didn't I insist he leave me be?"

She swallowed hard against the lump in her throat. Yes, she'd been a fool. A witless idiot to think that winning Ross could be so easy, to take for granted that he loved her as much as she loved him! In the end he couldn't even say it aloud, could he?

Meera must have noticed her tears, for her own eyes softened suddenly. "What is it, *piari?* What did the letter say?"

"He has gone back to her."

"Who?"

Maura's shoulders lifted in a helpless shrug. "The *kathak* dancer who lives in the zenana at the house of Walid Ali. The one with the courtesan's skills, the sloe eyes, the saris of perfumed silk."

The rival who would never be so indelicate as to be sick in Ross's presence!

Meera was looking at her, horrified. "Art thou riding back to Bhunapore to—to kill him?"

Maura uttered a brittle laugh. How she must look

381

the part, eyes wild and flashing, chin tipped with self-rightousness!

Only—

She collapsed on the bed, her unbuttoned riding habit slipping off one shoulder, and drew a shaky breath. "No, I don't intend to kill him."

"Then what?"

Maura lifted brimming eyes to the ayah's face. "I want to win him back."

"Then wait until morning. Thou art too weary to ride so many—"

"I can't wait that long! It will be far too late by morning!"

If it wasn't already too late now . . .

She dashed away the tears and caught at Meera's hand. "Show me how to win him back. Surely thou canst? It is said that thou wert raised in a zenana and in girlhood taught the ways of love."

"Nonsense! The kama sutra? Who told thee?"

"Lydia's ayah."

"Her head is stuffed with equal nonsense."

Maura's face fell. "Then it is untrue?"

"My mother was a courtesan," Meera admitted reluctantly, "but that was many years ago."

"But surely, coming of age in the same house, the ways of love did not remain totally unknown to thee!"

Meera scowled. "Oh, very well, the truth, then. Perhaps I remember a little."

Maura's eyes shone with sudden hope. "Please, Meera, please! Teach me what thou dost remember, no matter how unimportant it may seem. I am a quick learner. Please! There is so little time—"

"I should have stayed in Simla," the ayah grumbled, though she had begun to smile a little.

Chapter Twenty-five

Dawn had finally come to the zenana of the pink stucco palace. A silvery light had replaced the darkness and now a hot breeze stirred the windchimes. On a nearby rooftop a cockerel crowed.

Rising from the silken cushions where he had spent a restless night, Ross groaned and stretched his aching limbs. His head throbbed from the spirits he and Walid Ali had consumed. Naked, he crossed to the open archways that served as windows and watched as the last of the stars edged past the minaret of the nearby mosque.

In an hour, perhaps less, the household would be stirring and the merchants would begin setting up their wares in the bazaar beyond the garden. In an hour the heat would be brutal and he would be risking both his health and that of his horse by riding away.

Only a madman would do so.

Ellen Tanner Marsh

Then perhaps he was a madman, for he knew that he must. Although what would he say to Maura when he returned?

A mistake, he thought. I've made a bloody awful mistake.

Yet at the time it hadn't seemed that way. Perhaps because it had been so easy to trace the tainted meat Maura had eaten to the home of the local butcher, and easy enough to extract the frightened man's confession as to where he had come by it.

On the other hand, it had proven harder to follow the trail from the man who had bribed the butcher to the woman who had given the original orders and provided the bag of coins as reward.

And if he had been thinking clearly back then he would have realized that the biggest mistake of all had lain in coming here to Bhunapore to confront Sinta Dai after he had learned the truth. A mistake to have allowed her to think even for a moment that her plan had worked, that his wife was dead and that he had returned to Bhunapore to claim her.

He winced and put his head in his hands. Aye, and part of that mistake had lain in letting her kiss him, and kissing her back under the guise of passion when he had sought no more than a confession.

Yes, the ruse had worked and, yes, he had managed to erase his anger as Walid Ali had urged with a night of drinking and foolish, manly talk. But soon the sun would come up and the household would stir and then the events of last night would spread like wildfire: of how the nautch-girl Sinta Dai had attempted to poison the wife of Hamilton-sahib, how Walid Ali had ordered her taken from the house in the dead of night and banished far to the South, beyond Calcutta, beyond Poona, where none of the household had ever been, to a place where it was assured that she would never have the power to scheme again.

There were those among Walid Ali's advisors who had urged last night that the girl be put to death to avenge her attack on the memsahib. Ross had been surprised by the fierceness of their loyalty to Maura until he recalled all that she had done for the people of this house.

The knowledge had done much to calm his own anger, and he had realized that whatever should happen in the future, Maura would always find herself welcome here.

Which might not be a bad thing considering that she probably wouldn't wish to stay married to him once word of his exploits reached her.

Knowing Maura and her infamous temper, she wouldn't care two figs about the fact that he had exposed the person who had made an attempt on her life. All that would matter to her was the fact that he had appeared on Walid Ali's doorstep demanding that the nautch-girl be brought to him, and disappearing with her into the most secluded pleasure pavilion of the zenana.

"Oh hell," he muttered.

Only the Begum and a pair of attendants had seen him, but recalling their shocked expressions he realized now what hadn't dawned on him at the time: that to them his disheveled and wild-eyed appearance must have made him seem the victim of overpowering lust. Why else would he have ignored all the rituals of decorum and fairly shouted at them to bring him Sinta Dai?

Even Ismail Khan had misconstrued his intent, because Ross had felt the heat of the man's anger as he was escorted into the depths of the zenana where the nautch-girl, summoned from sleep, had been waiting. At the time he had been too consumed by the thirst for revenge to give the consequences any thought.

Which showed just how thoroughly he had taken leave of his senses.

But at least in the Pathan, too, Maura had a loyal friend. God knows she would need them. Because Maura, like all the members of Walid Ali's household, would initially believe that he had forsaken her for his former lover.

Knowing Maura as well as he did, he knew better than to hope that she would give him the chance to explain. The shame of his apparent defection would not be borne by any newly wedded wife, let alone one as proud and impulsive as Maura. Especially because Kushna Dev's spies had probably seen him take the nautch-girl in his arms and would have reported as much to her by now.

I only hope she didn't smash every last thing in the house, he thought grimly. I should have gone back last night and been the first to tell her.

But she had been so ill and he'd honestly wanted her to rest, although in retrospect he probably shouldn't have stayed here and gotten drunk!

Lord, what a mess!

Even if Maura did give him the chance to explain and forgave him his ungentlemanly behavior, she would never forgive him for leaving without confiding in her and shutting her out of his life once again. No, without trust there could be no hope for their marriage.

Why the hell, he thought fiercely, hadn't he told her he loved her when he'd had the chance? Why hadn't he begun to build the foundations of that trust during the intimacy of lovemaking, when she had looked up at him with such breathless expectancy and asked him sweetly, innocently, if he did?

Surely she must have known it then! Surely she had felt it in every one of his kisses and the way he had emptied the very essence of himself into her lovely, willing body!

Of course he loved her, to distraction, it seemed, and yet . . . he had been afraid to say those three simple words when she'd asked. Facing renegade tigers and Afridi assassins would have been easier!

And now he must pay the price for his cowardice, for his reluctance to lay the secrets of his soul into the palm of his wife's hand and so give her the power to wound him if she saw fit as he had so often and unthinkingly wounded her.

He cursed savagely. A fine state of affairs, this! What in hell had that damnable redhead reduced him to?

Yes, he should have returned to her last night, to scotch any rumors that had been sent her way the moment he'd showed up here on the Begum's doorstep. But instead he had taken the coward's way out, letting Walid Ali persuade him to hide behind an increasingly drunken discourse on the maddening mysteries of women and the hardships of marriage.

Given his behavior he didn't deserve to be forgiven. In Maura's eyes he had behaved just as abominably as Charles Burton–Pascal.

The memory of Maura's expression when the two of them had stumbled onto that scene of debauchery in Delhi hit him like a blow between the eyes. He straightened abruptly, ignoring the throbbing of his head.

He must go back and face her wrath, no matter how much her angry words would wound him. Never mind that the heat would probably kill him before he reached the Kishnagar bungalow that, last night, Walid Ali had presented him as a wedding gift—providing Maura wanted it.

He uttered a bitter laugh as he bent to splash water on his face.

Lord knows he wanted it! His heart literally ached with longing at the thought of turning it into a home for Maura and himself. Knowing her as he did, he knew that she would not hesitate to join him in working to encourage others to return so that the once thriving British station could come alive again.

Maura would be happy, he knew, with friends and family nearby. Perhaps Lydia and Terence would even agree to join them, as would kindly Dr. Moore, who would be resigning his commission in the army at the end of the year. Even if not, she would have plenty to do interfering in the lives of the locals, which she seemed to enjoy doing so well. There would certainly be enough to keep her busy: setting up a school for the native children and a clinic for the sick, and educating the daughters of the households to expect more than being courtesans and concubines.

To be honest, he wouldn't mind leaving the military and taking some civil service post himself where he could educate the village men on the modern methods of agriculture and irrigation so that the crops would not wither and their families starve whenever the monsoons failed to come.

Only what was the use in dreaming of a happy ending? By now Maura had probably gotten word from Bhunapore or figured out on her own where he'd gone and packed herself off to Simla. No doubt this time she had left him for good.

Before he'd ever really had her.

Oh, God.

Propping his shoulder against the carved marble

column he hid his face in the crook of his arm. Much as he tried he couldn't seem to swallow the lump in his throat or will away the ache in his heart.

Behind him the curtains rustled. He supposed it was one of the servants coming to awaken him. He remembered dully that he was standing there stark naked, but he suddenly did not have the will to lift his head, let alone demand that he be left in peace.

Bare feet whispered across the stone floor, coming nearer, but still Ross did not move. He was exhausted, beyond caring.

There was a rustle of fabric and then a touch on his arm, so light that at first he thought he had imagined it. And a scent of sandalwood perfume, so subtle and sweet, that his senses stirred despite himself.

"The sahib is ill?"

The question in whispered Hindustani was so unexpected that at first he could make no sense of it. Then he shook his head violently. "No. Leave me."

"I will not, sahib."

That voice, and the un-Eastern refusal to obey . . . He felt his heart grow still.

"I have heard that the sahib desires a woman. That he rode many miles to seek a particular dancing girl. Surely he would prefer the attentions of someone better?"

"And who might that be?" he asked, though he found that he had to clear his throat before he could speak.

Maura was leaning so close now that he could feel the lovely curves of her body brushing lightly against him. "A woman who brings thee the best of both worlds, sahib."

"Is this so?"

"Indeed. I delayed coming here in order to learn

389

from a famed courtesan a few tricks in the ways of love between a woman and a man."

"And what of the ways of my country?" Much as he wanted to, he found that he could not bring himself to look at her, as though he were afraid that by doing so he would make her disappear.

She gave a low laugh that shivered through him. "There is nothing to learn, sahib. Those ways have already been taught me by my husband, and he is a master in the art. May I show thee how well I have learned?"

At last, at last, Ross straightened and turned in her direction. But the words he meant to say went unuttered as he looked at her.

She was wearing a *choli* of deep blue silk that barely covered her breasts. The loose-fitting trousers that clung to the curves of her hips were of darkest emerald. The rest of her torso was bare, and a girdle of priceless pearls had been laid about her waist. More pearls adorned her throat and dangled from her ears. She wore a gossamer veil of silver-bordered peach, as lovely a thing as any that the mysterious Chota Moti had ever worn. But for once her face was bared to him and her hair, plaited in a thick red braid, dangled freely to her hips.

The Rajasthani enchantress and the lovely niece of the Resident of Bhunapore finally stood before him as one, a vision that branded his heart. How often he had dreamed of them, of her, and yearned, only to now find the reality a thousand times more striking!

And she had not left him. She had sought him here.

He found that he could not speak. He could only lift unsteady hands to cup his wife's exquisite face.

"The sahib approves?"

But he was quick to catch the slight tremor in her voice, and only then did he notice the uncertainty in her lustrous eyes, and realized why she had come.

So, she was truly not about to murder him. And he would not be abandoned, because she was here and not in Simla. And proud as Maura Hamilton might be, she had not come here to seek revenge, but to win him back, by baring to him her heart.

A wildly triumphant laugh swelled inside him.

"Aye," he whispered huskily. "The sahib approves."

In response the tears welled further in her eyes and, groaning, he lowered his mouth to hers. He could not bear to see her weep. His heart would simply not endure it. He must make certain for the rest of his life that she never again shed another tear because of him.

He kissed her slowly, lavishly, so that all the world grew still. Unable to get enough of her, he wrapped an arm about her waist and drew her up against him. The pearls around her waist chinked softly and the scent of her filled his senses.

Ah, how well she fit into his arms, into his heart! Unable to control the soaring of his being, he eased her back just enough to gaze into her wonderous eyes.

"I love you." The voice was not his own, for it was rough with emotion and entirely unsteady. "Oh, God, I love you. I thought—"

His voice broke and he could not go on. But he knew that he must. The only way he could make sense of what he felt was to let her know what was happening inside him.

"I love you. From the moment we met." Now his eyes, too, burned with emotion, and when she clasped the hands that cupped her face she felt the pounding of the pulse in his wrists.

"I love you," he repeated, wondering why he had fought so long to deny the words and the truth behind them, why he had ever feared them and the hold she had over him. "Did you hear me once and for all, you damnable, adorable, poison-haired enchantress? I said that I love you."

In response her lips curved into a smile so seductive that his breath was borne away. Going up on tiptoe she wrapped her arms about his neck. Slowly, slowly her body melted into his, a heated fusion that boiled through his blood.

"Yes, I heard you." Her lips nipped seductively at his. "Now come," she added in a whisper. "Show me, too."

He laughed again, exultantly. Swinging her into his arms he carried her to the cushions and laid her down. And show her he did.

The Magician's Lover
Flora Speer

Determined to locate his friend who disappeared during a spell gone awry, Warrick petitions a dying stargazer to help find him. But the astronomer will only assist Warrick if he promises to escort his daughter Sophia and a priceless crystal ball safely to Byzantium. Sharp-tongued and argumentative, Sophia meets her match in the powerful and intelligent Warrick. Try as she will to deny it, he holds her spellbound, longing to be the magician's lover.

___52263-2 $5.99 US/$6.99 CAN

Heart's Magic

Flora Speer

Bestselling author of *ROSE RED*

In the year 1122, Mirielle senses change is coming to Wroxley Castle. Then, from out of the fog, two strangers ride into Lincolnshire. Mirielle believes the first man to be honest. But the second, Giles, is hiding something–even as he stirs her heart and awakens her deepest desires. And as Mirielle seeks the truth about her mysterious guest, she uncovers the castle's secrets and learns she must stop a treachery which threatens all she holds dear. Only then can she be in the arms of her only love, the man who has awakened her own heart's magic.

___52204-7 $5.99 US/$6.99 CAN

THE LION'S BRIDE
CONNIE MASON

Winner of the *Romantic Times* Storyteller Of The Year Award!

Lord Lyon of Normandy has saved William the Conqueror from certain death on the battlefield, yet neither his strength nor his skill can defend him against the defiant beauty the king chooses for his wife.

Ariana of Cragmere has lost her lands and her virtue to the mighty warrior, but the willful beauty swears never to surrender her heart.

Saxon countess and Norman knight, Ariana and Lyon are born enemies. And in a land rent asunder by bloody wars and shifting loyalties, they are doomed to misery unless they can vanquish the hatred that divides them—and unite in glorious love.

_3884-6 $5.99 US/$7.99 CAN

FOR LOVE AND HONOR

FLORA SPEER

Bestselling Author Of *Love Just In Time*

Falsely accused of murder, Sir Alain vows to move heaven and earth to clear his name and claim the sweet rose named Joanna. But in a world of deception and intrigue, the virile knight faces enemies who will do anything to thwart his quest of the heart.

From the sceptered isle of England to the sun-drenched shores of Sicily, the star-crossed lovers will weather a winter of discontent. And before they can share a glorious summer of passion, they will have to risk their reputations, their happiness, and their lives for love and honor.

_3816-1 $4.99 US/$5.99 CAN

A FAERIE TALE ROMANCE

VICTORIA ALEXANDER

Ophelia Kendrake has barely finished conning the coat off a cardsharp's back when she stumbles into Dead End, Wyoming. Mistaken for the Countess of Bridgewater, Ophelia sees no reason to reveal herself until she has stripped the hamlet of its fortunes and escaped into the sunset. But the free-spirited beauty almost swallows her script when she meets Tyler, the town's virile young mayor. When Tyler Matthews returns from an Ivy League college, he simply wants to settle down and enjoy the simplicity of ranching. But his aunt and uncle are set on making a silk purse out of Dead End, and Tyler is going to be the new mayor. It's a job he takes with little relish—until he catches a glimpse of the village's newest visitor.

_52159-8 $5.50 US/$6.50 CAN